FALLEN AND FOUND

A Love Story

Jessica Mason

MURMURATION BOOKS

For the wayward.

AUTHOR'S NOTE

Dear readers, before you embark down this road, please know that *Fallen and Found* contains mature and often heavy themes, as well as explicit content and depictions of violence.

This content includes: infidelity, sex work, housing insecurity and homelessness, homophobia and hate crimes, mentions of abuse, drug and alcohol use, loss of a family member, foster care, mentions of conversion therapy, religious trauma, and bigotry.

I have attempted to the best of my ability to be accurate in my depictions of real life situations and issues, but this remains a work of fiction and is intended as such.

For additional specific content warnings, please visit my website at www.JessicaMasonAuthor.com, and do not hesitate to contact me with questions or concerns.

Thank you for reading.

1
Independence Day

sean

ON THE LONELY DAYS, Sean ignores the cost of gas and just drives. He climbs into his beat-to-hell Chevy Bel Air, feels the cracked leather against his back and the thin wheel under his hands, and goes. Sure, he doesn't own her in the legal sense, but she's his home, and the open road is hers. Can't take her too far though. Even with a ride like her, he's trapped in the sweltering city where he walks the street. In several senses.

His shoulders relax with the city skyline in the rearview, and he sneers his way through the sprawling suburbs. There's a church on every corner, and every house looks the same, with their too-green lawns and empty driveways. He drives into the country, through fields of corn and soy. Or maybe hay. Even the back-country roads are as straight as a die, perfectly perpendicular to the horizon. They go on forever, promising a horizon he can never reach.

He rolls past billboards asking if his soul is ready to be saved and pretends he's going somewhere. Once he made it to Independence, the famous start of the Oregon Trail, then a bit further, like a busted pioneer. There wasn't much there, aside from an ancient fill-up station. Felt like going back in time fifty years to when the Bel Air was new and her red paint was fresh instead of scratched and faded. The attendant told Sean a story about his first car, a '66 Thunderbird. They don't make them like they used to.

He doesn't make it that far today, even though he started before dawn thanks to some idiot having a loud argument with the voices in his head on the street at four AM. Sean didn't recognize the guy. Probably new downtown. Another bearded, lost soul in five layers, pushing all he owns in a grocery cart.

Sean hit the gas to get away from the thought that he was no better than that guy. A car has to be better than a shopping cart, right? Sean doesn't stink of booze. He's got all his teeth. He's only wearing three layers, for Christ's sake. He looks like someone who has a future, even if that's not true.

He's just south of the city when the old girl's motor starts making a sound he doesn't like. On the way back, every cookie-cutter house has an American flag up for the Fourth of July next week, dotting the beige landscape with alien color. The streets of St. Louis proper are the color of rust and red dirt, the looming rainclouds blotting out the sun and erasing the shadows.

Sean parks the Bel Air by a crumbling building on a patch of concrete with dead grass peeking through the fissures and starts walking. He's got an hour to kill before he has to be at the shelter, and he's hungry. He could duck into the diner and burn the last of his spare cash on crappy coffee and dry eggs, but he'd rather have a sandwich, so he drifts toward the brick façade of the rescue mission and hopes he's got the timing right. Sure enough, a cadre of generous souls with cardboard boxes and scripture in their hands scatter from the mission onto the street, like so many ants in polos and khaki.

Sean has names for all of them. There's Lurch, the tall, balding guy who looks like he hasn't smiled since 1982. Then there's Cuffed Jeans, a reasonably cute chick who at least tries to smile once in a while, but makes it look like indigestion. There're the Seven Karens, and the Vacuum Salesman.

Then there's Blue Eyes. He's handsome, in a pale, stoic, white guy way, with dark hair that resists the perfectly combed church look, a sharp nose, and a rugged jaw. Plus eyes like the autumn sky. Not summer. This is a deeper blue. If Sean were to guess, he'd say his friend is thirty or so, but his eyes look older. Sadder. He's the one Sean sees first today.

"PB&J again this week?" Sean calls out when Blue Eyes gets in range. He's usually paired off with Cuffed Jeans, but he's alone today and doesn't look happy about it. He gives Sean a sidelong look as he turns.

"It's always PB&J," he replies. His voice is deep, warm, and rough, and it occurs to Sean that he's never actually heard him talk before. He'd remember that voice.

"Can I get two?"

Blue Eyes hands him two sandwiches, neatly packed in plastic baggies, and Sean thanks him with a wicked smile.

"Would you like some reading material?" Blue Eyes stammers and rustles through his box for a scripture pamphlet. "I have it here somewhere."

"Don't strain yourself. I know I'm headed downstairs. Don't need a pamphlet."

Blue Eyes stares, and Sean can't tell if he's impressed or sad. Or maybe something else when his eyes dart to Sean's lips. "Is there any other way I can help you?"

"You take this ministry thing seriously, huh?" Sean asks back, and Blue Eyes looks at the ground. "You got a phone?"

"Yes, why?" The guy's pretty cute when he's confused.

"I just wanna know how long this rain will last."

Those blue eyes squint at him, annoyed. Also cute. "Why?"

"What's your name?" Sean asks back. "Can't tell you all my secrets without knowing your name." He flashes Blue Eyes a smile; the charming, flirty one that he usually reserves to land himself some easy money (depending on your definition of easy). He's not sure why he's flirting; he can't imagine a straighter arrow than one of these choir boys. Then again, maybe that's why. He likes poking the fire, even if it comes with brimstone.

"My name is Cameron," Blue Eyes – scratch that – *Cameron*, says.

"Huh, figured you'd have a Bible name. Hepzibah or something."

Cameron glowers at him. "What about you? Have you got a name?"

"Yup."

Cameron's perturbed scowl deepens, and Sean grins, really grins for the first time in at least three weeks. "Sean. My name's Sean. Nice Irish Catholic name for a not-so-nice, not-so-Catholic boy." He waits for a comment on his green eyes or his freckles that doesn't come. Maybe his brown hair saved him.

"Why do you want me to tell you the weather, Sean?"

Sean keeps up the smile. He knows he's pretty too. "Rain's bad for business."

"Panhandling?"

"Pans are definitely not what I handle."

Cameron looks scandalized, just like Sean hoped. "I should go," he mutters, and Sean scoffs.

"Come on, you didn't even tell me the weather."

When Cameron looks back at him, Sean can't tell what he's feeling, which is weird because Sean prides himself on reading people. Cameron takes his phone out but doesn't look away until it's unlocked. "Rain starting this afternoon and going into Wednesday," Cameron recites and starts to turn away, then thinks better of it. Sean smirks as Cameron meets his eyes again. "There will probably be a rush for shelter beds. You may need to get in line early."

"I'm cool. I'm sure I'll find somewhere nice and warm to settle in," Sean smirks, and the blush on Cameron's cheeks deepens. That's what he likes about these faithful types: they're an easy game. Spin 'em up and watch 'em go.

"Well, consider your options," is all Cameron says before turning away.

Sean heads the other direction, not looking back. He walks and takes in the dust and dirt of the city. It's not too different from the country. Flat, empty and dried up, with a cold underneath that even the brightest summer day can't burn away. Same empty blue sky, looking down like there's nothing to see.

It does end up raining on the Fourth. And the days after, flooding the dusty streets like empty riverbeds. Sean struck out looking for work, but he wasn't trying hard. Last year, he did great on the Fourth of July: loitered at the edge of the milling crowds watching the fireworks over the Arch. Country music blaring in the muggy night; cheap beer and shit exploding got folks' blood pumping, and a good crop of idiots with cash in hand had stumbled into Sean's path. This year, he was stuck walking the empty streets while good people enjoyed their Jell-O salads and watched the fireworks on TV. God bless America.

He's still soggy and close to starving on Thursday, but ready to look in earnest for a goddamn job. He wants a real meal and a good movie, and Danny will need a new coat soon. Damn fourteen-year-olds and their growth spurts.

Sean finds a wall to lean on by a strip joint in the shittiest part of town and waits. The light fades, folk come and go, and his stomach cramps before a man catches his attention. It's the way he walks that does it. Sure, he's dressed too nice for this neighborhood – khakis and a pressed shirt – but he trudges down the dirty street past the graffiti and trash like he's walked for a hundred miles already. There's also something about him that's familiar. He stares at the 'gentlemen's club', then closes his eyes. Shit, he looks like he's about to cry.

"You lookin' for—" Sean stops and chuckles as blue eyes lock with his. Interesting. "Cameron, right?"

Cameron looks like he's been caught pants down with a sheep. Eyes wide, he turns to rush away.

"Hey!" Sean calls, and the guy freezes. "You got any of those sand-wiches?"

Slowly, Cameron turns, head bent in shame. "I don't have any food with me. I was—"

"Traveling for pleasure?" Sean smirks. Cameron looks at Sean like he just shoved a knife in his gut or kicked his puppy. Something bad and sad. Whatever brought this pillar of the church into Sean's path tonight's got him twisted up something awful. Sean braces himself. He shouldn't say something this dumb, but he feels sorry for the guy. And hungry.

"You can still do your charity thing if you want to get me dinner."

So that's how Sean ends up at the Moonlight diner, eating a massive burger while Mr. JC-Penney-catalog watches him from the other side of the booth like he might explode.

Sean doesn't know what to say, but it doesn't matter because the food is greasy and delicious. If he groans like a bit of a slut when he takes a huge bite of his burger, juice dribbling down his chin, just to see Cameron go pale, no one has to know.

Cameron fiddles with his napkin as Sean wipes his face with his shirt sleeve, watching Cameron's long fingers with professional interest until he sees the plain gold wedding ring. Oh. Cameron notices Sean noticing and pulls his hand back.

"She doesn't know I'm out," Cameron mutters. "She'd be upset I'm eating this." He nods at the burger he hasn't touched.

"That the only thing?" Sean asks, eyebrow raised.

"She doesn't buy beef. She thinks it's unhealthy and cruel – the way the animals are treated. She's not wrong, but..." Cameron shakes his head and takes a bite of his burger. He smiles for the first time Sean's seen, but it falls away when he catches Sean staring. "She likes that I go downtown. It's good to minister. Even though I'm not very good at it."

Sean huffs a laugh. "So, how's that work? Your whole 'onward Christian soldiers' thing." Cameron furrows his brows. "Like, do I have to tell you my sins and then say sixty-nine Hail Marys and then you get a notch on your punch card for another soul saved?"

"What? I'm not a priest. And I'm not Catholic," Cameron adds, hilariously offended.

"What are you then?"

"*Christian*," Cameron replies like it's obvious.

"So are Catholics!"

"No, they're not."

Now it's Sean's turn to be offended – at least on his ancestors' behalf. "What the hell are you talking about? They believe in Christ, ergo, *Christian*."

"They hold false idols." Cameron sounds like he's parroting something drilled into him. "Their deification of the Virgin Mary in particular is troubling."

"Come on, you don't actually believe that," Sean says, all his bravado and pretense slipping away. He's not even angry; he just feels sad for the guy in front of him who apparently has never had an independent thought in his life.

Cameron, for his part, answers by avoiding Sean's eyes and taking another bite of the burger. "I told you, I'm not good at this," he murmurs after he swallows.

"Oh, you're not so bad," Sean lies.

"We call it the good news," Cameron says quietly. "As if people will be surprised. Follow the right rules, and it will all be alright. You'll be saved. It's easy. Why would anyone argue?"

"Sounds like you don't buy it," Sean tries, curious. "That why you were heading into a strip club?"

Cameron raises an eyebrow, and it's kind of hot. "I wasn't sure if I was going to go in. Before I saw you, I was praying for strength. Or a sign. Turns out God has a terrible sense of humor."

"What's that supposed to mean?"

Cameron stares at Sean, really truly stares, and it makes Sean feel more naked than with a john. "How old are you?"

"Twenty-two. You wanna check ID?"

"You look younger."

"And?"

Cameron swallows, looking at Sean with unchecked hunger in his eyes. "And people – men – pay you. For sex."

"Yeah." Sean shrugs. It's good not to talk around it, but he's not sure what this has to do with why Cameron's out and about without the god squad.

"So, you're not actually…" Cameron looks down at his food like even thinking the word makes him ill.

"Queer? Oh, I am. I like dick; always have." Cameron looks up, shocked. "I like pussy too. But dick pays better. Why not make money doing what you love, huh?" He gives a shrug and an empty grin.

"That must be nice, liking everyone," Cameron says mournfully, proving every suspicion Sean had right.

"I guess," Sean says, 'cause he'd never thought of it like that. "Sounds like you like something specific."

"I've been trying to do the right thing," Cameron grits out, face twisting in pain. "I have prayed and *tried*. Then I find out the man I've sinned with in my mind sells that sin for cash. Then find him the moment I ask for a sign."

If that confession wasn't the saddest thing Sean's ever heard, the whole sinning with him in his mind thing would be really interesting. "You're right. God's a jerk."

"One might say that," Cameron sighs like the weight of the whole world is gonna crush him any second. Every inch of him is tense and dour, and Sean's heart would break for the dude if he cared. Sean's tired and sore, but this weirdo looks like he could stand to do more for himself than a secret cheeseburger and shitty conversation.

"Or *one might say* this is a golden opportunity: Because I don't care what God says about what anyone should want or do, if they've got the cash." Sean's trying to go easy, not scare a possible paycheck away. He inclines his head and looks up through his lashes with his most tempting expression. He knows it works because Cameron looks like he's drowning. "You got the cash, Cam?"

Something shifts in Cameron's expression that has Sean catching his breath. "Is there some place we can go?"

The clerk at the motel takes Cameron's money without blinking, and Sean claims his preferred room on the first floor. The walls are papered with a greasy, puke-colored honeycomb pattern, the carpet a rusted red that's deepened by the buzzing neon of the motel sign outside the window. Turning on the lamp makes the stains on the gold bedspread easier to see, so Sean looks behind him instead. Cameron looks nauseous when he walks in.

"You didn't need to pay for the whole night."

"I did. I thought you might like to stay. After." Even after the burger and polite conversation, that surprises Sean. This guy takes that kindness to the needy shit seriously.

"Thanks."

"What happens next?"

If it hadn't been clear before that this was Cameron's first time paying for it, that cinches it. He's so out of place in the dingy little room, standing stiff in his nice suit and sensible shoes.

"Money on the table. Literally," Sean orders. Cameron takes out his wallet without hesitation, and Sean's stomach clenches with guilt and glee when the guy pulls out three crisp hundreds. "Hey, that's—"

"Do you need more?" Cameron looks so sincere, Sean has the weird urge to hug him. Instead, he gulps and shakes his head. He needs the money.

"Nah, that's more than enough."

Cameron sets the money on the dresser and turns to Sean, cheeks red. "It may take a while for me to…" He gestures towards his lower half.

Sean can't stop himself from wheezing out a laugh. "Guys have trouble getting it up all the time, don't worry."

"My wife and I – it's been hard."

"Or not hard." Sean gets a glare for that. He deserves it.

"She thinks it's her. I was going to that club to see if I—"

"Could get it up for other women?" Cameron gives another sick nod. Sean steps boldly into Cameron's space, pressing his chest against him, and Cameron exhales, eyes rising to meet Sean's, full of lust. "But it's not women you get it up for."

Cameron shakes his head. "When I want to be intimate, I think about... men. I've thought about you. Many times. You're very beautiful."

"Well, now you've got me." Cameron heaves a quivering breath, and Sean takes that as his cue to palm him through his slacks. Sure enough, he starts swelling immediately. "Seems to me like everything is workin' fine."

Cameron closes his eyes, like he's feeling the spirit, and Sean tries to keep his cool. He fails when those blue eyes open again and look at Sean like he's magic or something.

"Can I kiss you?"

That's usually a big no. It's messy and creepy and way too intimate. But this guy... "Since you bought me dinner."

It almost hurts when Cam's mouth hits his with too much force, but it's worth it. Sean can't remember the last time he was truly and properly kissed, and it feels good. Cam kisses Sean and pulls him tight like he's the one thing he's ever wanted and never had. He kisses Sean like he knows he's a sin, but it feels like salvation.

Sean pulls back and starts stripping off Cam's clothes as fast as he can. As a nice treat, the guy's in incredible shape under his suit, and when Sean's got everything off, he's fully hard and leaking through his pale blue boxers.

"That for me?" Sean pants. Cam nods, and Sean doesn't think the guy could form words if he tried. "I got something for you too." God, he hates how corny it sounds, but he's committed to his part. Screw that, he's into it. He guides one of Cam's hands to his ass and the other into his pants and dick. Cam straight up gasps when he gets a hand around Sean, eyes going out of focus.

Sean slips out of his clothes with Cam jerking him, and it feels awesome. There's usually some physical response on the job (bodies are bodies), but this is different.

"On the bed," Sean orders.

Cam nearly falls as he obeys, pushing himself up on his elbows to watch as Sean pulls off his boxers. "Don't come," Sean warns and proceeds to do his second (fourth?) really stupid thing in an hour as he takes Cam's dick in his mouth. Damn, it's nicer without a condom. He can feel the texture, the little twitches. There's something about knowing this is the first time in a long time, or maybe ever, that a guy has done this to Cam that gets Sean high on pride and the horrible thrill of defiling something good and pure.

"Sean, that's – Fuck." Cam keeps swearing and making filthy sounds as Sean shows off his best moves, but not for too long. Cam groans when Sean pulls off and retreats to his discarded jacket. "What are you—"

"You paid for more than getting sucked off." Cam looks thunder-struck. Did Sean call this wrong? "You do wanna fuck me, right?"

"Yes, but I've never…"

Sean's not surprised. "Lay back and relax, you're with an expert."

Cam scoots further up the bed as Sean returns to straddle him, condom and packet of lube in hand. Sean tosses Cam the condom, then rips the cheap single pack of lube open with his teeth. He squeezes a good dollop on his fingers while Cam rolls on the rubber. Sean shifts so Cam has at least a partial view to watch him reach back and start opening himself up. Cam stares up at him like he's seen, well, not the face of God. Maybe the opposite. Still something beautiful and astonishing.

"Wanna make sure I'm ready for you," Sean pants. "Slick yourself up too."

Cam fumbles with the lube and complies as Sean keeps up his prep. He's used to the burn. Even likes it. This is already more than he usually gets and a hell of a lot more control. Instead of getting pounded from behind, he gets to sink slowly onto Cam's cock and watch his eyes roll back in his head.

"You feel like heaven," Cam sighs. Sean doesn't remark on the choice of words. He starts moving instead, riding Cam at an easy pace while he moans and bucks underneath him. Sean's concentration is on Cam (customer and all), but it's easy to get lost. If he gets the angle just right, Cam hits the sweet spot and Sean joins him in the chorus of groans. "Sean, I—"

"Whatever you want." Cam takes him at his word and tugs him down by the shoulder. He kisses him, rough and wet, as he flips them and starts driving into Sean with a fury that has Sean seeing stars. "Yeah, that's right. Let it all go," Sean murmurs over the sound of their bodies moving together.

"I'm close," Cam warns. It's fast, but Sean's not judging.

"It's okay, sweetheart. Go ahead." Cam grunts as his hips stutter. Sean gets a hand on himself, jerking feverishly so that he comes right as Cam's eyes open. He figures that's what he'd like to see the first time he fucked someone, and Cam looks adequately impressed.

Cam pulls out and falls back, panting and staring at the ceiling in some kind of shock. Sean can't imagine what he's feeling, but it doesn't look like happy post-coital rainbows. "You okay?"

"I just broke my marriage vows, God's laws, and man's. And…" Cam sounds like he's confessing to murder. "It was so good I don't even care."

"Put that on my Yelp page." Cam turns to Sean with sincere confusion on his face. "Holy shit, I'm joking."

"Oh."

More than the sex or the food or even the kindness, the sweet-serious nod Cam gives makes something warm churn under Sean's ribs. And that's not okay. Sean heads for the bathroom to clean up so he doesn't have to think about it. He comes back to see Cam throwing the condom away and looking at Sean like he's a miracle.

"Is that normal?" Cam asks, nodding to where Sean's wiping the mess from his stomach.

"Me coming? Uh, no, actually. But that was… different." Cam searches for his pants, confusion and guilt creeping back into his expression. "You were good. Very hot. I liked it."

"I did too," Cam rumbles, low and honest.

"That I got."

Cam gives a weak smile as he puts back on his rumpled suit, and Sean slips on his jeans. "Thank you."

"Just doing my job," Sean shrugs and settles onto the bed. It's creaky and ancient, and it's gonna feel so good for the next nine hours. Cam pulls out his wallet again. "Dude, you already paid and covered the whole night."

"This is for you to get a decent breakfast," Cam rumbles as he adds one more bill to the pile.

"That your way of balancing this out? Fucking a dude is okay if you also show him the Lord's charity or some shit?" Sean knows it's petulant, but he doesn't want pity.

"Something like that." Cam looks down at the carpet, deflating rather than bristling. Sean swallows his argument. No reason to turn down cash. Cam doesn't seem done; he's writing something on a card. "This is my full name and phone number. You can call me if you need help."

"You know I'm not going to," Sean laughs, deciding not to be offended.

"It will ease my soul if I know you have it." Cam sets the paper next to the cash, and Sean watches as the weight of the world settles back on his shoulders. "Thank you again. For the conversation, as well as the... For everything." He opens the door and gives Sean a look like Sean just walked on water or healed the sick. Jesus, Sean's dealt with closet cases before, but never one that made a quick fuck seem like a revelation.

"Any time, Cam. You know where to find me."

Cam gives one last sad nod before disappearing.

Sean slumps back onto the bed and wonders if he has a new regular. The look in Cameron's eye was like a junkie after their first taste. The only mystery is if Cam will come back to Sean or go looking for someone else to try. Part of Sean hopes he doesn't. He doesn't wanna be some charity case. But if the guy's issues earn Sean a few more dollars, he'd be okay with it. Probably won't say no to a sandwich if he shows up around the neighborhood again. Sean's not going to think about it. Hoping Cam will find him again is too much like planning for a future he doesn't have.

2
RECEIPTS

cameron

CAMERON FINDS COMFORT IN routine. Not pleasure. Or joy. Just something resembling peace. He leaves for work every day at 7:30 and pulls into his parking spot at the hospital at exactly 7:58, which gives him just enough time to make it into his office on the ground floor at 8:00 precisely. Lunch at noon. Off at 5:00. Variable time stuck in traffic depending on the weather and the quality of his audiobook. Home for dinner, chit chat, television, run, showers, and bed before 10:00. Kayla makes fun of him for it. She's always been the spontaneous one.

Cameron's schedule leaves time for the things that don't fit. Like lying awake at night, going over how today was just like yesterday, and will be just like tomorrow. His whole life melting into an ocean of sameness, slowly drowning him. The usual. The routine is safe complacency and blissful numbness. Not peace.

He masturbates in the shower to thoughts of strangers. He pretends to pray. He avoids looking at the sweet picture of Christ that his mother gave them that hangs in the hall, and doesn't touch the Bibles because he's unclean. He keeps up the routine of the man he is supposed to be. He moves along in monotony and lies to himself that it will get easier.

The week has a rhythm too. Tuesdays are family nights. Friday is date night. Saturday is community service. Sunday is church, of course, and another family dinner if he's unlucky. On Thursdays, Kayla has her night shift. Thursdays are the days that Cameron usually goes for an extra-long run, then watches the medical shows that Kayla hates. Sometimes, he'll sneak out for a burger.

He could tell himself that's all he did tonight. He could convince himself that the receipt from the diner that he's been staring at for fifteen minutes as he sits parked in the open garage is simply evidence of the burger that he shouldn't have eaten. He could tell himself a lot of things. He's very good at that.

He doesn't know why he took the receipt. He paid with cash, the way he always does when he goes somewhere unauthorized. Heaven knows he doesn't need to deduct this. Keeping the receipt was a habit, and now Cameron doesn't know what to do. He should tear it up and throw it away in the garage trash. Kayla never checks out there. But if he throws it away, there will be nothing left to prove Sean was real.

Sean.

Saturdays are community service, when Cameron volunteers with the rescue mission and hopes to see the beautiful boy with green eyes, then comes home lost in fantasies of that mouth and face. On Sundays, he prays for forgiveness.

What do you do when your sin has become more than a filthy urge? Cameron didn't feel dirty or wrong with Sean. Didn't feel guilty kissing him. It was the most intense experience of his life, and at the same time, it didn't feel real. It still doesn't. Except for the little piece of paper in his hands. Solid as sin.

Cameron heaves a breath, nausea surging through him. He barely makes it to the edge of the driveway before heaving into the bushes. He vomits up the remains of the dinner he wasn't supposed to eat, tears springing to his eyes, then staggers back, panting. The pain in his chest remains, acid searing in his emptied stomach. He deserves it.

"Damn," he whispers, swallowing back the bile.

Kayla's more likely to notice that mess than the receipt now sitting in the footwell of his car. The idea makes his heart race and his stomach churn, as if his body is trying to expel even the memory of Sean and his touch. Something else to be discarded and ignored. Forced down and forgotten.

Cameron staggers back into the garage. Kayla's space is still empty, as it should be. She won't be home until past midnight. If she had come home early on this night of all nights, it would be a certain sign that God was punishing him, but she didn't.

He retrieves the receipt from the car, shoves it in the glove compartment, and heads inside. He doesn't want to forget. Not yet. He punches in the alarm code and doesn't bother turning on the lights. The two-story great room is cavernous, and his steps echo in the dark.

He shakes as he undresses for the shower, thinking back to how Sean peeled off his clothes and the taste of the other man's debauched lips against his. His cock stirs at the thought, followed by a new surge of acrid shame in his gut. He can still smell the grease of the diner and the stale stink of the hotel room on his clothes. And Sean's sweat on his skin. Cameron shoves his clothes to the bottom of the hamper and climbs into the shower. The water is ice, but his erection persists, mocking. He turns the water to scalding and scrubs and scrubs. He closes his eyes and sees Sean above him, smiling with bravado and so incredibly beautiful. He'd laugh at Cam now.

He takes himself in hand, remembering Sean tight and warm around him. He wanted it to feel wrong. Even when he kissed Sean, he prayed for disgust. It *should* have felt wrong because it was, but the memory has Cam biting back a groan. He masturbated to thoughts of a stranger for months. Green eyes, sandy hair, and perfect lips. Now he knows his name and how it feels to fuck him. Now Cameron is damned forever. He comes on the perfect marble tiles of the shower, on fire with the memory. Does it make the fire Cam is destined for worth it?

He pretends the moisture on his face is just water.

He takes a sleeping pill, the ones Kayla gives him worried looks about, but she's not here, so she'll never know. She won't know any of it. Ever.

He brushes his teeth until his gums bleed.

Cameron climbs under the covers as the orange glow of the street-light through the tree outside casts shadows on the ceiling like a mosaic. Kayla hates it when he leaves the blinds up, saying it's indecent that their neighbors might see into their bedroom. He leaves them open.

Their bed is so soft compared to that creaky hotel mattress. There was a spring stabbing his hip at some point, he thinks. He's not sure – he was distracted. Sean seemed so grateful for a bed to sleep in. He's probably sleeping easy for the first time in a while. Cam did that. He helped. It was the least he could do after Sean treated him so...

He can't find the right word.

He falls asleep trying to find it.

He dreams of Sean, of course. Dreams that he never left that room. Dreams of waking up next to him. Until Kayla walks in the motel door. Or is it his mother? He can't tell. They both look disappointed.

Cameron wakes up at the normal time on Friday to the insistent beep of his alarm, with Kayla asleep beside him and the blinds closed. She's snuggled close to him like nothing is different, and he didn't betray her. He doesn't get sick this time, but it's a close thing. He gets dressed too quickly, doesn't bother with shaving, and trudges downstairs for breakfast.

On Fridays, he has frozen waffles. The organic kind is all he can get away with, but since this is the day Kayla sleeps late, she's not there to make a smoothie or dole out yogurt with granola on it. He can't even stomach the sweet indulgence, so he grabs some fruit.

He sits in his car in the parking lot for five minutes when he arrives, fingering the receipt fished from the glove compartment. They didn't give him one at the hotel. He laughs bitterly at the idea of a receipt from Sean. He could imagine Sean making a joke about that. He was witty.

Cameron finally makes it out of the car, not even bothering to lock it. He slogs down the line of identical sedans, his own silver Corolla blending in and disappearing immediately. The hall to his office is similarly sterile and dark. Not in the way the rest of the hospital is sterile, but in the featureless uniformity of each door and wall. The administration offices are shoved in as an afterthought, stuck in the basement, where no light makes it in the windows because the patients need sunshine more. The door to the claims department is so innocuous that he's walked right past his own office several times.

"Good, you're here. I thought you were dead." Despite her small stature, Flor never fails to look imposing, and her (currently) sherbert orange hair and black clothes have something to do with it. Cameron can't tell if the silver accents on her shirt are safety pins or spikes or both, but he's sure the whole ensemble is against dress code. Knowing Flor, that's entirely the point.

"I'm only a few minutes late," Cameron grumbles, heading directly to the office kitchenette for coffee.

"And you look like shit," Flor says. Cameron can feel Lee glare at her from across the office.

"Profanity, Flor," Cameron mutters.

"Coffee, Cam."

Cameron scowls as he pulls out his favorite chipped mug and fills it. "I'm putting cream in."

"And I was making a factual statement." Flor looks smug as Cameron passes her to get to his office. He's the only one who has a real office. Lee, Flor, and Nate share the main office space with dozens of file drawers, copiers, and one window that only has a view of shrubbery and dirt. It always smells like warm paper and stale coffee.

"Are you alright?" Lee asks.

"I have some crackers if you'd like," Nate adds.

The two of them are hard to tell apart sometimes; their hair is the same shade of brown, though Lee's is longer. They both favor conservative office clothes, with Lee's being slightly more exciting. That might just be the difference between men's and women's fashion. Now they have identical looks of worry on their faces. Cameron wonders how bad he must look for this level of concern.

"I'm feeling under the weather." It's not a lie. "Stomach. Again."

Lee gives an earnest nod, as Flor glares at the coffee in his hand. She's usually the one who brings it to him and hides his mugs when Kayla drops in, so this is uncharacteristic.

"You know I was reading about the effects caffeine can have on impulse control," Nate offers from his desk. "Mr. Osborn had some interesting thoughts."

"I'm sure he does," Lee mutters. She's probably thinking the same thing as Cam – that their pastor has opinions on everything.

"That explains the ass tattoo I got at the Starbucks drive-through," Flor smirks, and Nate looks at his keyboard, scandalized.

"I can't imagine where you found room," Lee snarks, but Flor only looks flattered.

"I'll be fine, thank you all for your concern," Cam cuts in. "Let's get to work."

"Take your medicine!" Flor yells after him. He washes down a double dose of antacid with the coffee and appreciates the irony.

Cameron dives into his usual sea of numbers and claims. Black and white and orderly. His mind drifts when he stops for sips of coffee or to look out the sliver of a window at his glimpse of sky beyond the shrubs. He allows himself flashes of Sean's face, painted red by the neon of the motel sign, awash with pleasure. His guts twist, and his heart races.

Does he only look sick, or does he look different? Guilty? Sinful? What would they say if they knew? His monitor goes black from inactivity, and Cameron catches his blurred reflection. He can't see any difference, but then again, he's always known what was inside.

He means to skip lunch, but Flor barges in with cottage cheese and an English muffin at two. He gathers from her expression that his appearance hasn't improved.

"Are you sure you're okay?" Flor asks, waiting to see if he eats before she leaves.

"I'm fine. I told you." He's always been a good liar, by necessity, but maybe he's losing his touch.

"Are you and Kayla fighting?"

"Flor, I'm fine." It comes out too harsh, and Flor draws back.

"Bullshit, you look like you're about to pass out."

Maybe Flor would understand. She's his only friend who doesn't go to his church. She sneaks him coffee and makes off-color jokes. She listens to occult music, votes blue, and worst, doesn't want to get married. She would tell Cam that what he did was, if not alright, understandable, but the thought of putting it into words makes him dizzy and cold. He doesn't deserve consolation.

"I'm…" *I'm sick because I fucked a man for the first time last night and now I know what I am and…*

"Cameron?" They both look up at Lee, poking her head through the door. "I wanted to say goodbye."

"Goodbye?"

"I'm spending the rest of the afternoon with my cousin. He flies out tomorrow, so I won't see you downtown either."

Lee volunteers at the mission on Saturdays too. Images flash into Cameron's mind of what he could do if he were downtown alone. Sean's mouth and the *possibilities*. Then he thinks of hellfire and seeing Kayla afterwards.

"I won't be there either. I think I am sick," he says as a wave of shame hits him. "You're all right. I should go home to rest."

"Feel better soon. We'll add a prayer for you tonight." Lee means so well, but it makes Cameron feel worse.

"Good thing you're married to a doctor," Flor says, as smug as possible.

Cameron considers not going home. It's a nice day, he could go to the park or walk, but he fears that if he strays, he'll end up back downtown. It would be so easy. He's seen Sean in the same neighborhood for months since he started volunteering in the spring. The fact that he's considering breaking the law and cheating on his wife *again* is the very reason he should go home.

When he walks into the house to see his wife, with the summer sun streaming through the high windows of the home they've made and the bright green of the garden visible out the back door, there's comfort to it. It's a lie, but it's a beautiful one.

It's been so long since he's seen Kayla painting. The sun catches her strawberry blonde hair, and she turns to smile at him. He remembers when he'd find her in the studio at school. He remembers the sun in her hair the day they got married and all the hope he felt then.

"Hey, babe, what are you doing home? You okay?" Kayla asks, dropping her brush in a cup by her easel and coming towards him. "You look awful."

"I think I'm coming down with a bug, so I decided to come home."

Kayla switches into doctor mode instantly, hand on Cameron's head. "You're warm, but that could just be the day. Is it your stomach? Have you been—"

"I've been nauseous on and off since last night."

"Is that why you skipped your run?"

Of course she noticed his running clothes weren't in the hamper. Luckily, the receipt is stored carefully in the back of a drawer at work. Just like the memory of Sean: tucked away safely, unable to do harm. Cameron is pliant as Kayla leads him to their big white couch and pushes him down.

"Yes. I came home late and got sick in the bushes."

"Babe, why didn't you tell me?" She rubs his shoulder, concern in her wide brown eyes and voice. He doesn't deserve it, but he takes it.

"I don't know about date night." He was planning to take her to dinner at her favorite restaurant, once he asked his mother what that was, to make up for their Fourth of July fight. And the date night before that. And so much else.

"Don't worry. We can stay in and watch a movie. No pressure." Her smile is kind and genuine. "Do you want pink medicine or white?"

"Neither." He's been told many times that he's a terrible patient, usually because he doesn't want people to bother, but today he doesn't want to feel better. He shouldn't be allowed to.

"*Babe.*" Kayla waits, looming above him with an eyebrow raised. He knows that look. He remembers her in college, before they started dating. He remembers how she'd make him go home from the library and bring him pastries and tea in the morning. Once Kayla decides she's caring for someone, it's settled.

"White."

"I'll make you some tea too."

He feels better by the time they're in bed. They watched old movies (a date night staple when they don't feel like going out) and chomped on popcorn. No salt or butter, of course. He plays with Kayla's hair as she rests her head on his chest while they watch the ten o'clock news and sigh at the state of the world.

Kayla kisses him gently before turning out the light. Her hand snakes down his chest and to the drawstring of his sleep pants, and Cameron's heart seizes.

"Are you still feeling sick?"

"Yes," Cameron stammers, panic rising. "I don't think I'll even be up for going downtown tomorrow."

"That bad?" There's disappointment in her voice.

"I'm sorry." He truly is. In ways she'll never know.

"It's okay. Next week." He hates the sad resignation in her voice. She's not even surprised.

Cameron stares into the shadows as Kayla falls asleep beside him. He considers praying, but he doesn't know what for. Maybe the strength to stay home tomorrow. Maybe that Sean will need something and call him. Maybe to forget.

He dreams of green eyes.

sean

For a guy with a car, Sean sure walks a lot. As much as he loves a long drive, he has to be careful with the Bel Air. The motor's still giving him trouble, and she's not the most inconspicuous vehicle. He's proud of that, but he doesn't need attention. The fake tags are up to date, but if he ever gets pulled over, he's completely screwed. No registration, and something tells him his fake IDs won't cut it with an actual officer of the law. Hence the walking.

His feet know the way downtown, where the color has drained from everything, leaving faded, dirty buildings and people. He blends into the wash of brown and gray like another piece of debris, and no one looks his way. Everything is spread out and half-empty here, especially after the last few years, but this is where the only shelter in the city with free phones is, and Saturday is his call with Danny. No way in hell he's missing that.

So what if he hits the area early today and has an extra eye out for someone with a box of sandwiches? He's hungry and curious. He puffs on a stale cigarette a john handed him with his cash a week or so ago, and watches the volunteers trickle out of the mission. They all look so out of place in their nice, clean windbreakers and sensible shoes. He wonders how many of them are lonely and broken like Cam or if they know him.

Half an hour passes, and no blue eyes or messy black hair. No surprise. He's not paying attention when some blonde chick shoves two sandwiches into his hand. They're just bread and cheese, not the usual PB&J, and the woman looks straight through him.

Sean heads to the park that's devolved into the main homeless camp; an outpost of tents and tarps the city keeps threatening to clean out - if they ever get the money. He finds Lyle in the back. The marine insignia on his cap is obscured by grime, and the green of his old fatigues is fading. He jumps up to attention when he sees Sean. "Morning, Major!"

"Lyle, how many times do I gotta tell you, I ain't my dad."

Lyle's eyes focus, and a genuine smile spreads across his face. "Hey, Sean, how's it going?"

"Just about as good as you'd think." Sean hands Lyle one of the sandwiches, avoiding the beady-eyed glare of the guy who camps next to him. "Scram, Ulrich, nothing for you."

"You can't afford to buy something for your friend? Gotta bring him the free stuff?" Ulrich sneers back. "Cocksucking not paying out this week?"

"Fuck off." Sean turns his back to the other guy, hiding the twenty he slips Lyle. "Get a shower, okay?"

"Yes, Sir," Lyle says with a salute. Sean walks through the winding, trash-strewn paths of the camp. He sees a few other faces he knows. Eddie's still there, with a set-up nicer than half the houses Sean ever lived in. Joan is a few spots down, and Sean puts a few fives in her jar and pretends to take one of the cups of coffee she has on offer.

"Yo, Orson, you got the time?" Sean asks the grizzled Black man by the makeshift desk at the front of the camp. Orson keeps the whole place running; deals with the police (something that takes more balls than Sean can even comprehend), and takes the donations from upright, clean folk handing off their half-finished party platters so they can feel better about themselves.

"10:47. Ain't you got some place better to be than annoying me?" Orson shoots back.

"That I do."

Sean heads towards the shelter. Thankfully, there's not a line. Sometimes he misses having a phone, but it's hard to pay a damn cell bill when you don't have an address. He could buy burners, he guesses, but it's not like he has anyone else to call. He thinks of the number for 'Cameron Steward' wedged neatly in his wallet and shakes his head. The sap would never answer.

Danny picks up after one ring.

"Sean?" Danny sounds exactly like a puppy would if it could talk.

"Who else would call your lame ass?" Sean smiles into the phone. "How are things in Cleveland?"

"Boring," Danny sighs, as put upon and petulant as only a four-teen-year-old can be. "I'm already done with summer reading, so I've been at the library looking at the junior curriculum."

"Nerd. It's summer, you should be hanging out with your friends."

"Yeah, sure. All those friends I made in the last month of the year at a new school." Sean hates the bitterness in Danny's voice. "No one wants to hang out with the foster kid anyway."

"Screw anyone who says that. You're a dweeb, but you're cool enough."

"Thanks"

"The Weavers treating you okay still?" He tries not to sound nervous. Foster placements are always a crapshoot. Never know if you'll get a touching story or a story of touching.

"They're fine. I get fed. They get their checks. Nothing new to report."

"You need anything? I'm working on the coat," Sean asks, hopeful until Danny takes too long to answer.

"I'm fine, Sean. You don't need to worry. And you know—"

"I'm your big brother; worrying about you is my job."

"I checked out that book you were talking about," Danny says, ending the discussion. Not subtle.

Sean keeps up his attention as they chat about books and movies, but his smile fades. The call ends the same way it always does: with Danny suddenly having to hang up, and Sean telling him to watch his back. He doesn't bother with the "see you soon" lie anymore.

Sean hangs around the neighborhood after, unsettled. It's probably because he hasn't worked for a few days, thanks to Cam overpaying. Even with that thought in his head, he sticks around the area, walking bored laps past husks of abandoned buildings, empty windows, and rotting wood over gaping doors. Empty as his hope.

He doesn't see him. He doesn't see any blue eyes. He doesn't see dark hair or a man walking like he's going to an execution. He only sees uncaring face after face.

The streets smell of piss and exhaust, and dust stings in Sean's nose as his route takes him past yet another derelict church. The fourth, by his count. It's Catholic, this one – Saint Anthony's – and it's seen better days. Windows that used to be colorful are now caked with grime, but when Sean finds himself inside, it's still echoing and quiet and smells holy.

Mom would always mutter a prayer to Saint Anthony whenever she lost something, usually her keys. *Saint Anthony, come around, something's lost that can't be found.*

Cam probably goes to one of those gross megachurches. Or one that's indistinguishable from an orthodontist's office; all clear glass and beige siding.

Sean sticks a dollar in the little box and lights a candle in front of the Virgin Mary. He never thought his mom was an idolator for praying to her, but Cam does, so screw him for that and for not coming with sandwiches today. Some things are lost, and shouldn't be found, and that's fine. The prayer Sean says isn't for him anyway.

3
AGainsT PLan

cameron

"WELCOME HOME!" KAYLA'S BRIGHT voice cuts off Cameron's thoughts as he enters the house on Friday. The table is set with candles and food, cupcakes on the counter. "I thought we could do an at-home date night for a change."

Cameron makes himself smile to cover his panic. He did so well for the last week pretending things were normal (aside from nearly weeping in church, which no one noticed, and masturbating in the shower to memories of Sean once after a particularly vivid dream).

Last night had been torture, of course. He got in and out of his car seven times before going on the longest run he could imagine, all the way to the gas station where he'd bought a jumbo-sized bag of flaming hot Cheetos, carried them home, and eaten the whole bag before crawling up to bed with his stomach trying to kill him. Actual flagellation might have been easier on his system.

All because he wanted to be somewhere else. He wants nothing more than to be there now.

"Where did you order from?" he forces himself today.

"The natural market. I got you that macaroni salad with the garlic you like so much. And…" Kayla pulls a DVD out from under a napkin.

"*Sunset Boulevard*, Blu-Ray special edition. Do you remember watching this together at the old Paramount in college?"

Cameron remembers going home after with impure thoughts of William Holden. "You thought it was a musical."

Kayla grins, and Cameron tells himself to be proud that he's making her happy. She says the blessing over dinner, asks for it to nourish and heal them. She tries to make him smile by reminding him about the time the pastor and Cameron's brother Luke tried to convince them that brown rice was one of those socialist, heathen plots to force diversity on good, God-fearing people. Cameron's other brother, Vincent, and Kayla had corrected the assumption, saying it was healthier. Reverend Osborn and Luke had tutted and said there was no need for healthy food, just prayer. Cameron prays all the time and eats the healthy food his wife puts in front of him. He's still sick.

The movie is as beautiful and tragic as Cameron remembers. Norma Desmond, desperate to hold on to the one person that makes her feel wanted, is as haunting as ever, and William Holden is still handsome, acerbic, and doomed. When Norma is ready for her close-up and the credits roll, Cameron tries to keep his breath steady. Kayla excuses herself upstairs to clean up. He's expected in five minutes.

All those years ago, at the Paramount, he drove Kayla home, his thoughts distracted. He'd been thinking of William Holden when she kissed him. Her hand had found the bulge in his jeans, and she'd gasped. The shock of her unzipping him, pulling him free, and stroking him with an unsure hand had been exciting. The sensation had felt good, and Cameron had been young and desperate. When he came with a gasp, he told himself it was her hand he liked, not the visions in his mind.

That's how it works. Or used to work. Cameron's skill at summoning up a dream faded over time as fantasies were replaced with cold reality, and he could perform his duties as a husband less and less. He tried so hard to do it right, but for the last year, sex had been worse each time they tried, no matter how much he prayed. He never knows what's more painful: his shame at his failures or his guilt for the heartbreak on Kayla's face.

Cameron finds himself in their room, barely aware of coming upstairs. Kayla is there in lace, the lights turned low. She's beautiful, with gloss on her pink lips and hope in her brown eyes. Against his will, Cameron's mind fills with the image of different lips and green eyes. His stomach churns, and his skin prickles as Kayla approaches.

"Is there something you want to try tonight?" she asks uncertainly.

"No," Cameron says too fast, pulse already racing.

He closes his eyes when he kisses her, the lip gloss sticky against his chin. Her mouth is softer than Sean's, her kisses wetter, but more tentative. She's shorter, so the angle is wrong, but it's a warm body. In his mind, Cam stands in a dingy hotel again, with Sean's hand at the front of his slacks. He can nearly hear his husky laugh. Kayla is the one touching him, but Cameron remembers everything. Ratty jeans, firm arms, stubble on his lips. The smell of Sean in the stale air. The heat of his sinful mouth on…

"Oh my God," Kayla whispers, palming Cameron's weak erection with trepidation. "Oh my—"

"In the bed," Cameron manages. He strips fast, fighting to keep Sean in his mind as he takes his place where God intended. Kayla's hands are small and delicate, and nothing is the same as how Sean sank onto him, hot and slow. Cam lets his body take over, chasing the memory of the fire Sean kindled under his skin. He pushes away the sound of Kayla's pleasure and does his duty, bites back Sean's name, and comes, quick and weak.

He should have lasted longer, should have tried to bring her some pleasure too, but at least she smiles when he pulls back. That's something.

It has to count for something that he was able to do it, doesn't it? Maybe *this* is God showing him he can be good. The voice that sounds like Sean's whispering in Cam's ear says no. He was only able to do it because of his sin. Because tomorrow is Saturday, and he won't be able to hide for long.

Sean

Sean gets so tired of being uncomfortable *all the time*. Not that he doesn't make it worse for himself. He'd done everything he could this week to forget about Cam. He'd wasted cash on three movies and more on food and booze, but it hadn't eased the sting of not seeing him again. Sean doesn't know why he expected the guy to find him again, if only so he could con him into another night at a motel.

His body aches from walking and the general travails of being, as the PC dorks call it, 'chronically unhoused.' After spending too much time on his knees in a dirty bathroom on Thursday to forget being ditched, Sean's knees started aching and got worse all through Friday, so he gave in and crashed at the shelter. The showers were crap, but feeling clean for the first time in a week is worth it. Spending the night meant he was closer to the phones. Good thing, because there was a line today.

"How you doin' on shoes?" Sean asks Danny when there's a lull in the conversation. "I've got enough for you for the fall coat. Do you need shoes too?"

"I'm fine, Sean. You don't need to waste money." Sean hates the tension in Danny's voice.

"It's already done, okay? I just need the address to send the money."

Danny is silent, and Sean imagines him looking across some dirty room to a foster parent staring him down. "You know I can't tell you that," he almost whispers.

"It's not like I'm gonna come and snatch you! How many times—"

"I have to go. I need to get a book back to the library."

"Danny, come on."

"Use the money for you, please. Bye, Sean."

The line goes dead, and Sean stares at the pockmarked wall until the dial tone comes back. He was so sure Danny would tell him this time.

"Hey, buddy, you done? Other folks are waiting!" some rando yells.

"Yeah, I'm done," Sean growls, slamming the receiver down and pushing past the line of grimy faces. He stalks out of the shelter, walking fast just to be moving until he crashes into some idiot wearing a knit cardigan in July and sends a box of sandwiches spilling onto the sidewalk. "Goddamnit! Watch it!"

The dude gasps. Sean knows why the instant he looks up into gorgeous blue eyes. Of course, *now* he runs into the fucker. Sean turns on his smile like a weapon and watches the guy go pale. Messing with a closeted weirdo probably isn't the best way to process his rage, but it's all Sean's got.

"Fancy meetin' you here, Cam."

Cameron's eyes dart to a woman with brown hair further down the street, and he looks like he's about to burst an ulcer. "Sean."

"Oh, you remember?"

Cam squints at him like he's insane. "Of course." He keeps glancing at the other volunteer. "I…"

Fine. He'll give him an excuse. "You see me around all the time," he says with a wink as he kneels to pick up the scattered sandwiches, looking up through his lashes. "Missed you last week, by the way."

"I was ill," Cam mutters.

"Uh-huh. Sure." Sean piles the sandwiches into Cam's flimsy box before taking two for himself.

Cam looks at where his fellow volunteer is walking away. Finally, his pal disappears, and Cam relaxes slightly.

"I got some acquaintances that could use these," Sean says, holding up the sandwiches.

"Your friends?"

Sean shakes his head at Cam's innocence. "People round here don't have friends."

"That's very sad." He looks down at his lumpy pile of sandwiches, chewing his lip and fighting a bad decision. "Can I buy you something hot?"

"Buy me something hot or buy you—" Sean catches his breath at the glare Cam gives him. Okay, he found the line. Good to know. "Fine. There's pizza a few blocks away. We'll drop these at the camp with Orson."

Sean starts walking to the tents visible down the street. He heads past Orson, trusting Cam knows what to do, and stops by Lyle's corner. The guy's face is barely visible inside his filthy sleeping bag, and his eyes are closed, so Sean leaves a sandwich. The other ends up shoved in a pocket of Sean's beat-up leather jacket. He finds Cam at the front, avoiding Orson's eyes, but empty-handed.

"How far?" Cam asks.

"Four blocks." Sean walks fast, but Cam keeps up, looking around nervously the whole time. "Are you worried about getting jumped or getting caught with me?" Sean asks before jaywalking over the railway tracks and turning down the street to Dante's as Cam rushes after him.

"It's broad daylight." Sean guesses that's an answer to both questions.

They order three slices of pepperoni, and Cam leaves a nice tip after paying in cash. Sean attacks his pizza like an animal as soon as they're seated. The chairs are wobbly and sticky, and the pizza is dripping grease, but damn it's good. Cam looks suspicious of, well, everything.

"Not allowed pizza either?" Sean asks through a mouthful.

"Not really."

"Damned if that's not the saddest thing I've ever heard," Sean smirks as Cam scowls and douses his slice with parmesan. He watches with interest as Cam takes a bite and then groans around it. "I promise not to tell." Sean takes another large bite and considers. "Someone else might though. Tattle that is."

Cam looks up in panic. "Who? Why?"

"No one specific. I'm just saying that if you don't want to worry about someone blackmailing you, don't give people your real name. Or your number."

Sean has obviously planted a nightmare scenario in Cam's head. "People *do* that?"

"Hey, breathe. I'm not gonna rat you out. For anything. I'm just telling you, in the future when you go looking for fun: be careful."

"I have no intention of looking for more *fun*," Cameron says thickly. "But thank you for the advice."

"Really?" Sean very pointedly draws his thumb over his bottom lip and licks off a few drops of grease. Cam's cheeks blaze red at the sight. "You got it out of your system?"

"Yes," Cam says through gritted teeth, like he's fighting with everything he has not to jump across the table and kiss the smirk off Sean's face.

"Just doing the Lord's work then?" Cam takes another big bite and nods. "So work me for the Lord."

"I don't think that anything I say would convince you to leave behind sin," Cam sighs.

"I'm offended," Sean scoffs back, but Cam doesn't take the bait. He doesn't do anything but stare. "We can still talk, you know."

"I told you: I'm not good at talking," Cam mutters, finally looking down. Is he waiting for a blessing or something?

"You know, my mom wanted me to be a Priest," Sean blurts out.

Cam glares at him dubiously. "Really?"

"She liked church – the real kind, with candles and saints and chants," Sean goes on, enjoying how annoyed Cam looks. "She led a choir. I'm crap at singing, so I thought for a while I'd do what she wanted." Sean takes a big bite before he says something corny about how he wanted to be in the church to be closer to her, not God, because that's none of Cam's business.

"Why didn't you do it?" Cam asks before taking his bite.

"Mainly cause I figured out priests don't get laid," Sean says casually, and Cam chokes. "Or they shouldn't."

"Not allowing clergy to marry is one of the reasons there's so much abuse with the Catholics," Cam wheezes with no conviction. "Or, that's what our pastor says."

"He's probably not wrong," Sean says with a sigh. "Is he married?"

"Mercifully for all women, no," Cam says, and Sean barks out a laugh. "Ouch."

"I shouldn't have said that. It was rude," Cam tells his feet.

"So buy an indulgence. Wait, y'all don't get those either, do you? No wonder you never have fun." The glare Cam gives him is frankly amazing and weirdly hot. Sean licks his lip again and nudges Cam's foot with his. "You sure you're not in the market for fun? Really on the straight and narrow?"

"I need to move my car," Cam declares, standing and managing to bang the table. Sean's got a good idea of why he's walking funny.

"Come on, no one is going to jack your Prius!"

"I'll have you know I drive a Corolla," Cam snaps, and he stares down at where Sean still sits, slouched against the pizzeria wall.

"So, if you didn't want my services, why'd you buy me lunch? The guilt thing? Or you just don't have the balls to misbehave today?"

Cam scowls and stalks away as Sean snickers. He liked the way Cam fucked him; he's not denying that, but he didn't like the way he made him feel. Or, more precisely, that he made Sean feel at all. Better to be rid of him. Sean's able to convince himself he's glad he was an asshole for about two minutes before the regret sets in. By then, he's walking again.

cameron

Cameron refuses to be sick. He refuses to let the panic and lust swimming inside him burst out, even though he can feel the burn of it. The damned pizza doesn't help either. His hands are shaking, his pulse is racing, and he has no idea where he even is. He was headed in the direction of his car, he thought, but he's not even sure what street he's on.

"Goddamnit," he mutters, relishing taking the Lord's name in vain. He'd prayed this morning for God to spare him temptation. God probably knew it was lip service and could see his true, shameful desires. Just like Sean could. The well-behaved part of his mind is praying for help now, to make this all go away, to find his car, undo and unknow everything for the last few weeks. Cameron spins, hopelessly trying to find a landmark or even a damn street sign.

"Jesus Christ, do not tell me you're fucking lost." Cameron rounds on Sean. Of course, he found him again. Cameron settles for grabbing

Sean by the arm rather than punching him, though the impulse remains. "Hey, easy!"

"*Sean.*" The word is barely above a whisper, but Sean hears it, probably because Cameron is only a few inches from him. Far closer than is appropriate. Sean's eyes are locked on him, and Cameron prays with all his soul that right now Sean can read him. He can't say it, but Sean has to know what he's asking.

Sean's eyes darken. "You got forty?"

Cameron gulps, tongue thick and heart racing so fast he feels like he might explode. He nods.

Sean leads them to a building with boarded-up doors. They take the alley along the side and then a creaking door into the decrepit place. Maybe it was a business, but in the dusty half-light, Cam can't make out any identifying details. He doesn't care. Sean backs him up against a wall, hands on Cam's hips, chest pressed close, and Cam stops caring about anything but Sean.

There's no kiss. It's a blessing because a kiss might kill him. Instead, Sean's hands move to his ass, pulling the two of them flush so Sean can feel how shamefully hard Cam is and give a smug laugh. He groans as Sean grinds against him, then gasps when he pulls his wallet from his back pocket.

"Don't worry; not taking more than I quoted."

Cam doesn't speak, just nods again as Sean opens the wallet and pulls out two twenties. He doesn't snoop or comment. Doesn't entice Cam to confess that Sean could take it all, and he wouldn't care one bit. Sean replaces the wallet, grinding again. He's hard too, and Cam takes some pride in that. Then Sean drops to his knees and unzips him.

Cam bites hard on his lip to hold back his moan when Sean's mouth finds him. "You can look, you know. Watching's half the fun."

Cam can't resist Sean's honeyed drawl, dark and low. He looks down and whimpers at the sight of Sean's perfect lips wrapping around his dick. It's better than the first time. The soft flicks of his tongue, the way Sean hollows his cheek when he takes more of Cam in. He digs his nails into the crumbling wall behind him as Sean licks and sucks and drives him mad. Sean starts bobbing his head in earnest, and his hands on Cam's hips aren't a warning; they're encouragement to move. Sean catches Cam's eye through his lashes, then hums as Cam starts to thrust into his mouth. Sean's warm, expert mouth is everything. Everything he's wanted for so long.

Cam grits his teeth, fighting to breathe as his pleasure spikes, rising to a crescendo he can barely keep back. He wants this to last, wants to stay here, hidden in the shadows with Sean swallowing him down and never return to reality, but Sean does something bordering on witchcraft and takes all of Cam into his throat.

"Sean! I—" Cam comes, eyes falling closed, head thrown back, body shaking as he pours down Sean's waiting throat.

Sean pulls off with a wet noise and a filthy laugh. Cam collapses back against the wall, panting, eyes still locked on Sean as he gingerly tucks Cam back into his pants.

"Give me another twenty."

"What?"

"Just trust me."

Cam can barely make his appendages work, but he manages to fish out his wallet and fumble Sean his last bill. Sean pockets it with a grin and immediately undoes his fly, pushing down his underwear and revealing his own leaking member. He starts stroking himself, fast and rough, and Cam groans. "Fuck."

"Can't give you this show for free, but damn." Sean's breath hitches as his hand flies over his length. Cameron desperately wants to touch, but he doesn't think it's allowed. He's too dazed to be of much use anyway. "Never get this turned on giving head; you know that?"

Sean jacks himself faster, biting his lips as he stares at Cam, not blinking until he comes, spilling onto the dirty floor. "Glad I found you," Sean chuckles as he rights himself.

"I didn't—" Cam doesn't know why he's trying to explain himself to literally the only person who doesn't care.

"Yeah, yeah, you didn't start your day planning to get your cock sucked."

"No. I did."

Sean looks up at Cam, impressed.

"I wake up every morning since that night and think of you," Cam confesses, his focus intent on his shoe. "I thought about you when I was with my wife last night."

"With her like *with* her?" Sean echoes, green eyes bulging. "Wow."

"Still, my plan today wasn't this." He shakes his head. "Things weren't supposed to be like this."

Sean gives him a look that's equal parts pity and amusement. "Things are what they are, man. You like guys sucking you off, I like doing it and getting paid. It's meant to be. Some shit you just gotta go with."

"So there's no point in fighting?" Cam asks with an empty laugh.

"Depends what you're fightin', I guess."

Cam nods and straightens up, beating the dust from his sweater. That's a good enough answer. "Can you help me get back to my car?"

"Uh, sure. You okay?"

"No, but I'll manage." Sean leads him out into the daylight and within sight of the mission. "Thank you," Cam says, because it's polite.

"Seriously, are you gonna be alright?"

There's real concern in Sean's eyes when Cam meets them. Every time he looks at them, he's amazed by how beautifully vivid the green is. Everything about Sean is beautiful. "Are you going to be at the same place on Thursday?"

Sean looks surprised and amused. "Outside the bar or at the diner?"

"Does it matter?"

"Waiting around at the diner is a hell of a lot more comfortable," Sean says with a shrug. "'Especially after dark."

"That would be good."

Sean nods slowly in understanding, licking his lips. "See ya around, Cam." Sean doesn't wait for a reply, just turns and walks away, a bowlegged shadow cast behind him.

Cameron forces himself not to dwell on it. He just did something horrible and then made a plan to do it again. It didn't feel horrible, of course. It felt better than anything in his memory.

Kayla is in the garden when he gets home, pulling weeds. "Hey, babe," she calls, peering out from under her sun hat. "You wanna take off the Mister Rogers sweater and help out?"

"You bought me this sweater."

"Which is why I don't want you getting it dirty."

Cameron squats next to her. "The tomatoes look good this year." He plucks a beautiful ripe one from the vine and pops it into his mouth before Kayla can stop him.

"Hey! You know that's not good for your stomach!"

Cameron smiles, lips together as he chews, and the acid-bright flavor explodes in his mouth. It tastes like the sun. "One won't hurt me."

"No, but you never eat just one. I remember the guy who ate fifteen burgers in one day."

"They were on sale."

"Uh huh." Cameron moves to grab one more tomato, and Kayla playfully smacks his hand away. "Get changed and maybe you can have some more."

"Yes, Ma'am."

Cameron changes quickly and pops a few antacids before heading back outside. If he's careful, he'll be fine. He can enjoy the sun and the tomatoes and all sorts of things, if he's just careful. Some shit you just gotta go with.

4

Technicolor

sean

SEAN SPENDS A DAY or three ignoring the little electric charge under his skin each time he thinks about Cam. He hangs out at the library, sees a movie, services an idiot in a back alley who's so drunk he pays Sean twice, and he doesn't think about Cam. He walks by a church on Sunday, listens to the muffled warnings about sinners in the hands of an angry God, and instead of that tingle, he gets a pit in his stomach. So he walks faster.

It's stupid. Cam is just another john. Yeah, he's hot and his dick is nice and he overpays – he's also a mess. Still, there's something about him that Sean can't turn away from. He's had his share of repeat customers or guys that'll seek him out. He knows what they like, the kind of show to put on, and what he can get out of them. Cam is in a different world from those assholes, but Sean's not gonna waste his energy figuring out how.

Maybe it's to remind himself of what his regulars are supposed to be like that Sean ends up at Big Rig Paradise leaning on a wall and waiting until a trucker with a sallow face and hard eyes waves him over.

"You up for a party?" the guy drawls, nasal and lewd.

"Depends. Just you?"

The big guy gets a cruel, hard look in his eye and shakes his head.

"Got some friends all need some relaxin'. One at a time."

"Sounds like my kind of party."

He manages five customers in the stinking bathroom. His jaw aches, and his throat is sore. It's awful, but this is where he belongs, in the dark on his knees. The guy who brought him in pulls his hair and mumbles about fucking Sean raw and all sorts of other bullshit. Sean wants to take a bite out of him, but he shuts his eyes and thinks of England, and soon it's done. He throws the money on the ground for Sean to scramble after while he takes a bump of something. He doesn't even have the decency to offer Sean a hit. Asshole.

The taste of latex permeates Sean's swollen mouth, but he stumbles out with close to two hundred in his pocket. Not bad for night's work; not that Sean's keeping much of it. Some is earmarked for the bottle of rotgut he's gonna buy to wash out the memories. Maybe that Taco Bell by the liquor store on tenth is still open. It's a good idea, one that keeps him moving back towards town in the Bel Air as he massages his aching jaw.

The booze doesn't work. He huddles in the back seat, parked under a quiet overpass, and drinks and drinks and still he can't wash the memories out of his head. Or Cam.

Cameron Steward. He of serious expressions and repressed desire. He would never treat Sean like any of those guys tonight. He's the kind of person who's incapable of cruelty like that. Sean could see that the first time he offered him a sandwich.

Cam would be repulsed by Sean's night; he can't kid himself, but right now, in the dark wash of memory, Sean pretends he'd look past it. He wants that little scrap to hang onto before Thursday comes and reality sets it on fire. Sean doesn't fantasize about specifics, just the way Cam looks at him. The way he might still look at Sean in a few days if neither of them chickens out. Like he's something good, or beautiful. Sacred.

cameron

Cameron feels like he's watching a movie. Something noir, like *Double Indemnity*. He watches himself go through his day and lie to Kayla over lunch about his evening plans. Watches himself go to the ATM and withdraw cash from his private 'rainy-day' account. The sky will be clear tonight, but the cash is useful.

He watches himself pick at the salad designated as dinner, then throw it away in the garage. He feels entirely detached as he drives into the city, a clear plan of infidelity and depravity in his mind. When he takes the off-ramp, it's excitement, not terror, that tingles in his gut. His focus shifts, and suddenly he's in his body again, parking and walking briskly into the worst part of town.

Cameron passes the strip club he never went in. It's a helpful landmark to find the Moonlight diner. The place must have been a draw in the fifties, but its glory days are long gone. The chrome trim is scratched, the vinyl is torn on the chairs, and the pictures on the walls are crinkled and faded. Even the bell above the door is old, and the dull sound barely registers with the three patrons seated at the counter. The only person who looks up is sitting in the farthest booth.

It's a movie again, but this time it's that scene from *The Wizard of Oz* where Dorothy walks out of her sad, sepia world into glorious Technicolor.

Sean smiles, and Cam knows he must be making some ridiculous face. He doesn't care. Sean is there. Tonight, Sean is here for him. Like a miracle.

Cam ungracefully takes a seat in the booth, and Sean takes a circumspect sip of the coffee in front of him. "I had you at about a sixty-forty chance of showing," he drawls, all swagger and smugness. "Never know about you careful types."

"I'm glad I didn't disappoint you," Cam mutters, forcing himself to be calm. "Have you been waiting long?"

"Not too. They got decent coffee."

"You haven't eaten?" Cam asks in real concern, and Sean looks annoyed.

"You don't gotta buy me dinner every time."

"Are you saying you're not hungry?"

"No, but—"

Cam waves down the waitress as Sean shakes his head. "One cheeseburger, please. No pickles."

"Same," Sean grumbles. The waitress leaves, and Sean looks at him carefully, expression softening. "You're less nervous this time."

"I'm sure it will come."

"As long as you're sure you'll—" Sean stops himself, thanks to the shock on Cam's face. "Sorry. Can't talk like a human."

"It takes practice. Or so I'm told." He can see Sean holding back another smartass remark. That's progress. "How… was your week?"

Sean stares at him for a beat before giving him another shrug. "I saw a good movie, I guess. You know the old Paramount theater over by the university? They do vintage nights. They had *Notorious* playing on Monday."

Cameron's mouth twitches in a sad smile. "I know the theater. That's a good movie."

"You seen it?"

"It's one of my favorites," he admits, like he's confessing a secret.

"Man, Ingrid Bergman was hot," Sean grins. "Cary Grant too."

Cam looks around, wishing he had some water for his suddenly dry mouth. Sean is curious when Cam dares to look back at him. "I… always liked Claude Raines."

A grin spreads over Sean's face. "Respectable choice."

"He was so elegant, and his voice was very alluring." Sean nods, a glint in his eye. "I've never told anyone that. I mean. I have, but they—"

"Just thought you wanted to be him, not that you wanted to be with him."

Cam nods, cheeks hot. Thankfully, the waitress arrives with their food. Despite his protests, Sean looks more than happy to see the meal, and they tuck into their burgers without any ceremony. It's not until halfway through that Cam works up the courage to speak again. "What other movies do you like?"

It turns out the answer is all of them. Movie theaters are a sanctuary for Sean: some place secure and temperature-controlled where he can disappear for a few hours. Sean will see anything, and he delivers an extended monologue on the virtues of the Marvel Cinematic Universe versus the recent failures of the DC one. He then has to explain the whole concept of movie universes in general to Cam, to his great frustration. When Cam earnestly asks if the music Sean favors could be considered 'yacht rock,' Sean nearly chokes on his fry and informs Cam he appreciates 'the classics.' That doesn't include Bach or Brahms, so Cam continues to be confused.

It's normal. Relaxing. Enough so that when Sean nods for them to leave, that feels normal too. Cam keeps the receipt again.

The man at the front desk of the motel still doesn't look up from his newspaper when he hands Sean a key and takes Cam's money. Again, he pays for the full night. It's even the same room.

The nerves set in when they close the door, and Cam sees the dirty walls and rough red carpet. *This* isn't normal. This is a premeditated crime on both their parts, a betrayal of everyone that has ever had faith in him. Of God.

"Hey, ground control to Major Cam."

Cam blinks. Sean is there, standing close. "I'm sorry."

"It's okay, you said you'd get nervous. Don't matter to me." Something has changed in Sean's demeanor. It's softer, warmer. Enticing. He licks his lips, and Cam's heart starts to pound.

"You've seen it all, I gather?"

"Something like that." Sean looks more sad than proud when he says it, but Cam doesn't want to think about all the awful things he's seen.

Finally, Sean touches him. He runs a hand over his cheek, into Cam's hair, and pulls him into a kiss. Technicolor bursts in his mind, all over again.

Sean kisses him, gentle and unhurried, like he's savoring as much as Cam. That's impossible, but Cam will take the dream. Sean pulls away, and Cam feels dizzy, fighting the urge to tug Sean back and kiss him forever.

"Uh..." Sean looks nervously at the door. No, the rickety dresser by the door.

"Oh. Yes." Cam pulls out his wallet and sets out the bills. It doesn't make him feel guilty, just confident. The deal is done. For the rest of the night, Sean is his.

"That's *really* more than—" Sean's words cut off with a small intake of breath when Cam pushes back into his space, one hand on his shoulder, another on his hips. Sean is the one staring now, examining Cam's face with what one might call wonder. "Fuck."

"Is something wrong?" Sean stops his mouth with a kiss. It's more intense now, and Cam's mouth is frantic in return. He's never been kissed like this and never wanted to lose his entire self in lips and teeth and tongue the way he does with Sean.

Sean starts undressing him, something Cam is infinitely grateful for. He's sure his hands would shake if he tried. Sean licks his lips when Cam's chest is revealed. Then his lips are on Cam's skin, a gentle noise catching in his throat. Emboldened, Cam tugs at the hem of Sean's tee. He lets Cam strip him, revealing warm skin and a smug smile. He pulls their bodies flush, and Cam's caution dissolves into desire so deep and sharp it hurts.

They fumble at belts and flies between them. Sean starts to pull his pants off, and Cam feels like another force moves him. He finds himself kneeling at Sean's feet, batting his hands away and pulling the last of his clothes off so that Sean's beautiful cock springs free.

Cameron has been drunk a few times in his life. (He wasn't a complete shut-in in college, no matter what his brothers claim.) He remembers the way his head spun, like his mind was loose from his body, traveling at a different speed. Now, kneeling before Sean, he feels the same: dizzy and unmoored. And free. He's never been in this position outside of his most secret dreams. Now he's here, overcome by the salt tang of Sean's scent, the heat of him radiating towards Cam's lips, just an inch away.

"Cam, you don't have to—" Cam gives his first experimental lick, catching a bitter drop of precome on his tongue. Not so bad. He licks again, slower, then wraps his mouth around Sean's girth. "Oh God…"

Cam knows he has no technique or finesse. This isn't about that. This isn't even about making Sean come. This is about having something that was always impossible, the taste and weight of it on his tongue. He sucks and licks and holds onto Sean's hips for dear life, each sound and shudder he draws from him a triumph. On bended knee before the object of his sin, it's a strange sort of worship.

"Jesus fucking Christ, *Cam*." His name on Sean's lips is the greater blasphemy to Cameron's ears, and he relishes it. "I need…" Sean pants, voice breaking.

Cam pulls off, amazed to see how flushed and wanton Sean looks above him. "What do you need?"

"I need your pretty cock in me," Sean answers with a strangled laugh.

"No one's ever commented on its quality before," Cam comments, smiling as he rises.

"Well, I'm an expert, and it's nice, and I want you to fuck me with it right now."

Sean's good at this, at convincing Cam he wants it. So much so that Cam lets himself believe it's real, that he's wanted like this, by this beautiful man. Sean stumbles away, grabbing something from his pants. Lubricant and a condom. Of course. "Do you want me to? Or do you?"

Cam draws a shuddering breath. "I'd like to. If that's acceptable."

"Yeah. Fuck. Sure." Sean looks debauched as he scrambles back on his elbows, and Cam follows, magnetized. Sean presses the supplies into Cam's hands. The steadiness of his hands as he tears open the packet of lube and squeezes it onto his finger surprises him.

"Let me know if it hurts." It's a simple courtesy, but the words seem to overcome Sean more than the first touch of Cam's slick fingers. Sean's mouth hangs open, and he makes quiet, pleased sounds as Cam works. The heat of him is even more searing than Cam remembers.

"Fuck, I take it back," Sean sighs, arm slung over his head, a sheen of sweat on his chest that catches the orange light from outside. He's the most beautiful sight Cameron has ever seen.

"Take what back?"

Sean looks at him, eyes lidded, breath quick. "I ain't never seen anything like you."

sean

Sean doesn't have good days. He's living in his car, turning tricks when he needs money, with nothing on the horizon but a wait for people who may never come home. He has days that are less shitty than others, but he's not delusional enough to call them 'good.' Or he wasn't. Lately, he's had a few definitely-not-shitty days that make him reconsider.

For instance: today. It's sunny and he's got a book, a good spot on the grass, and an icy bottle of Coke. It's the good kind too, the shit from Mexico with real sugar. It's his second of the day. He downed the first with the flautas that Cam had looked at so dubiously. He'd trusted Sean when he told him the little place in the back of the tienda was the best Mexican in town. Sean tried real hard not to make a spectacle as he ate, but it was a dick-shaped food and he'd had Cam's dick in his mouth twenty minutes prior, so Cam blushed his way through his tamales anyway. Cam paid for the food, naturally, but Sean bought his own second Coke. It's an indulgence, but, hey, once in a while, he wants something nice. Cam's getting him used to nice things.

Over a month now they've been meeting up, and the weeks have fallen into a rhythm. They meet on Thursdays, eat, and fuck. Cam worries about Sean's health and comfort, but Sean doesn't mind because the money is good, and the sex is better. The sex is actually incredible. He tells Cam that, in his way, whispering filth into his ear about how good he feels and how hard he makes Sean come. Cam knows it's a show, but Sean knows it kind of isn't.

No client has ever done to Sean what Cam does, never laid him out, and just *adored* him. The guy asks what feels good for Sean and does it.

And damn if it's not nice. Maybe it's because Cam's learning, or because he's never had this, but everything he does to Sean, he savors and studies. It makes something magic vibrate in Sean's bones when Cam takes him apart, careful and slow.

He doesn't tell Cam how all that shit is special, unique to him. He doesn't let many guys fuck him; he usually doesn't have to. The service he provides is usually quick and dirty, out in a back alley or bathroom stall, and done in a few minutes. What he does with Cam is different, and he keeps that secret. Sean doesn't want him getting too much of an ego. Or feeling like more of a weirdo.

Cam doesn't ask about what's normal, of course. All part of the story he tells himself. It's that whole 'boyfriend experience.' Some of the time when they're together, Sean likes to pretend it's real too, so he gets why Cam wouldn't want to break the illusion and ask if it's usual for a whore to make out with customers. Cam has got to know the blow jobs aren't normal, at least.

Sean smirks to himself as he takes a long sip of Coke, the sweetness contrasting with the memory of bitterness in his mouth from Cam's come. He likes Saturdays too.

Thursdays, they fuck. After that, Sean gets a night in a bed, takes a long-ass shower, and eats a good breakfast. Fridays, he wanders until nightfall, drinks, and hustles pool. And Saturdays Cam ditches the God squad, depositing his sandwiches with Orson, and finds Sean near the tents. They eat again (either before or after) and find some spot for Sean to suck Cam off. Then Cam returns the favor. Sean's never heard of a guy getting paid to get a blow job, but he doesn't complain. Cam's mouth is gorgeous, and he's getting better at using it every week.

Sean wasn't even sure Cam would show up after their second fuck. He told himself he had to be in the neighborhood anyway, to call Danny, but he's not gonna deny the flip his stomach did when he caught sight of Cam across the park, carrying his box of sandwiches. Cam's never been rough, but that day he hauled Sean off with a fervor before he fell to his knees in the shadows and dust, and did what he wanted, hidden away.

"Cam, you don't have to do that." Sean said it then, and it still makes up half of their conversations since.

"I want to. Please, Sean."

Sean's getting paid to do what Cam wants, so who is he to say no? So Cam blew him, clumsy and frenzied, and Sean came biting his hand to keep from yelling. Sean made sure that Cam came just as hard when it was his turn, teasing him until Cam screamed. Then they went for shitty Chinese, and Sean gave Cam a hard time for his sweet and sour pork order.

Sean's quit complaining about the food thing. Again, it's the *Pretty Woman* lie Cam wants, and Sean can always use the grub. Plus, it's when they get to talk. He still sucks at polite conversation, and so does Cam, but they're getting better. Cam is dorky and literal and really fucking smart, and Sean genuinely enjoys talking to him. Not that they talk about much. Their topics are: Movies (Cam has barely seen anything made after 1985), Music (Cam is a complete nerd, but Sean's learned more about Mozart than he ever wanted to. Sue him if he didn't do some listening at the library, and he's working on educating Cam about AC/DC because Sean was raised by two parents who loved few things more than classic rock), and Cam's work. He does something in an office, with lots of numbers, and he low-key hates it.

Cam doesn't intentionally talk about his wife, but stuff slips out. He'll mention a conversation they had or what she thought of a movie. Every time she comes up, Cam looks so fucking sad. It's not an 'I hate the old ball and chain' sad, either. It's this mantle of regret that doesn't recede until they're alone and mouths and hands are finding dicks and skin.

Sean wonders what she looks like and if there was ever a point where she made Cam happy.

Sometimes they talk after they fuck, but not a lot. Everything's too raw, and the quiet is too nice to break. Sometimes Sean thinks he likes that best of all. Just the quiet. The calm between the storms. Each time they lie together a little bit longer, Cam kisses him a little bit deeper before he gets up to leave.

"See you soon."

Then there's the way he looks at Sean. It's so fucking intense it makes Sean squirm because what the hell is Cam looking at? Sean's gonna need to work to keep his ego in check if Cam keeps it up. Maybe that accounts for how the rest of his week usually goes, since Cam.

The changes aren't big. He drinks a little less, reads a little more, and is a little pickier with customers. He still works, of course, but he's less inclined to service some trucker in a washroom when he knows he's got $300 on the way on Thursday. He's more likely to sit in the damn park reading in the sun and enjoying a Coke.

Tomorrow is Sunday. It's always the shittiest day. The farthest away from the next time he sees Cam. He tries not to linger on that thought. He spends Sundays trying not to wonder if Cam is sitting in church thinking he's on his way to hell because of what he does with Sean. He can't think of anyone he's met in his entire sorry life who deserves hell less than Cam Steward. He's good and kind, and Sean knows all the saints Cam doesn't believe in and the scriptures he does say he's tainting and destroying him every time they touch, but they've got to be wrong.

Sean spots a figure across the park who sends him a wave. It takes him a second to recognize the dude. Last time he saw Eli, he was sporting the ugliest goatee in creation, but he's clean-shaven now.

"Hey, Sean! It's been forever!" Eli calls.

"Yeah, where the hell you been?"

"Let's just say orange isn't my color," Eli says, shoving his hands in his pockets.

"Damn, feel like I shoulda known." Now Sean thinks about it, he does remember some chatter about a dealer getting collared. "They really wasted a cell on a two-bit pot peddler?"

"Hey, I resent that." There's no bite to Eli's word. "We're having a welcome home party over at my place, you should come."

Eli's couch used to be one of his favorite places to crash and he'd give Sean a discount on weed if he serviced a friend or two. "Sure, sounds good."

"Okay then, see you there. You know the place."

Eli retreats. Sean watches him go, savoring another sip of Coke.

He's glad he has some time. It's a nice day, and there's so little light and green in his corner of the world that he doesn't want to leave. Not when he just worked up to taking off his jacket. He already feels the hint of a burn on his skin, the light melting away the cold that settled into his bones years ago. He doesn't want to go back to the grey, to the dark. Not yet.

5
summertime

cameron

CAMERON NEVER KNOWS WHO'S coming over for Sunday dinners, but it's not as if he has a choice about showing up. Today it's his mother, brothers, their wives, and the pastor. Ted Osborn's balding head is burning in the sun, his dark eyes squinting over the barbecue chicken. Cameron is seated between Kayla and his mother at the new patio table, the sweat drying under his collar as the horrible topic of local politics comes up.

"Susan, have you met Don Boyle? It's such an honor to have someone from our little parish running for office," Osborn crows.

"I have," Cameron's mother smiles. "His platform is certainly something."

"Now, Mom, I know you don't like political talk at the table, but I do think this city council election is important," Luke says with a smile as cold and sour-sweet as lemonade.

"Change has to happen at the local level," Osborn says, swallowing a mouthful of iceberg lettuce drowned in ranch. "We've made so much progress nationally, but the city is a mess!"

"Yes, I agree," Cameron says, perking up. "There's a lot to be done. Just the homeless situation since the Salvation Army shelter closed is atrocious."

"That's why Boyle is advocating for a no camping ordinance," Luke says, waving a cob of corn for emphasis. "Treat them like the criminals and junkies they are."

"How will that help?" Cameron asks, surprising everyone with his dubious tone. "What about funding for actual services? There are more people in need than there are beds, and the ones they have are barely adequate."

"Well, that's because of that disgusting 'non-discrimination' ordinance the liberals got in," Osborn spits. "If the shelters had the power to turn away the deviants, they could provide more services to the deserving."

"To good people," Jill, his brother's odious wife, sneers. Cameron knows she means, straight, cis people that look like her, all mashed potatoes covered in mayonnaise.

"Yes, well. Those rules are going to be the first to go," Osborn says. Vincent, Cameron's eldest brother, doesn't say anything, but he gives an approving nod. "Maybe soon we'll be able to clear them all off the street like the trash they are."

"Thank the good Lord people are coming to their senses about this and the employment rules. Never mind sheltering these useless burdens, can you imagine being forced to hire homosexuals? At a school? Or a church?" Luke adds in horror.

"That's why we're glad we have real, Christian people fighting for us," Courtney smiles.

Cameron turns, readying himself for a brave objection. "I don't think—"

"We wouldn't want our kids around that. The media is already bad enough," Vincent says, taking Courtney's hand as if to comfort her against the very thought.

"Speaking of," Osborn says through a mouthful, eyeing Kayla. "Are you two planning yet? The clock is ticking."

Cameron feels his wife tense beside him, and a different, but equally familiar sickness bubbles in his gut.

"At a certain point, some people start wondering when they'll be grandmothers," Cameron's mother smiles.

"You *are* a grandmother, Susan," Kayla says, falsely cheerful. "Or are we all pretending Jake and Meghan don't count?"

"I'd like to sometimes. Jake's been a demon lately," Luke laughs.

"You know what I mean," Susan says.

"I think there's lots of time," Courtney blessedly interjects. "They're just enjoying married life right now. As we all do."

"It's wonderful, isn't it? Coming home every day to your best friend," Kayla says, turning to Cameron, the sun turning her brown eyes a bright shade of gold. "I'm grateful to God every day for the person I get to spend my life with."

Cameron stares into his wife's face and forces a smile as green eyes flash in his mind. It's not the same now as when he uses those fantasies and memories to do his duty for her (and he's been very good about that lately). This memory is nothing but regret and longing. "We're both very lucky."

"We're all very lucky to find men we can serve and hold up," Jillian adds with a barely concealed sneer. She never shuts up about the fact that Kayla works and makes more than Cameron. At least Courtney has the decency to work in a support role for Vince.

"See, *that's* what's important," Osborn says. "Husbands and wives, supporting each other. That is the foundation of our society."

"That's what we need to protect," Luke agrees with a slam of his palm to the table. Cameron nods on reflex. There's another person he becomes at home, at church, in moments like these. A stranger that steps into his skin, who's the complete opposite of who he is when he's tangled up in a dingy motel with a man he pays for sex.

In no time, the guests are sent back to their shiny cars, and he's alone with Kayla again. A weight lifts when it's only the two of them doing the dishes and discussing what ingredients his mother shoved into the dessert she brought besides marshmallows, Jell-O, and canned fruit, and how Osborn ate three servings.

"You know we didn't donate to Don Boyle, right?" Kayla says as they close the washer.

Cameron lets some tension go from his shoulders. "Really?"

"Of course not." Kayla rolls her eyes. "He's an asshole."

Cameron lets out a thin laugh. "I thought I was the only one thinking that. The things he wants to do to 'help' the poor—"

"It's disgusting," Kayla scowls. "Jesus would punch him in the face if he knew what he was using his name for."

"I'd like to see that." Cameron follows Kayla to the couch, and they sit together.

"Hope the new assistant pastor is less of a—"

"Fatuous blow hard?"

"Cameron Steward!" There's only laughter in Kayla's voice, no anger.

Cameron finds himself smiling. He's glad of all the people he has to pretend around; there are still ways he can trust her. "You know, I'm down there every week, and the people they want to drive out? They're not bad. They're good people who have had bad things happen to them. I have friends there, and I wish—" Cameron bites his lip. "I wish I could do more."

"You do a lot, hon," Kayla says, squeezing his shoulder.

"You save people every day. I save money."

"I can only save people because I have you next to me," Kayla says, drawing Cameron's attention back with a finger under his chin. "I'd be nothing without you. You know that."

Cameron finally meets Kayla's eyes. "I still wonder if it's enough."

"Babe, come on." He doesn't deserve the kindness in her expression. "You're a better example of doing as Christ would want than any of them. You're the best person I know."

Cam means it when he smiles, even though it hurts. "You haven't met you."

Kayla rolls her eyes and gives him a quick kiss. "You're sweet." She snuggles under his arm, fishing for the remote. "I didn't know you'd started making friends downtown. Anyone interesting?"

Kayla clicks on the TV without the sound. It's one of the news programs she likes that makes Cameron want to tear his hair out at the mess the world has become.

"There's one young man," Cam says carefully, and he has no idea why he's even talking. Maybe he's punishing himself. Maybe he wants to remember. "His name is Sean."

"Sean?" Kayla repeats, looking up at him with furrowed brows. "How long have you known him?"

"A month or so," Cam replies. The concern on her face is troubling. She probably thinks he's taking advantage. If only she knew. "He's very caring. Sometimes he helps me hand out the donations."

"Does he take anything for himself?"

"Only when I make him," Cameron can't add that Sean doesn't think he deserves anything more.

"That's sweet of you," Kayla says, concealing a yawn. "Tell him your doctor wife says malnutrition can have serious effects paired with stress and, you know, whatever."

"I'll be sure to mention it," he lies.

sean

Sean likes it when Cam swears, and Cam swears a lot when he's about to come. "Fuck… fuck, God. Sean…" the litany goes, and tonight it's fantastic. Sean feels his orgasm building too, racing Cam to finish. He tangles his fingers into dark hair and pulls Cam to him, crashing their mouths together and groaning as he comes first. He shakes and bucks as he shoots between them. At least, he thinks it does. He's kinda distracted, even more so when Cam pants "Sean," one more time and comes himself.

Sean pulls back so he can watch. He used to think that everyone's O-face was ridiculous, but Cam's is hot. When he's free and soaring on what Sean can do to him.

"Beautiful," Cam says, breathless, as he plucks the words from Sean's mind. "So fucking beautiful."

"You know, flattery's supposed to come before the fucking."

Cam smiles, blue eyes searching Sean's as he pushes a few sweaty strands of hair from Sean's forehead with tenderness that makes Sean shiver. Cam looks at him like there's something on the tip of his tongue. It makes Sean feel split right open and carved out, electric charges replacing his breath.

"Are you alright?" Cam asks, eyes darkening because whatever moment Sean is having must show on his face. "Did I hurt you?"

"I'm fine," Sean manages to say, trying to hide that the question itself is a gut punch. "Don't think you could hurt me if you tried."

"I would never mean to." Cam pulls away to get out of bed. Sean's hand moves faster than his brain to stop him, and Cam looks at him, confused. "The condom…"

"Throw it on the floor. We don't need to keep the place clean."

Cam looks dubious, but he obeys and moves easily when Sean pulls him back. He wipes his hands on the scratchy sheets as he pulls them over their bare bodies. There's still come on Cam's stomach as Sean settles close, head on Cam's arm. On impulse, Sean runs his thumb through the mess, pressing it into Cam's skin and earning a small gasp. "Don't you wanna take a bit of me with you?"

"I always want to take all of you with me," Cam whispers back, completely sincere. Those electric eels in Sean's stomach spring to life again.

"Yeah, right."

"Sometimes I…"

Sean looks up through his lashes. He knows that's the look Cam can't resist. "Sometimes you what?"

"Sometimes I think about staying. Here with you. After. Just sleeping." Cam's breath catches again as Sean presses the last of his spend into

Cam's skin, marking him until it's washed away, so he can keep up his pretending. "Waking up next to you."

"Here I thought you were gonna get kinky on me," Sean says, trying to ease the tension that's thick in the air. It works, and Cam huffs a laugh.

"I don't think I'm capable of being very 'kinky.'" The air quotes he throws make it all the more adorable.

"I got faith in you. Just need to figure out what you like."

"I'm scared to ask what that means."

Sean rolls his eyes as Cam cards his hands through his hair. "Like, other positions and stuff, dumbass."

"Oh."

"Come on, you never wanted to get me on my hands and knees?" Sean says, turning the smolder up to eleven. "Bend me over a table or something?"

"I like seeing your face."

Sean wishes Cam would stop surprising him at every turn or reminding him how whatever they have going on is way too different and so fucking dangerous. "You still might like it." It would be easier if he did.

"Maybe. Or maybe eventually…" It's hard to see, but Cam's blushing.

"Whatcha thinkin'?" Cam tries to hide, and a grin spreads over Sean's face. "You want me to fuck you, don't you?"

"I have thought about it," Cam says, almost too quiet to hear.

Sean nuzzles at his face, forcing Cam to look at him and see him smiling before he kisses him, slow and encouraging. "We can see about that."

"I don't think I'm—"

"We'll work you up to it." Sean shimmies closer. The room is warm, the heavy August heat winning the fight against the clanging AC under the window. He still wants to be closer, even so. "That's what I'm here for."

"Thank you."

Sean runs a hand up Cam's arm. "For what?"

"For giving me something to look forward to." Cam takes a long, deep breath. "For getting me through the week. For getting me through."

"Like I said, that's what I'm here for," Sean replies. If Cam can't guess it's the same for Sean, he doesn't need to know.

cameron

The first person Cameron sees when he gets to the mission on Saturday is Arnold Isaacs. A top member of the hospital administration, he's another older white man with a face as dour as the bronze busts in the hospital lobby. He wears his greying hair in a military style despite having never served, which only makes him look more severe. His sharp, pale eyes catch Cameron the moment he walks in, with an air of judgment that makes Cameron's skin crawl. He sends the man a wave and escapes to the basement to join Lee.

The two of them have their routine down, able to churn out a few dozen sandwiches quickly and efficiently.

"Did you tell Flor we'd be doing the amenities packages today?" Cam asks, handing a sandwich to Lee.

"She shoved forty dollars at me and said: 'Have at it.' I don't know why you keep asking her to come. This is through the church, not the hospital."

"The same church that nearly everyone at the hospital goes to and has representatives on the hospital board," Cameron corrects.

"Don't tell me you haven't heard her complaining about that too."

"I have. But, despite Flor's feelings about the church, she's still a good person." Lee raises an eyebrow. "She shows it differently."

"Whatever you say. Have you invited Kayla to join us recently?"

Cameron tamps down a flare of acrid discomfort under his ribs. "She's very busy."

"Sometimes I feel bad that I get to see you more than your wife."

"She sees me when it's important." Cameron keeps his attention on the sandwiches. He's given his wife plenty of time and attention lately, more than ever before, thanks to what his time with Sean allows him to do with her. "It's not the amount of time people spend together; it's what they do with it."

"Of course. I tell my cat that all the time."

They fall back into their usual, comfortable silence. They divide the food and care packages evenly among all the volunteers and join in the prayer before heading out. Cameron's heart flutters in excitement when he steps out into the street, late-summer sun pricking his eyes.

He wore a polo shirt today at Kayla's insistence, along with light khakis. It's the most casual the mission dress code allows, and (to Sean's horror), Cam doesn't own jeans. He doesn't care about his clothes or his stomach or the bags of food and socks in his hands. He simply wants to find Sean and lose himself. He wants Sean's laughter and the glimmer in his eyes and the weight of him in his arms that make him feel whole and real.

"Cameron?" He turns to see Lee at his elbow. "Would you like some help with those today? I know you like to talk to people, but since we're—"

"Heya, Cam."

Cameron looks up to see Sean, and his blood does that thing it tends to do when Sean surprises him – where it seems to jump right out of his veins and vibrate slightly to the left. Sean, for once, isn't wearing his old leather jacket. He looks smaller and younger without it, but still absolutely beautiful.

"Hello, Sean." Cameron tries to keep his voice steady and ignore Lee's confused look.

"PB&Js again?" Sean nods at the boxes.

"And some other things. Socks. Ponchos. Other amenities." Lee answers, drawing Sean's attention for the first time.

"Oh, nice," Sean smiles. "Sorry for not introducing myself. I'm Sean."

"So I guessed." Lee looks suspiciously at the hand Sean holds out to her. "You're a friend of Cameron's?"

"Yeah, we've been, uh, talking about all that good news of yours."

"That's wonderful!" The change in Lee's demeanor is as surprising to Cameron as it is to Sean. She shakes Sean's hand vigorously. "Cameron has always been shy about spreading the word, but I'm glad he's found a willing ear."

"He buys me lunch, so..." Sean shrugs.

"Sean helps me as well; he's very well connected around here," Cameron explains.

"Really? How do you think we're doing?" Lee asks.

Sean glances between Cameron and Lee. "I dunno. Folks get a little tired of PB&J sometimes."

"If you have any ideas, you should tell Cameron. Or we have a meeting about how we can best serve the community after services once a month."

"I'll consider that." Sean's smile is stiff and polite, but it's enough to placate Lee.

"Wonderful. I'll see you later, Cameron. Nice to meet you, Sean."

Cameron waits until Lee is half a block away before he dares to look at Sean.

"Sorry bout that," Sean says, digging his toe into a sidewalk divot. "Got excited, I guess."

"It's alright. Lee will be happy I'm finally spreading the gospel."

"I don't know about the good word, but you are good at spreading some things," Sean smirks as Cam blushes.

"Thankfully, you didn't say anything like that in front of her."

"Do you think she's got a clue?" Sean looks genuinely worried.

"No. It wouldn't occur to her that I could be..."

"Not straight?" Cam is glad Sean says it for him. He nods. "God, what a boring way to live."

"Are you hungry?" Cam asks, feeling strangely fond.

"Always, you know me."

"Hm."

"What do you mean, 'hm?'" Sean asks as they begin to walk.

"You usually complain at least once before you let me buy you food."

"Maybe I missed breakfast."

"Or?"

"Or maybe I'm gonna make you take me to the shitty Chinese place that has a lock on the bathroom door," Sean says as easily as discussing the weather. Cam doesn't trip, and he takes pride in that.

"I do like the sweet and sour pork there," Cam replies. Sean laughs, and the day is perfect already.

They move too fast and not fast enough, handing things out at the camp. Sean makes sure to get a poncho and socks for the wild-eyed veteran he always checks on when he doesn't think Cam is looking. He asks after people, gets satisfactory answers, and waves to a crowd across the park. The time before he gets Cam alone, after giving careful instructions on how long to wait and how to enter the bathroom, is interminable. Then Sean is there, locking the door, grabbing the crumpled bills from Cam's hand, and kissing him.

sean

Eli's place always has people in it. Sean's not sure if he likes or hates it. Lots of people means no one really cares when Sean sleeps on the couch, and there's always someone with smokes, weed, booze, or something stronger. Most days, though, there're too many fucking people. Which is why Sean notices the fact that he's the only one in the living room when he wakes up there on Thursday.

"Hey, you're still here," Eli says cheerfully, plopping next to Sean on the coach. The thing looks like it belongs in a landfill, but it's a hell of a lot more comfortable than the Bel Air's back seat.

"What time is it?"

"Uh, two, I think?" Eli replies through a yawn.

"Are you fucking kidding me?"

"What, you got somewhere to be?"

"Thanks again for letting me crash," Sean says through a yawn. "I can pay you for some of that weed by the way."

"Nah, it's cool. Did wanna talk some business with you though."

"Business?" Sean stretches and smirks. "I don't usually fuck friends."

"You know I'm not into the sex thing," Eli says. "I wanted to see if I could set something up for you. I do half my biz through the web, and it's a good way to score. I could help you out. For a cut."

"You wanna be my cyber pimp?" Sean's too sober for this.

"You're too small time, come on. Don't you want to do more? Guys like you can make bank bending over for CEOs and mayors and shit," Eli says through a mouthful, neon orange dust coating his lips.

"And you'd be cashing in on this new venture."

"Only fair." Eli shrugs and picks up a half-finished joint from an overflowing ashtray. "You want?" he asks, producing a lighter from his robe.

"Nah, man, I gotta stay clear. Working tonight."

Eli nods as he takes a long hit. "See, if you join the modern age, you won't have to worry about that shit."

"I'll think about it. See you around."

Eli waves Sean off and heads back to the Bel Air, where he drifts in thought as he drives, not going anywhere. He really shouldn't be surprised that Eli wants to sell him like another commodity. He's only as good to people as what he can provide for them. Eyes to watch Danny and an extra welfare check, small hands and an innocent face for a job, a willing body. No surprise that Eli wants the same.

Cam is the first person in forever who's tried to take care of *him*. Figures that the first taste of that sort of care Sean would ever get would be from a john.

Sean pulls into a nice, secluded spot on the edge of downtown. He's got hours until Cam, but his stomach is already buzzing in anticipation. If everything goes right tonight, he may get to fuck Cam, and it's been a very long time since Sean's done that.

The feeling in his stomach might also be hunger.

Whatever. He'll find something to eat, maybe see a movie to pass the time. Cam will be at the Moonlight at sunset. Fall is getting closer. That means rain and cold nights and general shittiness, but it also means nights coming faster, and less of a wait. It's not that Sean minds waiting, but life is a little bit better when Cam's there. Everything is.

6

cancelation policy

cameron

CAMERON CLICKS HIS PEN for the thousandth time and checks the clock for the hundredth. It's 4:45. So close to the hour of escape he can taste it. He usually keeps his excitement to see Sean in check, but tonight holds the promise of something he's wanted for a very long time. He can't be blamed. Also, the week was particularly miserable.

Kayla had worked late on Wednesday, leaving Cameron alone for the welcome party for the new assistant pastor. The poor man looked more uncomfortable than Cameron felt as Ted Osborn led him around. Cameron lurked behind the vegetable platter until his mother forced him to make an introduction. The small man stammered about his training in creative writing before going to seminary. Neither his mother nor Osborn had any interest, so they had started talking about... something else. Cameron can't be bothered to remember. Just like he can't be bothered to concentrate on the spreadsheet taking up his monitors. He glances at the clock again. 4:47.

No one would comment if he left now. Nothing says he can't get downtown early. He knows Sean lurks at the dinner, drinking coffee and reading the latest acquisition from the library. The amount of time Sean spends at the library is very endearing. Many things about him are.

"Babe?" Cameron jumps at the sound of Kayla's voice from the threshold of his office. "Sorry, I didn't mean to surprise you." Her voice is shaky, and her eyes are red-rimmed.

Cameron goes to her instantly. "What's wrong?"

Kayla collapses into his arms the second Cameron touches her, burying her face in his chest as he wraps her in a hug.

"Bad day. I'll tell you more when I—" Kayla gulps, her voice thick with tears. "I got off my night shift. I just want to go home. Can you drive? We'll pick up the car tomorrow."

Cam hesitates for only a heartbeat. Bitter disappointment and choking concern tearing at his insides. He doesn't have a choice though. "Of course," he murmurs.

Kayla doesn't talk on the drive home. She stares out the window, unshed tears in her eyes, as Cameron runs through a hundred different scenarios in his head. Somehow it's his fault.

"I'm sorry," he says aloud, halfway home.

"You don't even know what's wrong," Kayla says, sniffling.

"Preemptive."

"Thanks," Kayla replies, barely more than a whisper. "She wasn't even my patient before Tuesday."

Cameron glances at his wife. She's curled into herself like a bird with a broken wing. He remembers the first time Kayla lost a patient, during preceptorship, before she even graduated medical school. She had cried for days.

"People die—"

"The patient didn't die," Kayla says forcefully. "She wasn't going to die, but her baby – he wouldn't have had a chance. He wouldn't have lived, but it would have killed her." Kayla stifles another sob. "I had to do the termination. I *had to*. It's what she wanted. It was for the best, but I…"

Cameron pulls over, not even bothering with the parking brake before undoing his seatbelt and pulling Kayla into his arms. "You did the right thing," he whispers into her hair. "It's alright."

"Am I going to hell?" Kayla demands, the words thick and ragged.

Cameron pulls back, staring into Kayla's tearstained face. "No. Honey, no."

"I killed a—"

"Stop. No. You did your job, you did what was best. You're a good person. God would never punish you for this." Cameron isn't certain of many things when it comes to God, but he is sure of this.

"You don't know that. Everyone else is sure gonna punish me." Kayla wipes her nose on the sleeve of her white coat.

"We'll deal with it together." Cameron puts the car back in gear, mind racing as they drive the remaining miles home. Kayla is right, there will be repercussions for this, at work and in the church.

Neither of them is hungry, so they change and cuddle together on the couch. Kayla gives him details slowly, during commercial breaks. He reassures her each time that she made the right choice, that he doesn't blame her, that he loves her, and that there is no crime here to forgive. Her tears stop after an hour or so. Eventually, the sky fades to black.

Cameron wonders how long Sean will wait and how long the itch to find some excuse to leave and go to him will stay. There's no way to get a message to him. He thinks of Sean, waiting alone, and it's a stab to the heart. It's not the right thing to be worried about. Not right now.

"You'll feel better tomorrow," he says quietly, squeezing Kayla tight as they settle into bed.

"Thanks, babe," Kayla replies. "I don't know what I'd do without you."

sean

Everything hurts. Sean's head and shoulders and neck and, fuck, his *ass*. Everything. The sun through the window drives into Sean's head like a spike. He slams his eyes closed, but that hurts too. The last thing he clearly remembers is the guy that fucked him in the alley buying him a drink like it was a goddamn thank you. How'd he get in the car?

Everything after Cam stood him up is a blur of whiskey and who knows what else. He doesn't know how much he drank, only that it wasn't enough. He was drinking to forget, and Cam hadn't left his mind for a second. An endless loop of impossibilities: Cam showing up, Cam being hurt, Cam never coming back if he knew what was good for him. A bang on the window makes Sean jump. He can't focus, and the movement makes him sick as he struggles to sit up.

"Good. You ain't dead," a muffled voice says. A large, man-shaped figure is peering in through the window at him. Sean grunts and opens the door. The air smells of trash and piss and turns Sean's stomach. "Go ahead and hurl, won't make any difference back here."

Sean recognizes that voice. He always liked Joe's bar because of Joe himself. Burly, bearded, with a southern accent sweet as pecan pie. He knows what Sean is, but ignores it. If the guy doesn't mind that, Sean's pretty sure he's not going to judge him for stumbling out of his car and puking up an entire distillery behind a dumpster.

"Just get it out," Joe says. He sounds closer than a sane person should be, but Sean's headache is still too bad to look.

"Fuck." Sean spits out the last of the bile and forces himself upright.

"Here. Drink this." Joe hands Sean a bottle of water and guides him to some cement stairs to sit. Sean downs the whole thing in one swig, and Joe hands him a second. "Maybe go slower on that one. I got some Aspirin here for you too."

"Why?"

"You tellin' me you don't have a hangover that would make the devil weep?"

"No, why are you taking care of me?" Sean takes a smaller sip. Even moving his arm makes his whole body hurt.

"Would you believe me if I said it's the Christian thing to do?"

It turns out rolling his eyes makes him sick too. "No."

Joe laughs and hands him two white pills. Sean swallows them down, too tired to care if Joe's gonna drug him and steal his kidney. "How about I was a dumb kid with nothing once too?"

"Did you get me in my car last night?"

"After you got your ass beat down at the pool table, yeah."

The memory is hazy, but Sean does recall picking a fight with some asshole who (correctly) accused him of cheating and Joe dragging him off. After that… "Oh fuck."

"I've had nicer propositions, I must say, but never from anyone quite so pretty." There's no bite in Joe's words. "But I ain't a fan of paying for what I can get for free. Or taking advantage of someone hurtin' over someone else."

"Shut up. Someone let me down is all."

"Whatever you say. You wanna use the bathroom? Looks like you could use a wash. I got some pretzels and Hot Pockets if you're hungry."

"Yeah, thanks."

Sean cleans up as best he can. He still feels like pounded shit when he makes it out, but at least he's pounded shit that can move. He shoves his wallet into his pants and thinks about the phone number tucked inside for the thousandth time. What if Cam isn't okay? What if…

The same thought that stopped Sean every time before keeps him from asking to use Joe's phone. Cam didn't come because he didn't *want* to. He had better things to do, probably involving his fucking *wife* and their nice, picket fence life. Cam is fine, and for fuck's sake he's just another john. Sean doesn't need Cam, and Cam certainly doesn't need him.

"You gonna be okay, brother?" Joe asks, catching Sean before he can sneak out the back.

"I'm always okay," Sean replies with a fake smile.

"I'm sure you are. Take care."

Sean doesn't say anything back. 'Take care.' What the fuck does that even mean to someone like him? He's not gonna take care. He's gonna drive and sulk and go to Eli's and get so stoned he won't feel his body and sleep for as long as this godforsaken world will let him. There's nothing here worth taking care of.

cameron

Cameron knows Kayla has coffee hidden somewhere in the house. It's the horrible instant kind, but he doesn't care. There's a picture in his mind of the jar, the one with the sunrise on it and a logo from 1978. It's supposed to be lurking at the back of the pantry, where he wouldn't think to look for it, and it's *not there*. Maybe the guest room off the kitchen...

"I threw it away three months ago, babe," Kayla says from the stairs, and Cameron spins to face her. He's too worn out to even feel shame or lie (about this at least). "It's bad for you."

"I need some this morning. I didn't sleep well." They skipped date night last night, and Cameron had thought he was safe until they went to bed and Kayla kissed him and climbed into his lap. His mind was too full of worry and guilt about Sean that no fantasy could arouse him. They had given up and turned off the lights, but he could feel Kayla's disappointment in the dark, the way you feel cold radiating from a window in winter.

"There's tea. Or I can make smoothies."

"Tea is fine."

They move quietly through the Saturday routine, eating toast, reading the news, pretending everything is fine until Kayla plants herself in the chair next to Cameron and takes a deep breath, the way she always does before asking for something she knows Cameron will hate.

"Kayla..."

"I want to have the talk again."

The toast sitting in Cameron's stomach turns to stone. "Not today. You're still upset." He will do anything, anything at all, to not have this discussion.

"You won't talk about it when we're happy, and it doesn't work when we're angry, so I think sad is worth a shot." Kayla grabs his arm, stopping him from getting up to leave before he can even try. "It's a good time. Work is good. We're over the biggest hurdle in the bedroom."

"We're still not ready for a child." He hates the way the light goes out of her face when he says it, but it's the truth. How can they have a kid when the only reason their problems in the bedroom are solved is because he's been having the sex he really wants on the side?

"No one is ever ready. But, babe, it's what people do. Get a house and nice jobs and have babies and pets and *families*."

"Then we can get a cat!" Cam snaps, panic rising. "Why do you keep coming back to this? Why can't we just stay the way we are?"

"Because the way things are isn't working."

Cameron doesn't meet her eyes, but he knows the expression of despair and heartbreak he'd see if he looked. He feels empty, like his soul has been carved out of him, leaving a tired shell that is only good for lying and getting through the day. "Things are fine."

"Sweetheart, I love you so much. And I know you." Cameron looks up at that, nearly ready to snap and tell her how wrong she is on that count. "You're not happy. I see you, even if you don't think I'm looking. You're drowning. I want something we can have together. Something that can make us happy."

"That's not reason enough to bring a new life into the world. A baby isn't a Band-Aid for our problems."

"Then what is?" There's steel in Kayla's voice. "Just tell me what you need, and I'll give it to you. Please."

Cameron shakes his head, obstinately and hopelessly silent.

sean

Sean wakes to crashing and yelling, and for that, he's ready to kick someone's ass. He tries to say as much, but it comes out a garbled groan.

"Damn it, guys, stop shouting!" Eli's voice comes from somewhere. "People are sleeping."

"People *were* sleeping," Sean grumbles. He sits up and rubs his face, which has taken on the texture of Eli's couch. Great.

"Sorry!" someone yells. Sean still feels like it's coming through cotton. His mouth is dry and disgusting, and his stomach is unsettled.

"You want some coffee?" Eli plops onto the couch and hands Sean a cup.

"Thanks." Sean takes an acrid, sobering sip. He still feels like he's missing something.

"So I got a nibble on the thing we talked about. You free on Tuesday?"

"Tuesday? What's today?" There's a wall of smoke and booze between him and something he needs to remember, and he can almost get to it.

"It's Saturday, man. No rush."

Saturday. Cam. *And Danny.*

"God fucking damn it!" Sean's brain goes from blank to full-on panic in .2 seconds. "I gotta go."

It's a miracle Sean doesn't get in a wreck or pulled over the way he drives. This is why he should buy a damn prepaid phone. He could do that now, but he still has to get downtown and see if—

He stops himself. He doesn't *care* if Cam is there. Cam stood him up and can go fuck himself. Sean parks and flat-out runs to the shelter's bank of phones. His only stroke of luck is that he doesn't have to fight someone in line. He can barely focus on the buttons to punch in Danny's number.

One ring. Two. Three… Shit. Four. *Fuck.*

"Hello?" Sean barely recognizes Mrs. Weaver's voice.

"Uh, hi. This is—"

"I know who you are, Mr. Lockwood. You're supposed to call between eleven and twelve."

She sounds like a nun with a ruler. Sean's gonna be sick. "I'm sorry, I got held up."

"Luckily for you, Danny is still here."

Thank God. There's muffled muttering over the line, tense and terse, then a heavy, familiar sigh. "Hey, Sean."

"Hey, short stuff. Sorry for the delay."

"Are you drunk?"

"What? No!" Is that what his brother thinks of him? Does it suck more that he's right?

"You sound drunk."

"I'm just catching my breath. I had a rough morning getting here to talk to you." Sean's not even lying, but it feels that way.

"Because you don't have a phone." It's been a long time since Danny sounded this *done*.

"I'm working on that. I can get one, if you wanna call me." Sean tries to put on the charm that usually gets him out of trouble.

"I can't call you, Sean, you know that," Danny snaps back. "I can't call you or even *see* you because of the crap you pulled before you ditched me!"

"Hey!" Sean barks. "I did that stuff to keep you fed and keep Dad—"

"Why? Why take care of him after what he did?" Sean doesn't want to say that the disappointed, angry tone in Danny's voice sounds exactly like Jeff Lockwood.

"He's our dad, Danny. He's all we've got."

"Is that why you're in St. Louis? Calling me from a freaking *homeless* shelter every week? I looked up the number. Are you waiting for him to come back?"

Leave it to Danny to figure it out on his own and make it feel like a punch in the gut at the same time. "This is where he'd come," Sean whispers.

"We haven't heard from him in two years. He's probably dead, and he's definitely never coming back." Sean hides his face in his hands; he doesn't want strangers to see his tears. At least Danny can't.

"He might—"

"I'm not coming back either!" The pitch of anger in Danny's voice continues to rise. "I *can't* because my deadbeat brother's living on the street, selling drugs or something and—"

"That's enough, Daniel," Mrs. Weaver's voice cuts in. "Mr. Lockwood, please call on time next week. And consider using some of the services at your disposal. Daniel is worried."

"Yeah. Fine," Sean says numbly and hangs up. He walks out of the shelter in a fog.

Danny's right. Sean had one job in his whole life that mattered, and he messed it up. The money he has saved – money he sold himself for – is as useless as the car he can't drive for fear of getting busted. He can't get an apartment or a *real* job. He can't do anything. Hell, even if he could, Danny doesn't need him. Danny doesn't *want* him.

Sean walks, shoving past the people who get in his way. Dad could be dead, and it wouldn't matter to Danny. Sean could fall off a bridge, and it would make no difference to him. To anyone.

He pushes past a random body, and the asshole grabs him by the arm. "Hey, get the fuck off!"

"*Sean.*"

Cam.

He looks like crap, and Sean feels like he can breathe again for the first time in days. "I've been looking for you for an hour." Cam pulls him away from the sidewalk and into the shade of an abandoned storefront.

"Sorry," Sean exhales.

"No, I'm sorry. I…" Cam takes a deep breath, his vice grip on Sean's arm unrelenting. It makes it easier for Sean to tell the guy is shaking. "Can we go somewhere private?"

"It's the middle of the day," Sean says, thrown by the intensity in Cam's eyes. Cam tugs Sean closer so that their foreheads nearly touch. It's moments like this that Sean forgets Cam is shorter than him, because it feels like he takes up the whole world.

"I need you," Cam says through gritted teeth, and Sean feels it like an electric shock. "*Please.*"

"Yeah, okay. Come on." Sean wants more than anything to hold Cam's hand, but he also doesn't want to get his ass kicked or get Cam in trouble. Cam walks too close anyway, and that's good enough. They get there fast. Fred at the front desk looks confused, but the cash Cam slams on the counter keeps him from asking questions. Sean can see the tremor in Cam's hand as he takes the key.

There are questions Sean should be asking; anger he should be feeling, because Cam is the reason he's been messed up for two days and got so wasted he screwed up his call, but damn it, he doesn't care. The door slams, and Sean doesn't even have a second to consider how ugly the room looks in daylight or how the AC isn't on before Cam slams Sean against the wall and kisses him.

Cam's been enthusiastic before, but never like this. He's ravenous and rough, and Sean is wild for it. They practically tear each other's clothes off between bruising kisses. No marking has always been a hard and fast rule for Sean with Cam, but Cam seems to have no such hang-up as he sucks a red bruise into the sensitive skin on Sean's neck, drawing a needy whine. Sean can feel Cam hard against his hip, and he would usually comment, but he doesn't bother with the bullshit today.

They stumble out of their shoes and pants, falling onto the bed and grinding together, filthy and urgent. Sean feels like the last few days were a bad dream, and he's finally awake. He knows Cam feels it too. He sees it when he pulls back and fixes Sean with that ice blue stare, like Sean is the first sun he's seen after a long dark winter. It's breathtaking, and fucking terrifying.

"Get the— In my—" Fuck, he can't even form a sentence.

"I know." Cam disappears, and Sean tries to breathe. He's practically shaking with arousal and something else. Crap, not practically. He *is* shaking, and the room is spinning. When was the last time he ate? "Turn over."

Sean doesn't ask why, doesn't complain. Flipping over and presenting his ass to Cam is the easiest decision he's made all day. Cam yanks Sean to where he wants him, ass up and legs spread, and gets to work. The lube is cold, and Cam pushes in rougher and faster than he ever has before. But his fingers are thick and warm and, God, it feels good. In no time, he's pumping into Sean, hitting his prostate and punching little screams out of him.

"Please...Cam, please..." Sean whimpers. Cam's fingers disappear, and Sean is empty, waiting for an eternity while Cam puts on the condom. Sean doesn't even look; he can't. He trusts Cam, and that's so stupid and scary. He bites the pillow when Cam pushes into him, slow and hot. Cam goes still when he bottoms out, and Sean can hear the rough sound of his breath in the stale heat of the room. "Please," Sean whispers, not even sure what he's begging for. Cam gives it to him anyway.

Sean lets out a long moan as Cam starts fucking him, hard and fervent. He holds tight to Sean's hips, hard enough to leave a mark, but it feels good. Everything feels so fucking good, and Sean doesn't know what to do with it. He's used to being a warm hole to be utilized and discarded, but this... This feels nothing like that. Cam fucks him like he's determined to wring every drop of pleasure out of Sean. He hits Sean's prostate relentlessly, and everything is lightning and the sound of skin slapping into skin and the smell of sweat and Cam's breath on his neck and...

"Cam! Fuck!" Sean yells as he comes untouched for the first time in his miserable life. Cam fucks him through it, and Sean distantly registers the falter in his rhythm before he cries out something close to Sean's name and comes too, shaking and holding onto Sean for dear life.

Cam pulls out and tugs Sean with him onto the mattress, keeping Sean from the wet spot like a gentleman while he tosses the condom on the floor. They lie there as their breathing slows and the sweat cools on their skin.

"I'm sorry," Cam says softly.

"You don't ever gotta be sorry for doing what you just did."

Cam cracks a lopsided smile. "I meant for missing you on Thursday."

"It's okay. I'm sure you had a good reason."

"Kayla had a bad day. She didn't do her night shift. I needed to be there."

Kayla.

Cam has never said her name before. For the hundredth time, Sean wonders: what does she look like? What does she do? How did she and Cam meet? What do they talk about over coffee in the morning?

"It's fine. I get it. I made do."

Cam swallows, focused on the spot on Sean's shoulder he's rubbing gently with his thumb. "I'm sure."

"This is sorta late for you, for a Saturday, isn't it?" Sean asks, because the shitty last few days, hunger and endorphins still have his brain leaking out of his ear. "Is she gonna be worried?"

"She's fine. She's at an organic gardening class at Home Depot," Cam sighs. "So we can have *more* salad and steamed vegetables."

Sean chuckles back. "She sounds like Danny."

Sean realizes his mistake the moment the words are out, and Cam looks at him in confusion. "Who's Danny?"

Shit. Especially today, he doesn't want to have this discussion, but he can't lie. "Danny's my little brother."

Cameron gets that 404 error look and cocks his head into the pillow. "Where is he?"

Goddamnit. Why is he asking? Why can't Sean tell him to fuck off? "He's fourteen. He's in foster care in Ohio."

"Do you see him?" The sweet concern and pity in Cam's face make Sean want to scream.

"I get to talk to him on the phone once a week. I call from the shelter." Even in the stifling heat of the room, Sean feels cold. "Not that he wants to talk."

"You can't be his guardian?" To Cam's credit, Sean can tell he gets how dumb that question is the moment he says it. Still stings.

"I had this plan, you know?" Sean says, swallowing back the bile from the argument that's still fresh. "I was gonna save up. Get a job and a place or something, but that's impossible."

"It's not. There are places that will take you with the right referral and—"

Sean stops him with a glare. "They don't take people like me, Cam."

"You don't know that."

"I don't even have a real ID. They won't."

"Sean, I can help." Sean feels the dam inside him break. Finally. "I can—"

"Jesus fucking Christ, no, you can't!" Sean snaps, so loud and forceful that Cam winces back. Good. Sean stands, shaking his head. "This is not your problem. You don't get to save me, choir boy. I'm way past it."

"Sean." Cam's voice is insistent. Sean grabs their tangled-up pants from the floor and throws Cam's slacks at him before shoving his legs into his jeans. "You'd know that's not true if you would stop hating yourself for one minute."

Sean rounds on Cam, his blood boiling. "Seriously? You're gonna lecture me on self-loathing? The guy who wants to make me his own little Julia Roberts because he can't handle how much God hates his gay ass?"

"That is *not* what this is about. I just want—"

"To help?" Sean barks back. "When are you gonna get it, Cam? You don't need to help me! We don't have a relationship, we have a transaction!"

For a split second, Sean can see how deeply those words hurt Cam before his wall goes up. He takes a long breath, stoic and cold, and looks right through Sean. "Of course. You're so good at your job, I forget sometimes."

"Yeah, well, I'm a pro."

Cam doesn't say anything. He gets up and grabs his clothes. He's efficient and focused, transforming from debauched to a perfect pillar of the community before Sean's eyes in less than a minute. It's fine. It reminds Sean who this asshole really is. It's all fine until he takes out his wallet.

"I'm sorry. I won't forget again." Cam sets the money on the dresser as usual. "I'll see you."

Sean watches as Cam opens the door. He thinks Cam pauses, looking at Sean out of the corner of his eye, but it's probably wishful thinking. The clicks closed, and Sean slumps back onto the bed, eyes stinging and his body burning with shame and hurt.

He nearly let Cam fuck him without paying. It's probably for the best that Cam won't want to see him again after this, now that his little illusion is shattered. First Danny, and now Cam. Leave it to Sean to fuck up the only good things in his life in one day.

Sean dresses and grabs the money, because looking at it makes his stomach turn. He returns the key without a word to Fred, and he walks. There's a late summer storm brewing, darkening the skies and making everyone on the streets skittish. Sean walks blindly until he gets to the tent camp. He doesn't talk to Lyle, just pushes Cam's money into his hands and keeps moving.

He keeps walking when it starts raining. He doesn't flinch at the sound of thunder. He doesn't even look up at the sky.

7

THE STORM

cameron

"So, ARE YOU GONNA tell me what's up with you?"

Cameron looks up from his lunch. He's been staring at the same wilted cabbage for ten minutes, so it's not like Flor's interrupting. He still frowns as she sets her tray across from him and sits. She's in a black blouse and plaid slacks today, with several belts. With those and her multiple earrings, Cam wonders how she got through the metal detector.

"I'm fine."

"No, you're not. You've looked like someone killed your dog since Friday. You can't avoid me, I'm too chismosa to let up."

Cam sighs. He's too worn down to lie. "There was a fight."

"About?"

He knows she means Kayla, and it's half the truth. "Kayla and I want different things, so much of the time." Actually, they want the same thing, which is sex with men, and that's the root of the problem. His thoughts turn back to Sean and the sting of his words. "I thought we felt the same, but I was wrong."

"Have you considered, I dunno, talking about it?"

Cameron huffs a tired laugh. "We're not good at that."

"Not to Kayla. Like, to a counselor or, hell, your pastor or something. Lee was saying your new guy is pretty chill."

"No." A pastor would correctly say his suffering was God's payment for his sins.

"Then talk to me, because bottling this up is gonna kill you."

"Don't be over-dramatic," he says even as another pulse of searing discomfort radiates from his gut.

"Cam, come the hell on, I know you."

"Language, Miss Guerra." Flor turns to where Arnold Isaacs looms over them, glaring at Flor. "We have workplace decorum policies for a reason. And a dress code."

"Our apologies," Cameron says before Flor can snap at him. "How are you today, Arnold?"

"Walk with me, Cameron. It looks like you're done here," Isaacs answers and gives Flor a withering look as he guides Cam away. "I had hoped to speak to you after services yesterday, but you looked so ill."

"I was," Cameron stammers as he stumbles after Isaacs.

"At least you had the decency to come and worship," Isaacs says, low and ominous as he pulls Cameron into a deserted hall. "You're already in a precarious position. We wouldn't want you to lose face with the community now."

Cameron swallows down his panic. Does he know? "What do you mean?"

Isaacs advances on Cameron, cornering him like he's prey, and so close that Cameron can see every wrinkle and liver spot. "I know what your wife did," he growls.

Cameron's anger is greater than his relief. "That's confidential patient information."

"Neither should you, so let's not pretend confidentiality matters here. The point is that your wife helped a woman commit *murder*."

"That is not what happened," Cameron seethes, fists clenched. "Kayla was doing her job. She was within the bounds of the law, and she had to honor her oath."

"I think ending an unborn life counts as harm." Isaacs stares at Cameron, like he's daring him to contradict him. "Despite the loopholes in the law, this hospital is a Christian institution."

"What about the mother who would have died?" Cameron asks, careful of his tone.

"She would have been reunited with her child in heaven if she accepted Christ. We have to take a stand, Cameron, against the sin that has infected this country: The child killers. The sodomites. The unwashed hordes streaming in and the trash in our streets."

Cameron has heard it all for so long, but it's more repugnant now than ever because it's about his family and friends and whatever Sean is. And him. But he can't speak up.

"What do you want, Arnold? I can't undo what Kayla did. And you can't fire her over this," Cameron states. Isaacs is in charge of finances, above Cameron, not the doctors. The smile on Isaacs' face widens even so.

"No. I can't fire Kayla."

Cameron's stomach plummets. "What?"

"I know you're a good Christian, Cameron. I'd like you to prove it. Since you and Kayla will both be under scrutiny."

Cameron sets his jaw, his teeth grinding as he processes the threat. "Mr. Isaacs—"

"If anything goes wrong with the billing for the woman your wife assisted in sin – say, the claim doesn't go through or she gets charged for extra OR time – just… ignore it. That's all I'm asking." He says it with an empty smile that makes it all the worse.

"And?" Cameron asks.

"It will be God's justice. I knew you'd understand." Isaacs gives Cameron another cold smile as he leaves. "I'm glad we understand each other. Goodbye."

Cameron slumps against a wall as soon as he's alone, cold sweat springing to his brow. He wants to call Kayla, so she can tell him what to do. He wants to get in his car and drive until he finds Sean, beg his forgiveness, and disappear into his arms to be someone else entirely.

Someone free. He can't do either. He can't talk to anyone or make this go away or make things right. He can't do anything.

sean

Maybe they'll get a tornado. It's been a long time since Sean's seen one, and it feels like the right time. He stares at the darkening sky from Eli's collapsing porch and wonders if thinking a tornado would be nice counts as praying for it and if that makes him a bad person.

He takes another swig of flat, warm beer.

It's not that he wants a tornado. He knows it would hurt people, and that's bad. But it's the same feeling he got yesterday when he barely missed getting hit by a semi. He didn't get an adrenaline rush, just a weird feeling that if a wreck had happened, it wouldn't be the worst thing.

"You're gonna catch a cold, sweetheart," a female voice drawls from behind Sean. He looks up lazily. He's seen the chick around Eli's before, but if they've talked, he doesn't remember. She's too skinny, with dark hair and hands that shake as she lifts a cigarette to her lips.

"Yeah, well, it's the only way to get someone to make me chicken soup," Sean grumbles.

The woman – she's too old to be a girl – chuckles and takes a seat by Sean on the decaying couch that's probably got rats living in it. She offers Sean her cigarette, and he takes a drag. He takes everything people offer at Eli's, which will eventually end bad for him. Feels like waiting for a tornado.

"Come on, sweetie, you're so pretty I bet someone would make you a whole Thanksgiving dinner just for smiling." The woman takes back her cigarette, sucks a final puff before grinding the butt into the damp fabric of the couch, and tossing it away. "You a friend of Eli's?"

"Something like that. You?"

"Something like that." She smiles. Her teeth aren't great, but her smile's still nice. She was probably beautiful before life chewed her up and spit her out. "I'm Crystal." She holds out a thin hand, and Sean takes it.

"Sean."

"You wanna go inside and fuck around, Sean?"

Sean has to smile at the forthrightness. "That's a nice offer, really, but usually I charge for that sort of thing."

"Knew you were a hustler," Crystal laughs back. "But come on, one freebie? I got moves you've never seen. I'll make it worth your while." Sean doesn't say no immediately, and Crystal takes that as a cue to climb onto Sean's lap. She tastes like an ashtray when she kisses him, soft and slow. It's been so long since he kissed a chick, he almost forgot how nice it could be. Maybe he should fuck her. The booze and the weed and whatever else he's used in the last few days won't get Cam off his mind; maybe this will. "Mmm, knew you couldn't say no," Crystal purrs.

"I ain't said yes yet." Sean bites his lip, Crystal grinds into his crotch, and it feels… Like a body rubbing against him and nothing more. Is this how Cam feels with Kayla? Cold and empty and detached?

"Come on, baby, let's go upstairs and forget all our cares," Crystal whispers, ignorant of Sean's lack of interest.

"I—" Sean jumps as the door opens.

"Hey – whoa!" Eli yelps.

"Sweetie, we gotta work on your timing," Crystal says to Eli without malice.

"Speak for yourself. Sean, I got something for you," Eli says, winking.

"And that's my cue." Crystal pats Sean's knee and pushes off the couch. "See ya."

Eli waits until the door is closed behind Crystal before turning back to Sean. "You're welcome."

"Yeah, yeah. She woulda eaten me alive, whatever." Sean slumps back into the old couch. "What do you want?"

"I got a job for you," Eli replies with a lopsided grin that makes Sean fume. "One of the internet things I told you about."

"I never agreed to that. What the hell?" Sean gets up to drive home the point. Not that he has anywhere to storm off to except into the rain.

"Yeah, you did. Or do you not remember last night?"

"I was trashed six ways to Tuesday last night!" It's worse because Eli knows that what he came here for, not to be pimped out like another of Eli's products.

"Come on, dude! It's some guy from out of town. He's offering a cool thousand to fuck you. Have you ever gotten an offer that good on the street?"

Sean stares at the darkening clouds. He hasn't. Not even Cam ever offered that much. He could have asked for it, and Cam would have paid. Cam would probably give him anything. Because Cam is an idiot who thinks Sean is worth it. He isn't worth anything, and he needs to remind himself of that.

"Fine. Where?"

"Motel on the edge of town. I'll go with you. Can't be too careful."

Eli chatters away on the drive. It's good to be back in the Bel Air; it feels like home in a way nowhere else does, even with an alien presence there. He spent the second half of Saturday and all of Sunday driving, crisscrossing the city and glancing at the freeway. He could've got on the interstate and driven until he hit the ocean, bought a new life with the useless cash in his trunk. Instead, he drove through the suburbs and out past a dozen churches and looked for dark hair. He drove by a hundred cookie-cutter houses and tried to remember when home was a roof and walls and people and not four wheels and a sputtering engine.

Eli gives him directions. He talks about his cut. Forty percent sounds like bullshit, but Sean's past caring. The motel's in that twilight area between city and suburbs, all flat highways and bright signs glowing in the Missouri night. Everyone has them, even the big churches, asking, 'Is your soul ready for the end?'

Eli makes Sean pay for the room, which is bullshit, but he says he'll get him back. It's a classic shitty motel where the rooms open into the outside. Sean pays for an hour in cash, toying with his wallet as the clerk rings them up. The damn thing is so worn, with pieces of duct tape holding it together in places. He's got a few fake IDs and, hilariously, his library card in there with his cash. Tucked safely away is a card with a name and number written in hand on the back.

He's never taken it out. He's never touched it, but it makes him feel good, knowing it's there. Or it did until a few days ago when he ruined everything again.

Eli shoots off a text when they get to the room, and they wait. Eli has a phone like a normal person, and there's an ancient one behind the bed. Nothing's stopping Sean from using it. He has no idea what he'd say, but the chance to fix things is right there…

Sean jumps at a knock on the door. He's never done it this way, with a middleman. It's weird and skeeves Sean more than the unfamiliar hotel where everything is oriented the opposite of what he's used to, and the carpet is brown instead of red.

"Showtime!" Eli says with a wink as he opens the door.

Sean's not sure what he was expecting, but a drab, white guy that could be his dad in a different light isn't it. He's got that all-American, rancher vibe, with silver-dark hair, a rectangular face, and a deep frown framed by a goatee. He looks Sean up and down like he's sizing up a prize bull. The john turns to Eli, frowning. "I thought you said he was young."

"Hey, buddy, no one's holding a gun to your head. Everyone's the same in the dark," Sean snaps. He doesn't care if he turns this jerk off. There's more where he came from.

"He's spunky," Eli says, placating.

Sean nods, pretending to care. "I'm young enough, bucko. So, we doin' this?"

"My name is Jeremiah," he says like a threat.

"And I'm James Dean," Sean shoots back, and something sparks in Jeremiah's eyes.

"We're doing this." Jeremiah pulls out an envelope and hands it to Eli, who counts the money inside.

"It's good," Eli declares, moving to stuff the money in his jacket. Jeremiah grabs his wrist to stop him.

"Money stays here, in case your boy doesn't perform." Alarm bells are going off in the back of Sean's head, but he ignores them. He's seen guys like this before; usually it's them who have the trouble 'performing.'

Eli nods and sets the money on a dresser. "I'll be outside. Mazel tov."

Jeremiah looks after Eli as he closes the door, eyes narrow. "Of course."

Sean grits his teeth. It ain't his place to say anything, now that he's bought and paid for. "So, how do you want me?" Sean asks as Jeremiah, weirdly, rolls up his sleeves. "You wear a rubber. That's non-negotiable."

"How do you like it?"

It's wrong. The tone, the look in Jeremiah's eyes that's as much disgust as want. The weeds on the wallpaper and the smell of smoke. Everything's wrong. The only person who should ask that is Cam, and Sean's never gonna hear it again. He turns away, but he can feel Jeremiah get close, looming behind him like a thundercloud.

"I like it all, baby. That's why I'm here," Sean declares with all the bravado he can muster. Never let it be said he let a bad decision go unmade. He feels Jeremiah breathing down his neck, hot and hungry.

"You're here because the devil has sent you to tempt and corrupt good men." Sean doesn't have time to get offended before he spins and the first blow hits, right in the gut.

"What the fuck!?" Sean wheezes, trying to get his bearings.

"You spread evil and disease and laugh about it." Another blow to the ribs and something cracks. Then the face. One, two. Eye and mouth. A kick to the shin and a knee to the groin, and Sean's falling as the bastard calls him every filthy name in the book.

"Eli!" Sean tries to scream before a steel-toed kick to the ribs knocks the wind out of him. Jeremiah's boots are sharp and hard, and Sean gasps with each kick. He's had his ass kicked before, but never this bad. Never like this. Pain on top of pain wraps Sean like a chrysalis. He hits harder than Dad ever did.

"Are you ready to atone, my son?" Jeremiah asks from on high. "Make your peace with God."

Sean moves on instinct and grabs Jeremiah's leg, then pulls. The fucker tumbles to the shit-colored carpet with a cry. Sean scrambles up, hitting back at Jeremiah as he claws at him. This time, Sean's got the upper hand.

"Fuck you and fuck your asshole God," Sean growls as he delivers the hardest kick he can to the dick's dick.

"You can't run from your sin," Jeremiah wheezes from the floor. Sean kicks him in the face and then in the throat for good measure. Then he runs.

"Eli!" he shouts, his voice thick through the blood in his mouth, as he bursts from the door, but there's no one there. "Shit!"

He barrels down the stairs into the driving rain, relentless and cold. He can see the outline of the Bel Air like a beacon in the parking lot. He just has to get to it, and he'll be okay. He'll be home. His ribs are screaming, his vision blurred with rain and blood, but he makes it. Thank God, he makes it, and he's home.

Of course, he can't find his keys straight away. Of course, he can barely see to unlock the door in the storm. "Come on!" Sean yells as thunder rolls.

Finally, he gets the key in the lock and lets out a sob of relief. Then he hears an engine rev and sees the lights.

He thinks it's lightning, just for a second, before he looks up. Time slows, enough for him to wonder if this is where he's going to run or let the tornado take him. He sees Jeremiah's hateful face above the headlights of his huge truck, a vicious grill mounted to the front of it.

He wishes he could see Cam one more time.

The truck crashes into the side of the Bel Air, and there's nothing but pain and screeching metal.

Then black.

8
THE CALL

Cameron

WEDNESDAY IS MEATLOAF DAY in the staff cafeteria. It's the most depressing thing to be pleased about, but Cameron can't be picky. He has no idea if he has anything to look forward to tomorrow, so if a slab of breadcrumbs and what he hopes is beef covered in dubious gravy is the highlight of his day, so be it. Tomorrow, he fully intends to go downtown and look for Sean. Even if it hurts, Cam needs to see him.

The food sits like tar in his stomach as he buses his tray, trudges back to his office, and avoids eye contact with anyone he sees, including Flor and Lee. Nate is unfortunately standing next to his office door, more nervous than usual.

"What do you need?" Cameron asks.

"I, uh, need to clear my vacation request with you." That must be the paper Nate is holding.

"When is it again?" Cameron asks, already taking the paper to sign.

"September. Sorry, I'll miss your birthday." Nate goes pale at the perturbed glare Cameron gives him when he finishes his signature. "To be honest, it's not a vacation. It's a mission. I'll be in Honduras for a week, ministering to the locals. Mr. Isaacs is sponsoring—"

Cameron is relieved when his phone vibrates, even though he doesn't recognize the number. "Hello?"

"So this is the same Cameron Steward," a familiar female voice says over the line.

"Tamara?" He knows Tamara Hodge from volunteer work and a few church functions, though her church is different from his. He has no idea why she would be calling him.

"Actually, it's Detective Hodge today. Official call."

All Cameron's blood seems to leave his body, and his mind starts to race. Could she know about Sean? Has he been arrested and given up his clients? Cameron takes a deep breath, waving Nate away but not moving. "What's wrong?"

"We have a John Doe down here with a bunch of fake IDs and your name and number in his wallet."

Sean. Oh God. What Cam was feeling before wasn't panic or fear; not compared to this.

"What? Where?" He doesn't know if Tamara means the morgue or something else, and the thought chokes the breath from his lungs.

"Your neck of the woods. You're at Sullivan Mercy, right?"

Cameron's heart starts beating again at an alarming rate. "Yes. Are you – is he here?"

"ICU. Room 416."

"I'll be right there." Cameron ends the call with shaking hands and heads for the door.

"Hey, what's up?" Flor asks from her desk.

"I have to…" Cam is afraid he's going to be sick, but he keeps it down. "A friend has been hurt. I'll be in the ICU." He doesn't wait for a reply before rushing out.

Cameron finds himself pushing past other employees and patients to get to the distant elevator bank. The ICU is in the newer East wing, and the journey is interminably long. Every step has him thinking of something else that could have happened to Sean. The ICU means it's bad, and if he hasn't been identified, that's *very* bad.

Cameron catches sight of himself in the dented metal of the elevator doors as they stutter to a halt on the fourth floor: his face is pale and drawn, his expression grim, and the bags under his eyes are as dark as his hair. At least on this floor, he won't be the only one who looks so haunted. The ICU has a heaviness to it. Everything is hushed, even the distant beeps and whir of machines. He forgot how much he hates the smell: antiseptic over sickness and decay.

The ICU comprises twenty rooms arranged around a central island of nurses and equipment. No decorations here to disguise that this is a place where people are going to die. He spots Tamara Hodge, a sturdy Black woman in a police jacket, outside a room with the curtains drawn over its large glass windows. She's in deep conversation with a ginger-haired nurse Cameron knows, Blake Kramer.

"Wow, that was fast," Tamara says when she sees Cameron.

"Can I see him?" Cameron asks, eyes straying to the closed door of room 416.

"*If* you think you're up to it," Tamara replies, exchanging a nervous look with Blake.

"This guy's not in great shape, Cameron," Blake adds. "Prepare yourself."

For a second, when Cam opens the door and sees the man with purple-green bruises blotting his face, lost in a tangle of tubes and wires, he thinks it's not Sean. He hopes it's someone else, and this is all a terrible mistake. This broken, beaten person *can't* be Sean. Then Cam looks at his hands. He knows those hands in every way. Their shape and texture and taste. Suddenly, the floor is dissolving under him.

"Sean," he whispers.

There's a tube down his throat, and compression devices on his legs, hissing steadily in counterpoint to the beep of the monitors. One eye is swollen shut, and there are cuts visible between the bruises on his cheek. He has an IV in his arm and wires sticking out from his hospital gown. One faded red mark below his jaw that doesn't match the rest of his injuries, Cam knows, because he put it there.

"Cameron."

Cam turns to see Tamara beside him. "What?"

"I asked if that's his name – Sean?"

"Uh, yes. His name's Sean. What happened?" he stammers, not sure where to focus or if he can.

"Hit and run, but it looks like there was a fight before. We're trying to figure it out. Docs called me in since it's in the obvious felony category. Why don't you come out to talk?" Tamara's voice is steady, calming, like she's speaking to a scared child.

"No, I–I'd like to stay here, if that's alright," Cam says, half to her, half to Blake.

"Fine. Don't touch anything. I'm paging his doctor," Blake sighs and leaves. Cameron and Tamara shuffle past the bed and over to a table, chair, and small couch meant for a family that won't ever come.

"Please, tell me what happened to him," Cam asks again, looking at the whiteboard on the wall across from the bed. It lists Sean's doctor (Miriam Elliott, Cam knows her) and other information: John Doe, trauma, surgery at 3:56 A.M. "He had surgery?"

"Let's slow down. I need information from you first." Tamara pulls out a notepad and flips it open. Cam feels like she's talking from across a crowded room, and he has to strain to hear her. "You said his name was Sean? Last name Lockwood sound right?"

"I…" He never asked. That wasn't part of the arrangement. "I don't know his last name. Where'd you get that?"

"Same wallet we found your number in. Bunch of fake IDs and a library card for a Sean Lockwood."

Cam shakes his head, smiling bitterly. "He likes the library."

"And how do you know Sean here?"

"We… I…" *I pay him for sex, and sometimes I think he's the best thing in my life.* "I volunteer with the unhoused population, downtown at the mission. I met him there. I buy him lunch sometimes. He's a friend."

Tamara jots down a note. "So, he's homeless?"

"He lives in his car." He recalls how touchy Sean is on the point that he has a place to live, it just happens to be on wheels.

"Big ol' red Chevy?"

"A Bel Air. I think."

Tamara flips back in her notes. "He was found by a vintage Bel Air in bad shape and half on top of him. That tracks. As far as you know, does Sean have ties to any criminal elements? Drug dealers? Gangs, maybe?" Tamara asks it so casually that Cam can barely process it.

"No." That's a lie. To a police officer. Sean is a criminal, in the strictest sense, and so is Cameron. But he can't expose him like that. "He never mentioned anything like that."

"Hm." Tamara scribbles and looks back at Sean.

"Can you *please* tell me what happened?"

Tamara sighs. "Your boy here was severely beaten in a motel parking lot bar out at the edge of town, and someone saw fit to ram his car while he was trying to get into it. It wasn't an accident. Right now, our theory is a drug deal gone wrong, since the guy who called it in is a known dealer."

"He never talked about drugs," Cam whispers, turning to look where Sean rests in the bed, unnaturally still. If it wasn't for the heart monitor, Cam wouldn't even be able to tell he was alive. The thought comes unbidden of having this conversation at a morgue, over a body he couldn't even recognize. He imagines Sean's blood splattered on some anonymous street and thinks he might be sick. "He's a good person."

"He's alive but for the grace of God. Sounds like the bad guy had some sort of grudge." Tamara shakes her head. "We won't know for sure until Sean here tells us. If he can."

Cam shuts his eyes. Sean is at least here. He's safe. Maybe. "Will he be alright?"

"The patient sustained multiple blunt force trauma injuries, the most severe causing a break to his pelvis on the left." Cam and Tamara turn to a severe brunette in a white coat at the door.

"Miriam," Cam nods. She's in the same year of residency as Kayla but older, having spent much longer working between college and medical school. She looks extremely perturbed.

"Cameron. I gather you know John Doe here," Miriam asks, picking up Sean's chart.

"His name is Sean. He's a friend," Cam says. "There was surgery?"

"Yes, on the pelvis. Dr. Villanueva had to do a serious reconstruction. We don't know the extent of the organ damage, so we're keeping him under for a few hours to allow him to heal and see how his function comes back." Miriam sounds downright bored.

"*Will he be alright?*" Cam repeats, patience thin.

"The first twenty-four hours after surgery are the most delicate," Miriam says. "We have no idea if there's brain damage or other complications. He may not wake up, and even if he does—"

"Thank you, Miriam," Cam says with enough force that she takes a step back. "Is there anything I can do?"

"Call his family? Is there anyone who might want to be with him?" Tamara suggests.

"He has a brother, but he's not in the state," Cam replies. The anger and hurt from their one discussion about Danny seems unimportant now. "There's no one else I know of."

"Okay then. I'm going to head back to the station and consult with my partner about what she's found on her end," Tamara says, forcefully upbeat. "The hospital will call me if he wakes up. I'll let you get back to work." There's a question in her voice, and out of the corner of his eye, Cam can see Miriam looking at him with similar curiosity.

"I'm staying here." Cam doesn't look away from Sean as he sits down to make his point.

"He's going to be under sedation for a while; there's nothing to wait for," Miriam says carefully.

"He shouldn't be alone," Cam replies, soft as a prayer.

Miriam and Tamara give him similar dubious looks but leave the room without comment. Cam doesn't let himself break or blink or even breathe until the door is closed and he and Sean are alone. Even then, he waits a good thirty seconds before he lets his head fall and his shoulders slump.

He has no idea how, but this is his fault. That's the truth that finally brings tears stinging at the corner of his eyes. He wanted to protect Sean, and he failed completely. Now Sean is being punished for Cameron's failures. He dares to look up again, at the bruised face in profile, eyes closed, and tubes shoved down his throat.

"I'm sorry," Cameron whispers into the silence. There's an oxygen monitor clipped to the end of his index finger that Cameron is careful of when he slips his hand into Sean's. He's never felt Sean's hand so cold, but all that matters is holding it. "I'm so sorry."

He holds Sean's hand, matching his breathing with the buzz and hiss of the leg compressors. He counts heartbeats and memorizes the bruises on Sean's face. He wonders if Sean is dreaming and what of.

He waits.

The nurses are supposed to check on Sean every half hour, so Cam watched the clock. It's an ugly thing with big red digital numbers in clear view of the bed. By his calculation, he has seven minutes left when the door opens again. He slides his hand from Sean's and attempts to look detached and professional. Until he sees his wife at the door.

"Kayla?" He wonders if there's guilt on his face to match the complete confusion on Kayla's.

"So, I just had an interesting talk with Miriam." The brightness in her voice is forced as she holds up a file. "She shoved these at me, asked me if I wanted to take this case since my husband didn't trust her care of a – how did she put it – a beaten up nobody. Care to explain?" Kayla looks back at Sean nervously.

"I was going to call you." He's sure he would have remembered eventually. "This is… the friend from downtown I told you about. Sean."

"Sean, as in – oh my God." The confusion in Kayla's face is gone, replaced by horror. She looks back and forth between Cameron and Sean, her breath shaky and her eyes wide. "He's so young. He—"

"He's twenty-two," Cameron says automatically. It's one of the only details he knows. "Maybe you should add that to the chart."

"Right. Chart." Kayla grabs Sean's chart and scans it. Cameron looks back at Sean. The hospital bed makes him look so small. "Blunt force… Full left pelvic… Broken ribs… Possible organ… Jesus Murphy, how did this happen?"

"They don't know. The police were called to investigate. He had no valid ID, and Tamara Hodge found my number in his wallet." Kayla looks at Cameron in fresh confusion. "I gave it to him. In case he needed help."

"Are you the only person they've been able to reach?"

"I'm all he has, right now." He knows he's staring at Sean too long, and looking at him hurts in so many ways, but he can't tear his eyes away. Kayla slips her hand into Cameron's. Her hand is small, soft, and warm, and she responds when he squeezes it. He wishes it were Sean's. "He doesn't deserve to be alone."

"No one does," Kayla says softly as they both stare at Sean, seeing two very different things. "Do you want to ask someone to bring your laptop? I don't think the nurses will mind if you camp out here and work."

Cameron raises an eyebrow.

"Remember when I was studying for boards and so anxious I made myself sick? You took three days off work, even though your boss hated you already, and you kept me rested and hydrated and managed to stop me from studying myself into an early grave."

"What does that mean?"

"I know you're not leaving." Kayla smiles as he says it, releasing Cam's hand. "Call your office. I'll bring you some dinner before I head home. Dr. Tong is on for tonight. She'll probably remove the breathing tube."

"Do you think…" Cameron has no right to put his worry about his secret lover onto his wife, but there's also no one in the world he trusts more. "Miriam wasn't very positive about his prognosis."

"We're monitoring, but we won't know for a while. If he was dealing with malnutrition or other complications we don't know about that could be bad." Kayla shakes her head, and Cameron feels all the warmth she brought leave him in a wave. "Patients have better outcomes when they have support present, so it's good if you're here."

That could mean two things, and Cameron doesn't want to think about one of them. Kayla gives him another chaste kiss on his cheek and leaves, casting one last thoughtful look at him as she does.

Cam sinks back into the chair and, after a few more empty minutes of staring, he sends a text to Lee. Blake comes in and checks Sean's vitals, face grim as he avoids Cameron's eyes. He does change the name written on the board, from 'John Doe' to 'Sean Lockwood'. No longer anonymous.

Lee arrives ten minutes later with Cameron's laptop, files, and coat. Her concern and shock are different, since she's the only person in his life to have met Sean, but she doesn't ask questions.

Cam tries to work. For the first time in a while, it's an escape. He catches up on the accounts receivable reports he'd been avoiding and starts in on the quarterly projections and claims trends. Nothing changes.

Blake comes and goes. At four, he's replaced by a dark-haired woman named Dawn, who comes in two minutes early and almost catches Cam holding Sean's hand. She's a friend of Kayla's, he thinks, but doesn't attend their church, so Cam doesn't really know her. She smiles with familiarity, though it's a sad, pitying sort of smile. She does the same checks. No change. He can't bring himself to ask if that's good or bad.

Kayla returns after five with a salad and several dinner rolls from the cafeteria, along with a Coke. She looks at the notes on the chart and doesn't smile. "His temperature spiked, then stabilized. Kidney function could be better."

"What does that mean?" Cameron places the food next to his work to be ignored and rises.

"We'll know more when we remove the sedation." No good news then. "You can call me any time if you have questions or if anything happens, alright?"

"Are you sure you're alright with this?" He asks because it's the right thing to say to your wife.

"I'll be okay for a night. You stay with your friend." Without warning, Kayla pulls him into a fierce hug, and Cameron melts into it. For a few seconds, it feels like coming home. "I love you, okay?"

"I love you too." He says it automatically all the time, never thinking about it, but he means it entirely right now. He squeezes Kayla tight and kisses her hair. When she pulls back, her eyes are bright and her lips tremble.

"I'll be praying for him." It's the kindest thing Kayla could say, and the weight of it isn't lost on Cameron.

"Thank you," Cameron whispers.

The door shuts, and Cameron retakes his seat. He watches Sean, barely blinking. Maybe if he concentrates hard enough, this will feel real, and the future won't be completely terrifying. Maybe he can convince himself that things will be alright. Sean will wake up and be fine, and things can go back to how they were. Or things will go back to how they were before he met Sean, desolate and stale and empty, because Sean will be gone.

The thought has fresh terror exploding inside of Cam, the kind that makes him sick and cold and ready to tear his hair out because that would actually be doing something. He doesn't tear out his hair; he goes back to work because it's the only way he can accomplish anything. He manages five minutes before looking up again.

He can't lose Sean, not now. If he just keeps watching him, he won't. If he concentrates hard enough and doesn't look away, he'll be fine. He'll be fine.

Dawn comes and goes. Visiting hours end, but no one tells Cam to leave. Privileges of being staff or married to one of the doctors. He eats a few bites of salad. He holds Sean's unmoving hand on and off when he can't concentrate. He's completely ahead of work for the rest of the week by eight o'clock when a small Asian woman in a white coat comes in with Dawn and another nurse he doesn't recognize.

"I'm Dr. Tong. You're Dr. Steward's husband, right?" She doesn't bother extending a hand to Cameron. She's too busy snapping on latex gloves.

"Yes. Cameron." He stands, scooting the chair back from where he'd moved it close to the bed.

"We're taking him off sedation and we're going to remove the breathing tube," Dr. Tong explains. "You can stay in here or wait outside if this isn't something you want to see. It'll be fast."

"I'll stay," Cameron says quietly, and Dr. Tong nods.

Dr. Tong and the nurses move quickly and are well-practiced in the procedure. IV bags are changed, and something is injected into the line. Machines are turned off, and the tube is pulled carefully from Sean's throat and mouth. It's longer than Cameron would have guessed. He wonders if it hurts or if Sean is too medicated to feel anything. They watch his heart monitor, a stethoscope on Sean's chest as well. Cameron holds his breath until Sean takes a shallow one on his own. Dr. Tong looks moderately satisfied.

"That's good at least," Dr. Tong declares, slinging the stethoscope back around her neck. "It's up to him now."

"We'll keep checking. Page us if you need anything, alright?" Dawn adds, looking after Dr. Tong as she leaves without another word.

"When will he wake up?" Cameron asks. He had been expecting something more.

"Like the Doc said, that's up to him," Dawn says as Cameron stares at Sean. "If you can, get some rest. It might be a long night."

He doesn't rest. He watches the light fade from the windows and turns on the lamp next to Sean. The overhead fluorescents make him look too pale beyond the bruises. The steady rhythm of the machines doesn't change. Dawn offers him the remote when she makes her checks after nine o'clock. Cameron doesn't take it. He drinks some of the lukewarm water on the side table after he finishes the Coke.

After ten o'clock, he finally manages to speak. "This is the longest time we've ever spent together, isn't it? Though maybe this doesn't count." He looks at the clock, the machines, the dark window, and back at Sean. "I'm still not good at small talk."

Silence.

"I've never seen you wake up. It was always something I dreamed of," Cam whispers. "This isn't how I imagined it." He sniffles and wipes his face. He hadn't noticed the tears, but he's glad of the dark and the quiet in case anyone comes in. Or if Sean wakes up.

By the time Dawn makes her next check, he's more composed.

Kayla sends him a text just past eleven: "miss you. Going to bed." He sends back a heart and turns off his phone to save the dwindling battery.

Sean doesn't move.

He keeps breathing, steady and slow, his chest barely moving, and he doesn't wake up.

Cam is tired and scared in a way he hasn't been for a very long time. Perhaps ever. He thinks of Kayla and church and his mother and brothers and feels like a fraud. He remembers Sean's mouth and his smile. He thinks of the blasphemies he uttered when he was with Sean, how in those moments together he felt closer to something holy than any other time in his life. He remembers a friend from high school whose mouth was so beautiful, but whose name he's forgotten. He remembers praying to God to make him not think the filthy thoughts about that boy and his mouth. And God had done nothing.

God didn't create thoughts, or stop them, or change them. He only judged them. Or so Cam was told. Still, Cam had prayed. He prayed for God to help him when he went to that strip club. Then he'd seen Sean.

"Every time I pray, it's selfish," Cam says out loud. "I pray to be saved. To be changed. I don't pray enough for those who need it. I'm sorry."

He takes Sean's cold hand in his, but he's not talking to Sean, not right now.

"I'm sorry that I'm a selfish, sinful man, but, please… If you're listening, if there was ever a time I could beg for something more important than me, please listen now. Please, let him wake up. Please, let him be alright and whole. I can't offer you promises that I'll live better or that I will suffer more, but just please… Save him. Please, God, I'm asking you. Please."

When tears choke the words, he keeps the prayer up in his head, or his heart. It's been there all day, unvoiced and unanswered. *Please fix this. Please save him. God, I need him. He's good, and he doesn't deserve this. Please save him. Please.*

Minutes tick by as Cam waits and prays until his head droops in exhaustion.

The twitch of fingers in his jolts him like a gunshot. Cam looks up, heart racing, wondering if he dreamed it, and sees green eyes.

"Cam?"

9

VISITING HOURS

sean

SEAN

Everything hurts. Sean's thought that before, but he was so fucking wrong. *Everything hurts.* It's not sharp, fresh pain either. It's dull and deep and *everywhere.* His vision is swimming, and Cam is there. Cam is *here.* He's holding Sean's hand, and that's the only thing that doesn't hurt, but how?

"Did I…" die? No. That's a stupid question. They're not dead. This isn't the afterlife because there's no fucking way he and Cam would end up in the same place unless somebody really screwed up their admission policies. Or Cam was right all along. Cam looks really worried and kinda out of focus. "What—"

"It's okay," Cam says. It is not okay. Sean hurts, and he's really confused. He feels sick too.

"Fuck," Sean struggles to sit up and, oh shit, that was a stupid, stupid move because it makes him hurt more, and he *can't.* Cam's moving, doing something with buzzing and beeps. Suddenly it's way too bright.

"Don't try to move," Cam orders and disappears. Sean would really like to call after him, but he's gonna be sick and he can't fucking get up and shit, this is *a lot* of pain. Why is Cam here? Where is here? Why does it *hurt*?

"Why can't I move?" His legs are trapped, and his eyes aren't focusing right because this isn't their normal room. Squinting hurts. Opening his eyes – eye? – hurts. Cam gets back, though he's sort of a worried-looking blob with another blob beside him that's vaguely purple.

"Sean, I'm going to sit you up," a calm female voice says. "Just stay still, okay?"

"I'm gonna hurl," Sean groans as the bed moves and his upper body is slowly tilted up, and that hurts too. "Where—"

"You're in the hospital, Sean," Cam says. That makes sense. Kind of. There's a very concerning amount of pain going on right now, but why would he come to the hospital? He can't afford that. Fuck, his stomach really wants to flee his body.

"Right here, Sean, it's okay," the chick says, and there's a gentle hand on his neck.

Sean lets go and pukes into the bucket, and it hurts everything – his chest and his head and his hips – fuck *his hips*. He doesn't remember drinking enough to be hungover, and this doesn't feel like that. No. Hospital. This is real pain. He feels like he went ten rounds with the Hulk… Or a psycho with a truck and a god complex. He hurls again as bits and pieces flash into his pounding head. He can't talk, so he reaches for something. Cam. He squeezes Sean's hand tight.

"I'm here, Sean," Cam says as another wave hits Sean. How does he even have anything left in him to throw up?

"You're okay, Sean, just let it out. The anesthesia makes people sick all the time, it's okay," the girl he assumes is a nurse says. Sean takes a deep breath, which is weird cause there's something shoved under his nose, and it smells too fresh over the scent of sick. "I'm gonna get rid of this. You can give him some water or ice chips."

The hand on his neck goes away, then Cam is there with a cup, and Sean finally manages to focus. He's able to at least help hold the plastic cup to his lips, though Cam does most of the work. The water is stale and lukewarm, but it's so good. It wakes him up enough to consider what the nurse said.

"Anastasia?" No. Wrong word. It's funny, though. Cam should be smiling, but he just looks worried. He always looks worried. "What…"

"You had surgery," Cam explains. "They had to do reconstruction on your pelvis. You're—"

"That fucking asshole," Sean groans. He remembers a truck barreling towards him and the Bel Air and an explosion of pain. "Who tries to kill a guy with his own fucking car?"

"So this was on purpose?" Cam says, horrified. "You have broken ribs too and—"

"I need to get to my car." Sean tries to get up again, and pain shoots through him from his hips. Shit, he forgot. He's fucking *broken*, and so is his car.

"Sean, shhh, don't worry about that," Cam says, soft and soothing. Sean blinks, and Cam is right there, leaning in close with a gentle hand on Sean's face, brushing his cheek and up into his hair. "All that matters is that you're okay."

"You call this okay? We gotta raise your standards." Sean argues because he always argues. Cam's fingers are careful in Sean's hair, his forehead against Sean's. Oh. So this is a dream. He can't think of any other explanation for tenderness like this, not for him.

"I know, but I'm just—"

"Sean?" It's the nurse. Cam springs away, and everything hurts again. "I paged the doctor. We need to do some tests before we let you rest, okay?"

"Yeah, fine," Sean says, keeping his eyes on Cam. He's the only thing that makes sense. Except he doesn't. "Why are you here?"

"They found my number in your wallet." Cam's face is worn and sad, even more so than usual.

"You look like crap," Sean says. The nurse gives a small laugh as Cam finally cracks a smile and shakes his head.

"So do you," Cam shoots back as the nurse starts to fuss around Sean. There's something in Cam's eyes that's relieved and amazed. Sean wishes he would touch him again.

"Oh, I think he's still pretty cute," the nurse says in that kind way that means Sean must look even worse than he feels. He feels really, really shitty, for the record.

"Thanks," Sean exhales, melting back into the mattress.

"No sleeping yet," a new voice says. Sean turns painfully to see an Asian woman at the door. "It's nice to see you up, Sean. You had Cam here pretty worried. I'm Doctor Tong. I'm going to do a few tests, okay?"

"Uh, sure," Sean says. He watches as Cam backs out of the way, next to a dark window.

"Ain't it past visiting hours?" Sean asks, wincing in pain as the doc pokes at him.

"I'm staff," Cam replies with a shrug. Did Sean know that?

"What day is it?"

Cam glances up at a big clock on the wall, and it looks like he might have a breakdown right there. "It's technically Thursday."

Sean doesn't say anything as Cam meets his eyes. Not the way he wanted to keep their date, but at least Cam isn't pissed at him anymore.

"Okay, Sean, I'm going to need you to look at my finger," Dr. Tong says, bringing Sean's attention back to her. He cooperates as best he can as she shines lights in his eyes and asks him who the president is ('a fuckwad' isn't the right answer, but it makes Cam laugh before Sean gets it right) and what Sean's pain level is (all of it). After what seems like forever, the doctor nods. "No apparent brain damage, so that's great. And your organ function is doing okay, so we're going to give you some more medicine for the pain and to help you sleep."

"Thank fuck," Sean groans.

"Your friend's quite the firecracker," the nurse says as Dr. Tong leaves. "Do you need anything?" she asks Cam as she injects something into Sean's IV.

"I'm fine, thank you, Dawn," Cam says.

"Just let me know." Dawn gives Sean one more smile and leaves.

Sean's suddenly very aware he's in a room alone with Cam and not being paid for it. That makes absolutely no sense. Whatever weird guilt or sense of obligation kept Cam here should be gone now, but Sean doesn't want to watch him walk out another door. Cam turns off the overhead light and returns to Sean's side.

"Do you want to adjust the bed or—"

"Please don't go." It comes out hoarse and pathetic, but it gets the job done. Cam takes Sean's hand and looks at him with all the seriousness in creation.

"I have no plans to leave you, Sean."

"Will you get in trouble?" Sean murmurs. Whatever Dawn gave him is working fast because he feels heavy and tired already. That's good though. Cam staying. That's good.

"I don't care," Cam replies. Idiot.

Sean nods, or he means to nod. His head is so heavy that moving it is impossible. The bed reclines on its own, or thanks to Cam, maybe. Sean can't see; he closed his eye at some point. There's something warm close to him, breath on his face, and a soft touch on his forehead. Lips? He must be dreaming again. Already. Someone takes his hand.

cameron

Cameron wakes to a hand on his shoulder and opens his eyes to see his wife's face. This is confusing. He's uncomfortable and starving. Why did Kayla let him fall asleep here?

"Come on, I brought your stuff," Kayla says softly, over the sound of machines as he looks around. He's in a chair. In a hospital room. He fell asleep next to Sean.

"Is he—"

"He's fine. Still sleeping. Come on."

Cameron lets himself be led out of the room. "What time is it?"

"About 7:30. Got here early. I thought my husband would appreciate some clean clothes." Kayla holds up a canvas bag. And a cardboard cup.

"And since you probably didn't get a lot of rest, I got this from the place down the street. I know you like them better than the cafeteria coffee."

"You got me coffee?" Cameron asks with a groggy wave of guilt as Kayla gives him a knowing look. "If it makes you feel better, my stomach is fine this morning," he adds, cautiously taking the coffee.

"That's probably because you slept in a chair. It keeps the acid down. I was going to suggest that for at home. Not a chair. Pillows or something." Kayla's face darkens, but she shakes it off. "Drink up. You can shower and change in the residents' lounge. Come on, I'll let you in."

"Thank you." Cameron follows Kayla out of the ICU. She has a huge coffee cup of her own, which is uncharacteristic. "You don't look like you slept well."

"It was just one night. Still probably better than yours," Kayla says, turning to him with a brave smile. "I'll have you back tomorrow. Sounds like Sean is out of the woods. It's a miracle."

"I guess." Cameron watched Sean for a while after he fell back asleep, counting his breaths and trying not to think about the future. The last he remembers looking at the clock, it was past two. He feels unreal and hollow to be so outside of routine, and the hunger and inadequate sleep don't help. They walk in tired silence, Kayla leading the way to the elevators and letting them off on the second floor. It smells less like sickness than the fourth.

"I brought your charger too," Kayla says as they get to the lounge. "I guess you turned off your phone, or it died."

"Oh, yes." Cameron pats his pockets until he finds the phone. Kayla takes it from him before he can turn it on and uses her key card to enter the lounge. It's simple: Lockers, a TV, a few couches, and some doors that lead to cots and a nice bathroom.

"I'll plug it in for you. Go ahead and shower." Despite his few hours of sleep, Cameron is too exhausted to argue. Kayla gives him a peck on the cheek when he heads into the shower.

The hot water feels amazing, and Cameron indulges for far too long. The coffee is starting to work too, and he nearly feels human. Or at least good enough for his mind to clear and the reality of his situation to settle in. Sean is okay. Sean is still very hurt, with nowhere to go. Sean and Kayla are in the same building. Kayla is Sean's doctor.

Cameron blinks as the water streams down his face. He's completely screwed.

He finishes washing quickly and exits the shower to the empty lounge. His phone is plugged in next to the bag of clothes and food with a message to him in the notes app: "Got paged. Will check on Sean too. Let Lee know you're alive."

"Shit."

sean

Sean doesn't hurt *as* badly when he wakes up. The pain is distant, a quiet throb in his ribs and hip. The heart-stopping terror is way more concerning. His head's clear enough to realize that he's in a fucking hospital because some crazy bigot beat him to a pulp and destroyed his car, and nothing is okay.

Sean scrambles for the controls on the bed to sit up. Maybe he can just leave. No, that wouldn't be cool for Cam. Wait. Was that a dream? Sean looks around the room. He's completely alone. Of course he is. He probably hallucinated the whole Cam thing because there's no reason Cam would be there with him. So he can leave, if he could only... move.

"What the fuck?" There are things on his legs making noise, and struggling brings back the pain in his hip full force. Right. Broken fucking pelvis. Shit. "Um. Help? Is someone there?!" Sean rasps. There's gotta be a call button or something, right? He turns to look and fresh pain spikes from his hip. "Hello?" Oh, yelling hurts too: his throat, lips, and jaw. Fantastic.

"Hey, it's alright," Sean looks to the door where a woman in a white coat with strawberry blonde hair stands, looking more confused than frustrated. "Settle down, Sean. You're okay."

"Doc, have you got eyes? Do I look okay by any definition of the word?" Sean snaps. To his surprise, the doctor smiles and shakes her head.

"You got me there. Let's get a look at you." Instead of actually looking at him, the doctor retrieves the chart hooked to the bottom of Sean's bed and reads.

She's pretty. Very pretty, actually. Shorter, with soft curves, and a cute nose. She's the kind of girl Sean might flirt with if he weren't a freaked-out, broken mess. Hell, he'll flirt anyway.

"I thought doctors were only this cute on TV." Sean tries to smile, which is hard when most of your face doesn't work. The doc smirks, clearly amused as she puts the chart back. "You know I don't usually get into bondage on the first date. What are these things on my legs?"

"They prevent blood clots after surgery when the patient can't move for a while. We'll be removing them now that you're awake, don't worry."

More cloudy memories of the night before coalesce. Waking up, seeing Cam (or not), puking because of anesthesia. Doctor Tong examining him. "Wait, my doctor last night was an Asian lady. Or did I dream that too?"

"Oh, I'm sorry. I should have introduced myself. That was Doctor Tong," not-Doctor-Tong says. She steps close and holds out a delicate hand. "She was on call for the night. Today you've got me. I'm Doctor Steward."

"Doctor Steward like…" No, there's no way. *There's no fucking way.* But there it is, embroidered on her white coat: 'Kayla Steward, MD.' He takes her hand, more so to make sure she's real than out of politeness. "You're Cam's wife."

"So, he did mention me," Kayla says softly and squeezes his hand tight.

"Yeah," Sean says, fully aware he's staring like an idiot. "Never said you were a doctor. Now you're my doctor?"

"Fate's a funny thing," Kayla says. "You'll see a lot of us in here. Your case is pretty interesting. The malnutrition from your lifestyle may have exacerbated the breaks, and pelvic fractures like this are pretty rare in your age group."

Sean's head falls back as he groans. He doesn't want to be an interesting case. "Great."

"Sorry, I didn't mean to get all clinical. So, how are you feeling this morning?" Kayla smiles at him, and Sean can only think of how Cam sees that smile every day.

"Um, shitty?" Even shrugging hurts. "Does Cam know I'm here?"

Kayla tilts her head, her face falling. "I thought you saw him last night?"

Sean looks down at his hands and thinks of how real the dream was where Cam held them. He thinks back to Cam's face close to his, and maybe even a kiss, before Sean faded away. "I thought I dreamed it. Didn't think he'd stick around for some guy he barely knows."

"Cam stayed with you the whole night," Kayla says flatly. Is she mad or worried? "I made him go change and shower, but he should be back soon."

"Oh. Cool." Sean knows he sounds like an idiot. He *is* an idiot. How Cam ever tolerated his conversation when he's married to fucking doctor is a goddamn miracle. Or Cam really liked the sex and was too polite to tell Sean to shut up. "You got any idea how soon I can bust out? I don't think I can afford, well, any of this."

"A few days, minimum. Do you—" Kayla starts to ask as the door opens.

Cam still looks like crap, but the sight of him has never been more of a relief. He stares between Kayla and Sean, face pale and conflicted, and Sean still can't believe any of this is happening.

"You never said you married a doctor," Sean says, grabbing onto the first thought he can to break the tension. "Good work."

"I wasn't a doctor when we got married." Kayla looks at Cam, and the love and pride in her eyes are jarring.

"You were halfway there," Cam replies, warm and familiar, like this is a bit they do all the time.

"Wait, are *you* a doctor?" Sean asks Cam. "You said you were staff. I thought you had an office job?"

"I do," Cam sighs, like a weight resettled on his shoulders. "I'm a billing and claims administrator. I deal with insurance companies and medical bills."

"That sounds boring as hell," Sean says.

"I told you." Cam shrugs and finally steps fully into the room. "How is he?" he asks Kayla.

"Dude, I'm right here," Sean protests.

"Yes, but you'll lie and say you're fine," Cam replies without missing a beat.

"Sounds exactly like someone else I know," Kayla says, smirking. "He's doing well. We're moving him to a regular room in a few hours. Depending on his pain levels, we may try to get him to physical therapy tomorrow."

"See, I'm fine," Sean says, though he doesn't like the sound of physical therapy. He doesn't like any of this. "Uh, speaking of pain levels."

"We'll get you something for that," Kayla replies quickly. "That reminds me: I brought this for you too." Kayla turns to Cam and hands him a bottle of pills from her coat pocket.

"Kayla, I'm fine," Cam groans.

"I know you said you feel fine, but I also know it gets worse with stress," Kayla says, in full doctor mode.

"Should I ask?" Sean will blame the meds if he's stepping over a line.

"They're just for acid reflux," Cam says, shoving the pills in his jacket pocket.

"Don't minimize it," Kayla scolds and looks at Sean. "It's Gastroesophageal Reflux Disease; it can be very serious."

Sean thinks back to all the times Cam looked warily at his food or avoided spicy shit. Sean thought it was because he was one of those boring white suburbanites afraid of pepper. "You never mentioned that."

"I didn't think it was important," Cam mutters. Sean wonders if Kayla knows Cam's lying face too – the white lie one he's got on now. Judging by her dubious look, she does.

"I'll get the nurse in here with some pain meds, and I'll be around for the day. Babe, you have to get down to the office." Kayla's so familiar and soft with Cam, and Sean sorta hates it.

"I…" Cam looks between Kayla and Sean, clearly conflicted. Kayla places a gentle hand on Cam's arm, a warm touch she probably thinks nothing of, but jealousy and guilt blot out Sean's pain for a second before he shakes his head.

"Don't let me keep you. I know you've got way more important shi-stuff to do," Sean says, turning on his professional smile. "Go save the hospital money or something."

He's still not sure what Cam's job entails, because Cam never told him. He never told him his wife was a beautiful doctor with a kind smile who worked in the same place as him and kept Cam from getting himself sick. Cam never needed to tell him because that's not what they had. They ate and talked about nothing and fucked, but the guy standing next to his wife and looking at Sean like a bomb that might explode? That guy is a stranger.

"Are you sure?" Cam asks uneasily.

"Yeah, go ahead. I got some TV to catch up on," Sean replies. Cam keeps his focus on Sean as he gathers a laptop and jacket from a table Sean hadn't noticed.

"Come on, hon, let's let Sean rest." Kayla tugs at Cam's sleeve, and he moves easily.

"I'll visit later," Cam says automatically. A pleasantry.

"Sure. I ain't going anywhere today." A few more polite smiles and a wave, and the couple is gone. Sean watches their silhouettes retreat on the other side of the window, walking close. He closes his eyes tight and tries to breathe. Not too deep, that hurts too much.

Just enough to carry on.

10
HISTOrIES

cameron

CAMERON HAS NO IDEA what to do with himself in his office. He reorganizes his work from the day before and returns missed calls. He's bleary and seriously considers taking a quick nap at his desk, but he's too wound up, especially after a text from Kayla letting him know Sean's moved rooms.

He looks up at the sounds of a knock on his door, and Lee pokes her head in.

"I wanted to see if your friend was doing better," she asks without ceremony as she enters. "I assume since you're here, he's out of the woods." Cameron sees she's holding a package.

"Yes. He's awake and doing as well as can be expected. What is that?"

"I know the food isn't the best here," Lee explains, clinical and stiff as she hands Cameron a bag of Oreos. "They're all that I had in the pantry."

"That's a very kind thing to do for someone you've barely met."

Lee shrugs. "It's very kind of you to be there for your friend. I assume you'll be visiting for lunch."

Cameron's surprised to see it's a few minutes past noon. "Yes. I will be."

"Good luck then, if that's appropriate." Lee gives her best approximation of a supportive smile and lets Cam out of the office. Flor is at her desk, already enjoying salmon, which Cam knows she'll store in their kitchenette solely to annoy Lee.

"Leaving again?" Flor asks.

"I'm going to visit my friend. I have my phone if you need me," Cameron answers.

"Since when do you have other friends?" Flor calls after Cameron as the door closes, and he hears Lee start to admonish her. He acquires a healthy, if bland, selection from the employee cafeteria to go with Lee's cookies and tries not to rush to be in Sean's presence.

Sean is staring out the window, a tray of food untouched in front of him. His bruises are less vivid, but his skin is still ashen. Is it wrong to think he's beautiful, even like this? Cam clears his throat, and Sean turns to him with a look that's equal parts confused and weary.

"Didn't think I'd be seeing you again today."

"Why?"

"You ain't responsible for me," Sean says, staring Cam down in a resigned challenge. "Whatever guilt you've got going, you can drop it. You don't need to—"

"Sean, shut up." Sean's eyes go as wide as possible (which isn't much more for the right). "We don't need to have this argument right now. Just accept that you're more than a…" He can't find a word for what Sean is that he can risk saying aloud, or that won't reduce Sean to something dirty and cheap. "I care. I know you don't think I can, or should, but I do. And I thought you might be hungry."

Sean scowls for a beat, then relents. "More like you knew the grub here was crap."

"That too." Cam comes close enough to get a good look at the brown and beige globs on Sean's tray. "Is that supposed to be beef?"

"They called it Salisbury steak, but I think it might actually be dog food."

Cam takes the tray away and replaces it with the cookies, ham sandwich, chips, and soda. "I also have a salad if you—"

"Goddamn, I haven't had Oreos in forever." Sean tears into the package and gobbles a cookie without further ceremony, moaning around the mouthful in a way that makes Cam blush.

"Those are from Lee." Cam takes a seat while Sean scarfs down two more cookies.

"Tell her thanks. These are the best thing that's happened to me all week," Sean says through a mouthful, and Cam can't help but roll his eyes. "The bar is low."

"Are you going to tell me what happened?" Cam asks when Sean swallows.

"A friend found me a job. Turns out it was one of your buddies from bible study who wanted to kick my ass in the name of Christ or some shit." Sean says, bitter but resigned and oblivious to Cam's horror. "It was my own fault for being stupid. Never shoulda taken the gig."

"It wasn't your fault," Cam says softly, automatically. He's ready to weep. This is *his* fault. Not just for failing Sean, but the hatefulness of his own community. "Sean, I'm so sorry. Men like that... Christ would condemn them. And if I hadn't been thoughtless, you wouldn't have been there."

"Hey," Sean snaps, and Cam looks up, blinking away tears. "I'm my own person. It's done. No use sobbing over it."

Cam sniffles and wipes his nose with the back of his hand. "How are you doing now?"

"Really damn shitty, how 'bout you?"

Cam smiles and shakes his head, glad that Sean's humor is intact. "I guess things could be worse."

"Yeah, you could be stuck with a broken pelvis and a pile of goddamn paperwork." Sean gestures to the small mountain of forms next to him. "I don't even know where to start with this crap."

Cam picks up the first form, skimming over the innocuous boiler-plate. It's questions most people wouldn't think twice about. Address, phone number, and emergency contacts. Things Sean doesn't have. "Just put down what you can. It's mostly for billing anyway."

"Oh yeah, fun times. You got any idea how much this vacation is gonna cost me?" Sean asks around a mouthful of cookies.

"You had surgery, an ambulance ride, medication, x-rays, and will be here several nights, and will get physical therapy," Cam rattles off as Sean grows even paler. "You're looking at upwards of sixty thousand dollars."

Sean laughs, shaky and high. "Holy crap. Yeah, I'll just put that on my credit card." Sean looks up, shaking his head with another hysterical giggle. "*Fuck.*"

"We'll figure it out," Cam says and gets a withering look for his trouble.

"There's no 'we' here, Cam. There's only me and the colossal mountain of crap I'm under."

Sean stops at the sound of a knock on the door before it opens. Cameron isn't sure if he's happy to see Tamara Hodge walk in. It delays the fight, but it means more questions and stress for Sean. "Tamara – Detective Hodge. You're back," he says, rising.

"Yeah, Kayla called. Protocol," Tamara says, looking sympathetically at Sean.

"Detective? Jesus, Cam, do you know everyone?" They both ignore the outburst as Tamara approaches and holds out her hand to Sean.

"Glad to see you're up. You gave this one quite a scare." Sean shakes her hand uncertainly, glancing at Cam. "Detective Tamara Hodge, St. Louis PD."

"I know Tamara through our churches and some volunteer projects," Cameron explains. "Same way I met you." He doesn't think Sean will reveal anything, but the possibility makes the acid that had been quiet all day jump in his stomach.

"My job is to arrest whoever did this to you," Detective Hodge smiles.

"Sorry to disappoint, but I didn't see him," Sean says, flat and cold. Cam opens his mouth to protest, but Sean shoots him a look. "I drove a friend to meet someone, and I got jumped. Angry Guy. I fought back. He fought harder. Got mad and got his truck. Don't know what he wanted. Woke up here."

Cam watches as Tamara jots something down in her notepad. She knows Sean's lying. "Sean, I know that you may be scared, but we don't want people like that on the street."

Sean's expression is grim as he stares Tamara down, a silent conversation happening between them. "I didn't see anything."

Tamara shakes her head and stows her notebook. "I'm sorry to hear that. If you do remember anything, call us. Please. We understand that you've been through a lot and won't hold it against you if your statement changes."

"What about my car?" Sean demands.

"The old Bel Air with fake tags and no registration that's in the shape of a croissant now?" Tamara asks back with a raised brow.

"She's mine. Everything I have is in that car." Cam didn't think it was possible for Sean to look this worried.

"Not legally, she's not. But don't worry, I won't collar you for possession of a stolen vehicle."

"I didn't—"

"*Since* it's evidence and has no legal owner, it's been impounded," Tamara explains, and Sean looks like he's been hit all over again.

"When can I get to her?" he grits out.

"Once we close this investigation, she'll get sold at auction. There's a salvage yard that picks up most of the classics we get."

"You can't..." Cam can see tears in the corner of Sean's eyes. "Damnit."

"I'm sorry, kid. But there's no evidence that the car is yours." Tamara does seem to mean it, not that it matters to Sean. "Call me if you remember anything." Tamara places her card on the bedside table before leaving.

Sean looks desolate, and Cam feels absolutely helpless. "There's got to be a way to—"

"Cam, get back to work, okay?" Sean says, holding back emotion. "Thanks for the food. As usual."

Cam stares. He wants to hold him and lie that it will be okay. All he can do is grasp Sean's hand and force him to look into his eyes. "I'll come back later and bring you dinner."

"You don't—"

"And don't worry about the bills." Cam gulps. "I'll handle that. My boring office job has its uses."

Sean shakes his head, but he squeezes Cam's hand back. For the moment, it's enough. "Thanks, Cam."

Leaving is hard. It always is. Standing at a door and looking back at Sean on a bed, beautiful and lost, always tears at something inside him. It's worse today, and when the door shuts behind him, Cam feels like his insides have been carved away and replaced with molten lead.

He doesn't head back to his office. He walks right past Arnold Isaacs' secretary and into his office without ceremony. Isaacs, for his part, looks bored and smug when he deigns to notice Cameron glaring down at him. "Mr. Steward, I hope you're here to tell me the billing matter with your wife's patient has been handled?"

Cameron braces himself. "It will be once you do me a favor."

sean

Sean's decided the only thing worse than hospital food is hospital TV. He was excited, since it had been a long time since he had a TV to himself, but like everything else in this hellhole, it's crap. No food shows. No good reruns. Just talk shows and soaps, five Christian stations, the shopping network, C-SPAN, and the weather. Sean settled on the weather after trying and failing to follow *Guiding Hospital of Our Lives* or something. Turns out Missouri is hot in August, but not as hot as Texas. Shocking.

His heart does a stupid jump when the door opens, then stops when he sees who it is. Kayla: holding a clipboard and papers. She doesn't have much makeup on. Sean wonders if that's a church thing, a doctor thing, or a personal thing. She's pretty without it.

"Hi, Sean, how are you feeling?" Her tone is the sort you'd use with a child or nervous animal.

"Crappy," Sean replies, refusing to squirm under her scrutiny.

"How's your pain?" Kayla pulls up the chair beside Sean's bed.

"Uh, better. The move was a bitch, but I think I'm like a three, right now."

"Good. That's good." Kayla looks down at the clipboard, then back up to Sean. "I know you're probably tired, but we need to get your medical history."

"No." Sean snaps. Not this. Not for her.

"Sean, I know you probably don't want to talk, but this information is important. I can tell you some about me if you want to even it out."

"You're offering a trade?" It's transparent, but he knows he's not getting out of this. And he can't say he's not curious about the woman who gets to share a life with Cam. Kayla watches him expectantly, and Sean huffs. "Fine."

"Great! The first part's easy: place of birth. We already got the date."

"Here. I mean, not this hospital, but in St. Louis. I think it was St. Louis General."

"Really? Hm." Kayla writes down the answer and then pauses with her pen an inch from the paper. "I was born in Ohio. Cam was born here too."

"I didn't know that," Sean says, and it's true. "Doubt we ever met. We left when I was ten or so, and Cam is, you know, old."

"Thirty isn't old, be quiet. Do you remember what vaccinations you've had?"

"Some? We stopped with that stuff when we moved. Obviously haven't been in for a checkup in a while."

"Considering that and your circumstances, I'm going to order a tetanus booster." Sean winces and groans. "Sorry. Do you drink? And if so, how many drinks a week?"

"I dunno, ten?" Kayla makes an interested face. "Too many."

"Smoke?"

"Once in a while, don't buy my own." Sean's skin is starting to prickle with discomfort even as Kayla keeps scribbling.

"Drugs?"

Sean pauses long enough that Kayla looks up, eyes serious. "Nothing hard, okay? Just weed. Maybe once a week?"

"No needles?" Kayla's deadly serious.

"*No.*" The vehemence of the answer satisfies the doc, and she goes back to writing.

"Sexually active?" The tone is too light, too forced, and Kayla pointedly avoids his eyes. Maybe she's just an uptight Christian. Or maybe she's asking if Sean screwed her husband. He doesn't know, and he's not going to give her this.

"Not a lot of love connections happening in my circumstances. Chicks don't really dig the whole living out of my car vibe, so…" He makes sure to say chicks, not people. Kayla still looks tense. "I always used protection. I'm not a complete idiot."

"I don't think you're an idiot at all," Kayla says softly. He can't tell what she's thinking, but she makes a note. "I assume you haven't been tested recently?"

"Uh, no."

"We'll run a panel, just in case, okay?"

Sean can't argue with that, even if a positive STD test would be the cherry on the shit sundae that's his life right now. "Fine."

"Next is family history."

"No." If Sean could walk, he would get up and storm out right there, but all he can do is stare petulantly at the window.

"It's not complicated. We just need to know if there's any history of illnesses, causes of death, if any. Simple stuff. Not your life story." Kayla actually sounds concerned as she says it, but Sean scoffs anyway.

"I don't know most of that shit."

"Try. Mother's side first. Can you tell me her name?"

Sean closes his eyes. He's teared up more today than in the past month. "Marlene Lockwood. Maiden name was O'Brien. Her parents died before I was born."

"Is she still–"

"Died in a wreck when I was nine. And I don't know her medical history," Sean spits, turning to glare at Kayla. He regrets it when he sees the pity in her face. "Next."

"Father's side?"

"Granddad: Greg Lockwood. He ditched my dad and grandma, and they found him with a bullet in his head a year later. Grandma was Betty. Died of a heart attack before I was born."

Sean waits for Kayla to ask it. He's not even sure how he's going to answer.

"I've seen your X-rays, you know," Kayla says quietly, and Sean's anger snaps to confusion. "I saw the old broken ribs. Where they've healed. And your left wrist. Do you know that with some injuries, we see them enough that we can guess the cause? What you had looks like a defensive injury."

"You're making me feel kinda naked here, Doc."

"My father wasn't a nice man either," Kayla begins, sincere and quiet. "He drank a lot. Liked to hit people. Had one of those tempers you had to tiptoe around all the time. I… hated him, and I hated that my mother never stood up to him. Not that she was much better. She liked pills more than drinking." Kayla's gaze is unfocused, not seeing Sean at all.

"You know how most kids rebel by smoking under the bleachers and drinking at parties? That wasn't me. Some friends invited me to church, and that was my rebellion. I found people who talked about forgiveness and grace, and how Christ knew me and loved me and died for me. My parents hated it. There was an older couple in the congregation, and they took me under their wing. I moved in with them, and they fought in court to get me away from my parents. When I went to college in St. Louis, they moved here to stay close."

"They sound like good people," Sean says quietly, and Kayla gives a sad smile.

"They were. My dad – adoptive dad – died when I was a junior in college. Cancer. That's what made me switch from art to pre-med. Took some doing, but Cam helped me. Mom made it long enough to see me graduate from medical school, then passed away two years ago. She stayed with us at the end. We didn't want her in a home. House still seems empty without her."

Is this supposed to make Sean feel worse? To make him understand her or trust her? He has no idea, but he sure feels worse than before for screwing her husband. "Doc, I—"

"Call me, Kayla." Sean doesn't know why that sounds like a challenge.

"Kayla." He takes a deep breath as Kayla holds his gaze. It's time for him to give as good as he got and suffer too. "Fine. Fair trade. My dad's name is Jeff Lockwood. He wasn't great before Mom died, but he got by. Not after. You can write down alcoholism on your little sheet. He carted my brother and me around from job to job for years until we ended up in the system. He hit us when we got out of line. Well, just me. I got between Danny and him when shit happened. Haven't heard from him in two years. Don't know if he's alive." Is he supposed to feel better saying it all out loud? He just feels empty.

"I know saying I'm sorry is trite, but—"

"Then don't." Kayla doesn't argue. Cam would have, and he's glad Cam isn't here.

"You have a brother?"

Sean looks up. "He's fourteen. He's in foster care. And no, I do not want to talk about it." The fight with Cam about Danny seems a hundred miles away now, but it still stings.

"Okay, uh..." Kayla trails her pen over the forms on the clipboard. "Any allergies?"

Sean snorts. "Good transition. Do cats count?"

"I'll put it down." Kayla stands, looking resolved and satisfied. "Thursday is my night shift, so I'll be around until midnight if you need anything."

"Thanks." Now he knows what Kayla was doing all those Thursday nights while Cam snuck out. Leave it to Cam to walk in at that very moment with two bags of food and a surprised expression on his face.

"I didn't know the hospital did delivery," Kayla says. "What'd you bring us?"

"Cobb Salad, no bacon, extra avocado," Cam says without missing a beat and hands Kayla a bag. "And several things you won't approve of for Sean, since *he* appreciates the finer things in life."

"You didn't have to do that," Sean mutters.

"No, I've seen the patient food, he definitely did," Kayla answers before Cam can. Sean gives an awkward smile as Cam hands him the bag. It smells fantastic, but he's not sure how much he can eat. Getting your worst memories brought up when you're already feeling chewed up and spit out by the world doesn't do a lot for the appetite.

"Thanks, Cam," Sean says anyway and pulls out a warm, greasy fry. "You steal any of these on your way here?"

Cam avoids Sean's eyes. "They're better warm. Someone had to appreciate them."

"There's soup at home, with actual vegetables in it," Kayla says, and Sean pretends the stab of pain he feels is a rib. "Doctor's orders are no run tonight. Just get to bed."

Cam opens his mouth to protest, looking between Kayla and Sean. Sean's not sure why Cam even wants to stay; there's nothing that Sean can give him right now other than poor company.

"You look worse than me, Cam. Go home. I'm in good hands," Sean says. "I'm just gonna eat this and ask the nice nurses for something to knock me out."

"Sounds like a good plan. The physical therapist is going to see you tomorrow, see how well you move." Kayla replies.

"I'll stop by," Cam says, kind and useless.

"I'll see if I can fit you in. I'm awful busy with callers." Cam and Kayla both smile.

"Goodbye, Sean," Cam says for both of them, and they leave. Together.

Sean imagines Kayla holding Cam's hand all the way to the elevators. Kissing him on the cheek. He imagines Cam driving home alone in his nice car and standing alone in his nice, big house. He imagines Cam missing him, Cam showering and jacking off, thinking of Sean instead of Kayla. It's easier to think about Cam's sad life than his own, so he forces himself to think of Cam lying awake in bed and thinking of him. It's a weird fantasy, but it does the trick.

Sean eats the food Cam bought him and falls asleep aching in a bed Cam probably paid for. Typical Thursday.

cameron

Cameron wakes up groggy and overheated, a film of sweat between his skin and sleep clothes. Kayla's holding onto him tight. Yesterday morning was the first morning in a while he hadn't woken up and wondered what Sean was doing, what it would be like to wake next to him. He wonders it again now.

It's early, so he takes extra care washing and dressing. More armor against the day.

"Babe?" Kayla calls from the bed before Cameron can creep out of the room. "Coffee won't be good for Sean right now, so don't use him as an excuse. Just donuts, okay? Say hi for me."

"Of course," Cameron says dutifully, and the words settle in his stomach like stones.

"Love you," Kayla says through a yawn and settles back into the bed.

"You too. See you tonight."

He's shaking when he gets in the car. He drives a different way to work, picks up a dozen donuts, and barely avoids getting sideswiped because his mind is spinning.

She knows. Kayla knows him better than anyone and can guess every transgression before he does it. Of course she knows. Or suspects. He can't be sure without asking, and the risk there is too great. He's been acting without thinking for months, telling himself that what he was doing with Sean was alright because no one knew, and no one was hurt. That's not true anymore.

Cameron feels guiltier sneaking to the fifth floor with a box of donuts than he ever did driving downtown for a sexual encounter. He should have felt that yesterday. Should have been more careful. Christ, he kissed Sean when he first woke up.

He's surprised to find himself standing in Sean's door, fear reverberating through him. Sean's staring out the window, face so blank that Cam wonders if he's still asleep.

"Sean?" His voice doesn't shake. Small victory.

"Hope you got cream-filled ones," Sean says tiredly as he looks at him, and Cam doesn't know if he can move. "You okay? You look shittier than I feel, and I feel really—"

"Did you tell Kayla something?" He shuts the door and lowers his voice. "About us?"

"What? No!" There's no lie in Sean's face or eyes, but Cam's panic doesn't ease.

"Are you sure? Because I think she…" God, he can't even say it.

"I didn't say anything! She got my medical history. That's it. I lied about the bad parts. She doesn't know the whole fucking guys for money thing. Hell, I told her I was straight!"

Cam squints at Sean in surprise. "You did?"

"I lied to the cops for you, you think I wouldn't also lie to your wife?"

"Thank you," Cam replies, shocked.

The weariness settles back around Sean like a haze, and he slumps back into his bed. "Hand me a damn donut."

Cam hands Sean a chocolate frosted one and takes a plain glazed for himself. "I think she knows there's something. She knew I was planning on getting coffee for you and using it as an excuse to get some for myself. The way she said it – maybe she only suspects."

"If you're worried about her knowing…" Sean looks like he's having as hard a time saying it as Cam is thinking it. "You shouldn't be here."

"Sean."

"Cam, come on, you're putting yourself at risk." Sean finds something very interesting to look at on the sheet. "It's not like I'm any use to you now anyway. You can quit hanging around."

"Use?" Cam's brain can't process that.

"I mean, I could probably blow you in the right position, but I'm on the bench for a while." Sean's returned to his old mask of bravado and flirtation, though it's cracked now.

"You still think this is about sex?" Cameron asks dully, and Sean shrugs. "Of course. We don't have a relationship; we have a transaction. Isn't that what you said?" The hurt and anger from the forgotten fight hang above him like a lifeline he can take to get out of this.

"It's true."

"You know it's not," Cam says, soft and insistent, and Sean's mask falls.

"It's better if it is. Get out of here, Cam, you've got work to do." Sean doesn't sound angry, just resigned.

Cam shakes his head, stubborn and defeated at the same time, "I'll see you," he says, taking the donuts and barely noticing Sean's little wave.

"Bye, Cam." It feels more final than usual.

sean

Sean feels worse today, which he didn't think was possible. Maybe it means he's healing, or maybe they're giving him fewer drugs because they flagged him as a potential addict. Maybe it's that gut-churning fear that he's entirely messed up Cam's life. Or the weird ache of worrying Cam won't be showing up again if he knows what's good for him. Not that Cam ever cared about what was good for him. That's why Sean turns to the door with a stupid surge of hope every time it opens.

It wasn't Cam the first four times. It isn't Cam this time.

It's his physical therapist – a scarecrow of a man named Wayne – back with the oh-so-helpful handouts about recovering from pelvic fractures he promised. Sean wants to use them as a cudgel to kill the guy, but that would mean moving again, and that's not happening.

PT hurt, and it hurt bad. Sean's amazed by how exhausting it was too. He'd thought he was in okay shape, but man was he wrong. He never worked harder to do less and ache more.

Sean doesn't want to be the guy who asks for more drugs, but he wants more drugs.

"Now, read this and thank the Lord that today was a good, solid start," Wayne says, grinning. "Another session tomorrow and you'll be good to head home and continue recovery there!"

"I'll *what*?" Sean squawks. The idea of getting out has Sean's heart racing. "But I can't – I can't *move*."

"You'll need to take it slow for a few weeks. Gonna take at least six before you're all healed up." Wayne remains cheerful, completely oblivious to Sean's panic. "All in the pamphlet."

"Six *weeks*?"

"I'll have a list of exercises for—"

"I can't be laid up for six weeks!" Sean can't breathe. This can't be real.

"Now, Sean," Wayne's voice deepens in what must pass for serious-ness for him. "I know it's probably tough with the active life a young man like you must live, but if you don't let yourself heal, things can get real bad real fast. The bones may not set right or rebreak, and there could be organ damage, infection, or even death."

"Just great." Sean wants to slap the guy because that's not the problem. He'd love to sit on his ass in bed for six weeks, but that requires a *bed*.

"I'll be back by tomorrow, okay? Get some rest." Wayne gives one more goofy smile that Sean doesn't return and leaves.

He waits until the door is closed to fully collapse. Maybe if he can make it to the tent camp, he can hole up there and pray for help. If the city doesn't clear it out, and he doesn't die from exposure, since he has no gear.

What else can he do? He'd sooner shoot Eli than talk to him. Shelters won't take a single male long-term. Cam would probably give him anything he needed, but Sean's an idiot who told Cam to back off.

Sean looks at the clock. It's a few minutes past five, which means Cam is on his way home. Sean remembers how Cam was meticulous about his schedule to the minute. Cam had said that like it was something he was ashamed of, as if the boring certainty of his life was a mark on his character. Sean would kill for that right now. He had two things to look forward to each week – Cam and Danny – and that had been enough to make the streets bearable.

Crap. Danny.

What the hell is he going to tell Danny? How is he even going to call him?

"It was fried Friday in the employee cafeteria," a deep voice says from the door. "I hope you like rubbery popcorn shrimp and tater tots."

"Jesus, Cam," Sean sighs as Cam sets the food in front of him on the little swingy tray thing. "I thought you were gonna keep clear."

"I spent all day keeping clear," Cam replies, fishing a cookie and a can of soda from his pockets.

"And?"

"It was unpleasant. Eat."

Sean rolls his eyes and pops a tot into his mouth. It's not very warm, but it's better than that crap he had for lunch. "You ain't eating?"

"It's been a stressful day." Cam pulls a roll of antacids out of another pocket and takes one. "I'm meeting Kayla for dinner."

"You talked to her?" Sean suddenly finds it hard to keep chewing.

"Texted. She didn't say anything."

Sean has no idea what that could mean, and obviously neither does Cam. "Guess that means you can't hang around."

"I'm sorry," Cam says with such genuine regret that Sean can't look at him. "I'd much rather be here."

"Nah, I get it. You've got..." *A life to live without me in it.* Better get used to it. "Stuff to do."

"Do you need anything?" Cam asks, and Sean dares to look up into those ridiculous blue eyes. It's Cam making the offer, but it feels like he's begging Sean for something.

"Yeah, actually." Screw dignity. "I need a phone? Tomorrow's my weekly call with Danny, and I can't miss it."

"Of course. You can use mine." Simple as that. Idiot.

"I may need it for a while, I gotta make some other calls." Sean gulps, shame heating his cheeks. "Sorta need to figure out where I'm going when they kick me out of here. Turns out I gotta sit on my ass for six weeks or something."

Cam's eyes widen in worry. "Are you talking about a shelter or friends or—"

"I don't know!" Sean snaps, the breathless panic returning. "I kinda don't wanna die. Yet. Which is dumb, cause my life is fucked."

"We'll find somewhere for you to go. I'll come in tomorrow, and I won't leave until we have a solution." It's exactly what Sean knew Cam would say, but it breaks something in him to actually hear it. "What time do you need the phone?"

"Call's supposed to be between eleven and twelve. Used to do it at the shelter. That's why I was always downtown when you were on sandwich duty." Cam looks down, and Sean realizes he's said something wrong. "I came for you too."

"You don't need to flatter me. I understand. Are you going to tell Danny what happened?"

"I dunno," Sean whispers, tears pricking his eyes. "I don't wanna let the kid down again. That's all I've ever done."

"I doubt that," Cam says, because he's the kind of moronically optimistic person that still believes that people are good; that *Sean* is good. The thought of how wrong Cam has always been about him makes something ugly and sharp twist inside Sean.

"Did Kayla tell you? About the crap she got out of me?"

"No. Among other things that would be illegal, and she wouldn't do that."

"Figure it's only fair that you know too," Sean sneers. In his mind, he sees Jeremiah looming above him, and his face melts into Jeff Lockwood's. "My dad was a drunk. And an angry one too. He kept it cool, mostly, when my mom was alive. I always stood up to him. Told mom he'd get better, but she died when I was nine. She got hit by a drunk driver after storming out of the house. She and my dad had a fight about me, so it was my fault."

"Sean…"

"I failed her. After that, Dad was never the same. We hit the road, jumping from place to place every time he got fired or collared for fraud or something. I had to raise Danny and keep him safe from Dad too."

Cam doesn't offer empty words of comfort; he just takes Sean's hand. "I should have gotten him straight. It's a miracle that Danny and I stayed out of the system as long as we did, but once we were in, it got worse. I was in and out of homes and juvie for doing what I could to keep us fed. When I turned eighteen, they dumped me so fast it made my head spin. I found Dad. Helped him on jobs, kept him in booze and smokes. Then two years ago, I woke up and he was just gone."

"Gone?"

"Gone. The Bel Air was still there, so who the hell knows where he went, but I looked for him instead of sticking around for Danny. Figured he'd come back here if he came anywhere, so this is where I ended up. He hasn't come back. I'd turned tricks a few times before, and it was easy money, so I kept it up. I was saving up to get Danny back, nearly everything I earned, but all my cash was in my fucking *car*."

"It will be okay," Cam says so kindly that Sean wants to scream.

"No, it won't! How do I tell Danny I got the shit beaten out of me by a john that wanted to send me to hell?" Cam winces at that. "Should I tell him that the one nice guy I know, who also liked to pay me for sex, is helping me out 'cause of some weird guilt complex?"

There's so much ice in the glare Cam gives him that Sean gets a genuine chill. "You know that's not why I'm here."

"Cam, I'm not your problem to solve or your burden to bear." Sean knows that's a dumb thing to say to the guy he's begging for help, but it's also the truth. "I'm not your anything."

"That's not true. You're my friend." Sean wants to laugh at that. He's had this guy's dick in his ass multiple times and enthusiastically come on his face. That's not friendship territory. More than that, it's just plain stupid on Cam's part.

"Did you not hear what I've been saying? All I do is let people down." He pulls his hand out of Cam's, knowing he doesn't deserve that warmth.

Cam grabs it back. "You haven't let me down yet." Cam's voice is firm, his hand steady as stone, and the earnest look in his eyes almost makes Sean believe him. He stares for too long, letting himself be the person Cam sees, just for a little while. Until Cam's phone buzzes with a text alert. Letting his hand go isn't easy.

"It's Kayla," Cam says, looking at his phone. "Asking if I'm on my way. I should go."

"Go ahead. Get out of here. Thanks for... For everything."

Cam gives him another long look. "I'll be back tomorrow. We'll figure something out." Sean notes the tension in Cam's shoulders as he turns to go. He's off to face a wife who may or may not confront him for a whole menu of bad.

"If you can't come for some reason. I get it."

"I'll be here," Cam says firmly.

Sean doesn't have the energy to argue, so he gives him a weak smile and a nod. "See ya, Cam."

"Goodbye, Sean."

He's never really liked watching Cam leave, so he doesn't look when he walks out the door. He stares at the window instead. It's a beautiful sunny day, but the view outside feels like a cheap piece of art. Just like the room, it's empty and cold.

cameron

The restaurant Kayla's chosen for tonight is full of laughing young people taking pictures of their food with their phones. Cameron waits for Kayla and can't decide what to worry about, so he dwells alternately on everything.

"Hey, babe." He spins at the feel of Kayla's hand on his elbow and plasters on a smile before bending to kiss her. He takes a bit longer than usual, and when he draws back her face is warm and amused. "Good to see you too."

"We still have about ten minutes to wait," Cameron tells her. "How are you?"

"Good. Had a nice day. Got some things sorted out."

"Sorted out?" It sounds ominous, but she doesn't seem in the mood for a confrontation about infidelity, and they're in a public place, but he's not very good at judging things.

"Don't worry. I did some painting. Went to that ladies' luncheon with the new assistant pastor. Your mom says hi, by the way."

"I thought you were skipping that?"

"I missed the big party, so I figured if I was free, I should go. Drew is interesting." Interesting could mean a lot of things.

"I didn't really get to talk to him much."

"I did. He had some good thoughts." Cameron's nervous again, wondering if he was a topic of conversation. "Then I had coffee with your mom, came home, and curled up with a book. And cramps. You're off the hook tonight, by the way. How about you?"

"I stopped a fight between Flor and Lee over the last donut. Nearly lost an eye. Finished the quarterly projections."

"How's Sean?" Her voice is light. Almost too casual.

"He's fine. I think. I didn't see him much," Cameron says carefully.

"His chart says he started PT, and it looks like he's good for discharge soon." Cameron raises an eyebrow. "What? I log in on my day off to check on patients I like all the time."

"You like him?" This is very much not where Cameron thought this conversation was going.

"I do. I can see why you two get along." Kayla continues to smile, and Cameron's mind keeps racing.

"About that. Sean, I mean," Cameron intended to discuss Sean after he'd fulfilled his obligations, but the topic is open now. "He asked if I would come by tomorrow. He needs a phone to call his brother and some help sorting out where he's going."

"Of course," Kayla says, easy as anything. "Does he know where he's going?"

"No. He's..." Better to make the leap now. "He doesn't have anything, Kay. No ID, no money. Nothing. I know it's a lot, but I was hoping we could help him."

When he looks at Kayla, she doesn't seem suspicious at all. In fact, she's smiling brightly. "You haven't called me Kay in forever. And of course, we can help Sean."

"Maybe we can find him a hotel?"

"Or we could put him in the guest room."

11

QUIET

sean

SEAN WINCES AS THE nurse helps him ease back into the bed. They upped the pain meds last night, so only about sixty percent of his body hurts now, but things are still smart like a son of a bitch when he moves the wrong way.

"Hear they're releasing you back to the wild soon," Dawn says as she helps Sean arrange himself among his scratchy blankets.

"Yeah, they're talking about it," Sean says, noting the rise of Dawn's eyebrow. "Why, you lookin' for a date?"

"In your dreams, hot stuff."

Sean deflates. He tried not to look at himself in the dark bathroom mirror while he was in there, but he wasn't successful. The swelling on his face has gone down, leaving green-purple bruises behind that go great with his pale skin and sunken eyes. He's lost weight, despite Cam's best efforts, and he's looking gaunt. The few days' worth of beard helps some and hurts some. Hot stuff indeed.

"Buzz me if you need anything else," Dawn says and leaves him alone in the quiet.

It's never fully silent in the hospital. There're always people walking outside, the sound of wheelchairs and walkers; nurses scurrying by in their sensible shoes. He can make out distant beeps and pages over the intercom and sirens when some other poor schmo gets brought in. He doesn't remember coming here, not really. There're flashes of pain and red and noise, like remembering a nightmare, but that's it. Leaving is gonna be a hell of a lot different, but still terrifying. A knock on the door startles Sean out of his panic spiral. He knows it's Cam before he even turns, and he can't help but smile.

"Right on time—" he stops at the sight of Cam's wide, worried eyes and pursed lips. A head of blonde hair emerging behind Cam explains the look. Oh no. Is this the confrontation?

"Hey, Sean," Kayla says with a smile that does nothing to stem Sean's terror. "Hope you don't mind me tagging along. We'll let you make your phone call soon."

"That's fine," Sean stammers. "Do you have to bill this as overtime?"

"No, she's salaried." Cam's mouth snaps shut as Kayla and Sean give him the same look. "Oh."

"We wanted to talk to you together, actually," Kayla goes on, shaking her head.

"It's nothing bad," Cam says quickly, doing his mind-reading thing. It doesn't help. "I mentioned to Kayla last night that you didn't have anywhere to go when you get discharged."

"I know that you don't know us, particularly well," Kayla picks up. "Especially me, but we do want to help, and we have a perfectly good room in our house and—"

Sean wonders at what point he started hallucinating. "You have a *what*?"

Cam gives Sean a strained look. "I suggested a hotel, but Kayla—"

"This was *her* idea?" Sean has no idea if he's offended or terrified.

"This is cheaper and much less stressful," Kayla replies. "The room is on the first floor, right by the kitchen, with its own bathroom. It's where my mom stayed when she was sick. Cam never took down the bars, so it's set up for limited mobility, which you'll have for a few weeks."

"We have streaming and cable too," Cam adds weakly.

"You're talking about me living in your house." Sean doesn't think he needs to convey to Cam what a colossally bad idea this is, but he's gonna try. "Eating your food and getting in your way and... No. Dude, that's too much."

"It's the best option," Kayla argues with a churchy sort of warmth. "We can help you get back on your feet. And you'll have a doctor right there."

"Is this some 'what would Jesus do' thing?" Sean asks.

"Maybe a bit," Kayla replies with a shrug. "I know Cam has been talking to you about the church. You can join us at services, if you want to, once you're moving."

Sean's going insane. He can think of nothing more awkward than going to church at some evangelical purgatory with the guy he's extensively fucked *and his wife*. Maybe that's proof there is a God and he's punishing Sean specifically. "I... Uh..."

"I know you would do the same thing if you were in our place," Cam adds, infuriatingly reasonable. "Please. It would be the best thing for you."

Sean wants to snap that Cam should, for once in his life, think about what would be best for Cam. Instead, Sean sighs. "I'm not winning this, am I?"

"Nope," Kayla grins, triumphant.

"I see why you two get along," Sean murmurs. "I'll pay you back. When I can. I promise." It's the only thing he can say to ease his shame.

"Here," Cam says, pulling a phone from his pocket. "It's prepaid. Keep it for now."

"Thanks." Sean checks the clock. A minute to eleven. Perfect. "Don't you have to get downtown for sandwich patrol?"

"I had something more important today," Cam says, too sincere for comfort.

"We'll let you make your call while I talk to the on-call about your discharge." Kayla's all smiles, and Sean honestly doesn't know what to make of it. No one is this good, not without an angle, and especially if they think the guy they're helping is shtupping their husband.

"Great. Thanks. Again," Sean mumbles. It's too early for this shit. Yes, he knows it's eleven.

"Are you alright?" Cam asks, low and careful.

"I'm fine, Cam. Lemme talk to Danny."

"Of course."

Sean stares at the phone in his hand after the door shuts. It's not fancy, but it's the first cell he's held in – he can't remember. How sad is that? He dials and waits.

"Hello." Danny sounds fed up already, but damn, it's good to hear his voice.

"Hey, short stuff," Sean says, voice breaking.

"Are you okay? Why are you calling from a blocked number?" Danny demands, half-angry, half-concerned.

"I, uh – I got in a bit of an accident. I'm in the hospital. I'm okay—"

"Holy crap, Sean! What are you – oh my God, your car!" Even after so long apart, Danny knows him pretty damn well.

"She's in bad shape, but I'll get her fixed. Somehow."

"What about you? What's going to happen? Are you okay?" Danny usually sounds older than his years, but not right now. Right now, he's a scared kid, and it breaks Sean's heart that he even cares.

"You know me. I'm always okay. I'm gonna stay with some friends for a little while to heal up though."

"Friends?" The 'you have friends?' remains unspoken.

"Yeah, nice God-fearing folk in the burbs."

"Seriously? And you met them how?" Danny sounds rightfully dubious.

"Cam – the husband – he volunteers downtown where I hang out. We made friends. Don't worry about it."

"You just told me you're in the hospital and you're going to live with some strangers; of course I'm gonna worry."

"I'm just staying there while I sort stuff out. Don't stress." Sean's going to do enough of that for the both of them. "Tell me about you. How's summer?"

"It's fine. My worker got me into some camp thing for foster kids where we're gonna climb ropes and learn not to be delinquents or something. Might be cool."

"You like your new guy? You said what's-her-face got reassigned, right?"

"Yeah, Anthony's pretty cool. Kinda serious, but you know, well-intentioned."

"Sounds like a friend of mine."

"He's been really cool about trying to get me in the advanced classes in school, since the Weavers don't care."

"What sort of classes you lookin' at?" Danny launches into an extended monologue on statistics and trig and getting into calc a year early, and a familiar pride settles under Sean's battered ribs. Danny's okay and not too pissed. Thank God for small miracles.

The call is winding down when Danny asks, "So, this place you're staying, are you gonna have, like, an address?"

"I guess. Why?"

"I was talking to Anthony about ways we could be in touch more, and he said maybe letters? Like you can get him the address, and I can give him letters, and vice versa. I know it's stupid but—"

"Danny, shut up." Sean can't keep the dumb amazement out of his voice. "I'll get you the address."

"Great. I gotta go! Take it easy and get better, okay?"

"Yeah, bye, short stuff."

"Bye, dork."

Sean ends the call and fiddles with the phone, trying to think what he'd even write in a letter to Danny and failing. He'll deal with that later; for now, he'll focus on not freaking out about other shit. He takes some time to explore the phone. It's not a smartphone, but it's got Tetris and Pong, so that's cool. He decides to add Danny to the contacts, so it won't be empty. To his surprise, there're already a few names entered: "Kayla," "Cameron," "Doctor," "Wayne" (why). And "Home."

"Jesus Christ, Cam," Sean whispers to himself. Of course, it's possible that Kayla could have programmed it, but Sean has a feeling she didn't.

He could still say no. He could figure out some way to get out of here without anyone knowing and… die on the street or something. Danny and Cam would be sad, but it would hurt less than becoming part of someone's home – Cam's home – and leaving. Anything would hurt less than that.

He thinks about how he used to drive around the burbs, sneering at the cookie-cutter houses and manicured lawns. He told himself he hated it because thinking of a nice, clean life like that being within reach made him ache too deep to breathe. He thinks of seeing Cam every damn day and how it's been a week since they kissed and how much Sean misses his touch. He's going to have to look at Cam the way he used to look at those nice houses, judging and yearning, instead of admitting that he wants the thing he can see but never have.

"Hey, Sean?"

He looks up at Kayla's voice. She's standing in the doorway with Cam lurking behind her.

"Yeah?"

"So, it sounds like if Wayne gives the okay, you can leave later this afternoon," Kayla says.

"This afternoon? Oh. Wow." Sean wonders if they'll load him up with drugs before he goes, because he will definitely need some chemical assistance to deal with this.

"We'll get the room cleaned up, get some clothes for you, and come back," Kayla plows on, perky and unquestionable.

"If that's alright," Cam adds.

"Yeah, that's fine," Sean says. "This isn't how I thought the day would go."

"I'm sure." Cam's 'me neither' is clear in his face.

"God always has surprises in store," Kayla says with a smile that Cam tries and fails to imitate. "We'll be back in a few hours."

"I'll be here," Sean laughs hopelessly to himself.

cameron

Cam enjoys trips alone to the store. He likes being on his own but not secluded. No one at Wal-Mart is going to ask him anything besides if he's finding things alright, and he can wander the aisles and think. The hope of finding something soothing was what made him offer to do the shopping while Kayla fixed up the guest room. It's not working. As it is, he's trying to pick a shampoo Sean might like and not have a panic attack.

What the hell are you doing? The voice in his head that sounds suspiciously like Sean asks. He's going to share a roof with the man he cheated on his wife with and still lusts for. Every day will be a test he'll surely fail. All at his wife's suggestion.

He chooses a generic shampoo and heads two aisles over for more antacids. He's going to need them.

"Cameron?"

He doesn't know the voice, but he turns anyway. It takes him a moment to recognize the small, scruffy man looking at him. It's not the face but the twitchy, nervous set of his shoulders that finally clicks. "Mr. Barons?"

"Please, call me Drew." The new assistant pastor shifts his basket from one hand to another with a distinct clink of bottles and holds out a hand to Cameron. Drew's palms are clammy, and he winces at Cameron's grip.

"Nice to meet you. Again."

Drew's attention falls on Cameron's cart. "So, are you, uh, stocking up on... pants?"

"They're for a friend," Cameron says, as if that's a perfectly valid reason to have that many pairs of sweats in a cart. At least they cover up the packages of socks and underwear.

"A friend?" Drew echoes, voice high. "Kayla mentioned you had a friend who was hurt? Is he getting better?"

Cameron squints at the smaller man. Did Kayla tell him something, or is this simply how Drew is? "He's recovering. He's going to stay with us while he recuperates."

"He's going to – oh, uh, wow. That's really nice of you." Drew shuffles as Cameron wonders how long he has to talk to him before it's socially acceptable to walk away. "Very Christian."

"He has nowhere else to go, and we have space," Cameron says, repeating the argument Kayla made multiple times last night.

"Of course, that's great. I hope I can meet him."

Introducing Sean to members of his church is something else Cameron has no desire to think about. "I need to go now."

"Sure. See you tomorrow!" Drew calls after him, and Cameron suppresses a sigh.

It will be fine. He's going to buy some food for Sean and go home and unpack and get in the car with his wife and retrieve his injured friend from the hospital, and everything will be *fine.*

They have a past, yes, but that's over. It was physical and monetary, not emotional. At least not on Sean's side. Cam cares for Sean, of course, and he still desires him, but he's under no illusion that Sean feels the same way.

They take Cameron's car because it's bigger than Kayla's aging Mazda.

"Are you sure this is okay with you?" Cameron asks as they pull up to the hospital.

"I was about to ask you the same thing," Kayla says. "This was my idea, remember?"

"Yes, but I don't want you to think this is something you have to do because…" Words fail him again, and Kayla gives him another tolerant look.

"Cam, I know you're not good with people, but you know Sean, you like him. This will be fine. I think it could even be a blessing for us."

There is absolutely no way he can tell Kayla how much he likes Sean and in what way and how that's the entire problem. He's about to enter a personal hell that he completely deserves, and like always, he will be fine.

sean

The ride is quiet. Sean focuses on the relief of putting the hospital behind him and breathes through the pain of sitting in the back seat. Wayne didn't go easy in their final session, and Sean was so tired and sore at the end that he was sure he wasn't going to be cleared to leave. He'd be lying if he said that he wasn't actually hoping for that, but, no, Wayne and Dr. Tong agreed he was good to go. So, after an hour of meds, discharge notes, and every lecture in the book about staying off his feet and taking it easy, they'd dressed him in sweats, handed him his bloodied old coat and things, and rolled him to the car.

He tries not to notice Cam's eyes in the rearview or how tight his hands are on the steering wheel.

It's easier to look out at the neighborhood as it passes by. Everything is clean, bright new construction, with trees too small for their plots, waiting to grow. The houses are all variations on the same theme, bordered by lawns growing unnaturally green in the summer heat. Parents are running after kids and dogs, and someone is kneeling in a garden. Shit, there's an honest-to-God white picket fence in front of one place. Sean feels like he's gonna get arrested by the homeowner's association the second he steps outside the car.

"Are you hungry, Sean?" Kayla asks, shattering the silence.

"Uh, not right now," Sean replies and catches a disapproving flash of blue eyes in the rearview.

"We'll figure something out later. Neither of us can really cook," Kayla goes on.

"Hey, Cam makes a hell of a PB&J," Sean says. He can't see Kayla's expression, but her laugh is encouraging.

"I'm also familiar with the theory of several other sandwiches," Cam rumbles.

"I love a good BLT," Sean offers and gets a sigh for it. He's not sure whose.

"We don't do much bacon," Cam says.

"Or tomatoes," Kayla adds with a glare at Cam. "But, hey, remember the egg sandwiches you used to make for us when we were in the dorms?"

"No, that was our first apartment," Cam corrects. "Before you broke the oven. And the stove."

"It was an honest mistake."

"Uh huh."

Sean feels like he should hate the banter, the easy familiarity of it all. But it reminds him so much of the way he talks with Danny that it makes something very different ache inside him.

They pull into a driveway that Sean can hardly distinguish from all the others on the block, except for the rosebushes on the side. The garage is normal, full of boxes labeled in neat Sharpie, with bikes at the back that don't look like they've been used in a few years. At least there's only one step up to the door.

Sean startles as his door opens, having completely spaced on Cam and Kayla getting out of the car. Cam holds out a hand, and Sean's pretty sure he's about to have the first of many panic attacks.

"Do you need help up?" Cam asks, even though he knows the answer. There's no reason besides Sean's pride to try it himself, except for his very vivid memories of all the places that Cam's hands have been. Sure enough, when Sean gives up and clasps Cam's hand, electricity shoots through him. He meets Cam's eyes and knows he feels it too, which makes Kayla standing right there holding out crutches for Sean even more awkward.

"It'll hurt getting in, but then you can rest and not move for as long as you like," Kayla says, probably taking the face Sean's making as pain.

"Sounds great," Sean grits out. He makes it into the house with a combination of Cam's help and the crutches. At least Cam's gentle hand on his back is a nice distraction from the very real pain in his hip (or pelvis or whatever). Cam lets go once they step into what Sean would call a mud room combined with the laundry, and Sean starts breathing again. Kayla and Cam toe off their shoes, because of course they're no-shoes-in-the-house people. Sean awkwardly does the same with the slippers they brought him to leave the hospital.

"Through here," Kayla says, opening another door and letting them into the main part of the house. Sean gives a long whistle, because *holy crap*. He's never going to feel bad about Cam overpaying ever again.

To say it's the nicest house Sean's ever been in doesn't mean much, but it's beyond anything he's seen outside of TV. The main area is huge and open, with the kitchen, dining, and living room all in one big, airy space. Massive windows look out into a vibrant garden; there are shiny hardwood floors and a giant cushy white couch facing a flat screen. It's something out of a catalog or a Pinterest board, and Sean feels like he's getting it dirty just standing inside and gawking.

"Damn, I should have gone to medical school," Sean breathes. "This is amazing."

"Thanks, we like it," Kayla says.

"You seriously don't cook? Your kitchen is insane," Sean goes on, moving further into the house on his crutches, awkward and halting.

"I've wanted to learn, but haven't had time," Cam murmurs.

"You're right through here," Kayla says, rushing in front of Sean to a door next to the kitchen. "The sheets and towels are clean, and we put the extra clothes in the dresser."

"Yeah, that's…" Sean means to say it's fine, but his mouth stops working. It's not a particularly special room, but it has a big window looking out on the garden, a clean bed with white sheets and a nice quilt, and for a little while, Sean gets to pretend it's home. There's a painting across from the door, above the bed. It's abstract; bright splashes of red and blocks of blue that look like they're at war, with other colors sparking in between.

"Sean? Are you okay?"

He nearly jumps off his crutches at the touch of Cam's hand on his elbow. "Yeah. I'm – This is real nice."

Sean looks back and forth between his hosts. Kayla looks as concerned as Cam. Sean gets it. To them, this is just another room. They don't see what it is to Sean: a taste of so many things he never thought to want. He's not even going to think about how he can't keep it.

"Good!" Kayla pipes up, her smile returning. "Bathroom is right through there, and we can give you the tour of upstairs some other day."

"It's not very interesting," Cam mutters.

"I'm sure." Sean's not going to say how relieved he is that he doesn't have to see the room they share.

"We'll let you get settled in," Kayla says. Sean makes his way to the bed and nods.

"I'll get started on those egg sandwiches," Cam adds. Sean can't tell if it's a peace offering or avoidance because the bed is heaven, and he doesn't care at all right now.

Kayla and Cam leave Sean alone with a click of the door. He carefully arranges himself on the bed, letting the pain ebb as he eases back onto the pile of pillows and looks around again. This is really happening. He's really here in Cam's house and life, and there's no way to run.

The room smells fresh, like the windows were open this morning. The quilt under his fingertips is soft, and it's so quiet. No yelling or sirens or trains. Nothing but the soft whoosh of the air conditioner, the occasional birdsong, and the distant sounds of Cam and Kayla moving in the house. The AC shuts off after a few minutes, and Sean can make out the low rumble of Cam's voice, his steady footsteps, and the clink of plates. Then it's quiet.

"Sean?"

Sean startles awake at the voice. "Yeah. Come in," he says, voice rough and groggy as he rubs his eyes.

Cam is alone when he opens the door, a plate in one hand and a big glass of water in the other. "Did I wake you?"

"Sorta, but it's cool. That dinner?" Cam nods. The smell of eggs and warm bread is fantastic after the hospital slop he had for lunch. "Great, wouldn't be a Saturday without a sandwich from Cam." Cam hesitates in the threshold, eyes on the food instead of Sean. "Are you waiting for me to get up or an invitation?"

That gets Cam moving, albeit with an annoyed sigh. Sean struggles to sit up, missing the magic hospital bed. Cam sets the food on the nightstand and reaches out to help. Sean recoils, and Cam grimaces.

"I'm sorry. I know you want to do things on your own."

"That's not…" He really doesn't need Cam touching him right now. Especially with his goddamn wife loitering nearby.

"Sean," Cam bites down on his lower lip, and Sean has never had a more inconvenient urge to kiss someone. "I want you to know I don't expect anything from you." Cam looks up at him, all serious and sincere.

Sean doesn't understand. "Expect?"

"This isn't a trade or a payment, you being here. It's the right thing to do, even if the intimate part of our acquaintance is over. Which I know it needs to be."

"Oh." Cam doesn't want him anymore. Of course. Why would he? "Fine. Yeah. Thanks, I guess."

"Sean—"

"No. That's good to get out there," Sean goes on, voice brittle. "Business arrangement over. No hard feelings." Sean's proud he doesn't make a dirty joke of that.

"Good," Cam says with a nod and a serious look.

"Good," Sean echoes. "And you don't get what you don't pay for, so don't go getting fresh, okay?" Sean tries to make it sound like a joke and fails. Cam looks down at the floor like a scolded child.

"Of course," Cam murmurs. "Enjoy the food. Kayla and I are going to eat in the kitchen. Call if you need anything."

"Yeah, sure," Sean says. Cam gives Sean a pathetic excuse for a smile as he leaves, the door closing behind him.

Sean retrieves the food and takes a bite of the sandwich. It's good. Fancy bread with seeds and stuff in it, mayo, salt, and warm eggs. He eats in the quiet, clean room and wonders if the house feels like this for Cam too: secure and bright and empty.

12
MaraтHоn

cameron

CAMERON IS ALWAYS THE first one out of bed on Sundays. He showers, shaves, and makes it downstairs before Kayla even stirs. His efficiency gives him ample time to stare at the guest room door while the water for his tea boils. He wishes he could brew coffee, so the smell could let Sean know he was awake. He needs the caffeine too, thanks to a restless night, tossing and turning with Sean one floor below him. Knowing Sean doesn't desire him should have made it easier, but it just gave him more fuel for an endless thread of dark thoughts until he'd taken a sleeping pill at one AM.

It doesn't matter that Sean was only with him because he was paid to be. Cam can't stop wanting him, any more than he could stop wanting to live. So Cam stands outside Sean's door and listens for the sound of movement for five minutes before knocking gently.

"Sean?"

Cam hears sheets shuffling and the creak of the bed frame, then a low grunt. "Yeah, I'm decent."

Cam cracks the door, keeping his eyes down for his own sanity more than Sean's modesty. "I'm making breakfast. Do you want anything?"

"Dude, you don't gotta wait on me."

Cam looks up in time to see Sean wince as he pushes himself upright in the bed. "Are you saying it's easier to do it yourself?"

"Fuck you," Sean replies through a yawn. "Fine. Whatever you're having. No rush, this is gonna take me a while."

Cam retreats, closing the door behind him and taking a steadying breath. That wasn't so bad. Maybe somehow, through the grace of God, he can manage this. On the other side of the door, Sean groans. It's a sound of weariness and pain, but it reminds Cam so vividly of more pleasurable times that he has to dig his fingernails into his palm to control the heat that goes through him. Maybe he can't do this.

Cam putters in the kitchen, taking longer than usual to cut fruit and pour two glasses of real milk for him and Sean and almond milk for Kayla. By the time he remembers he was going to make tea, the water is already cold again. All the while, he listens through the walls: water running, the thump of crutches as Sean makes his way through the room. Cam still jumps when the door opens.

"Hey." Sean hesitates, leaning heavily on his crutches and looking between the kitchen island, where Cam has set up the food, then back to his bed. "Yeah, I think I'll eat in—"

"Oh, you're up!" Sean's eyes widen as Kayla comes down the stairs. Cameron turns to her with a nervous smile. "And you convinced my husband to make breakfast. Good work. Morning, babe." Kayla presses a quick kiss to Cameron's cheek and takes her milk. "Oh, Sean, let me get you a pillow so you can sit at the table."

"You don't have to." Kayla ignores Sean's protests and grabs a throw pillow from the couch. "Thanks."

Sean does fine on his own, using the crutches to get to the table and easing himself down. He's wearing a plain cotton t-shirt and dark gray sweats, and he looks soft and comfortable as he nods in appreciation when Cameron sets a bowl in front of him. "It's just yogurt, granola, and fruit."

"It's Sunday; haven't you ever heard of pancakes?" Sean says as he starts in.

"Are pancakes those puddles of lumpy batter with burnt stuff on the bottom?" Kayla asks with a devious smile.

"I still should get credit for the effort," Cameron grumbles.

"Yeah, no criticism from the chick who broke an oven," Sean adds and then tenses until Kayla laughs.

"You're not wrong. We'd starve if we had to actually cook anything," Kayla says.

"I mixed three separate foods; that counts as cooking," Cameron retorts.

"Sure, Cam, whatever you say." Sean smiles at Cameron over his glass of milk. "This is good though. I think Danny would like it. He's always on about whole foods and stuff. Friggin' hippie."

"Sounds like a smart kid," Kayla says.

"You have no idea, he's off the charts," Sean beams. "Kid's going into sophomore year, and he's already on the senior reading list and all the advanced classes."

"Sounds like intelligence runs in the family," Cameron says, and Sean scoffs immediately.

"Dude, come on. I barely got a GED."

"Considering what those years were probably like for you, that's very impressive," Kayla says carefully. Cameron can see Sean's cheeks redden beneath his scruff and fading bruises.

"And you read more than anyone I know," Cameron adds.

"Because I have a lot of fucking time on my hands," Sean shoots back. "Sorry. Trying to mind the language."

"It's okay," Kayla smirks. "We're all fucking adults."

"Kayla," Cameron gasps as both his wife and Sean burst out laughing. Cameron shakes his head. "Don't listen to her. We don't stand for that shit around here."

Sean grins at him, and even with his healing bruises and scruffy cheeks, it's the most fantastic thing Cam has seen all morning. "Uh, speaking of," Sean says, cheeks still bright. "The reading, not the cursing. Do y'all have a bookshelf somewhere I can raid?"

"Of course, we have an office over there," Kayla indicates a door they'd neglected to show Sean yesterday, located near the stairs. "The books are mostly Cam's history doorstops, so we'll get you set up on Netflix and the cable before we go."

"Go?" Sean echoes, looking nervous.

"Church," Cameron says.

"That sounds fun. At least there's wine, right?"

"That's Catholics," Kayla says warmly. "But they think it's blood."

"Yeah, I remember. My…" Sean swallows. "Mom was Catholic. Or raised that way and dragged us to mass sometimes. Dad never was into it, and after she passed we stopped going. So, uh, what do y'all do? I'm guessing no Latin?"

"Sermons, some community news, most weeks, people will come up to testify – tell stories of how the Lord has worked through them and touched their lives. There is communion, but with grape juice," Cameron explains. "Music too. Sometimes it's not terrible."

"Drew says he wants to improve that," Kayla adds. "Today we also promised your mother we'd join her for lunch. We missed dinner on Tuesday."

"Just her?" Cameron asks, hoping to estimate what level of scrutiny he'll be under.

"She mentioned that Vince might be there. Luke can't make it."

"Who are Vince and Luke?" Sean asks.

Cameron fails at suppressing a sigh. "Older brothers," he answers. "Luke has a farm in the country. Vince runs the local Christian radio station."

"The one Lee kept turning on to piss off Flor that one week?" Sean asks.

"No, that was the Christian music channel. Vince runs the AM talk radio one," Cameron explains.

"What was it Flor kept switching it to? Rap?" Kayla asks.

"Death metal." Cameron shudders at the memory. "I didn't even know we had that kind of station around here."

"She was probably using an internet radio, you can find anything on there, according to Danny," Sean says. "I stick to radio and tapes, so it's a mystery to me."

"Better than this one's boxes of vinyl records he's never touched," Kayla replies, and Sean perks up.

"Gotta say, Cam, never pegged you for being that cool," Sean says.

"They're not—" Cameron looks down into his bowl and away from Sean's crooked smile. "They have sentimental value."

"I get that," Sean says. Cameron remembers Sean's poor, battered car and thinks he does.

"So, did you sleep okay?" Kayla asks, blessedly changing the subject.

"I slept great, actually. Nicest bed I've been in, like, ever." Cameron watches from the corner of his eye as Sean pokes at his yogurt with his spoon. "I, uh, really can't say enough how much this means, y'all taking me in."

"We're glad you're here," Kayla says for both of them. "I think it's going to be a good thing for everyone."

He and Sean smile and nod. Cameron knows he'll be doing a lot of that today.

sean

Sean can't pace, so he's clicking. Netflix asked "Are you still watching *Serial Monsters?*" one too many times for his pride, so he's finally exploring the ridiculous amount of channels to keep his mind off Cam coming home soon – without Kayla for the first time this week.

Cam and Kayla are almost always home at the same time. It's good, in the sense that he has a reason not to jump Cam's gorgeous bones, aside from the fact that Cam doesn't want Sean's broken ones. It's not like he doesn't get time alone with Cam. They had a good talk when he and Kayla got home from church and lunch on Sunday, which sounds like it was a blast (of hellfire). Sean clicks angrily past the church channels and wonders what it's like to hear that crap from your family all the time, especially growing up gay and thinking you can pray it away. He wonders if Kayla thinks that way, but he has no intention of asking.

When Kayla's around, even in another room, Sean feels like any wrong word will bring everyone's life crashing down. On Monday, Kayla brought home Sean's STD test results, and he was sure they were about to find out he had given the whole family chlamydia right there in the kitchen. But, miracle of miracles, it'd been clear and they'd just eaten dinner. Sean clicks on past a talk show where their problems aren't nearly as complicated as his.

The shopping channels make Sean think of Cam's family, and the hideous plates with Jesus's face on them, which his mother apparently thinks are the best gifts a person could ask for. Most of the art in the house is better, since it's Kayla's. They're all vibrant and abstract, washes of color and movement that tell a story Sean doesn't know.

He pauses briefly on the sports channels, trying to remember what seasons are even going on before news about the Cardinals reminds him it's baseball. Boring. The talking heads on another channel discussing the coming football season make him think of his Dad passed out with a game on. Next. How many damn ESPNs are there? This one's showing some track meet, and Sean's mind jumps unwillingly to Cam again. Specifically Cam's thighs. Sean's seen them before, obviously, and knew that Cam did something to stay in shape. He hadn't anticipated Cam appearing after a run on Monday, soaked with sweat, while Sean was just minding his business on the couch.

Fuck those thighs. Seriously. He wants to *fuck* those thighs. And those arms and that chest. And all the shiny, hot parts Cam just paraded around like Sean wasn't there trying not to have a horny aneurysm before the guy's wife came downstairs. He hadn't said anything besides 'hi' and then watched Cam take a long drink of water before he disappeared to shower. The image of Cam's flushed face and shimmering skin stayed with Sean after. He'd made sure not to be around when Cam got back from his run on Tuesday, but on Wednesday, he was weak and made sure he had a good seat. At least his dick hadn't betrayed him until later that night. Luckily, Cam and Kayla have the kind of nice house where there's Kleenex by the bed, and Sean only mildly hurt himself dealing with the situation before bed. If only he could flip channels in his brain.

Next up are the news channels, and no fucking thank you to that. Then history, which is also a nope. Kid's stuff. When did Ninja Turtles come back? Next are reruns and movies Sean's not in the mood for, so he ends up on the food channel. Someone is trying to make an omelet on a scimitar over an open flame while some other guy is blindfolded. Now this is quality television.

Sean gets into the show pretty fast, enough that he jumps when he feels a hand on his shoulder.

"Jesus!" Sean exclaims as Cam pulls back like he's been burned. "Ow, fuck," Sean adds, pain rippling from his healing bone and bruises.

"Sorry. I thought you heard me come in." Cam looks bashful and awkward, as usual. He holds up a paper bag. "I got dinner."

Sean sniffs. "Fried chicken?"

"The best Colonel Sanders has to offer."

"Oh, thank God," Sean sighs as Cam comes around the couch and sets the bag on the coffee table. "No offense, but I'm getting real tired of salad and keno."

"*Quinoa*," Cam corrects as Sean attacks the food, pain be damned.

"Hell yeah, you got extra biscuits too." Sean looks up to where Cam is still standing, conflicted as Sean's ever seen him. "Are you gonna sit down or what?"

"I, uh…" He's thinking of what they used to do on Thursday, before everything (including Sean) got broken.

"Sit down, Cam." Cam glares but complies, seating himself a respectable distance from Sean. They divide up the food and eat in awkward silence for a few minutes as the cooking show finishes. "So, uh, what did you do on Thursdays all alone before?"

Cam looks guiltily at his cup of mashed potatoes. "This, mostly. Get something to eat that Kayla doesn't like and come home. Sometimes I skip the run. Watch… something frivolous."

"A specific something?" Sean catches the embarrassed pink in Cam's cheeks and has a sudden, all too vivid, vision of Cam jerking off to gay porn. Doesn't seem in character, but the image of Cam with his dick out, face red with arousal, stays bright in Sean's mind.

"Just a show I like, nothing inappropriate," Cam reassures him. "Kayla thinks it's silly, and my mother thinks it's demonic."

"Okay, now you gotta tell me what show," Sean says through a mouthful.

Cam scowls at Sean's bad manners, then gives a defeated sigh when Sean swallows and doesn't look away. "It's called... *Serial Monsters.*"

"Holy shit."

"I know it's stupid, but—"

"I've been watching that show non-stop for the past three days."

Cam finally looks at him without any fear or nervousness in his eyes and grins. "Are you serious?"

"Yeah, I kinda love it. Got behind the last few seasons, obviously. Can't believe it's still on."

"I think they made a deal with the devil to get it renewed. I've never met anyone else who watches it."

"That's 'cause you don't hang out with emo teenagers," Sean sighs, knowing that says something about him too.

"The new season doesn't start for a month, so it's a good time to get caught up," Cam says shyly. "Where are you right now?"

Sean smiles. "They defeated the demon king, but now they have to deal with his accountant or something? Who do I think is also his cousin?"

"Ugh, then they call in the eldritch goo monsters," Cam groans. "What kind of demonic weakness is *soap?*"

"Hey, spoilers!"

"Apologies," Cam says, obviously not meaning it. "It's only really resolved in the musical episode and—"

"There is *not* a musical."

Cam takes a bite of chicken with a glint in his eye. "I guess you'll have to find out. I don't mind rewatching."

"Yeah, sure. Just no more blabbing, okay?"

They finish the food halfway through the episode (where a monster hunter has to give some witches marriage counseling while somehow also getting turned slowly into a bee), and Cam clears the detritus. Sean doesn't say anything about how Cam makes sure to throw away the bags in the garage, not the regular trash. The guy certainly has his systems down.

Cam sits back down, and Sean also doesn't say anything about how he's a little bit closer this time. Not close enough to touch, but he's not treating Sean like he's radioactive anymore either. Sean shifts his own position, telling himself he's getting more comfortable and manages to drift a few inches closer to Cam too.

The tall, sexy monster hunter is having a crisis about whether he'll ever be able to save his vampire girlfriend (who totally won't die like all his other girl friends) while his shorter, sexier brother broods and tries to punch his best friend, who happens to be a sexy ghost.

"You know, I think Ross would be better off with Dimitri than any of the girls he hooks up with," Sean says, trying to sound casual.

Cam gives him a sidelong look and a knowing smirk. "He does have more chemistry with him than with the women. And they'd make a very attractive couple."

Sean smiles. He knows Cam doesn't ever get to say anything like that in front of anyone else. Must be a relief.

Finally, Tristan finds out that the vampire girlfriend was secretly lying to him all along, and maybe also a witch, while Ross and his ghost friend just stare at each other until the credits roll.

"Do you want to watch another?" Cam asks, politely hitting pause.

"Yeah, but uh…" Sean swallows. Somehow, they got even closer in the second half of the episode, so now he can feel a trace of the warmth from Cam's body. It's distracting. "I wanted to ask you something."

"Anything," Cam says it so easily and sincerely that Sean doesn't know what to do with himself.

"I know why Kayla went to med school and all; she told me about her adoptive dad." Cam looks surprised. "It was a whole thing. But, uh, why do you do what you do? "

"Why are you asking?" Cam asks back, giving Sean the sad sense that no one has shown a genuine interest in getting to know him in a long time.

"I know more about Kayla than you. I wanna fix that." Sean fiddles with the material of his sweats. "You can, you know, talk to me."

Cam stares at him, and Sean's certain he's gonna get up and leave rather than actually let Sean in. Then again, Sean already knows too much about Cam for comfort, and he wouldn't blame Cam for saying he's finally crossed the line.

"I wanted to go into language and history. Classics, actually." Sean waits. "That means Greek and Latin history. I wanted to learn about the battle of Marathon, not run them."

Sean looks up at Cam, holding his breath. "Yeah?"

"I liked reading. Even though my mother would have killed me if she caught me with half the books I liked. Fantasy. Novels. Murder mysteries. History. Poetry. When I got to college and was finally on my own, I thought I could pursue that. Maybe I could study Biblical Greek along with Latin poetry. I could understand God better that way. I wasn't suited for it though. My mother made the point that it wasn't viable, and I needed something practical. I was good at math; business and accounting seemed like a good fit." There's brittleness to Cam's words, a tension that Sean recognizes from when Cam is saying things he knows he has to say.

"Okay. That's a nice story, but what's the truth?"

Cam looks out the window into the darkening night, his eyes clouding with memory and regret. "There was a professor. In the first Greek class I took," he says quietly. "The class was amazing, and he was handsome and vibrant. We learned so much about the world back then and what was expected of men. The way he read the language—"

"You had the hots for him?" Sean asks with a grin.

"I... Yes, I did." He's never heard Cam's voice so small and vulnerable. "But the thing that truly stood out at our little Christian college was that he was gay. I'd never met someone who was out before. All I ever heard about was perverts dying of AIDS and predators and groomers.

Horror stories. Then there he was, living his life as boldly as could be. It was amazing. *He* was amazing. I switched my schedule so I could take two classes from him in the spring term, and he was happy to advise me about anything I asked; books, different programs. Even studying abroad," Cam goes on, wistful. "Kayla kept warning me that my family wouldn't like that. We were just friends then, but she knew what they'd all say about me associating with a known homosexual. I didn't listen. All I saw was him and a chance to be… free."

"Were you and him, like, a thing?"

Cam scoffs, shaking his head. "No. I wasn't so bold, and he was much older. I had fantasies, of course, but nothing came of it." Cam peers at Sean with a warmth that makes Sean's heart jump. "You're the only man I've ever known that way. If that's something you care about."

Sean wasn't going to be jealous, he told himself that when he asked, but it still satisfies something deep inside him to know he's the only one. "So what happened?"

"At the end of the year, someone reported him to the administration and said he was being inappropriate with students. Everyone knew about his sexuality, and rumors started to swirl and spread. I know none of them were true, but he wasn't well-liked in some circles."

"The Christian ones," Sean supplies.

"Yes. I don't know if he left or was fired, but the next year he was gone, and I realized…" Cam shakes his head. "I finally truly understood what sort of life I would have if I let that part of me out. I already knew I was damned, an abomination, but I hadn't really considered how people would react to someone like me. I wanted to teach too."

"Cam," Sean says softly. He wants so much to touch him, offer some kind of comfort, but he's afraid that if he does, Cam will slap him away.

"So, in the fall, I declared as a business and accounting major and started dating Kayla at my mother's suggestion. It was easier to go along with what was for the best." The coldness is back in Cam's voice and face, that stoic resolve that Sean wishes he had the balls to shake out of him. "So that's why I do what I do."

"Yeah." He knows Cam is talking about more than his job. "Thanks for telling me."

"You're the first person I've ever told," Cam replies and leans a little closer to Sean. "Thank you for asking."

Sean clears his throat. The itch in his palm to touch Cam is still there, but he settles for sliding it closer to him. "Since we're getting at the big stuff, can I ask you one other thing?"

"Of course."

"You, uh, talk about your mom a lot but not—"

"He left."

Sean's own fatherly mess could be as easily distilled into the same two simple words, but it wouldn't scratch the surface either. "When?"

"I was three. Luke was five, Vince was six. I don't remember much about him other than one day he was just gone. My mom doesn't talk about it."

"Jesus, that's shitty." Sean studies Cam's profile: the tense, sad set of his jaw and downcast eyes. "You know, I still don't know why my dad bailed on me. Some days, I hope he ended up dead because that would mean he didn't choose to ditch us. It still sucks though. Getting left behind."

"It does. My mother was alone with three children and hadn't worked for years. She had to get a job and take care of us. We couldn't have done it without the church helping. People brought us food and watched me, Vince, and Luke while she looked for work."

"Guess they can be nice when they're not being dicks about where people put their dicks," Sean mutters, and Cam laughs softly. "Sorry."

"I think he liked music, my father. All I have left of him is a box of vinyl records."

"The ones Kayla was talking about?" Cam nods. "Does she know who they belonged to?" Cam shakes his head in the negative. "You ever look at 'em?"

"No. One day, maybe." Cam's eyes return to Sean, a soft smile playing across his features. "Would you help me? You likely know the artists better."

"Yeah, I could do that," Sean nearly whispers.

"Thank you." Cam turns back to the television, somehow inching closer to Sean in the process. "Should we go on to the next episode?"

"Sure." Sean shifts carefully, getting comfortable again as Cam hits play and sets the remote aside.

Somehow, this feels more illicit than anything else they've ever done. Just sitting here, being together, with Cam revealing things to Sean that Kayla's never known. It feels cruel, in some way, that Cam gives him so easily what Kayla must have to pry out of him. But Cam's secrets are his, just his.

Cam doesn't say anything when Sean's hand finds his, ten minutes into the new episode, but they stay that way for the rest of the night.

13

HELPING HANDS

Cameron

CAMERON PLANS TO LEAVE the house for his volunteer shift and stop for the largest cup of coffee that Missouri can offer. He doesn't care if he'll spend the rest of the day hurting, because he deserves that as much as the sleepless night he spent next to Kayla after last night's unsuccessful date night. But first: a run.

Running in the morning used to be meditation. Now he's just running from things. From the woman in one room whom he can't look in the eye, and the man in another he can't stop looking at. He runs until his lungs burn, his knees ache, and his empty stomach churns and cramps. He doesn't even think about his route and shocks himself when he sees the bright yellow roses in front of the house.

He considers turning away, but he's starving and thirsty, and there's no point. He still tries to be quiet coming in and lets out a small sigh of relief at the sight of Sean's still-closed door. He grabs a glass of water, downs the entire thing in one long swallow, then refills it and starts gulping more down.

"Jeez, be careful, Cam. You ever heard of dry-drowning?"

Cam very narrowly avoids spitting water over the counter at the sound of Sean's voice from the couch. He's seated with a book in his hands and a sardonic expression on his face.

"Sorry, didn't mean to frighten you."

"You absolutely meant to frighten me," Cam shoots back, and Sean breaks into a laugh. "It's not funny."

"Your face was."

Cam sets his glass down. "How are you this morning?"

"Slept like shit. Really wish you had coffee."

"From your mouth to God's ears," Cam mutters to the counter tile before looking back up at Sean. "I'm sorry you slept poorly. I did too if that's any consolation."

"Really? Thought you'd been chill. Kayla said y'all had date night, or whatever. How was that?" Sean asks, voice a tone too high.

"Uneventful."

"Oh." Sean blinks at him, lips parted as he processes Cam's meaning. "*Oh.*"

"That's why I slept poorly," Cam adds. "My failure caused some awkwardness."

"Yeah, uh—"

"We shouldn't talk about this." Cam gestures towards the ceiling.

"Right. Not my business." There's an argument to be made that it is very much Sean's business, especially since Cam feels like he's betraying *Sean* each time Kayla touches him. That's ridiculous, considering they aren't intimate anymore, which is why it also felt wrong to use the memory of him to become aroused. "How was your run? You training for a marathon or something?"

"It helps me calm down. Or it's supposed to."

"Danny was saying he wants to do track, but his school doesn't have it, which I don't get," Sean says. "Like, what kind of shit school doesn't have a track team?"

"Probably budget cuts."

"I can't imagine that weirdo on track," Sean goes on, wistful. "Kid was all shins and elbows last time I saw him."

"Are you talking to him today?" Cam asks as he drifts closer to Sean, pulled in by his gravity.

Sean nods. "Yeah, got the phone all charged and ready. What're you planning?"

"I have my volunteer shift, then I promised Kayla I'd go with her to... I don't remember what. I think it's at the mall."

"She's swapping out her phone," Sean says, rolling his eyes.

"How long were you two talking while she was home yesterday?" Cam doesn't know if he's jealous or terrified, so he settles on annoyed.

"I dunno, a while? We got to the story about her trying to do yoga and the church shutting the class down for being pagan, and then she had to go meet you." Sean sounds defensive, and Cam sighs. It had all been so much easier on Thursday when it was only them in the soft light of the TV, no one watching over their shoulders.

"Are you hungry?"

"You offering to cook me some yogurt?"

"Oh, me too!" They look up to see Kayla coming down the stairs. "Actually, I'll handle it, babe. You're disgusting. Go shower."

Cameron opens his mouth to protest, but thinks the better of it. Being in the same room with both of them is more than he can handle right now. He retreats to the shower and lets the hot water beat down on his already flushed skin. Sean's bruises are almost all gone now, and his face was ruddy and bright this morning. So were his lips.

Cam's arousal stirs at the thought, and he's too tired to fight it. He needs this, and at least this way, he's not using Sean for a lie. It only takes him a few strokes to get fully hard, and he comes with embarrassing speed, remembering Sean's heat around him, stifling a whimper with his fist when he remembers he'll never have that again.

Sean and Kayla are huddled together on the couch when Cameron comes back down.

"Listen to me. That noise? I'll bet you all the dollars I don't have that it's the fan belt," Sean is saying as Cameron sits down in front of his fruit and yogurt.

"Should I take it in, or can I live with it?" Kayla asks.

"Not for too much longer. No one wants that busting while you're driving, but I don't want some mechanic to gouge you."

"How easy is it to fix?" Kayla replies, and Cam stops chewing.

"Replace a fan belt? Simple if you know what you're doing." Sean shrugs.

"Which you don't," Cameron reminds his wife, who sends him a glare over her shoulder.

"No, but Sean does, and he can help."

Cameron feels like he's slipped into some strange dream, and Sean looks just as bewildered. "Wait – what? I don't think I'm in good enough shape to do that, Doc," Sean stammers.

"You can tell me what to do. I'll go out and get the part, and we can figure it out today or tomorrow." Kayla grins. "If I can't do it, Cameron can figure it out. He's pretty mechanical."

"I nearly killed myself building an IKEA shelf, and you've never let me forget it," Cameron interjects.

"Can you make it out to look under the hood at least?" Kayla asks.

"Yeah. Sure, maybe after I talk to Danny?" Sean says.

"No problem. Babe, you're gonna be late," Kayla says, and it takes Cameron a second to realize she's addressing him. He rushes to grab his things and gives Sean and Kayla the most cursory of goodbyes.

He should have kissed her, he thinks as he drives downtown. He feels far guiltier for that than for the coffee he buys. He should have made more of an effort. He should have made more of an effort last night instead of making up excuses about feeling embarrassed about sex with a guest in the house. There are so many things he should do. So many things he should be. He doesn't want any of them.

sean

"So these people really are just letting you stay in their fancy house for free?" Danny asks over the line.

"I told you. Cam's a friend. We met downtown."

"Sean."

Sean squints up at the sun and imagines Danny's exasperated face.

"What? I was living in my car, he had free food, and we got talking," Sean replies, fidgeting. "He's dorky, but he's sorta cool, so he gave me his number if I ever needed help."

"Why you?" Always trust Danny to get to the heart of it. "I mean, I'm sure he meets a lot of people."

"I dunno." Not like he can tell Danny that he and Cam connected over (fantastic) sex (for money). "It worked out. Someone found his number on me after the accident, and it turns out his wife, Kayla, was my doctor."

"That's like divine intervention levels of crazy."

"Yeah, seriously." The kid doesn't know the half of it. "They felt bad about my, uh, situation and offered me a place. So here I am."

"Is it nice?" Danny asks, voice garbled as he chews something.

"Don't talk with your mouth full, kid." Sean looks around the patio where he's sitting, at the shiny, barely-used grill, pots of flowers, and soft green grass. "Yeah. It's way nice. Like, Martha Stewart nice."

"Who's Martha Stewart? Is that an old person thing?"

"Shut up." Sean perks up at the sound of a door closing inside the house. "I gotta go. I'll send your guy my address and stuff, okay?"

"Great! Talk next week!" Danny says. Sean hasn't heard him sound so perky in a long damn time, and it warms him more than the sun.

"Good luck in school, if anyone gives you shit, tell 'em you got a big brother that's gonna kick their ass from Missouri, okay?"

"You gonna beat them with your crutches or something?"

"I can still kick *your* ass."

"Bye, dork," Danny laughs.

"Bye, short stuff." Sean ends the call and stares at the Post-It in his hand.

"Hey, thought I'd find you out here." Sean looks up as Kayla comes out of the house, her red-gold hair catching the sun perfectly as she takes it out of a ponytail. He punches down his disappointment at seeing the wrong Steward as she hands him a bottle of water and takes the chair next to Sean's lounger.

"I'm nothing if not predictable," Sean smiles back. "Unless doctor's orders are to go inside?"

"Nah, fresh air and sun are good for you. There's like tons of research on it."

"Sure, there is."

Kayla laughs as Sean takes a long drink of water and fiddles with his phone and note. "How's Danny?"

"He's good. Starting school next week. Can't believe it's September."

"I'll wake you up when it ends," Kayla says. Sean squints at her, and she sighs. "It's a crappy music joke. God, you're as bad as Cam."

"Come on, no one's as bad as Cam. I had to explain ABBA to him."

"You know ABBA and not Green Day?"

"Shut up." Sean smiles as he turns back to the garden. He's always amazed at how bright and green it is. So vivid and alive compared to the concrete and decay he lived with for so long. "It is really nice out here. You do a good job."

"Eh. Sometimes it works. I've been trying to grow decent roses for years."

"The ones out front are nice. What are you talking about?"

"They're the only ones that lived. I've planted red ones three times back here and they all got sick." Kayla follows Sean's gaze through the garden with a sad smile. "I like it out here too."

"It's so quiet." Sean gets a look for that. "I hung out in the parks a lot downtown, and there were always cars and people shouting, dogs fighting, trains. This is better."

"I bet." There's an irregular heaviness around Kayla that worries him. She's usually cheerful and sharp, not wistful and subdued. He can guess why.

"So, uh, how was the date last night?" Sean asks carefully. He at least owes her a sympathetic ear after everything.

"Cam took us to Red Lobster." Kayla says it like Cam took them to kick kittens.

"Are you allergic to shellfish or something?"

"The last time we went there was after my mom – adoptive mom – after she died. It was the most depressing meal of my life. I hate it."

"Oh. Does Cam know that?"

"Obviously not," Kayla scoffs. "So I can't really hold it against him, but the whole date night has been more hassle than help lately. I think we're running out of ideas."

Sean scratches at a spec of dirt on his chair cushion. He feels like a double agent, trying to talk normally without letting on that he knows exactly why their dates are crappy. "What's with that anyway? The date night thing?"

"It's…" Kayla bites her lips and looks askance at Sean.

"Not my business." Sean means it. He spent the whole of last night stewing over Cam and Kayla out for a romantic evening, then coming home to fuck a floor above him. Now he feels like shit for feeling happy to know it went badly.

"It was his mother's idea," Kayla says. "She was worried about us not getting time as a couple."

"Because of work and stuff?"

"And stuff," Kayla mutters, cheeks heating, and Sean wants to sink into the ground.

"Susan knows Cameron. She knows that he does better with routine; when he has set rules and expectations." Kayla goes on, as if this is something she's repeated to herself many times. "He tends to drift when there's no structure. That's what was happening. We were drifting, so we set up date night."

"So Cam likes it?" Sean asks, trying not to sound too dubious. Cam's been drifting a lot in the last few months, date night or no.

"Did he ever tell you how we met?"

Sean raises an eyebrow, not sure where this is going. "College is all I know."

"It was a study group for Classics 101," Kayla explains. "He didn't really need the group, because he did so well in the class. The professor adored him. I knew he was smart and, well, cute, so I started the group and invited him. He didn't notice when it was just us after a while, but we eventually got to be friends, and I didn't mind that he was oblivious."

The little smile Kayla gives as she recalls what sounds like an epic crush makes Sean's stomach twist. Of course, Cam didn't notice her or any other girl throwing themselves at him; he only had eyes for the professor. "I don't get what that has to do with dates?"

"When he finally asked me out the next fall, it was like a switch had flipped. He did everything right," Kayla says with a smile. "Everyone was jealous, and we were such good friends already, it was natural. Once he was a boyfriend, it was all different. When he has parameters to fill, he does well. So date night has been helpful. Especially lately, it's been good. Or it was."

I thought about you when I was with my wife last night. Sean had tried not to think about it. He'd always felt like the biggest hypocrite in the world for not liking the idea of Cam with anyone else, but he'd still known. He'd known that Cam fucked his wife, fueled by the memories of the filthy things he did with Sean. Now things are right back to shitsville.

"It'll be fine," Kayla says, taking Sean's silence as awkwardness. "Cam always comes around eventually. Sorry, I don't mean to unload on you."

"Gotta earn my keep somehow." Sean looks down at the phone and bites his lip. He's always been good at making himself useful. "By the way, can I use your computer? I need to send an email."

"Of course," Kayla says without any hesitation. "Can I ask who to?"

"Danny's social worker. Gonna give him my address and, you know, get him updated on me and stuff." Sean doesn't add that he's fucking terrified about getting a reply back that he can never talk to Danny again, but he's got to take the chance.

"That's great, Sean. Do you have an email address set up for yourself?"

Sean lets out a weak laugh. "Guess that's step one."

"I'll help you. Then we can go over the car stuff."

Sean has no idea how he's going to manage the fan belt, but he's got to try. Sort of applies to this whole scenario. He sends the awkward email and talks Kayla through getting under the hood. They're in the garage when Cam comes back, looking as uncomfortable and tired as he did this morning.

"It looks like you two are having fun," Cam says dryly as Kayla wipes a smudge of grease from her hand and Sean adjusts himself on his crutches.

"Oh yeah, Kayla's a natural," Sean smiles, and Cam's frown deepens.

"It's apparently a miracle this thing hasn't exploded yet," Kayla adds. "We need to stop at the Auto Zone after the mall. Let me change first."

"Are we going *now?*" Cam asks. Sean doesn't miss the disappointed glance he gives him.

"They close at five, and then we've got to get to that thing at Miriam's," Kayla explains, and Sean really wishes they would get a calendar or something, so he'd know when to expect a night alone on the couch and when to look forward to a meal with all three of them.

"That's tonight?" Cam asks, sounding as disappointed as Sean.

"Yup. Sean, can we bring you something home for dinner, or are you okay with the pantry?" Kayla asks, ignoring Cam's pained face in a way that makes Sean bristle.

"I'm fine on my own," Sean says.

"Great. I'll go get cleaned up, and we can head out," Kayla declares

"Cam, can you help me back in? Need to get off my feet," Sean hears himself ask as Kayla heads inside ahead of them.

"Of course." Cam's at Sean's side in the blink of an eye. He's too eager, but Sean doesn't care. He doesn't care that this is an admission that he's weak and needy. He just wants a few more seconds alone with the guy before Kayla whisks him away again. Cam hovers as Sean hobbles back into the house, his hands a few inches from Sean, but never really touching him.

Holding Cam's hand on Thursday feels like a dream, especially since it's the only time Sean's touched anyone in near a week. He never thought about it much, but his job was physical, especially his time with Cam. Now he feels like he quit a drug cold turkey. Maybe that's why he stumbles and leans into Cam when they make it into his room. He feels Cam tense, but his hand on Sean's chest stays firm, then slides up to his shoulder. It feels so good that Sean almost sighs.

"Are you okay?" Cam asks, voice tight, eyes boring into Sean like he's looking for his soul.

"Yeah, fine, I just need…" He needs to keep touching Cam so badly he can taste it. This is a mistake. There's a good reason for them to stay apart, and it's not just the woman upstairs. It's the helpless pull he feels to Cam with nothing but heartache and regret waiting at the end of it. "I need some meds. Can you grab one for me?"

Cam nods and lets go of Sean, the warmth of his touch fading too fast as Sean eases back onto the bed. He brings Sean a tramadol, and Sean washes it down with stale water from the glass on the nightstand.

"Thanks," Sean says. Cam nods and lingers, looking too pensive for comfort. "Don't you gotta head to the mall?"

"I missed seeing you today," Cam says softly, eyes downcast.

"You're seeing me right now," Sean starts before he realizes what Cam really means. He missed Sean getting him off while he dodged the Bible brigade. "Oh."

"Sorry. I know I shouldn't bring it up."

"Yeah, that's, uh, in the past or whatever."

"I'll see you later then." Cam turns to go, and Sean grabs for him without thinking. He means to catch his wrist, but ends up with Cam's thick, soft fingers trapped in his own. One more hit of contact. Cam stares at him, breathing shallowly, and Sean knows he's on the high as well.

"I'm here for you. Whatever you need, Cam," Sean tells him, not even sure what it means. Maybe he wants Cam to know that, despite spending that day with his wife, Sean is still here. Still his.

"Thank you, Sean," Cam says and tugs back his hand. "Have a nice evening."

Cam closes the door after him, and Sean listens to the muffled sound of steps, then the garage opening and closing as he hangs on to the ghost of a touch. The meds are starting to work already, making him loopy and carefree. Well, as carefree as he can get. He lies back in the nice soft bed and gives a hollow laugh, because what else is there to do?

How did this all get so fucked up? Why can't he pick whether he likes Kayla or hates her? Why can't he decide if he wants Cam any way he can have him or not at all? What's the point either way when Cam's over it?

He doesn't want Cam to be over it. He doesn't want Kayla here. He wants Cam with him, moaning his name, and that's insane because Sean isn't being paid to want that. If he had any decency at all, he wouldn't lust after the husband of the nice woman who's saving his life.

He doesn't have any decency, though. He rubs himself through his sweats until he's hard, then takes his dick out in broad daylight and jacks it fast and tight to thoughts of Cam. He comes with a whimper into a wad of tissue, whispering Cam's name.

14
Labor

cameron

CAM.

He dreams the sound of the name so clearly that it gives him chills. Sean echoes in his mind, the feel of him more than a memory and less than reality. *Yes, fuck, Cam, you're so good. No one fucks me like you.* Just like the lie of those words, the lie of the dream sets Cam on fire. He's so hard it hurts, and that's what wakes him, halfway at least. There's a warm body against him, and Cam turns into the contact. He wants relief, Kayla makes a soft, surprised sound, and he blots it out with the echo of Sean still fresh in his mind.

Yes, Cam, want you so bad. Look what you do to me.

He keeps his eyes closed as they push off their sleep pants and he finds his way into slick heat. Wrong. The bones of her hips poke into his. Wrong. The weak grasp of her thighs. The scent of her. Wrong wrong wrong. But he needs to prove this to her while he can. So he thrusts hard and fast while she gasps and coos beneath him.

"Yes, baby…" *Fuck yes. Cam. "So good."*

He comes with a grunt and opens his eyes. He's never been so sad to see Kayla's face, even when she's smiling.

"Wow. Good morning," Kayla says, searching his face, cheeks still flushed.

"Sorry, I didn't mean to wake you." Cameron's heart is pounding; the brief release of the orgasm replaced entirely by guilt and dread.

"I'll never complain about that. It's the nice kind of surprise."

"I know," he says weakly.

"Stay for a little while, okay?" Kayla asks, readjusting them so that she's draped on his chest. "No run this morning. Let's just enjoy this."

He's never wanted to crawl out of his own skin more than for the minutes cuddling with Kayla, but eventually he makes it to the shower. He washes too forcefully and prays for some peace. He knows there won't be any. Asking God to change him is fruitless, with the devil always whispering in the back of his mind.

Sean's shower is running when Cameron and Kayla make it downstairs and start breakfast. Kayla makes smoothies and toast, and Cameron watches the door. They're done by the time Sean comes out, damp and scruffy and so ridiculously beautiful Cameron wants to scream.

"Morning, folks," Sean says with an uneasy smile.

"Good morning! Glad we caught you before church," Kayla says, grinning brightly. "You're welcome to join us."

"Maybe some other time," Sean evades, looking at Cameron.

"It will be there for you if you need it," Cameron replies, and Sean's smile wavers. Was that insulting? Does Sean think Cam wants him to be saved? Selfishly, he's never really wanted that. Cam didn't want to be damned alone.

"Come on, babe, we'll be late," Kayla says before Cam can wonder more about Sean being "there for" him and the state of their souls, and pulls him away.

Maybe he's being paranoid, but Cameron feels like Kayla's been doing that more than usual lately, guiding him where to go and telling him what to do. It used to be an easy thing to accept, but now it feels like she's steering him constantly – away from Sean.

They pull into the parking lot of the church, the angular, beige building squatting amongst the overgrown rhododendrons with doors open wide as the congregation makes their way inside. His mother is already in the lobby with Vince, and she zeroes in on Cameron and Kayla the moment they enter.

"It's been too long," Susan says, giving Cameron and Kayla dry pecks on the cheek.

"It's been a week, Susan," Kayla smiles.

"Darling, will you take your brother and get the pastries for today? I want to talk to Kayla about this new – what are we calling him? A *roommate*?" Susan says, chilly as always.

"We're calling Sean what he is, a friend," Kayla says before Cameron can.

"Come on, little bro," Vince interjects, tugging Cameron the other direction as Kayla and Susan fall into conversation. "You two are quite the topic today. You're certainly taking your ministry seriously."

"It was Kayla's idea," Cameron says, like that makes it normal.

"Hope you know what you're doing. People get ideas, especially about strangers," Vince replies. "I'm sure Mom will have all sorts of things to say."

Cameron nods. He's sure she will.

sean

Sean wakes up resolved. It's the start of a new week, and he's decided this one will be better than the last. If not for him, then for Cam. Cam looked like, to put it mildly, warmed-over crap most of yesterday. At first, Sean thought it was church, but Cam didn't improve over the rest of Sunday. He mowed the lawn, helped Kayla and Sean fix the fan belt, and went for a run. He barely touched the dinner salad (not that Sean blames him), then disappeared, looking sad and worn. So today Sean's awake early and fucking resolved to do something for the poor bastard.

Today, that's French toast. It wasn't his first choice, but he's living with monsters who don't buy bacon, and he doesn't know how anyone likes their eggs. The bread was getting stale too, and it's an easy recipe even if it's a little hard to cook using one crutch. The amazed look Cam gives him when he comes downstairs is worth the effort.

"You can cook?" Cam asks.

"Better than you losers, yeah." Sean pushes the plate piled with finished slices towards Cam. "Dig in. I've got one more to flip and I'm done." He can feel Cam staring at him as he serves himself and sits at the counter. He glances over as Cam takes a bite, and the noise he makes should be illegal.

"This is fantastic," Cam declares through a full mouth, and Sean beams. It's the first time he's seen Cam actually smile in days, and it feels like the sun just came out. Maybe it's a holdover from before, but he likes making Cam feel good. Someone has to.

"What's going on here?" Sean nearly drops the tongs as Kayla appears, but he manages to keep his composure. "Oh Mylanta, is that French toast?'

"Thought it would be a nice change. I was getting paranoid that I might turn into a bowl of granola." Sean turns off the stove, plating the last slice. "Y'all need syrup."

"We need a lot of things," Cam mutters, and Kayla swats him playfully. "This is fantastic without it anyway. Did you add something?"

"Some orange? I kinda saw it on one of the cooking shows," Sean confesses, scratching the back of his head.

"Amazing," Kayla says around a bite. "You learned all of this from a week of TV?"

"I figured out my way around the kitchen when I was a kid. Someone had to keep Danny fed," Sean explains, spearing himself a bite. "Cooking's a lot easier when you've got a full stove and the ingredients aren't from a gas station."

"Well, thank you, it's delicious," Kayla says.

They eat and chit-chat until Cam takes the empty plates while Kayla gets ready to leave. The kitchen is big, so there's no reason for Cam to walk so close to Sean that he brushes against him, but he does. Sean shivers at the fleeting contact and barely notices Kayla saying goodbye.

"Have a good day," Cam mutters as he straightens his oxford under his sweater vest.

"Yeah, you too," Sean replies, holding Cam's gaze and feeling stupid for thinking one breakfast might fix things. Cam doesn't say anything else before leaving, but there's still something warm about his presence that's missing when the door closes behind him.

Sean's still getting used to how quiet the burbs are. He can hear a clock ticking in the office and the buzz of an airplane overhead. A dog barking three houses over. It makes the rumble of his own thoughts absolutely deafening.

He heads to his favorite spot on the couch, right in the corner, and turns on Netflix. The food channel is still infomercials at this point in the morning, so he starts up an episode of *Serial Monsters* and tries not to feel bad for watching without Cam. The episode ends up being a monster-of-the-week snoozefest about a haunted computer where some poor girlfriend gets murdered for no reason again. At least it's better than the ghost ship...

Sean is halfway through another episode just as the sound of the door startles him. He swivels to see Cam coming in, his face etched with annoyance. Cam looks less put-upon when he sees Sean is there, but not much.

"You forget your lunch or something?" Sean asks.

"Apparently, it's a federal holiday and my office is closed."

Sean doesn't even try to stop himself from laughing. "You forgot you had Labor Day off?"

"I've been distracted." Cam shoots Sean a glare that gives him the good type of goosebumps, heads straight for the couch, and sits by Sean, his eyes on the television. "Which episode are you on?"

"Uh, Ross just died again." Cam nods, and Sean hits play. "Are you okay?"

Cam gives him a withering 'of course not' look. The theme music starts, and Sean tries to concentrate on the screen, not on the man beside him. Cam seems to be doing the same, but much more easily than Sean, which is annoying. He gets up after ten minutes and heats the remaining french toast, and when he sits back down, he's a few inches closer to Sean. It makes Sean's skin prickle, and he clenches his jaw.

"I didn't like this storyline with him dying," Cam says as he chews, and Sean grunts in agreement. "They did it too many times."

They make stupid small talk over the rest of the episode, and when Cam returns his plate to the kitchen, he sits even closer. Maybe he's trying to kill Sean, or maybe he doesn't know he's doing it. Sean scoots towards him, though, and *he* absolutely means to do it.

He wants to touch Cam, but that's the last thing he should be doing in broad daylight. Who knows if Cam wants to be touched by the pathetic mooch with the ratty beard in the ugly Wal-Mart sweats? Sean thinks Cam might be relaxing a hair until Ross and the hot chick of the week (who happens to be a ghost) start making out in a mausoleum after Ross shared a totally heterosexual confession with Dimitri the scene before. Meredith is definitely not the ghost he should be kissing, but Sean doesn't think that's why Cam looks downright green.

Sean hits pause, and Cam looks up at him like he's been caught in some sinful act. "Hey, seriously, are you okay?"

"I'm fine," Cam replies too quickly.

"No, you're not. You've been twitchy since yesterday."

Cam scowls and starts to get up. Sean catches his wrist to stop him, and he looks up at Sean like he punched him in the stomach. "Sean, please—"

"Did I do something? Or say something wrong?" Sean pushes. "I can't fix something when I don't know what's broken."

Cam stares at him, his mouth opening and closing in confusion. "I had sex with Kayla. Yesterday morning." Cam actually looks like he's going to be ill.

"Hey, man, it's fine. I didn't think you'd stop." He's lying. Saying what he has to for Cam to feel better. "It's okay."

"Nothing about this situation is okay!" Cam snaps. "I *used* you, and I shouldn't have, and it was a lie. I keep lying. To everyone."

"No to me," Sean says, catching Cam's face in his hands. It's too familiar, too intimate and forward, and Cam gives a small gasp at the contact. "Have you ever lied to me?"

"Never." Cam says it with the intensity of a storm, and Sean has no idea how things went from zero to what-the-fuck-are-we-doing in a few seconds.

"Then it's okay." Cam grabs Sean's hand and squeezes tight, and, God, it feels so stupidly good. "You're not lying to everyone as long as you don't lie to me."

"Then I should tell you—"

The sound of the doorbell makes them jump like a gunshot. "Who the hell is here?" Sean yelps.

"I don't know," Cam grumbles as he goes to the door.

Sean doesn't even know what the guest interrupted, but he'd really like to kick them in the jewels on principle. It's probably a damn salesman ignoring Cam and Kayla's polite 'no solicitors' sign.

"Mother?"

Sean's heart drops through the floor, and he spins painfully to see Cam blocking an older woman's entry to the house. What the *fuck*?

"I hope there's room in the fridge. Vincent is just behind me, and he's got more coleslaw and beer than I know what to do with," Mama Steward says, as if she's continuing a conversation that's been going on for an hour and breezes right past Cam. She's a handsome, midsized woman with brown hair in that curly bobbed style every woman her age seems to like. She's wearing a lavender sweater set, and a stern expression that reminds Sean of every teacher who ever hated him.

"Vincent?" Cam echoes.

"Luke's running behind, but since Kayla won't be off work for a while, it's fine." Sean can tell from Cam's pale, horrified face that everything his mommy dearest is saying is news to him.

"Kayla's working all day," Cam says. "Why are you here?"

"Darling, she told me yesterday that she'd be off at noon in time for the barbecue. Didn't she mention that to you? She was saying how little you get to use that new grill of yours, and since Vincent's porch is getting done, we agreed that it was best to bring the party here."

"She *agreed*? She didn't – I mean, I don't—" Cam stammers, and his mother waves off his concern like it's nothing.

"It's not as if you aren't already hosting guests," Mrs. Steward says, and her eyes fall on Sean with the focus of a sniper. "Please introduce me to your friend, Cameron."

Crap. So that's what this is about. Sean grabs his crutch and struggles ungracefully to shuffle towards the Stewards.

"Mother, this is Sean," Cam says tensely as Sean extends a hand. "Sean, this is my mother, Susan."

Susan looks at Sean's hand like it's a dirty sock she has to pick up off the floor. "Does Sean have a last name?"

Sean's proud that he doesn't flinch at the ice in Susan's tone, nor does he let his hand fall. "Lockwood. It's a pleasure to meet you, ma'am. Cam has said a lot of great things about you."

"That makes one of us," Susan says with that particular sort of sweetness rich folk use to insult people to their faces, but she finally relents and clasps Sean's hands with more force than thought possible. "Now, I'm sure you'll want to change before the family gets here, Sean." Susan gives a glance at Sean's baggy sweats. He drops Susan's hand and looks to Cam.

"Yeah, I'll uh…" Sean starts.

"I'll get you some other clothes," Cam says under his breath.

"You're providing him with clothes too?" Susan asks. "What happened to yours, Sean?"

It's too early in the day to go punching friends' mothers, but Sean considers it. "They were all in my car," Sean says, mock-cheerful. "But she's stuck in police impound right now. Cam and Kayla were nice enough to get me a few things."

"Hm," Susan says before heading to the kitchen.

"I'm sorry," Cam whispers. "I'll be right back. Can you—"

"I'll call Kayla, my phone's in my room."

"Thank you."

Sean's more than happy to retreat to the guest room. He dials Kayla while he sits and tries to calm down.

Kayla answers after a few rings. "This is Doctor Steward."

"Kayla. It's Sean, uh…" This is weird. Calling the wife of an ex-client he has an inappropriate thing for during work like they're friends in weird, but helping out Cam is more important.

"What's going on?" Kayla asks, her doctor voice dropping away.

"Did you know anything about Cam's mom and the rest of the fam showing up for a nice Labor Day barbecue today?"

"*What?*"

Sean lets out a breath in relief. He knew this wasn't Kayla's style. "She says you were all for it."

"She mentioned something after church, but I didn't think she meant coming to our place." Kayla sounds tense and tired. "I explained I had work for the morning, but I'll try to get out of it. Make sure Cam doesn't burst an ulcer before then, okay?"

"Any advice for dealing with these folks?" Sean cannot believe he's the one dealing with Cam's bitchy mother.

"Do not mention politics under any circumstances," Kayla orders frantically. "Or global warming. Or Dungeons and Dragons. Or recycling."

"*Recycling?*"

"Luke thinks it's a liberal conspiracy."

"Jesus fucking Christ."

"Don't say that either. I'll be home as soon as I can." The line goes dead. Maybe Sean can stay here until everyone's gone. The knock on his door indicates otherwise.

"Sean?" Cam's voice is muffled and hesitant outside.

"Come on in." Cam enters with a faded pink polo and a pair of khakis. "Ugh. Remind me to make you buy some goddamn jeans."

"If we live through this, we'll put it on the agenda."

"This is about me, isn't it? The ambush. Your mom ain't happy I'm here." Sean starts to pull off his shirt, and Cam's eyes go wide in horror.

"Sorry, I forgot..." That they aren't like that anymore, and Sean can't just go getting naked in front of the guy.

Cam takes a deep breath and trains his eyes on the floor. "It isn't not *not* about you. My mother worries about corrupting influences everywhere."

"Great." Sean doesn't want to know what that means. "Go entertain the clan, I'll get decent."

"Sean, you don't have to do this." Cam looks so crestfallen that it breaks Sean's heart just a bit.

"I know, but I'm gonna."

Cam leaves Sean to change. He takes his sweet time because moving is still not his best skill, and also, he's terrified. Checking in the mirror is a sobering experience too. He needs a damn haircut and a shave, but he's just going to ignore that. At least all his bruises are gone, and he's not so gaunt.

Sean emerges to find Susan in the kitchen with a shorter woman with long hair that's just between brown and blonde in a dress that's a touch too nice for a simple family barbecue. A small child runs past them as a man with dark hair enters, along with Cam. Sean can tell immediately they're brothers. Same chiseled noses, blue eyes, and stern good looks. They don't look much like Mrs. Steward, so they must favor the long-lost dad. Sean's sure that's super easy for Mrs. Steward.

"Here, let me get those, hon," the woman, who Sean assumes is a wife, says and takes the grocery bag, shooing the child. "Meghan, out of the way."

"Can I do anything to help?" Sean asks. He knows it sounds stupid because he's still rocking one crutch, but it's the thing you say. The family members turn to him, and he can't tell if the look he's getting is suspicion or disgust.

"We're fine, don't worry," Cam murmurs kindly.

"So you must be the new... Guest? Boarder?" The brother asks, striding to Sean.

"I prefer the term house boy," Sean says, and Susan blanches. The brother laughs, thankfully.

"You're funny. I'm Vincent Steward. Call me Vince." He shakes Sean's hand (what is with this family and their vice grips?) and looks Sean over before nodding towards his wife. "This is Courtney. The munchkin that ran by is Meghan."

"Nice to meet you, I'm Sean. Lockwood." Sean's hand smarts when Vince lets go. Courtney gives Sean a weak smile.

"Lockwood," Susan echoes. "You know, I remember a mechanic by that name, over on the other side of town." The way Susan says 'other side' makes Sean's hackles rise, but he smiles through it.

"That might have been my old man. He used to have his own shop."

"So you're a local boy?" Vince asks, jovial in a way that makes Sean suspicious.

"Not exactly. We left when I was ten. Moved a lot. I ended up back here a few years ago."

"Were you homeless then as well?" Susan asks with a sickly sweet smile.

"*Mother*." Cam sounds more offended than Sean feels. Vince and Courtney just look uncomfortable.

"Yeah, I was. Though I had my car. I always felt like she was home, so it didn't bug me," Sean replies, unblinking.

"The car that's currently impounded?" Susan asks back, and Sean grits his teeth.

"It's evidence, in the case against the—" Cam starts.

"Honey, I think I just heard Luke's car!" Courtney yelps. Sure enough, the sound of a car door comes from outside. Susan turns away with a frown and heads to the front.

"Don't worry, you'll like us all a lot more once you meet Luke. He's the character of the family," Vince mutters just as a burly man with lighter hair, brown eyes like Susan's, and a grin Sean immediately wants to punch off his face bursts in.

"Are you warning Cameron and Kayla's new stray about me?" the man who must be Luke asks loudly.

"Not that a warning would help," Vince shoots back. "And I don't think Sean here enjoys being called a stray."

"Charity case then?" Luke goes on undeterred.

"Just Sean is fine," Sean says, coolly, holding out a hand to Luke. "Nice to meet you anyway."

"So, let's get this out of the way: how'd someone like you end up here?" Luke asks as Sean gets yet another crushing handshake. "When I heard someone was staying in Cameron's house, I was sure it would be some brown drifter taking care of the lawn."

"Now really, Luke," Susan sighs.

Sean opens his mouth to argue, but Vince speaks first: "My impression is that Cameron was ministering to Sean and they struck up a friendship."

"Yeah, and Cam and Kayla did the Christian thing when I got busted up and had nowhere to go," Sean adds.

"That's so inspiring." The words come in a too-sweet female voice, and Sean notices the other people behind Luke: a lumpy woman with a sour expression holding a toddler with sandy hair to match his father. "I'm Jillian, and this young man is Jake. Nice to meet you."

"You too," Sean says. He's gonna need a chart for all the names.

"Do you like trucks?" Jake asks with a lisp. He looks about three and somehow, sticky.

"Not really," Sean grimaces, and he can't tell the rugrat that a truck nearly killed him. Jake seems unimpressed and disappears with his mother into the house. Leaving Luke staring at Sean.

"Now, Cameron, you're gonna have to stop that nonsense downtown if word gets out about the shelter you're running. The vagrants will be beating down your door like it's a welfare office," Luke sneers.

"You aren't a very charitable man, are you, Luke?" Sean asks back, barely holding in his contempt.

"Charity is an excuse for theft by those who can't take care of themselves," Luke counters, unfazed. "That's how this country ended up in the mess we're in."

"The Lord you profess to love would disagree," Cam says, low and dangerous, but Luke just rolls his eyes.

"It's time for you men to get out on the deck and talk about sports or hunting or whatever it is you don't like us girls hearing," Jillian calls from the kitchen. "We'll bring you some meat to throw on the fire when it's ready."

"We can help," Sean starts but shuts up when Cam shakes his head.

"Wives belong in kitchens, men belong at grills, that's the way it is," Vince says, laughing at himself. "Can I get you a beer?"

"No, I don't think that would mix well with my meds." As much as Sean would love to be intoxicated right now, he needs all his faculties to deal with this clusterfuck. He limps out to the porch to see where Jake and Meghan are already playing happily in the grass and takes his favorite seat at the edge in the lounger, close to the lilacs.

"Now, Sean." Sean jumps at the sound of Vince's voice above him. The other man smiles as he pulls up a chair. "I'm glad to hear that Cameron has been witnessing to you."

"Uh, well, we mostly talk about regular shi-stuff," Sean stammers. Is he going to get a scripture quiz? He knows his 'father, ghost, and holy spirit,' but he honestly doesn't know if these guys even believe in that.

"That's part of it. I'm sure through talking with Cameron you've learned the joy and peace a life lived through Christ can bring." Vince smiles, and Sean gulps.

"Oh yeah, Cam's been really good on that front." Maybe if Sean's lucky, he can end up suffocating in a closet with an ulcer and cheating on his wife too.

"Good, good. Now, the next step is to truly understand that Christ has a plan for you, and this is all part of it. He died for you," Vince goes on, and Sean settles in. He smiles and nods as Vince gives a well-rehearsed spiel about God's plans and the beauty of his sacrifice or something. There might be a bit about sheep, but he's not sure because he keeps most of his attention on Cam across the porch as he avoids Luke and plays with the kids.

Meghan is cute: curly brown hair and a big smile and she follows Cam like a puppy. Jake is a terror, but it's still cute at this age. The women come in and out, replenishing drinks and eventually carrying a platter of burgers and sausages.

"Is Kayla okay with this menu?" Sean asks, probably interrupting Vince. Luke and Susan turn to him, both looking curious and a little impressed.

"Has Kayla gotten you with her 'farm-industrial complex' speech already?" Luke asks. "Because you know that's all propaganda created by the liberal media to undermine American industry."

"What now?" Sean balks.

"I think Kayla understands that getting back to the earth and the natural way we live and eat is another way of expressing traditional values," Courtney offers. Sean had never thought of it that way, and suddenly, Kayla's hippie food fetishes make a little more sense.

"It's one step from veganism, and that's a road to satanism," Luke cuts in as if what he just said is logical and not completely insane. "Animal activists are as bad as the socialists. They're trying to tear down the things that keep this country on top: our farms, our marriages, our guns, and our liberty. It's all a bunch of lies."

"Sean doesn't want to talk politics," Cam tries, hovering behind his brother. Luke waves him off. "No one does."

"This isn't politics, it's about the soul of our country and the people that want to destroy it who work for the devil," Luke counters, and Sean's never heard that kind of contempt outside of cable news. It makes his skin crawl. "Who did you vote for in the last election, Sean?"

"Well, they don't really let you vote when you don't have an address or valid ID, so..." Sean hedges.

"Doesn't stop the migrants the other side hires to flood the ballot boxes. Every one of *us* good Christians should engage in a civil society," Luke replies. "Otherwise, the sodomites, feminists, and foreigners will take over along with the socialists, and then where will we be?"

"I dunno, California?" Sean tries. No one laughs. He can see Cam trying to hide behind a porch umbrella, and he really, really wants to make Luke bleed just for that.

"Luke runs a farm out in the country," Susan says, placating. "He's very invested in the issues."

"It's a slaughterhouse, not a farm." Everyone looks up to where Kayla has appeared at the back door. Sean sighs in relief.

"Auntie Kay!" Meghan squeals and runs for her.

"At least you know the burgers are fresh, sis," Luke smirks. Kayla glares at her brother-in-law over Meghan's head. Sean's never liked her more.

"No more politics, today is about family," Susan declares, with a sigh.

"And others," Jillian says with a cold glance at Sean.

"Speaking of," Courtney pipes up, coming to stand next to Vince, who slips an arm around her waist. Sean watches as Kayla takes a place by Cam and notes the difference, how they barely touch. "We were waiting until everyone was together to share some good news."

"Oh, sweetheart," Susan coos.

Sean doesn't understand until Meghan starts jumping. "I'm gonna be a big sister!"

"Oh, wow," Sean says. Everything is a bustle of hugs, congratulations, and fussing over Courtney. Sean keeps his eyes on Cam, enjoying the genuine smile on his face as he hugs his brother and sister-in-law. Kayla's smile is much thinner and doesn't reach her eyes.

Sean keeps to the edges of things when the excitement dies down, trying to stay out of the way as the 'men' grill burgers while Kayla and Cam get caught by Susan, Courtney, and Jillian. He ducks away when he hears Kayla assuring Susan that her IUD isn't witchcraft. Sean can't think about Kayla and Cam having kids, and he doesn't want to admit how relieved he is that it won't happen anytime soon.

He doesn't mind being left alone, since one more conversation with Luke might result in bloodshed. It's Kayla who finally makes it over with a plate of food and a soda for Sean.

"You don't have to serve me," Sean says automatically.

"It's fine," Kayla shrugs. "Sorry for all of this. Susan wanted to get a look at you, I guess."

"Can't blame her. Strange guy moving in – not exactly normal. And hey I wanted to meet the crew too. They're... nice." He should be better at lying by now.

"They're not so bad," Kayla sighs. "Most of them."

"Can't imagine who you mean," Sean snarks, and Kayla finally smiles. "Are you really sure it's okay with them? Me being here?"

"It is. Having you here... It's better." Kayla sounds sincere, and Sean, for the life of him, can't tell what that means.

"Kayla, will you help me with the coleslaw?" Susan calls, and Kayla plasters on a smile and heads off. Sean watches her go and shifts in his chair. He's starting to hurt again, and he could really use a pain pill. Or one of those beers. He settles for food and chows down on his burger. It's really good, and he hates himself for enjoying it. He washes it down with a Coke and closes his eyes to enjoy the sun.

"What happened to your leg?" Sean looks over into a set of big brown eyes. Meghan has seated herself beside him, examining his crutch.

"Meghan, don't be rude," Cam chastises, rushing over.

"It's okay," Sean says, smiling at the kid. "My leg is fine. It's the part on top here that got hurt. Broken actually. But I'm getting better."

"Did you fall off the monkey bars?" Meghan asks seriously. "My friend Aidan fell like that and broke his leg, and he had to miss school for *two weeks*. Did you miss school?"

Sean and Cam both chuckle at the forwardness of a five-year-old. "I didn't fall. And I'm not in school. I do have to sit down a lot to get better. That's why I'm staying here with your aunt and uncle, so I can get better."

"Are you really Uncle Cam's friend? Daddy says he doesn't have any friends, and I think he's lying because Uncle Cam is nice and nice people have lots of friends."

Cam grimaces as he sits down next to Meghan and Sean. Sean meets his eyes over the kid's head and smiles. "Uncle Cam is my best friend, yeah."

Cam looks surprised by that, and hell, Sean's surprised he said it. But it's true. No matter what their past is, Cam's treated Sean better than anyone else in his damn life, and that matters. Just the soft way he's looking at Sean now makes him appreciate it.

"Mommy says I'm gonna have a little sister or brother. I hope it's a sister, so she can be my best friend because Sally down the block had to move," Meghan goes on. "Have you got sisters and brothers?"

"I've got a little brother, yeah," Sean replies, a pang hitting his heart.

"Where is he?"

Sean's smile wavers. "He's still in school. He's much smaller than I am. But I check in on him. That's the important thing with little brothers and sisters – you have to take care of them. That's your job. You gotta take care of your mom too. Babies are tiring."

"I'm gonna!" Meghan grins. "I won't let anything happen to her."

"You're on the right track then."

"I'm gonna go get more corn now." Without ceremony, Meghan jumps up and leaves Cam and Sean alone.

"No one will question if you disappear. Though I'll be envious." Cam stands and offers Sean a hand to help him up. Sean holds onto him too long and not long enough.

"I don't want to leave you to the wolves out here."

He's learned a lot of information about Cam and his family today, and he's not sure how to process it or if he's ready for more. He's certain that Susan would rather that he kept out of sight for the rest of the afternoon now that he's been evaluated, but then Cam would be out there alone. Sean can at least deflect some of the attention from them. It's not going to solve anything in the long term, but it's something. So Sean gathers himself back up on his crutch and returns to the fray. Resolved.

15
CLean UP

cameron

CAMERON SLAMS THE CAR door and makes sure the food didn't get too wet. The weather finally broke, and it's been raining on and off all day. It makes everything smell fresh and clean, but the roads are a nightmare. That means it's going to take him longer to get home to Sean, and so he's decided that, for today, he hates the rain. Luckily, the taco truck wasn't too far out of the way, so maybe he can dim the hate to a smoldering dislike.

He feels the same thrill driving home with burritos as he used to going downtown. Since the disaster barbecue on Labor Day, the closest he's come to a moment alone is when Sean caught him before leaving this morning and requested Mexican. There had been a sparkle in Sean's eyes when he said it. Sean could ask Cameron for a kidney with that look, and he'd reply: 'Which one?'

Despite his excitement, Cameron stays in the car once he's parked. He needs to temper his expectations. This is not a tryst. This is dinner with his friend. Yes, a friend he used to have sex with and who he desperately wants to have more sex with, but a friend he cares for and respects just the same.

His best friend.

Cam smiles at the thought and walks into the house to find Sean standing from the couch to greet him, and his smile widens. "Hello."

"You actually got burritos."

"I wasn't about to turn down the request of an injured man."

Sean takes the bag of food, and Cam sheds his coat and jacket. "Yeah, yeah. Just don't die from eating this, okay?"

"It's stress more than anything that exacerbates the reflux," Cam admits with a shrug, and Sean scowls.

"That doesn't sound promising."

"This is the least stressed I've been all week," Cam says with a smile that Sean returns. "I did pick up something else - in case the food gets to me." Cam nods to the second bag, and Sean pulls out a pint of ice cream.

"You're a genius."

"Thank you."

They walk back to the couch and sit, Sean moving slowly without the crutch, but much better. Cam isn't sure how he feels about Sean healing. It means approaching the day Sean has to leave, and he's not ready to think about that.

"These are amazing," Sean says through a mouthful of burrito. "Where'd you even find them?"

"A little truck on the edge of town. They used to park near the hospital until they were forced to move, but I kept track of them."

"Forced to move?" Sean asks, eyebrow raised.

"One of the higher-ups, Isaacs, didn't like having foreigners feeding us. Said it sent the wrong message." Cam makes no attempt to hide his disgust.

"Sounds like he and your brother would get along."

"They're very good friends, yes." Cam knows it was a joke, but there's no point in sugar-coating things.

Sean shakes his head. "Cam, I don't know if you know this, but your brother is a giant bag of dicks."

Cam hangs his head and huffs a laugh. "I noticed."

"I don't mean to hate on your family, really," Sean goes on, kinder than Cam deserves. "I guess Vince is okay for a church guy, and the little ones are cute. The wives think they'll get rabies from me, though, and your mom wants to murder me in my sleep. Yikes."

"She's set in her ways."

"That's one way of putting it."

Sean takes another bite as Cam regards him. "You know, I didn't really notice it; how bad she is, how close-minded and cold. It's like a bad smell," Cam muses. "After a while, you barely notice until you get some fresh air."

"You callin' me fresh?" Sean smirks, and Cam rolls his eyes. He takes another bite and savors the taste of rebellion, then lustfully watches Sean lick a grain of rice from his lips and enjoys that transgression too.

"I guess I'd take her over Luke. What a piece of work."

"The result of just enough education to be dangerous and the un-questionable conviction that every thought that occurs to him is right. The backbone of America."

"Don't forget cable news."

"The people that argue with him are simply unenlightened or liberals intent on spreading evil, so nothing they say has any effect." Cam balls up the wrapper from his burrito with too much force and drops it on the coffee table. He doesn't want to mention the devil, because especially right now, he knows Satan is working inside of him. Or maybe that's just the burrito.

"So, no one's ever gonna get through to him. Great." Sean looks carefully at him as he crumples up his foil and tosses it next to Cam's. "Kind of a miracle you turned out so good, coming from all of that."

"Debatable. By their definitions, I'm quite the embarrassment. And they don't even know that I'm…" It occurs to Cam that he's never really said *it* out loud, or even in prayer. Maybe he's holding onto the idea that if he never even confesses, never speaks the words, in some way it won't be true.

"Cam, there's nothing wrong with you." He looks up. Sean's face is open and sincere, and Cameron doesn't understand.

"I've done some very bad things," Cam argues softly.

"We all have, man, but liking dick ain't one of them." Always trust Sean to be so blunt that it makes him blush.

"Sean—"

"Cam, it massively sucks if I'm the first person that's ever told you this, but: You're not broken." Cam takes a shuddering breath when Sean's hand squeezes his arm. He didn't think words he never even imagined hearing would affect him this much. "This situation is screwed up, I'm not saying it's not, but there's nothing wrong with *you* and fuck anyone that makes you feel like it is."

"You don't know how many times in every conversation I want to tell them all to go screw themselves," Cam confesses unsteadily.

"Why don't you? I get things are complex, but, really? These are the people keeping you in the closet?"

Cameron winces at the term, even if it's accurate. "It's much more than that." He doesn't want to talk about God or his sins right now, and how every desire he feels for Sean every day is a betrayal of the sacrifice God made for him.. "They're my family. And you saw that they can be kind and good too. They raised me, and I love them."

"All of them?"

"Most of them."

Sean gives him a crooked smile and rubs his shoulder. Cam leans into it, the way he does every time Sean touches him. "I know about not giving up on shitty families, so I guess I can't tell you what to do," Sean says, slumping back into the overstuffed cushions. Cam follows, chasing his warmth.

"Danny doesn't sound shitty," Cam says, looking over at Sean. He likes the way Sean's eyes light up anytime he mentions Danny.

"He beat the odds. Kinda like you." Sean's eyes remain gentle as they meet Cameron's.

"And you."

Sean scoffs. "I ain't nothing to write home about."

You're everything, Cam wants to say, but keeps it inside. "I think you're quite remarkable. If that wasn't clear."

He can make out the barest hint of a blush behind Sean's beard and freckles. "Shut up. I'm kinda useless."

"Not to me," Cam says before he can stop himself. "There's no one else that I'm... out to. Having someone I can talk to matters."

"That's good, I guess," Sean says quietly. He turns his attention to the television and clicks it on. At the same time, he slips his hand into Cam's like it's nothing. Like this is normal, and this is just what they do. What they are. Maybe for a little while it can be.

They watch two episodes as it gets dark, they argue about who should date who and the questionable ethics of exorcism, demolish the pint of ice cream together, and end up talking about books between episodes. It's without a doubt the best evening Cam's had in a long time. They're halfway through their third episode when Sean says, "I hate the British guy. He was funny once, but he got overused."

"At least he's cute," Cam argues, easy as anything.

"Ugh, no, he looks too much like my dad for me to wanna hit that." Sean's comically disgusted face is beautiful in the blue glow of the television. They haven't managed to turn on the lights, and it feels like a different house or a different world. A liminal space only for them.

"Were you... out, to him?" Cam asks.

"My dad? Not really." Sean keeps his eyes on the screen. "He caught me with a guy when I was sixteen, screwing around in the back of the car. Smacked me a bit, but I think he was angrier about me taking the car. He was hammered, and he never talked about it after. I messed around with enough girls that it wasn't really a big deal."

"I used to hope I was bisexual. That maybe I'd meet a girl that made me feel the way men did," Cam says softly. "It would have been easier if I had any attraction to them. I kept trying but..." Cam gives his own shrug, and he knows Sean understands.

"It's not that much easier."

"For a while, I thought that maybe I didn't even feel sexual attraction at all. I'd been infatuated with men and fantasized about them, but it was never *consuming*. Maybe I was just not a sexual being."

"Used to?" Sean's question is innocent, but it quickens Cam's pulse anyway, and he looks away.

"Until I met you," Cam says, low and careful. "I've never wanted anyone the way I want you," he adds, barely above a whisper. In his peripheral vision, Sean gulps and stares at him. "I'm sorry. That was inappropriate. I—"

"Want? As in present tense want?"

Cam sits up and turns to Sean, blinking. He must have misheard. "You thought I'd stopped?"

"Well, yeah." Sean looks absolutely flummoxed. "Look at me. I'm a mess. I figured you were only into me when we met up that night because I was, you know, there."

Cam rolls his eyes so hard he might give himself a concussion. "How could you *possibly* think that?"

Sean throws up his hands. "I don't know! My self-esteem isn't great if you haven't noticed."

"Sean," Cam takes a breath. "You were never just *there*."

"Oh." Sean scratches the back of his head, the way he always does when things get awkward.

"I thought it was very clear that my attraction wasn't situational. I understand why you'd think that, I guess. Given…" Cam bites his lips. He was going to say given the fact that he paid Sean to be attracted to him, but he's finally found something that he doesn't want to talk about. "Never mind. This isn't something we have to discuss. I know you don't feel the same. I'm sorry."

Sean keeps staring at him until Cam starts wondering if there's something on his face or if he's broken things irreparably. "You think…" Sean shakes his head. "Whatever. We got one more episode in this season. Do you wanna watch, or have you gotta get to bed?"

Cam wants to say that even when he goes to bed, he'll just spend an hour thinking about Sean; that he's afraid to shower because the temptation to touch himself will be too great, and that still feels like a violation. "I can stay a little bit longer."

"Cool," Sean says uneasily as Cam settles back into the cushions beside him. Sean shifts just enough so that their arms are touching, and Cam catches his breath. They're so close that every instinct tells him to drape his arm around Sean's shoulders and hold him close, but that's not going to happen. It can't. Nor can pulling Sean to him and kissing him until neither of them can breathe. Just touching him like this is good. Just talking to him is more than enough.

They watch two more episodes until both of their eyes start to droop. It's well past eleven, but the temptation to fall asleep next to Sean for once is so strong it takes every ounce of willpower Cam has to finally get up and turn off the TV.

"Thanks for hanging out. And dinner," Sean says as Cam helps him up, stealing one more touch. "How's your stomach?"

"Surprisingly good."

"So that means you're not stressed right now. That's good."

Cam isn't sure what Sean is trying to say; he's too distracted by his hand lingering on Cam's arm. Sean looks at the sea, and Cam speaks without thinking. "You were always the best part of my week, you know."

"Yeah, you mentioned that once or twice."

Cam resists rolling his eyes or glowering again and keeps eye contact. "I just want you to know: that hasn't changed."

Sean's bravado falls away, and Cam feels a charge in the air between them, something fragile and dangerous. His eyes fall inextricably to Sean's mouth as he licks his lips.

"Same for me, just... so you know," Sean says softly. His hand on Cam tightens, and they each take a deep breath.

It's been nineteen days since they last kissed. Cam has counted. It feels like a year, and if he simply moves an inch closer, he can reset the clock and change everything. It would be so easy.

"Thank you for this evening," Cam says, stepping back. "Goodnight, Sean."

"Night, Cam," Sean replies, distant. Cameron doesn't look back as he walks away and up the stairs. He doesn't hear the sound of Sean's door closing, or he can't hear it over the pounding of his heartbeat in his ears.

He almost did something very stupid. He's been given one sliver of peace, and he was still ready to ruin it for the sake of his lust. Doing anything with Sean would mean disaster. Even what they're doing now is skirting a line they shouldn't even be close to. Or Cam at least. Sean's probably not troubled by this. Or maybe…

Cam doesn't even let himself entertain the thought. Sean isn't weak like him. Sean isn't interested. Sean isn't his.

sean

Sean is fucked. He fell asleep with that thought ringing in his head, and it's the first thing that occurs to him once he's awake, staring at the ceiling. He is one hundred percent, absolutely, completely, totally fucked because Cam still wants him.

He realizes that his shock is kinda his fault. He's used to being a thing to people, reduced to the service he could provide. It was business. Cam never treated him like that. Cam bought him dinner and asked if Sean was hurt, and made Sean come and, Jesus, took care of him in the hospital, and *let Sean move in when he had nowhere else to go.*

For some reason, Sean had convinced himself that knowing him as a person meant Cam wanted him less, but that was (apparently) stupid on so many levels.

Sean goes through his morning routine, trying to avoid going insane. It's hard. *He's* half hard when he showers, but he doesn't do anything about it because he has to look Cam in the eye at some point today, and it's already weird.

He thinks they almost kissed last night. Or almost something-ed, but Cam held back. Despite all the evidence, Sean's not an idiot: he knows that Cam isn't making a move because he thinks Sean doesn't want him. He thinks Sean was only pretending because he was being paid, and hell, Sean hasn't been sending any signals to the contrary because of his own idiocy.

But he does want Cam. He really does. That takes him to a whole new level of fucked.

Sean lurks behind his door, fiddling with his plain t-shirt and sweat-pants. Why didn't he ask someone to get his clothes from his car or ask Cam for a damn razor? He doesn't want to walk out like this and face down Cam. In fact, going back to bed sounds like a really good idea. He's feeling extra achy today anyway.

"Sean?"

Sean jumps back from his door, right into a chest of drawers so hard he might have broken the other half of his pelvis. "Motherfucker!"

"Sean, are you alright?" Cam asks through the door as Sean hobbles over and opens it.

"I'm fine! Just tripped." Cam squints dubiously at Sean. God, his eyes are so blue and he's freshly showered and shaved and probably smells really good and Sean is *fucked*.

"You're usually up and about when I come down," Cam says. Did his voice get deeper? Is that possible? Does he know how hot he sounds when he's being all stupid and nice?

"I'm fine, just a little, you know, fuzzy. You kept me up late last night." God, he sounds like a moron.

"I'm sorry." Cam looks genuinely sorry, so Sean kicks himself internally.

"No, it's fine. No one else I'd rather stay up with." Jesus, *really*?

Cam gets that sad puppy-that-chewed-up-your-shoes-but-is-really-sorry-for-it look. "I'm apparently meeting Kayla for dinner and a gallery opening tonight, so I won't see you until we get home. Late." Of course.

"Or not at all," Sean garbles out. "I mean, I might already have turned in by the time you get back, and I know you've got, uh, stuff to do." Why did he bring up the sex thing? Why?

"We'll see. It's been…" Cam sends a guilty look towards the ceiling. "Dicey."

"I thought you banged?" Sean cannot understand how he keeps ending up in situations where he's counseling Cam about sex he doesn't want to have with a person Sean sorta wishes he could replace. "On Sunday?"

"Yes. Well. The only times I can perform with her is if I'm thinking about… things I shouldn't think about anymore." Cam's eyes rake over Sean so he knows exactly what Cam's talking about. So that 'I used you' weirdness meant Cam doesn't even think he's entitled to fantasize about Sean. What sort of martyr bullshit is that?

"Cam, you—"

"I'm going to be late. Have a nice day, Sean."

Cam turns and disappears so fast it makes Sean's head spin.

Sean floats around downstairs, unable to settle. He eats breakfast and watches a few old episodes of Good Eats without absorbing anything, his brain still foggy with thoughts of Cam. It's almost a relief when Kayla comes down.

"Hey, how are you today?" Kayla asks. She looks soft and casual, her smile as easy as ever.

"Not bad," Sean tries to lie and obviously fails.

"Really? You look uneasy."

"Just cabin fever. Been a long time since I was anywhere this long. Kinda gets to a guy."

"I'm sure," Kayla says as she gathers smoothie materials. "You're moving around pretty well. You could get out and about if you feel up to it."

Sean perks up in his seat on the couch. "Really?"

"Don't see any reason why not."

"Um, no clothes, no car, no cash. Pretty good reasons."

"You can borrow some of Cam's, then we'll go to the store and get you some new stuff," Kayla says with a wave. "Don't worry about the money. I'll put it on your tab, okay?"

Before Sean can argue, Kayla turns on the blender and effectively drowns out anything he might say.

"I'll pay you back for everything," Sean still says when the blender goes off.

"About that," Kayla says as she pours.

Sean grimaces at the pain from getting into his seat as well as the incoming awkward conversation. "I *will* pay you back. I swear."

"That's not what I'm asking. I just want to know how."

Sean feels that familiar lump of leaden fear in his stomach. Kayla doesn't look angry or fed up, but people can always surprise you. "How?" he echoes nervously.

"As in, what are you planning to do to get money?"

"I... I don't know." He's not lying. He's actively avoided thinking about his 'plans' because going back to turning tricks already feels impossible. "'Get a damn job' doesn't count as a plan?"

"You're going to need an ID for that. And references and an address and a resume and—"

"Christ, I know," Sean groans, raking his hands through his hair. "I've been trying not to think about it."

"You just need to go one step at a time," Kayla says, sounding way nicer than Sean deserves. "Let's start with the ID."

"Start?" Sean was under the impression this was a 'get your shit together, you useless idiot' talk, not actual planning.

"Yeah. You need something to get going, and you were born here, so while we're out, we can go down to the records office and get a copy of your birth certificate and start with that." Kayla passes him a smoothie as Sean stares at her, dumbstruck. "You can pay us back for that too."

"Um, okay." Sean doesn't know what else to say.

Everything is a blur until he's back on the Steward couch, running his thumb over his mother's signature and raised official seal. He's legally a person, and that shouldn't make him feel things, but it does.

"You okay?"

He looks up at the sound of Kayla's voice. She's changed into a black dress and her hair and make-up are done. It's the kind of effort people put into first dates. Sean wonders if she really thinks it's going to make a difference.

"I'm fine," Sean says. "You look really pretty."

Kayla actually blushes. How long since someone said that to her? She gives him a once-over and smiles at the successful makeover that took up most of the afternoon. "You do too. Well, not pretty. I mean, you are kind of pretty but in a very masculine way."

Sean smiles at how flustered she is. Pretty has always been the go-to word when people describe him, and he's used to it. "I get ya."

"Anyway. There's pasta in the fridge. And salad stuff."

"Thanks. Y'all have a nice time," Sean finds himself meaning it and returning Kayla's smile before she heads out the door.

The house is quiet once he's alone, and his thoughts return to the same refrain from the morning: he's so fucked, and it's even worse because Kayla doesn't deserve this messed-up situation any more than Cam. He's tried and tried to hate Kayla, and he can't.

He looks at the birth certificate in his hand: the first step towards changing his life, thanks to her. The idea that he even *has* a life ahead of him to change is too massive and daunting to contemplate. The clothes and shoes and whole goddamn house feel too small, and he wants to scream.

He heads out onto the patio. There're still a few hours of daylight left, and the air is clean and fresh from yesterday's rain. Sean still feels like he's suffocating, but it's not as bad with only the sky above him. His mom used to talk to the sky when she didn't think anyone was listening. If he were a praying man, he'd do it now, but that's Cam's thing. Not that it's done him much good.

He remembers finding his mother out in the backyard, saying the rosary, but looking up at the stars. It hadn't done her any good either.

He misses Danny. Even as a snot-nosed kid, he'd listen to Sean's rants and nod like it was gospel. He'd always have a pretty decent idea about what to do too. He tries to imagine what Danny would say now. Probably that Sean should behave, and everything will be fine.

Sean and Cam can keep up the status quo, and everyone will just keep drowning and drifting, but damn it, Sean doesn't want that. He wants to be greedy and hang on to the one good thing he has, even if it's not really good. Or maybe it is? Maybe doing something isn't so bad, especially if he's gonna be out the door soon... How is he even thinking this?

Sean stews and stares at the sky for hours before he returns to the couch that's developing a Sean-shaped dent. He watches mindless TV until he hears the garage open, and his stomach drops. Shit. Sean gets up to retreat because he's not as brave or as good as he should be.

Kayla comes in before he can get to his room.

"You're still up," she says. She looks nervous, and Sean can't blame her. He'd be nervous too if he were heading up for a scheduled bone session with a guy that may or may not follow through, who may or may not be cheating with the homeless guy that ended up in their house.

"I was about to call it a night, thought I'd say hi to Cam before you two, uh... that." Sean wants to punch himself. Kayla looks like she's going in that direction too. "I wanted to ask him about a book he was going to show me."

"Don't keep him too long," Kayla says. Sean winces at the clack of her heels as she heads upstairs, then looks up in time to see Cam walk in the door.

"Sean," Cam whispers, eyes wide and jaw slack, clear hunger in his face. The reaction makes the discomfort of the barber's chair and the Marshall's dressing rooms completely worth it.

"Kayla helped me get cleaned up," Sean says, mouth already dry. "How was dinner?"

"Bland." Cam is doing that thing where he doesn't blink, and Sean thinks he's trying to stare him into oblivion. Sean can feel his skin prickling and his cheeks heating.

"You okay?"

"Generally, no." Cam looks over Sean's shoulder toward the staircase. "I have an appointment."

"Hey, if you…" Sean stops. He doesn't know how to do this. He doesn't even know what he's doing, and the way Cam looks like he's going to execution isn't helping. "Can you loan me that medieval book that you were talking about last night? The columns of dirt thing?"

"*The Pillars of the Earth?*"

"Yeah, that's the one."

"Of course."

Sean follows Cam to the office, watching as he sheds his coat and drapes it on the banister. It occurs to Sean that he still hasn't been upstairs. The space that Cam and Kayla occupy as man and wife remains vague and unreal. The way their marriage isn't really real to Cam, because it's something he did because he had to, and not because he wanted Kayla that way. That thought makes Sean's next move feel easy. Cam goes straight for a bookshelf and doesn't notice Sean close the door. He barely has a second to react when he turns, and Sean is there in his space.

He drops the book when Sean kisses him.

Fuck, Sean missed this. He missed these soft lips and desperate hands on his hips, missed the way Cam gasps in shock and pleasure, how kissing Cam just makes sense. He pushes Cam against the shelf, and he moans softly, devouring his mouth. It's good and warm and everything he's been starving for. He grinds his hips against Cam's crotch, blood rushing to all the right places before Cam pushes him back.

"What are you doing?" Cam pants. They're still only a few inches apart. Sean can feel Cam's ragged breath against his wet lips. He tries to focus because he honestly can't remember what the plan was, if there even was one. "I didn't think you still… That you ever…"

Right. That.

"I do. I wanted you to know that I do. Want you. That way," Sean says, still too close to Cam and idiotically overcome by the need to keep kissing him. He settles for cupping Cam's cheek.

"I have to…" Cam shuts his eyes and clasps a hand over Sean's.

"You have to go upstairs and do what you gotta do, I get that. And it's okay. If you need to think of me to get things done, that's okay. I'm giving you permission."

"What?" Cam asks in wide-eyed shock.

"You don't have to feel guilty, not about this," Sean whispers, searching the blue eyes an inch from his. "If it makes you feel better, I'm gonna go back to my room and get off thinking about you. Won't be the first time."

Cam surges forward and kisses him again, so intense and hungry that it takes Sean's breath away. Good. Yes. Sean has to keep his hips in check because he wants to grind on Cam until they're both hard and begging, but that is not the goal. The goal is to give Cam what he needs to get through the next few hours. He pulls back slowly, Cam chasing his lips, and finally steps away.

"I…"

"Yeah. Same. Go." Sean backs up even further to let Cam by. He keeps his eyes down as Cam leaves the office, then waits a respectable thirty seconds for Cam to get up the stairs before retreating to his own room. His heart's beating like he ran a marathon, and he has to lie down to stop the room from spinning.

He could think about the incredibly stupid thing he just did, and he knows he should. Instead, he undoes his pants, takes himself in hand, and thinks of all the things he shouldn't.

16
LION'S DEN

cameron

"In these troubled times, it is more important than ever to remember that the foundation of our great nation and the path to a righteous life are built with the same stones: family. Family, as God intended, not as the liberals and heathens want to pervert it. Family built on blood and the institution of holy matrimony as the Bible sets out."

Cameron wishes Ted Osborn had a mute button. Or sudden onset laryngitis. A fire alarm might be nice. Osborn only has so many sermons, and in some ways, this one is better than last week's screed against the creeping danger of Sharia law and pagan worship in their midst. Cameron wishes he'd go back to warning people about how reading too much lets in the devil.

He closes his eyes and thinks about Sean's lips on his instead of screaming. He often wonders if God can see the transgressions of his heart and mind as well as those in the real world. Certainly, in His house it should be clear. Maybe Cam is expected to think on his sins, then pray for forgiveness. Perhaps that's why it doesn't feel particularly evil to remember the heat of Sean's breath mingled with his own or the pressure of his hands on Cam's body. He never quite gets to the contrition part of the contemplation. It's fine. He did enough mental penance the next day anyway.

Sean kissed him, and he went upstairs and copulated with his lawful wife as God intended. It took him hours to fall asleep after, even with the physical release. He stumbled downstairs the next morning to find that Sean had made them eggs, toast, and tea. Sean smiled like nothing had happened, and Cam spent the morning volunteering in a haze, wondering if he had imagined the entire thing. Then Kayla had taken him to the farmer's market and dragged him along to an engagement party for a friend from work.

"Hell is real, friends," Osborn's voice breaks through the fog, and Cameron winces. "The devil is real, and he and his servants walk among us, leading good men to sin and deviance. They spread lies, promise pleasure, and what they call freedom. They come in the most beguiling of forms."

Cameron hates it most when Osborn is right. He felt like he was in hell last night, with the devil right there at his side. They made it home for dinner, then Kayla suggested watching a movie. If there was anything more torturous than trying to enjoy *The Philadelphia Story* while seated between his wife and the man he'd had an affair with, Cameron couldn't name it.

He never really thought about it like that before last night – as an affair. The fact that he paid Sean for what happened had made it feel like something else. Maybe the fact that he thought Sean didn't *actually* want him back made it less of a sin. That isn't the case anymore. Sean kissed him. Without a cent of payment. And it was searing and dizzying and insane. Cam cast glances at Sean through the entire movie and caught him doing the same. The look in his eyes and the way he licked his lips had assured Cam that the kiss wasn't a dream. Nor was Sean's desire.

Perhaps it was cowardice or some lingering sense of self-preservation, but Cameron hadn't spoken to Sean afterwards. He went to bed, took a sleeping pill, and pretended everything was fine. He still doesn't know what he'll do when he gets home.

"No one will be witnessing today," Osborn says. "Instead, we'll be hearing from someone you've all probably met in the last few weeks and who is finally ready to take the pulpit." The clear contempt in Osborn's voice has Cameron very interested in this next speaker. "Mister Barons comes to us from – where was it again?"

"Illinois," a muffled voice supplies from behind Osborn.

"Illinois, that's right. I'm sure Andrew here has great wisdom to share from the land of Lincoln. Even if he forgot to give me a draft to review." Cameron raises an eyebrow. He hasn't formed an opinion of Drew Barons, but if Osborn dislikes him, that speaks highly of his character.

The congregation is silent as Barons takes the pulpit and attempts to adjust the microphone down to his height with a commotion of creaks and feedback. Not promising.

"Okay. Way to get thrown to the lions, huh?" Drew starts, voice tremulous. "Hope I end up like Daniel."

Silence.

"A little Biblical humor for you there."

In the back row, someone coughs.

"Okay, tough crowd. But that's fine. I wanted to talk about this part. The first impressions bit, and how it can be an opportunity." Drew's voice grows steadier as he starts reading from some crinkled paper.

"This should be interesting," Kayla whispers.

"First impressions are important, that's true, but they're never quite right," Drew begins. "We judge people too quickly. It's a problem. Just the other day, I met a woman at the grocery store, and I thought she was staring at me because she didn't like my beard. Turns out she recognized me from, uh, somewhere else. We got to talking, ended up having coffee, and now I can count her as one of my many new friends here in St. Louis. Anyway. It's only after we get to know someone that we really understand them. That's good. If we relied on first impressions, we'd never make friends or fall in love or do much of anything. It's the same with the obstacles God sends us in life."

Out of the corner of his eye, Cameron sees his mother's eyebrow raise imperiously.

"Now, I say obstacles, not punishments or trials, for a reason. Obstacles seem to stand in your way, but you learn and grow from getting around them. That's what God wants. I mean, I think it is, I don't talk with him directly—"

Osborn clears his throat, and Drew cringes.

"Never mind. Back to my point. Something bad can seem like a punishment or a setback but if you look closer – if you understand that God won't ever send you something you can't handle – you might learn that it's an opportunity to grow or change or be better. God loves us; he doesn't want us to suffer. So when you curse his name for something going wrong, think about that first impression. Think about what God wants you to do with the obstacle and go from there. It could be a blessing. It could be that the person you think you're meant to hate or fear has lessons to teach you. That people you're told are sinners—"

"And with that, we're out of time," Osborn says too loudly, and Drew jumps away as he retakes the pulpit. "Now, the sacrament for the month. And I'd like to remind you all how important it is to support the politicians on the side of Christ who are waging valiant fights for us at all levels of government - so give them a call or a cheep on social media if you can."

There's a murmur from beside the pastor. "I'm told it's called tweeting. And that it's not a thing anymore. Never mind. Let's continue to the blessing."

The grape juice and stale bread meant to be the blood and body of Christ are particularly off-putting today as Cameron chokes them down. So too is the reading from the Old Testament full of wrath and rage. The music is predictably terrible, but at least in a pedestrian sort of way.

Cameron endures the last few minutes of off-key droning before the congregation streams into the aisles and lobby to chit-chat. His mother accosting them is a welcome distraction.

"Kayla, dear, do you know how to set up one of those social things Osborn was talking about?" Susan asks before she's even finished giving Cameron a one-armed hug.

"Of course, let me see your phone," Kayla says before Cameron can object that the last person who needs to be on the internet is his mother.

"My phone? I thought it was on the computer," Susan grimaces. "I don't want those perverts on the internet getting into my phone. I have personal pictures on there."

"That's not how it works, Mother," Cameron sighs. "You can choose what to see."

"But what about what they see?" Susan shoots back, and Kayla stifles a giggle.

"Maybe it's better to write a traditional letter. Or use Facebook. I know you can manage that," Kayla says. "That's what I'm planning to do."

"What pressing issue is it this time?" Cameron asks. There's always some new issue or scandal online he hears about second hand months later, and it always makes him grateful that he's, as Sean puts it, so analog he should send telegrams. "You know, arguing with people online is the definition of useless. You'll never save a soul that way."

"This is a real problem, Cameron," his mother snaps back. "The sodomites are unhappy about the laws that allow good Christians not to serve their kind or be forced to participate in their ridiculous mockeries of weddings."

Cameron stares, bile burning at the back of his throat. "What?"

"The religious freedom act, hon," Kayla explains patiently. "It allows businesses to refuse to serve people based on their faith."

"That's horrible," Cameron says without thinking, but his mother nods.

"I know. Can you imagine it? Good Christians forced to condone that sinfulness! Catering to servants of the devil?" Susan goes on, misinterpreting Cam as usual.

"Oh yes, that's awful."

Cameron turns to Kayla, eyes wide. He must have misheard her. "What do you mean?"

"I agree with your mother; people shouldn't be forced to participate in something they don't support. And those people — the homosexuals and deviants," Kayla lets out a sigh and shakes her head. "The fact that they feel the need to strongarm others into serving their agenda instead of getting help is very sad."

"Thank God the nation is coming to its senses now." Susan pipes in. "The *things* they're exposing children to nowadays have to stop. Perverts reading to them in the library wearing their sexual fetishes like costumes, and men barging into girls' bathrooms!"

"That's not–" Cam tries to interject, but no one hears him.

"And they want to ban the therapy that can save those poor souls!" Susan laments and shakes her head.

"I just feel so sorry for them," Kayla sighs in agreement that hits Cam like an avalanche. "It must be so lonely, being that way, without a real family. Knowing they're bound for— Hon, are you okay?"

Cameron must look pale and stricken. He has the sudden urge to start running and never look back. "My stomach is bothering me," he lies.

"That's because you didn't eat breakfast," Kayla chides. "Sean noticed too."

"And how is *Sean?*" Susan asks, sweet acid in her voice. "Any progress on moving him along?"

"Yes, actually. We got his birth certificate, so he can get an ID and start looking for a job," Kayla replies, smug and smiling, and Cameron feels more sickened. No one told him that either. The thought of Sean leaving… He can't handle it.

"Well, that's nice," Susan says through her teeth. "Cameron, will you be saying hello to your brothers or joining us for lunch?"

"I need to get home," Cameron says before Kayla can answer yes.

"Of course, feel better soon, darling. We'll see you on Tuesday. Seven at Vincent's."

"We'll see you then," Kayla agrees. "Come on, babe, let's get you home."

Cameron follows, docile and numb. He barely engages in the conversation in the car on the short ride home. Kayla doesn't notice. She's been in a good mood all weekend, thanks to their successful Friday evening. That thought makes the emotion in Cameron flare hotter. It's not shame now, or even fear. It's anger. He doesn't know why he's shocked. Maybe he'd been so careful to never discuss anything close to his own affliction with Kayla that he'd never known her thoughts. Or maybe he just hadn't heard, or hadn't wanted to.

"What do you think you can stomach for lunch? Soup? Bread?" Kayla asks when they're in the garage. "The salad dressing you like has too much acid. Maybe some pasta?"

Cameron blinks. Why are they having this conversation? Right, because Kayla thinks he's sick because of skipping breakfast, not that he's appalled by everyone around him and sick with his own sin at the same time. "What about cream of wheat?"

"I know we don't have any of that," Kayla says, amused and oblivious. "I can run to the store if that's what you're set on; if you promise to take some meds and take it easy. You really don't look good."

"That would be an acceptable compromise," Cameron murmurs.

"Okay, get inside and take care of yourself. I'll be right back."

To Cameron's disappointment, Sean isn't on the couch as usual when he gets inside, and his door is open. That leaves one place he might be.

Sean looks like he's asleep on the lounger on the porch. His skin is golden in the sun, and his bowed legs are splayed apart, his jeans standing out in contrast to the light brown cushions. He's so beautiful, Cam wants to strangle him.

"Sean?" Cam calls from the door.

Sean startles and opens his eyes. "Hey, you're back," he says groggily, rubbing his face. "How's the God squad?"

"More terrible than usual." And they're always terrible, and Cam hates it.

"Are you okay?" Sean asks, standing slowly.

Cam shakes his head, his body tense as Sean approaches. "Not even remotely."

Sean freezes, looking at Cam like he's some wild animal that might snap if he gets too close. "Do you wanna… talk about it?"

"I don't see how that will help." Talking will remind him of all the reasons he shouldn't be here and all the ways his life is, as Sean might say, incredibly fucked up. Talking might convince him not to fuck it up more.

"Okay, then. Uh. I get if you're pissed at me for Friday. But in my defense—"

He doesn't so much kiss Sean as pounce on him, covering his mouth with his own and stifling Sean's surprised exclamation. Sean's hands find his jaw in a heartbeat, and Cam drags him back until they thump into the siding, barely avoiding a planter.

Maybe it's because they're kissing in the light of day, where any nosy neighbor might see them, or because Sean kisses him back with equal passion and not a cent has changed hands, but this feels more real and immediate than any other time they've touched. Cam feels alive and whole, and at the same time, like he's being torn apart from inside. Sean's fingers tangle into Cam's hair as Cam presses his whole body against Sean, hands pushing under his tee to find sun-warmed skin.

"Fuck, Cam, we—" Sean starts as Cam's mouth moves to Sean's jaw. Stubble scrapes against his lips, and Sean's protest dissolves into a whine of pleasure. For a few glorious seconds, everything is perfect: mouths, hands, breath, and heat. Then the distinct sound of a back door sliding open echoes through the quiet afternoon. Cameron jumps back, leaving Sean gasping.

It's not Kayla, but he can hear their neighbor, Marv (the obnoxious one who reports people to the HOA when their laws get too brown, or their Christmas lights are still up in January), talking on the other side of the fence. Sean is still braced against the wall, catching his breath, kiss-swollen lips glistening in the sun.

"Cam, what the hell?"

"I'm sorry, I thought you—" Cam's anger is gone, replaced by a familiar miasma of shame and guilt.

"I do. I *really* do. But... Kayla."

Cam bites back a few very choice words regarding his opinion of Kayla right now. "I just needed to – I don't know."

Very gently, Sean rests a hand on Cam's hip and uses the other to tug him closer by the lapel. "Did something happen?"

"You kissed me," Cam says softly.

"Yeah, I remember that." Sean's chest bumps against his as Cam stares up into green eyes and perfect freckles.

"Because you wanted to or because I needed you to?" He draws a shaking breath. That's the thought that's been tormenting his brain for days. The kiss, despite Sean's words, was another service. Another exchange of goods because Sean benefits from Cam's sham marriage staying on track.

"Can't it be both?" Cam winces and tries to draw back. "Shit. That was the wrong answer."

"Kayla's only going to be out for a few minutes."

"Cam."

"I told her I was feeling sick, I should go lie down and—"

Sean kissing him again is better than any medicine. He melts into it as they fall back against the wall again, Sean's tongue darting against his lips. Kissing Sean, deep and thorough, feels like the first rain after a drought. Sean's hands tangle in the material of his jacket, and he lets out a low moan as he braces himself against the wall. He holds Cam's lower lip between his teeth before pulling back an inch.

"I wanted to kiss you. I always wanna kiss you," Sean whispers. "It's kind of a problem."

"It is." Cam proves the point by claiming Sean's mouth again. He can hear Marv's imperious voice through the shrubs, giving some poor customer service representative a piece of his mind. He pulls back with great effort, savoring the lingering taste of Sean's lips. "We have to stop."

Sean gives a low growl of frustration. "You're killing me, man."

"If we get caught…" Cam closes his eyes on a spike of pain under his ribs at the thought. Sean's lips on his throat – teeth grazing skin so that goosebumps explode over Cam's body – drown out the pain and all other rational thought. Sean kneads his fingers into Cam's hips and pushes him to flip their positions, trapping Cam between him and the wall. The siding is so hot that Cam can feel it through his jacket. Sweat materializes on his brow as Sean kisses along his jaw and to his ear.

"Come on, Cam," Sean murmurs and grinds his hips against Cam's. He can feel a growing hardness in Sean's jeans pushing against his own, and he moans at the friction. "I can get you off fast enough, you know I can. I'll probably come just touching you," Sean gives another thrust for emphasis. "Or tasting you."

"Sean, please." He's not sure if he's begging Sean to stop or keep going.

"So what if we get caught? Would that really be so bad?"

Cameron pushes Sean back with such force that the other man nearly trips over the patio furniture. "Are you insane?" Cameron spits as Sean gapes at him.

"Cam, I'm—"

"No, shut up!" Cameron snaps, and Sean goes pale. "You have no idea what you're talking about! I have responsibilities, Sean. I have a family. I can't be exposed!"

"I didn't mean it." Sean moves towards him, and Cameron holds up a hand to warn him back.

"Just stop. I need to go." Cameron pushes past Sean and runs upstairs, slamming the bedroom door behind him.

sean

Sean's walking. It's his new thing. He's literally started taking walks because there's nothing else to do to burn energy or punish himself. He can't smoke. He can't drink. He can't fight. He can't even eat, and he certainly can't fuck. So, walking it is.

He started on Sunday. Not a coincidence that he needed air on the day he messed everything up with Cam. Again. Kayla gave him the all-clear and said some exercise was fine, even good. So he'd done a lap around the block, then lurked outside until the neighbor across the street gave him the stink-eye. His hip ached after, and he had to use the stupid fucking cane later in the evening, but, damn, getting out had been worth it.

He's tried again each day since, adding a little more distance. Monday was easier, but Tuesday was rough. He was aching and angry when Cam and Kayla went to family dinner, and Sean was left with another miserable salad full of dried fruit and something called freekeh. To be specific, Kayla had left it for him because she'd gone to meet Cam there. He worked late Tuesday, after avoiding Sean's eyes for too many meals.

It pissed Sean the hell off. So did Cam taking extra-long runs and hiding upstairs after. The fact that Sean had only himself to blame for the mess they were in made him even angrier. Sean knows he screwed up, and he could make it right if Cam would fucking *talk* to him.

He did two walks yesterday. On the second, he almost made it out of the subdivision and to a main drag. The trek back had been bewildering. The geniuses who designed the neighborhood wanted lots of meandering streets and green spaces so interlopers driving too slow in their confusion would be easy to spot. There are only five basic house types, and every one has the same landscaping and paint jobs. Sean had wandered, lost, for fifteen minutes until he spotted Kayla's yellow roses and limped home. When he got in, he discovered he'd missed Cam entirely, so he took two tramadol and passed out for twelve hours. He's convinced half of his pain meds only work because you can't hurt when you're unconscious.

Sean is determined to do better today because he has to have one concrete goal, at least in terms of navigation. He has no idea if Cam will even show tonight or what they're going to do when forced to be alone together. Maybe there'll be more excuses about quarterly reports, and Cam will come home after Sean's asleep again.

That possibility is why Sean's staring down the main street, wondering how far he has to walk before someone picks him up. Probably a few miles. Folks in the burbs don't pick up hitchhikers, and none of them would be headed somewhere good. Also, Sean has nothing but the clothes on his back and a bum pelvis, and disappearing again would be the last straw for Danny. And he'd probably die. Still, the open road is tempting. He wishes he had his car back, and he wasn't a prisoner in the house of salads and sexual tension.

"Can I help you, young man?"

Sean looks over to see an older Black woman with curly hair and an all-knowing smile. "Uh…"

"You're Cameron and Kayla's guest, aren't you?"

"Yeah. Are you a friend of theirs?" The woman has a scotty dog with her on a leash. It sniffs with interest at Sean's still-too-white sneakers.

"I knew Kayla's mother pretty well when she lived there, but I haven't stayed in touch as much as I'd like." The woman is still looking at Sean with an uncomfortably discerning expression. "I'm Wanda."

"I'm Sean." He offers his hand, and Wanda takes it without hesitation, even though her dog gives him a miniature growl. "You go to church with them?"

"No. Oh no. That church…" Wanda shudders. "They lay on the fire and brimstone a little thick for my taste."

Okay, so Sean likes her now. "So I hear."

"You didn't answer my first question: Do you need some help? Because you look like you're fixin' to make a bad decision." Sean looks between Wanda and the road, then heaves a sigh.

"You're not wrong. Don't really see how you can help though."

"You're probably right, but just in case, why don't you walk with me back to my place. It's only a few doors down from Cameron and Kayla." Sean raises an eyebrow as Wanda starts walking without waiting for him to agree. "Fergus here is good company, but he's shit for conversation," she calls over her shoulder as Sean stumbles to catch up.

"Fergus?" Sean asks when he reaches her, and the black little dog between them gives a yip.

"So, what happened that's got a nice young man walking slower than an old lady like me?" Wanda looks Sean up and down as he shuffles beside her.

"Got into a fight with an asshole. And his truck." He leaves out the part about the asshole doing it because he's queer and God told him to.

"Interesting. Most of the neighborhood gossips think Cam hit you with his car, and he's making it right by taking you in."

Sean bursts out laughing, startling Fergus. "Wow. Sorry to disappoint, but Cam's just a friend." At this point, friend seems like an inadequate word.

"I'm sure. He's not the kind to hurt people."

Sean's not sure about that, but he doesn't argue. Cam never means to hurt people, that's true, but he's still damn good at it. It's not the immediate kind of hurt like a knife, but something slow and hard to notice until it's happened, like a sunburn.

"Yeah, Cam's a good guy," Sean says, because despite all the hurt, Cam *is* good. He's confused and scared and frustrating, but he's good. Just like the sun again. He's bright and warm and, fuck, Sean needs to stop thinking like this. He's supposed to be mad at the guy, even though Sean's the one who screwed up.

"This is my stop, thank you for the escort," Wanda says as they come to a smaller one-story house with a beautiful garden in front. "When you're well, I'll come over and ask you to repair something. Seems like you need more people to talk to."

"You have no idea."

"See you again soon, Sean."

"Have a nice evening, Wanda." Sean watches as she and Fergus go inside and then turns his attention to the two-story house with the roses three doors down. The garage door is open, and Cam's Corolla is sitting there, which is weird. Even weirder is that Cam is still in the driver's seat. Sean sighs. Better deal with it.

Cam jumps when Sean opens the passenger door and sits down. Sean hits the garage remote and waits for Cam's face to lose the look of panic once the door rumbles closed to leave them in semi-darkness, but it doesn't.

"Were you thinking of not coming inside?"

"Yes," Cam says without hesitating. At least the guy is honest.

"Good thing I caught you then."

"I'm not sure about that."

Sean huffs and bites his lips. "You being an asshole makes it real tough for me to apologize."

"Apologize?"

"Yeah. It's a thing people do, or so I've heard. I was over the line, okay? I shouldn't have said what I said." Sean's cheeks are burning with shame. He's wished all week he could unsay those stupid words and go back to kissing Cam like a normal idiot. Then again, that's what got them in this mess. "I shouldn't have kissed you in the first place."

"Don't apologize for that," Cam almost gasps and fixes him with that hungry, desperate look that gets Sean going every time.

"You're still okay with that part?" Sean asks, reflexively licking his lips.

Cam places a tentative hand on Sean's thigh, and electricity jumps under his skin. "I want you. But this – us – what we've done or could do can never come to light. If I were caught, the consequences would be catastrophic. Not just for me."

"I get that. I do." Sean covers Cam's hand with his. "I ain't ever bringing that up again."

"I don't know how to reconcile what I want with everything else." Sean feels a stab of his own guilt as he watches Cam's downcast face. He's talking about Kayla. And maybe God and family and laws and shit. Good thing Sean's been practicing this same argument in his head for days.

"Think of it this way: we won't be doing anything that we ain't already done. Just sliding back into old habits." He doesn't think he's ever been more literally the devil's advocate, at least according to Cam's worldview.

"It's not the same, you know that," Cam says softly.

"Yeah, no cash but…" This is getting too close to something Sean knows he shouldn't say. Something that's going to turn Cam's world on its axis and that he should definitely keep to himself if he's smart. Too bad he's an idiot. "I always wanted you, just for you. From the get-go."

He hears Cam's sharp intake of breath, feels his hand tighten over Sean's, and he knows Cam believes him.

"I think we should go inside," Cam orders, low and careful

"Yeah. That sounds good." Sean doesn't know why he's even talking. Cam is out of the car and heading inside, and Sean has to struggle to keep up. He makes it into the house, somehow, and manages to get the garage door closed before Cam kisses him.

17
Relapse

cameron

GOD, CAM MISSED THIS so much. He missed the feel of Sean's hip bones under his thumbs. He missed the way Sean throws his head back when Cam kisses his neck. He missed the way he bucks up when Cam drags his nails down his back. He missed the taste and the smell and the heat and *Sean*.

"You feel so good," Cam groans as he traps Sean against the nearest hard surface, which happens to be the hall closet door. Sean tugs Cam's hair and kisses him again.

They're wearing too many clothes. He's not capable of much rational thought right now, but he knows that. He strips off his coat and jacket while Sean undoes his buttons and tie. Not soon enough, cold air touches his skin, and he breaks the kiss to pull off Sean's tee. They press chest to chest as Cam kisses Sean's neck. Sean's not as thin as he used to be, and his skin is ruddy and warm. Perfect. He's also hard against Cam's thigh.

"Fuck," Sean breathes as Cam's teeth graze his collar bone before he laves his tongue over Sean's nipple. "Fuck fuck *fuck*."

"Need to taste you," Cam purrs against Sean's stomach as he falls to his knees. He nuzzles against the bulge in Sean's jeans, then looks up.

Sean's mouth is agape, his plump bottom lip hanging heavy as he stares down at Cam. He gives the barest nod, and Cam opens Sean's jeans. They both groan as Cam takes Sean in his mouth. He missed this too: the bitter tang and velvet heat. It feels like forever since he's done this, and his senses are on overload.

"God *damn*." Sean slams his hand against the white door when Cam gives a long, slow lick. Sean's other hand finds Cam's hair and tugs him to the perfect angle, and Cam takes in all of Sean that he can, messy and uncoordinated. With each lick and swallow, he can take Sean deeper, using his hand as well. Sean makes high, strained noises as he thrusts shallowly into Cam's mouth to meet him. "Cam, Jesus, I'm…"

Cam hollows his cheeks, and Sean comes with a cry, spilling on the back of Cam's tongue and down his throat, bitter and hot. Sean nearly doubles over, grabbing onto Cam's shoulder as he shakes through his orgasm. Suddenly, Sean has pulled out of Cam's mouth and is truly falling, legs giving out as he collapses into Cam's arms in an ungainly heap, and they tumble together onto the hardwood.

"Jesus fucking Christ," Sean pants, resting his forehead against Cam's. "Always said no one ever made me come as hard as you. You believe me now?"

"I'm starting to," Cam whispers. Sean responds by kissing him, deep and long, like he's chasing his own taste in Cam's mouth. Cam grinds up against him, adoring each rush of pleasure from the friction and Sean's solid weight above him. "Missed you," Cam murmurs against Sean's lips, and Sean gives a dark, sinful chuckle.

"Same." Sean slides down his body and undoes Cam's belt and fly with swift precision. He gulps Cam down so easily it's like magic, and Cam groans in ecstasy. He feels like he's been hard for hours, and the touch of Sean's mouth sends his whole body into overdrive.

"God, yes." He doesn't even know what he's saying. Sean lets him fuck up into his mouth and takes Cam so deep he feels his cock hit the back of Sean's throat. Sean opens more, then swallows, and Cam just about screams. It's been so long since he's felt this, felt *Sean* around him and with him. It's a spark on a dry prairie, and he's bursting with fire. How can this be a sin or wrong or evil when it feels so good and right and holy and… "Fuck!" He arches off the floor and comes into Sean's waiting mouth, that same fire bursting behind his eyes and racing through his blood.

He doesn't even realize Sean's moved until he feels his lip on his mouth. They kiss for a long time, sprawled on the floor with their pants hanging off their hips and the taste of come in their mouths until Sean hisses in pain.

"Are you alright?"

Even in the fading light, he can see Sean's grimace. "Probably need to get somewhere softer." They struggle to get vertical and fix their pants, to no one's pleasure, and Cam helps Sean onto the couch before taking a seat beside him.

"Better?" Cam asks.

Sean shifts so they're shoulder to shoulder and pulls Cam in for another slow kiss. "Better."

"That was extremely corny."

"Shut up. You scrambled my brain with the blow job. I don't even know what I'm saying."

"Are you alright? Really?" Cam asks, running a finger over the still-bright scar that now mars Sean's hip.

"I was gonna ask you that too." Sean's voice is quiet, the humor gone and replaced with gentle concern Cam doesn't deserve.

"You're avoiding the question."

"So are you."

Cam runs his fingers up Sean's side and then back down his arm until he finds his hand and squeezes it. "I don't think I'm ever alright, but the only time I feel remotely close to okay is when I'm with you. Does that answer your question?"

"Yeah," Sean replies, voice small and tight.

"And you?"

"My stupid hip or pelvis or whatever is gonna hurt tomorrow," Sean says with a shrug, running a thumb over Cam's knuckles. "Fuckin' worth it though."

"Agreed." The silence around them, for once, is gentle and safe, as the sun fades. The thought of losing moments like this fills Cam with complete dread. "No one can know."

"I get that. I won't even joke about that again, I know I—"

"I would lose everything," Cam cuts him off. Just the thought makes his chest tighten in panic. "My family. My job. My home." Sean opens his mouth to protest, but stops when Cam looks up at him. His eyes sting, but he doesn't blink. "And I would lose you."

"Cam."

"I can't risk that. I can't. I—" Cam shuts his eyes, unwilling to let Sean see him break.

"Hey, hey, hey," Sean's thumb brushes his cheek as Sean moves to straddle his lap. He kisses Cam's mouth, warm and tender, then peppers kisses on Cam's cheek, chin, and forehead, even the tip of his nose. "I'm right here. I'm not going anywhere."

"We both know that's a lie." Sooner rather than later, life will pull them apart.

"Come on, it's not like we'd be picking out curtains or whatever if things were different. We just gotta take what we can, where we can, for as long as we can, right?" Sean kisses him again. He's throwing Cam a lifeline, and Cam needs to take it before he drowns.

"Alright, I'll… Alright." He kisses Sean and pulls him close. It's enough for now.

"Hey, you didn't even have to buy me dinner to get in my pants this time, I'm getting easy," Sean jokes when he pulls away, and Cam lets out a laugh that surprises him with its force.

"I guess that means you have to provide the food now, since the sex came first."

"You serious? You're gonna make the guy with the busted pelvis cook for you?"

"Exercise is good for you. And we both know if I'm responsible, it will just be sandwiches."

"I like your sandwiches." Cam rubs his hands up and down Sean's side and treasures the annoyed smile Sean gives him. "Fine. But I reserve the right to complain about the health food."

Complain Sean does. He keeps up a running commentary about what sort of crazy people don't have cream or bacon in their house and so on. Eventually, he finds chicken sausage and pasta, and Cam brings in some tomatoes from the garden. Sean works some sort of witchcraft, and in a few minutes, they have bowls of deliciousness to enjoy on the couch. They still haven't put on shirts, and they sit hip to hip and skin to skin as they enjoy the food and turn on an episode of *Serial Monsters*.

Sean's head finds itself on Cam's shoulder at some point after the food is done, and Cam responds by entwining their fingers. When the credits on the second episode roll, Sean hits pause and climbs back on Cam's lap.

They kiss and grind and touch, and Cam sucks a mark onto Sean's chest that will last for days because he wants Sean to have a reminder of this, even if it will fade like everything else. Sean only complains about his hip once when he crawls off Cam to remove their pants, then retakes his position. He takes them both in hand, and Cam adds his own fist. They rub together, perfect waves of friction and pleasure cresting and growing until they come seconds apart, whispering each other's names.

sean

Sean's beat when they make it back to Cam and Kayla's on Friday afternoon, but he has a shiny new state ID card to show for it. Not a driver's license, mind you, just an ID, because he had no social, and he needs the ID to get *that*. It was a slog, and supervisors were spoken to. After assuring Karen (and her manager) at the DMV that Sean wasn't some 'illegal' destroying the country, he got to give the camera a blue steel and get out of there with a promise that next week they'll make the fun trek to the Social Security office. Being a person is exhausting, and he hates how much society wants to make it hard for people without the right amount of money or the wrong birthplace to actually be a part of it.

Kayla, for her part, was a champ, and Sean doesn't want to think of how grateful he is to her while also remembering the things he did to her husband the night before. It's giving him a headache.

"Hey, you got mail," Kayla says as she comes in the front door.

"What?"

Kayla hands him a thick white envelope and starts sorting through a coupon circular. This can't be good, Sean thinks, as he tears it open. No one knows he's here, besides maybe the police and the hospital. If this is a bill, he's gonna burn it. Cam said not to worry, but...

"Shit." Sean stares at the papers in his hands, tears stinging his eyes. He can't make out the words right now, but the picture folded in with the letter he can see just fine.

"What's wrong?" Kayla asks. "Who is—"

"Danny." The kid – no, *teenager* – in the picture is taller than the little brother he remembers, and his hair is too long, but Sean would know him anywhere. "I gave him the address so he could write. I didn't think... Holy shit."

"How long has it been since you've seen a picture?"

"Two years. I..." Sean blinks, and his vision clears some, but his cheeks feel wet. It might as well have been a whole other lifetime. He starts reading.

Hi Sean,

So I'm writing a letter. Anthony said to make sure I say important stuff, not only the kind of things we talk about on our calls, but I don't really know what that is. School is okay. My bio lab smells like crap because someone left a bunch of dead frogs in there over the summer. The library isn't very good either. Anthony is working on getting me in the advanced program or to a magnet school, but it's tough, and Mr. and Mrs. Weaver aren't really into driving me. I bet you'd drive me if you were here, especially if you had the Bel Air. Have you heard anything about getting her fixed?

Sorry. That's probably not a good subject. But I'm writing in pen in Anthony's office, so I can't fix things. I started doing the crossword in pen too.

The Weavers are the last people on earth who get the newspaper. I can only really finish Wednesday, but I'm getting better.

I hope you like the picture. Anthony said you'd probably like to see one, and I thought it was cool. Yeah, I know I need a haircut, but I like it long. Maybe if things keep going well, we can Zoom or something (ask your friends what that is). Can you try to send one back for me in the meantime? I know getting them printed is a pain, but it'll be nice to have a newer one.

I really miss you, Sean. I don't say it enough, but I do. I hope we can visit soon, maybe for the holidays once you can afford it. We can go to the Rock and Roll Hall of Fame. You'll love it.

I hope you're getting better and that you're happy and that Cameron and Kayla are nicer than the Weavers. It sounds like they are. Stay out of trouble, okay?

Love,

Danny

Sean rereads the letter a second time, and it's still a punch to the gut. He hadn't thought Danny ever wanted to see him again, or that he even deserved a real place in the kid's life beyond that weekly phone call, but suddenly Sean misses him like a lost limb. "Fuck. He—"

Sean doesn't finish the sentence before Kayla hugs him. She smells like his mom: that female mix of perfume, fabric softener, conditioner, and something homey. Sean hugs her back, trying not to sniffle. He doesn't deserve it. He abandoned his brother, and he's banging her husband. Sean deserves a kick in the balls and a few more broken bones, not forgiveness from anyone. But he's a stupid, selfish bastard, and he'll take it.

"Sorry, didn't mean to get all emo," he mutters as he pulls away and wipes his eyes.

"It's okay," Kayla smiles. She picks up the letter and envelope Sean dropped and hands it to him. "I can get you some paper and an envelope if you want to write back. Wait, does that say Anthony Gardner?" Kayla's eyes are on the return address.

"That's Danny's social worker, why?"

"I went to high school with an Anthony Gardner. He was one of the first people to take me to church," Kayla muses. "You said Danny's in Ohio?"

"Outside Cleveland, yeah."

"That's not too far from where we grew up, wonder if it's the same guy," Kayla muses quietly, then looks between Sean and the letter. "You sure you're okay?"

"I dunno," Sean gulps. He knows what he has to do, but it's crazy scary to think about it. "I need to get my crap together, so I can get back in Danny's life."

"In Ohio?" Kayla sounds skeptical and maybe even sad. Sean can't blame her.

"If that's the only way."

"That's going to take a lot of... a lot." Kayla definitely looks sad, and Sean can't figure why. "Are you gonna tell Cam that's the plan?" Oh. That.

"Yeah, soon. Probably." It's not like he and Cam have a relationship. They're doing what they're doing *because* Sean's gonna be out the door sooner rather than later. "Cam cares about family. He'll get it."

"He does," Kayla says softly. "I'll get you that paper."

Kayla heads towards the office where he kissed Cam, past the spot on the floor where Sean sucked him off last night. What he's doing feels good, but it isn't. Still, he's going to keep it up until the day he finally can do something right.

18

MANY HAPPY RETURNS

cameron

"Before we get working, I'd like to introduce someone," Arnold Isaacs grumbles to the assembled volunteers in the mission basement. "I'm sure you all already know Mr. Barons, but he'll be joining us from now on as an outreach coordinator on behalf of the church." Cameron watches as Drew (who reminds Cam strongly of a rescued ferret) peeks out from behind Isaacs and gives a nervous wave. He's dressed far more casually than the rest of the group, in a hoodie and jeans, and Cameron can already see the people bristling.

"Does that mean we'll be focusing more on spreading the good news and not just feeding them?" someone asks from the back corner.

"I'm more interested in how we can more effectively serve the community," Drew answers, his voice reedy and thin. "Feeding people once a week is great, but there have gotta be other ways we can help."

Isaacs scowls and gives Drew a sidelong look. "They'll learn to help themselves once they've found peace in Christ."

"Yeah, that's a good start, but so is job training and…" Drew looks around the circle of his parishioners, and his eyes fall on Cameron. "I'm sure everyone has ideas. Cameron? Don't you have a formerly unhoused person in your house? What's important to him?"

"Why don't you discuss it while Cameron shows you the ropes?" Isaacs interrupts before Cameron can even open his mouth. Drew gives him a nervous smile, and Cameron doesn't even try to hide his sigh.

It's fine. He can handle Drew for one morning while Lee is off helping her cousin look for houses. He's feeling good, relatively speaking. He was able to perform with Kayla the previous night, and she seemed happy, so he could lie to himself that he was doing a good thing.

There's a nervous twitch of energy all around Drew when he approaches. "Hi, Cameron. Cam. Can I call you Cam?"

"I'd prefer not."

"Right. Uh, so," Drew shoves his hands into the pockets of his jacket. "What first?"

"We make sandwiches. Do you need instruction on that?"

"I'm good," Drew gulps. They start work, and Cameron is afforded a few blessed minutes of quiet before Drew pipes up again. "Do they ever worry about peanut allergies?"

"What?"

"Like, some people, a peanut can kill them, you know? I have this thing with mangos and one bite makes my whole tongue get tingly. Then after, hoo boy, let's just say I'm glad I put down a cleaning deposit at my old…" He finally notices Cam staring in horror. "But, ya know, peanuts."

"Peanut butter is protein-rich, the whole wheat bread has complex carbohydrates, and the jelly is a good source of glucose, which is essential to brain function and energy. The sandwiches keep without refrigeration, are portable, and cheap to make in bulk. And no one has died yet, that we know of."

It's Drew's turn to blink before going back to his work.

"You sure know a lot about PB&Js," Drew says after a few beats, long enough to make the comment incongruous. "But you're married to a doctor, so…"

Cameron thinks Drew expects him to reply to that. He doesn't. Another minute passes, and Drew moves to start bagging while Cameron finishes more sandwiches.

"So how is that?" Cameron turns to Drew slowly. "The married thing. To a doctor, I mean. Like, that's gotta be stressful, right?"

Cam squints. "For me or Kayla?"

"Both. Or you. Whatever you want to—"

"Are you married?" Cameron asks. Drew gives a brief, explosive laugh. "I didn't think so."

"Hey, now, it's not like I don't date. Things are complicated! Or were. I'm not sure what tense things are, but I am definitely sure that complicated is the correct word."

"That doesn't inspire confidence in your grasp of marital relations." Cameron realizes it's the height of hypocrisy for him to comment on someone else's understanding of marriage when his is in such a state, but his defenses are up.

"I can still counsel people," Drew protests. "That's my job. It's literally in the description. Believe me, I have read it *many* times."

"And the many books I'm sure Mr. Osborn has on hand," Cameron adds, allowing himself a little pity.

"I'm still working on those, to be honest." Drew looks green at the prospect. "I passed the test on the only one that mattered so that counts for something." Cameron squints at Drew, suspecting he should know what he's referring to. "The Bible. I'm pretty up on that one."

"Oh."

"Numbers is kind of iffy," Drew half-smiles. "I was never good at math."

Cameron lets out a ghost of a laugh through his nose, and Drew beams. "That's humorous."

"Deuteronomy, though, tough. I don't even like Andrew Lloyd Webber."

"What?"

"Crap. Lost you on the *Cats* joke."

"That's musical theater?" Cameron asks, his curiosity and amusement at this strange, small man slowly edging away his annoyance.

"Yeah. Not a fan?"

Cameron shakes his head. If Drew doesn't know that a man admitting to liking *musicals* is the first step to *rumors*, there's not much hope for him. "Next, we distribute the food. It's pretty simple," Cameron explains as he lifts a bag of sandwiches. "We're supposed to carry pamphlets and scripture verses, but no one takes them."

"No one? Didn't your, uh, Sean take one?"

Cameron avoids Drew's eyes by heading up the stairs and out of the building. It's a bright day, the last warmth of summer still in the air despite a few stray clouds. "We just talked."

"That's good. That's awesome. I'd really like to meet him sometime. If he's interested in coming to services"

Cameron can't think of anything he'd be less inclined to do than bring the man he's sinning with into the house of God. "Sean doesn't like crowds."

"Oh. Me neither."

Cameron turns to look at Drew, who is dwarfed by the bag of sandwiches he's carrying. "How exactly did you get this job?"

"I sort of have a friend who kind of knows Ted, and he put in a good word for me. In his way. I mean, well, Ted owed him a favor and, uh…"

Now it makes sense. "Your friend blackmailed Mr. Osborn into hiring you?"

"Blackmailed is such a mean word!" Drew squeaks, looking around in terror. "He persuaded him"

Cameron balks. "Why this job?"

"My friend knew I needed a job, but I wasn't super specific about things, so this was kinda a joke on me too? Also, I needed, you know, health insurance. So here I am." Cameron raises an eyebrow. "I went to seminary though! Top of my class."

Cam heaves a sigh. "You do seem to truly want to help people. That's a nice change."

Drew watches as Cameron hands out his first sandwich to a familiar man who stays in the general vicinity of the corner market. The cup in front of him changes each week, but not the red wool cap he wears despite the season. "You got a dollar?" he asks Drew, voice slurred.

"I, uh…" Drew nearly drops his bag fishing into his pockets. Cameron tugs him away without comment. "You don't think I should give him money?"

"It won't do any good. It only goes for drugs and alcohol." Cameron parrots the advice he's heard so many times, and for the first time, considers if it's true.

"Damn," Drew sighs.

They pass out more sandwiches. To the woman with the dog in the door of a decrepit laundromat. To the panhandler who keeps his cup on a fishing pole, so it hangs three feet above the sidewalk. To the man at the edge of the park with a sign that reads 'Starvin like Marvin.' Cameron doesn't know who Marvin is, but he gives the man two sandwiches. Eventually, they enter the park, heading towards the camp.

"I do really want to know where you think more can be done, or what Sean thinks," Drew ventures as they walk, his eyes wide as he takes in the tarps and trash. "I want to help."

"The first thing he'd tell you to do is come here," Cameron says as they reach the tent camp he and Sean so often frequented.

"New intern?" Orson asks from his seat, looking at Drew as Cameron places the bags on his makeshift desk.

"Go easy," Cameron mutters with a faint smile

"Never," Orson grins.

Cameron smiles back. "Lyle in the usual spot?"

"Nah. He went through a bad spell, did a few nights in the shelter, and some tweaker took his spot. He's over there for now. I'll give him his old digs back when Toothless gets mad about the no smoking in the camp rule and bolts." Orson points to a spot over by the edge of the camp, near the plywood precariously dug into the mud that comprises a makeshift fence. On the outside, there are signs and slogans posted: "Give us Dignity." "Our rights are Human Rights" and "ACAB" such. They're fading. In the corner is a pile of cloth that would be indiscernible as a person if you weren't looking.

Cameron approaches carefully, aware of the eyes of the camp following him. "Lyle?"

The lump startles and resolves into a human shape, complete with a wild-eyed face and a shaking hand holding up a sharpened stick. Cameron doesn't flinch, even when Drew stumbles back. *Lyle won't hurt you, don't worry.* He hears Sean's voice in his head. *He's twitchy, is all. He goes in and out, but he's harmless as a kitten. Just make sure he gets some food and maybe some cash. He won't use it for booze, I swear.*

"Air support is on the way! I've called in our location! Get back!" Lyle yelps.

"Sargent!" Cameron growls, and Lyle jumps to attention, dropping the stick.

"Sir." Lyle's eyes focus on Cameron, drifting in and out of recognition. "Sir?"

"Sean sent me, remember," Cameron says.

"Jeff's kid?"

"We wanted to make sure you got this." Cameron holds up a paper bag of food he's packed for Lyle specifically. There's an envelope of cash inside as well. "Sean told me to tell you to, in his words, 'think about getting your ass to the VA if things are too shitty.'"

"Things are always shitty." Lyle's demeanor shifts again, and he seems normal, if that's possible. "Sean doin' okay?"

"As okay as he can be. Please do think about the VA," Cameron says.

"I'll be fine once I get my spot back," Lyle shrugs.

Cameron shares a respectful look with Orson as he leaves. Drew follows him out of the camp with a look of awe on his face. "Okay. Cool, so…"

"If you want to talk to someone who has ideas on how to help best, talk to Orson. Or look at that place. People live there because the shelters won't take them, or they have too much stuff to move in and out of places every night. See if you can fix that."

"Thanks! I'll do that," Drew calls after Cameron.

Cam heads back to his car behind the mission and drives five miles over the speed limit to get home. Kayla's car isn't in the garage, and his heart jumps at the sight.

"So, are the pigs fascists or communists? I'm not following," Sean is saying as Cam walks in the door. He's sprawled on the couch, still in his grey sweats and a tee, phone to his ear, listening intently. His eyes widen when he sees Cam, and he gives a smile and a wave.

"Okay, so they're both. Like pork belly and bacon are kind of the same thing." A faint squawk of consternation is audible. "What? They're pigs! That's a good metaphor." Sean rolls his eyes as Danny replies, and Cam seats himself a virtuous distance from Sean on the couch. "Yeah, fine. Listen, Cam just got back from good person duty, and Mrs. Weaver is probably mad at you for talking so long. I should let you go."

"Please tell Danny I said hello," Cam ventures as Danny says something that makes Sean look wistful.

"Yeah, yeah. Hey, Cam says hello." Danny replies, and Sean's face scrunches in confusion. "Really? Why? You know he's a real person. Gardner checked the address and stuff. I – Fine." To Cam's surprise, Sean thrusts the phone at him. "He wants to talk to you."

"What?" Cam takes the phone automatically as Sean gives him a pleading look. "Hello?"

"Hi, Cam, nice to meet you. Sorta." Danny Lockwood's voice is kind and warm, like his brother's.

"You too, Danny."

"So, is he behaving himself?"

"It depends on your definition of behaving." Cam already has the sense that lying to Danny is neither easy nor advisable.

"Is he following the doctor's orders? Taking it easy?"

"Generally," he answers, giving Sean a look. "He doesn't mention the pain bothering him very much, but he's still moving slowly. Better though."

"You move slowly," Sean grumbles, pushing Cam with his foot.

"Yeah, he's a crappy patient." There's deep care in Danny's voice. "He got some bug when I was like, nine, and he wouldn't go to the doctor for days until he literally passed out. Dad nearly killed him for not saying anything."

That sounds like Sean. "Well, he's in good hands now," Cam assures the younger Lockwood. "He's a very pleasant guest too. We enjoy having him."

"How long?" Cam is surprised at the force in Danny's voice. It shouldn't be a shock that Danny is as indomitable as his brother.

"As long as he needs," Cam answers without hesitation, eyes on Sean, who smiles shyly.

"Good. And thank you. It means a lot to know someone is looking out for him."

"It's my honor to do it."

"Cool. I guess I should tell him bye. It was nice talking to you, Cameron."

"You as well, Danny. And please feel free to call me Cam." He doesn't say that he looks forward to meeting Danny in person someday, although he'd like to. He hands the phone back to Sean, a shiver rushing over his skin as their fingers brush.

"Okay, I'll talk to you next week. I'll get a letter back in the mail. Bye, shorty." Danny says something that makes Sean smile before he hangs up and looks at Cam. "How were things downtown?"

"Not too bad. I saw Lyle. He's doing alright, but not well. How's Danny?"

"He's good. Real good. Talking a lot more to me, which is awesome." He'd heard about the letter from Kayla first, but Sean had shown him the picture this morning. It was good to have a face to go with the idea of Danny. "He's so smart. Way better than the shitty school he's stuck in."

"That's good to hear. Where's Kayla?" She'd been there when Cam had left to volunteer.

"I, uh, don't know how long she'll be gone." Cam likes the slight blush on Sean's cheeks. It's good to know they were thinking the same thing, though it's disappointing they don't really have time. "Said she was heading to the mall, buying someone a present or something."

"Oh crap."

"You know, usually people like presents."

"Not if they're for me," Cam sighs. "Monday is… my birthday."

"Holy shit, really? Why didn't you tell me?"

"Because I don't like being celebrated." Even the mention of it has anxiety crawling under his skin. "Kayla always tries to do something big."

"Why? Does she know you don't like it?"

"She thinks if she orchestrates enough good birthdays, she can get me to like them. It worked with kale, so I guess she's optimistic."

"Okay, for one, the kale thing is called Stockholm syndrome. Two, it's your goddamn birthday, you should celebrate it the way you want."

"I don't think my wife would be amenable to how I'd like to celebrate it." Cam runs his fingers up Sean's thigh. Sean licks his lips with a wolfish grin.

"Oh. I know it's early, but—"

The sound of the garage opening makes them both jump, Sean with an added wince of pain. "Another time," Cam says with a sad smile as the key sounds in the lock.

"I'm gonna hold you to that," Sean replies in a whisper as Kayla walks in the door.

sean

Sean wakes up to an alarm for the first time in years. The anemic beeping on his phone eases him out of vague dreams, and he hauls himself up as much as his healing bones allow. He makes it into the kitchen before anyone is awake and decides french toast is the way to go, since it was a hit last time. Cam is the first one down, and Sean can't tell if he looks touched or annoyed.

"Please tell me you didn't do this because of me."

"No one should have to endure a kale smoothie on their birthday."

"I'll remember that for yours." Cam takes a seat at the breakfast bar, and Sean presents him with a plate.

"Well, that's in January, so we'll see." *We'll see if I even know you then,* Sean doesn't say. *I hope I do.*

"Wow, way to start the big day," Kayla says as she descends the stairs to join them, taking the air out of the moment. She bypasses the kitchen and heads for the mud room. When she returns, she's carrying a Macy's bag.

"Kay, no," Cam groans. Kayla smirks and hands the bag to Sean.

"What?" Sean squints at the bag.

"My husband is hard to shop for. You aren't. Happy unbirthday."

Sean still doesn't understand, but he pulls the box out of the bag anyway. "Oh, this is cruel," Sean laughs as he sees what it is: one of those fancy one-cup coffee makers. There's a pack of pods at the bottom of the bag too.

"Are you serious?" Cam says as Sean holds it up.

"Now Sean can have his coffee and it won't be too much of a temptation to steal it," Kayla says. Sean's certain she knows Cam is going to get some, but he's still strangely touched. It's been a long time since anyone bought him a present. "We'll set it up later; today I can get you a cup on the way into the hospital."

"Huh?" Sean and Cam say at the same time.

Kayla looks at them with an unconcerned expression. "Sean's got his follow-up x-rays and checkup today?"

"I do?" Sean's sure he would remember that.

"You'll come in with me, then you can help me with some errands in the afternoon. I'm taking it off."

"Kayla, that better not mean you're getting ready for company tonight," Cam says.

"Quiet, it's supposed to be a surprise," Kayla smiles. Sean sighs and turns back to finishing up breakfast.

Cam's gone when Sean finishes dressing and joins Kayla in the Mazda. It hurts not to say goodbye, but it's Sean's fault for lollygagging. He took a good five minutes freaking out after his shower about the goddamn *hickey* above his left nipple. Is someone gonna make him take off his shirt? Is *Kayla* going to examine him? He has no idea how to explain this, but he's good at thinking on his feet. He's sure he'll come up with a plan. Maybe he tripped and fell… into someone's mouth.

He's still waiting for the plan to come to him when Kayla leads him to a nice waiting area somewhere on the third floor of the hospital.

"Okay, they're going to call you for X-rays and then a nurse will come and get you for the exam," Kayla tells him.

"You won't be examining me, right?" Sean asks with a gulp. " Not that I don't trust you, but uh, seems kinda inappropriate."

Kayla gives him a wry smile. "Sean, I see your underwear in the laundry."

"Yeah, but—"

"The nurse will be looking at you, not me. I'll come in after I look at the X-rays. It's gonna take a while, so find a magazine."

Sean breathes a sigh of relief as Kayla goes. He's not happy to be back in the hospital. It's fifty shades of beige, and even in the waiting room that antiseptic smell lingers. The stiff seats are hell on his hip, and he doesn't like the way the older guy with a cast on his arm is looking at him. Sean decides he's being paranoid and turns back to the wrinkled old copy of *Good Housekeeping* he's been perusing. The best way to get the ten most common stains out of clothes doesn't include come, so he's dubious of the whole article.

After forever, he gets his X-rays and is sent off to another floor and another waiting room, where he lingers reading *US Weekly* until a familiar nurse calls him back for an exam.

"Hey, Sean, good to see you back," the woman smiles as Sean tries to remember her name. His brain was pretty fried last time he was here. "Dawn," she says, saving him. "Let's take a look at you."

He indeed has to get undressed, which is *great*. She gives Sean a look when she pulls down his gown to check his heart with the stethoscope, but doesn't comment.

After another interminable wait, Kayla finally reappears with a large set of X-rays and a smile on her face. At least Sean was allowed to get dressed. "So, good news, everything is healing well, just a little slow."

"Slow?"

"History of malnutrition will do that, but things are good. A few more weeks taking it easy, and you should be back to normal. If you had a job, I'd clear you to return to light duty."

"Yeah, yeah. Don't rub it in."

"Speaking of – did you tell Cam about your plans yet?" There's just a hint too much worry in her voice.

"To get to Ohio? No, I…" He doesn't want to hurt Cam like that yet, and he doesn't want that pain for himself either. "I figure I need something more solid before I do, you know? Not some vague 'here's where I'm going' shit."

"Uh-huh," Kayla replies, eyes narrow.

Sean really doesn't want this convo now. "Have you got more work to do, or am I in for more waiting?"

"I have to finish up a few things and then we'll get going."

"About that," Sean grimaces. "Are you really gonna throw Cam a party?"

"Just with his family," Kayla protests. "He says he doesn't like it, but he does."

"He really, *really* doesn't. Also, Luke and Susan are the definition of not fun." Sean stares Kayla down, pleading. He watches the argument take fire in her eyes, then fade with a sigh.

"Okay, fine." Sean lets out a breath in relief. "But we have to do something for him."

"Did you get him a present?"

"Of course. I got him some Blu-rays of the last season of the awful show you two watch."

"*Serial Monsters*? How did you—"

"I see the Netflix viewing history, Sean."

"I really need to make my own profile." Kayla laughs as Sean chews his lip. "Is that all?"

"What do you mean 'is that all?' I thought you didn't want to make a big deal."

Sean doesn't know if this is a bad idea or a great one, and it might just make things even weirder in the insane throuple situation he's gotten himself into. But he's gonna go with it. "I have some ideas, okay?"

cameron

Cameron sits parked in the garage, afraid to go into his own house. Again. The lack of other cars outside is promising, but he still finds himself hesitating. Flor and Lee took him out for lunch. The food was mediocre, but their bickering was amusing. At least there wasn't too much other attention besides a few texts from distant family and Facebook notifications. The yearly ritual of logging on to see that his high school classmates had been prompted by some algorithm to remember his existence and congratulate him for it continuing was even more depressing this year, thanks to all the political and news posts he'd seen.

Cam wants to go for a run, sleep, and wake up one day closer to Thursday.

He trudges inside, stomach churning and braced for an unwanted onslaught. It takes him several seconds before he processes that there was no yell of surprise, no lights flashing on. There's only the normal sound of Kayla and Sean's voices and the smell of something delicious.

Sean and Kayla turn to him and smile. It's a strange sight for sure, but certainly not unwelcome.

"Happy Birthday," Sean says.

"Welcome to your party," Kayla adds. "Hope the quality of the presents makes up for the number. Your family won't be joining us."

"That's the only present I need," Cam sighs in relief. "That and dinner. Do I smell—"

"One hundred percent GMO-free, pasture-raised, organic *steak*," Sean grins.

"Sean made the compelling point that supporting good farming practices was an important part of creating positive change," Kayla says with a begrudging smile.

"Also said a man deserved a damn steak on his birthday," Sean emphasizes the point by pulling a cast-iron pan containing three gorgeous steaks out of the oven. "We got vegetables too, so don't get too excited."

"Thank you," Cam says, awestruck. Sean has somehow worked a miracle. "You cooked this?"

"Not too hard," Sean shrugs.

"That's what he says," Kayla scoffs.

"These have gotta rest. Open your damn presents," Sean prompts. Cameron takes a seat at the table in front of two packages. He opens the small one first and laughs at the sight of *Serial Monsters* Blu-Ray. "Figure we can catch up on the season that's not on Netflix yet."

"I'm sure Kayla will enjoy that," Cameron smiles.

"I'll have something to read. I don't know what yet, but it's important," Kayla says. "The next one is better. Took us a while to find it."

It's the word *us* that sets off all sorts of feelings in Cameron. Cameron tears the wrapping off the package and opens the box. It's been so long since he's seen a record player, he almost doesn't recognize it.

"So you can finally listen to some of that vinyl," Sean says, and Cameron knows this was his idea. This *all* was his idea, and it takes every ounce of control Cam has not to walk across the room and hug Sean right there.

"Do you like it?" Kayla asks.

"I love it," Cameron replies softly. "The only thing that could make this better is dessert."

"Red velvet cupcakes in the fridge," Kayla says with a pleased grin.

For the first time in a long while, Cameron means it when he says grace and thanks God for the food and the company and everyone's safety. Even Kayla has to admit the steaks are amazing and perfectly cooked. It's not enough to convince her to let beef back on the menu permanently, but she says she'll consider bacon.

After dinner, Kayla is kind enough to sit through one episode of *Serial Monsters*, offering appalled commentary (on the misogynist language and how improbable it is that the sexy monster hunters seem to drive across the entire country in an hour) before she gives up and heads upstairs. She squeezes Cameron's shoulder and places a kiss on his cheek before telling him not to stay down too long.

Cam and Sean don't touch as they sit on the couch. Not with Kayla still awake upstairs. But they do sit close, so Cam can feel Sean's warmth a few inches from him. He would tell himself that he doesn't need it, but that would be a lie.

"Thank you for everything today," Cam says as the credits roll on the episode. "It's the first time I've had an enjoyable birthday in a while."

"I just redirected, okay? It worked out."

"Maybe we can use the record player later this week. Listen to some of those albums."

"Just us?" The question is pregnant with meaning that makes Cam's skin tingle.

"Just us."

Sean smiles crookedly and moves to get off the couch. "Help me up. I got one more thing for you."

Cam raises an eyebrow in interest, savoring the heat of Sean's skin under his palms as he hoists him up. Sean's hand trails down into Cam's, and he leads him confidently towards his room. "Sean…"

"Chill, it's not that." Sean shoots him a look over his shoulder and smirks. "Okay, it's sorta that."

Sean closes the door, and Cam's heart pounds; the thought of Kayla coming downstairs to look for him rings in his mind, but Sean's proximity screams louder. It's barely been a week of this change in their relationship, and they're already taking stupid risks and…

"Stop panicking," Sean whispers and kisses him, deep and tender. Cam surrenders so easily it's frightening. Sean pulls him close, and Cam embraces him in kind, lost in the contact until Sean presses something cool and smooth into his hand. Sean pulls back with a glint in his eyes. "Used a five-finger discount to pick something up while Kayla was getting produce."

Cam looks down at the object in his hand: a small bottle of lube. "You stole lube. For me. As a birthday present."

"I get to benefit too." Sean's cocky grin falters. "If you're okay with that."

"I am very okay with it." Cam's skin heats just imagining it. "Condoms?"

"No." The simple word has Cameron starting to harden in his slacks. Not convenient.

"You probably should get upstairs," Sean murmurs before kissing Cam again as he takes the lube back from his hand. "I'll keep this down here, but you think about what we'll do with it."

"That's a cruel thing to say," Cam grumbles. "Going up will be awkward and frustrating now."

"Why? Get some birthday sex."

"That's not a thing."

"That's totally a thing."

"It's not Friday." The look Sean gives him is overflowing with disbelief and pity. "Oh."

"Yeah." Sean rolls his eyes and tugs Cameron close for another kiss. "Go. I don't mind. Have fun."

Cam keeps a hand on Sean until he can't reach him anymore, letting his own movement decide for him when to end contact.

Kayla is in bed with a book when he gets to their room and doesn't immediately look up. "You done already?" she asks.

Cameron pushes the sound of her voice from his mind, even the image of her face, and pretends it's a different room he's walked into. In his mind, it's Sean looking warm and safe. Sean smiling at him from their bed. Sean.

"I thought it would be nice to spend time together," he lies as he crawls up the bed and to Kayla. She puts away her book with interest in her eyes and makes a soft, surprised noise when he kisses her.

It's not the same. It's never the same, and Cameron hates it, but it's what's right. The man making love to Kayla is who his family and God need him to be. She turns them over and rides him, and Cameron closes his eyes. He enjoys the sensation when she takes a small vibrator from her bedside table. He never begrudged her the purchase of any marital aids; in fact, he hoped that she could use them to get the satisfaction he was never good at giving her. He keeps a picture of Sean in his head as Kayla whimpers with pleasure above him. Distantly, he wonders if this is how Sean felt with other customers: touching as intimately as possible and completely separate. Sex with Sean never felt that way.

He feels it when Kayla reaches orgasm. It's a relatively alien feeling, given how long it's been since she finished with him inside her. His body responds to the novelty of its own accord, and he thrusts a few more times and thinks of the heat of Sean's mouth and comes weakly with a soft groan.

He's the first to retreat to the bathroom to clean up. He feels dirty, tainted. When Kayla snuggles next to him in bed, it's suffocating.

"Wow, that's one way to kick off another go around the sun, huh?" Kayla says.

"I guess so," Cameron replies. He's not superstitious, but he wonders if there's something to that. If the whole year will be like this. If that means Sean's close, that's a trade he's willing to make. He's willing to endure many things for Sean's sake. It scares him when he considers how much.

"I think it's gonna be a great year," Kayla says beside him. "I can feel it."

19
French Fries, Fenders, and THIGHS

sean

Sean waves goodbye to Wanda and Fergus from the Steward front porch with a crooked smile. He's tired from an hour helping her sort through boxes of donations, but it's the good kind of tired that comes from a job well done. Wanda served him sweet tea and chatted about nothing in particular. It was a welcome distraction from angsting about tonight, since it's Thursday.

He *wants* to think about fooling around with Cam tonight, so of course, all he can think about is that he's got to tell Cam he's planning to leave. Is he really, though? He has a destination, but he doesn't have a route or a timeframe. Does that count?

He sighs as he walks to the beautiful kitchen, running his fingers over the cool, polished white counters. Cam is taking care of grub tonight, which is exciting, though Sean's sorta bummed he's not cooking. He made dinner again last night, and it was a hit. Kayla's slowly letting him add things to the shopping list too, which everyone appreciates. He also offered to take over some of the laundry because he's honestly getting sick of Netflix and daytime TV. Hustler to housewife – how the worm turns.

As of now, the laundry is done, and Cam won't be home for a while, so Sean heads back into his room and opens the laptop that found its way in there last night after Kayla responded to Sean's complaints about boredom with the suggestion of online classes. Sean argued until Cam had the audacity to agree that it would be good for him to just look.

Sean still doesn't like the idea, especially if it means Cam and Kayla paying for more shit he doesn't deserve or need. He'd made it as far as a basic web search before he panicked so thoroughly he started shaking. Maybe this time he'll actually check a link.

Before he can try, his pants start quacking. He's started keeping his phone on him, but no one's ever actually called him. Cam or Kayla will text once in a while, but that's it. Sure as hell, his phone's ringing and with an unknown on the caller ID.

"Hello?" Sean answers unsteadily.

"Sean Lockwood?" A female voice replies over the line. "This is Detective Tamara Hodge. Remember me?"

Sean swallows, mouth dry and heart pounding. "Yeah. I remember. How'd you get this number?"

"The hospital. I'll get right to it. It's been four weeks, so unless a witness or additional victim comes forward in the case involving your assault, we're going to close the investigation."

"Oh." Sean doesn't know if that makes him relieved or ashamed.

"Unless you've remembered something about who attacked you." There's no mistaking the hope in her tone.

Sean shakes his head, even though she can't see. He doesn't want to think about Jeremiah. Once in a while, the bastard's face shows up in a nightmare, then it turns into Sean's dad, so he'll force himself awake and think of Cam. Not in a sexy way, just a 'he's in the same house, it's safe now' way. More than that, Sean doesn't want some pointless court case messing up Cam and Kayla's lives. "Nope. Still nothin'."

"Sean, I want you to know there wouldn't be any consequences, legally, for you if you changed your story. No one would hold it against you or prosecute you *for any reason*. Even why you were there that night."

Sean's insides turn to cold mush. Hodge knows what he is. "I don't know what you're talking about. Is that all?"

"No. The car found on the scene—"

"You mean *my* car."

"Since no rightful *legal* owner came forward to claim it, it belonged to the state," Hodge shoots back.

"What do you mean belonged? Where is she?" There's a cold sweat all over Sean now.

"Exactly where I said she'd end up: sold at auction this morning to Farnell Salvage." Detective Hodge pauses as Sean catches his breath. "You need to write that down? The owner's a friend, and I told him to expect your call."

"Farnell Salvage. Got it." Sean doesn't know why the detective is being helpful, especially if she knows what kind of person Sean was (is?). "Thank you for telling me. I know you didn't have to."

"I can open this case back up any time for two years," Detective Hodge replies. "Just so you know."

"Yeah. Okay." Sean does not want to think about that right now. One shitstorm at a time.

"Hope to talk to you again soon, Sean. You have my number."

"Bye, Detective."

Sean doesn't save her number. Instead, he goes to the laptop and looks up Farnell Salvage and dials before he can think better of it. It takes four rings before someone answers.

"Farnell. What do you want?" a gruff voice demands, and Sean winces. This is gonna be even more fun than he thought.

"Yeah, my car. She's a—"

"Beat to hell Bel Air I just spent my hard-earned cash on?" Farnell grumbles in a rough, southern drawl. "Tamara told me to expect your call."

"So she explained the car's mine, I just don't have the paperwork," Sean pushes, feeling desperate already. "I've got the keys though."

"Only paperwork I saw said the thing used to belong to a…" Sean hears the sound of shuffling paper. "Jeff Lockwood."

"That's my father. He gave her to me."

A pause, then a grunt. "You ain't talking about Jeff Lockwood that used to work at a mechanic shop down on 65th?"

"Uh, yeah? He left that job like twelve years ago." Sean's still freaked to the point of nausea, but now he's also confused.

"I have a good memory. As I recall, the bastard had two sons, which one are you?"

"Sean. Wait… Farnell. As in *Bill* Farnell?"

"The one and only." Memories flash into Sean's mind of rusted cars, summer sun, and Skynyrd playing on a busted porch radio.

"Holy shit, we've met! I was a kid, but Dad took me out to your place to do some work on an old Chevelle. I was six and I climbed up one of the stacks and—"

"Nearly broke your neck. I remember." Farnell does not sound moved. "You get any less stupid since then?"

"Not really." Bill laughs, dry and derisive. "But that means you know I'm not lying. That car – she's my home. *Literally* my home."

"Even if she weren't trashed, I can't just give some idiot kid I ain't seen since last decade a car," Bill says, and Sean's shoulders fall in defeat.

"Please, man," Sean pushes, and he doesn't care that it sounds like begging. " Everything I had was inside, and I *need* to get her back."

There's silence for too long. "I can't give her to you, but if you wanna come take a look at her, swing by this weekend. We'll talk, but no promises."

Sean would jump for joy if he could. "Oh my God, thank you! I'll be there around—" There's a beep, and Sean looks down to see the call has ended. "Damn." He falls back onto the mattress, running his hands through his hair and grunting at the pain the movement causes.

Like most details of 'what the hell happens next,' he'd thought about the Bel Air in only the vaguest terms. What's he going to do if he can't get his money from the car? What's he going to do if he can? Just leave when he's healed? Fuck off to Ohio on the off chance of being part of

Danny's life and never see Cam again? How would he even get there without a car? Where would he stay? What would he do when the money ran out? He can't go back to hustling, can he?

"Sean?"

Sean startles. Cam is standing in his doorway, looking very worried. "Hey. Cam, I—"

"I called and looked on the porch and…" Cam looks down at the floor. "I thought you'd left." A kick in the jewels would have hurt less than the fear in Cam's voice.

"No, man, no. I was in my head. Didn't hear you."

"Oh. Are you okay?"

"'Course not." Sean doesn't get up. Instead, he scoots over on the bed and makes room for Cam. He's carrying a greasy bag that smells like burgers and fries (aka heaven), and a huge milkshake. "We sharin' the milkshake?"

"It's peanut butter," Cam says as he hands Sean the food. He takes off his coat and jacket before climbing into the bed next to Sean. Sean distributes the burgers between the two of them, leaving the obscene amount of fries in the bag and setting the milkshake between them on the bed. "Will you tell me why you're not okay?" Cam asks after a few bites.

"You ain't gonna like it."

"That's alright." Sean gives Cam a long look. "Tell me anyway."

"Got a call from Detective Hodge. Said they're closing the case for now." Cam makes an interested noise as he bites into another fry. "So that's whatever, but they sold my damn car."

"Sold it?"

"Auctioned it. Got picked up by someone I sorta know, actually. Mean old cuss named Bill Farnell. Owns a salvage yard." Sean takes a petulant bite of his cheeseburger. It's so good it almost makes him forget the bullshit he's dealing with.

"And?" Cam asks through a full mouth.

"And I called him. He said to come talk to him on the weekend and I don't know if he's gonna give her back and, fuck, even if he does, she's too busted to drive and I don't know if he has my stuff or the money I saved and…" Sean stops at the feel of Cam's hand on his thigh, soothing and gentle. "No matter what, it's all crap I have to worry about for when… When I leave."

"Leave?" Sean can hear the sadness in Cam's voice. He feels it too.

"I've only got a few weeks of recovery left."

"It's not like we're going to dump you on the street once you're healed, Sean." Cam sounds exactly like Kayla, and it makes Sean smile.

"I know, and I really appreciate that," Sean sighs. Better to rip the bandage off now. "But I have to start thinking of how I can get… to Danny."

Cam doesn't say anything. In his peripheral vision, since Sean can't bear to look at Cam right now, he sees him roll his lips and breathe deep. "In Ohio."

"Eventually."

"But not immediately?" Sean finally looks at him. One more punch in the gut. "You need employment and reliable transport."

"I know. That's why I'm freaking. That's the long-term plan, and it's fucking terrifying."

"It is." Cam takes a sullen bite of french fry. "So let's talk about it later. Not today."

"In all of our copious time together. God, this discretion thing is a bitch." Cam gives Sean a worried look as he stuffs more fries in his mouth. "Dude, I ain't complaining. I'm not gonna say anything or endanger you or whatever."

"I know." Cam sighs and picks up the milkshake, but doesn't take a sip. "When I said I'd lose everything. I meant it. If people at work – certain people – find out I'm the way I am, I'd be fired. Without me there to protect her from those same people, Kayla could be fired as well. So would Lee and Flor. It would hurt Vince and Luke's businesses. I know you don't care for them, but they have families. My mother would never speak to me again and—"

Sean grabs Cam's hand, forcing him to look at him. "Cam. You can trust me. I'm not gonna get you busted. I know this is shitty, all of it.

Granted, I didn't know the goddamn *everyone will lose their jobs* specifics. But I don't want to hurt people. Especially not Kayla." Cam raises an eyebrow. "I like Kayla. She's a good person."

"But you're okay with stealing her husband?"

"Cam, you're a human, not a pair of candlesticks. I can't steal you." Cam looks down at their joined hands and squeezes. "I just borrow you once in a while."

"Why are you doing this, if you know it's bad?"

"Because it doesn't feel bad when I'm with you," Sean says with a casual shrug, because he doesn't want this to be more of a moment than it already is. "It feels better than anything, and we ain't gonna have it for long."

"It does," Cam says quietly.

They eat in silence until there's nothing left but dregs of the milkshake and a few bits of fries. Sean moves the detritus to a nightstand and wipes his greasy hands on the comforter before slinging a leg over Cam to straddle him. It hurts, but Sean tries not to let the discomfort show on his face. He must do a good job because Cam accepts it easily when he kisses him. He still tastes like salt and sweet cream, and Sean sinks into the kiss like easing into a warm bath, every muscle relaxing like he's finally come home.

"Help me out here," Sean whispers as Cam fingers the edge of his tee. Cam complies, and the shirt hides Sean's wince when he lifts his arm. Cam kisses at his collarbones and chest, open-mouthed and hungry. Cam scoots up, and Sean hisses in pain.

"Are you okay?" Cam asks in that tone that lets Sean know he won't take a bullshit answer.

"Just hurting a bit. It's nothing." Cam glares. "Let me move and…" he shifts so that his weight is on Cam, and he has one leg between Cam's thighs. "Much better."

It is better. Sean can rut against Cam as he gets hard and kisses his perfect mouth and gorgeous neck. He unbuttons Cam's shirt slowly, moving downward with his hands and exploring each inch of exposed skin. He pays the same care to his pants, avoiding Cam's crotch to kiss and bite his way down Cam's legs. He likes the tickle of hair against his cheek, the heated muscle under his fingertips. He steps off the bed to get rid of his own remaining clothes and smiles at his work.

"Been a long time since I've had you naked. Or in bed for that matter," Sean purrs as he climbs back on. This time, Cam does notice Sean's grimace. Cam pulls him close, keeping Sean on his good side, and runs his hands over Sean's back.

"Maybe nothing too strenuous tonight."

"You're not gonna break me."

"I don't want to hurt you, even a bit." Cam trails his fingertips over Sean's cheek so light and soft that it gives him goosebumps.

"Fucking hell, Cam."

Cam tugs him closer, brushing their dicks together, and Sean whines at the slight friction. "I didn't say nothing at all."

"Thank God," Sean whispers, and pulls Cam's body flush against his as he kisses him. Cam is a blanket of solid heat leaning over him, and it's so good. They kiss and touch and grind until Sean's digging his fingers into the meat of Cam's ass, desperate for little something more. "Hold up. I wanna try a thing."

"What are you–" Cam's sex-heavy eyes go wide when Sean fishes the lube from his bedside drawer. "Sean…"

"Not that. Just trust me." And Cam does. He lets Sean manhandle him into the perfect position, half on his side with a pillow wedged behind him and his legs together. Sean squirts a small dollop of lube on his fingers and raises an eyebrow at Cam's adorable look of confusion. "Been thinking about this for weeks. Every time you come in from a run."

"What?"

"Keep your knees together," Sean orders and proceeds to spread the lube on Cam's glorious thighs. Sean slides into the tight clench of Cam's legs and groans. It's not the same as fucking Cam, or feeling him inside him, but it's hot and close, and having Cam surround him is its own kind of heaven. He locks one hand around Cam's shoulder and another on his hip as he chases his pleasure, Cam's cock nudging his belly with each thrust. He comes, sighing as he paints Cam's thighs and the comforter with his spend. It's messy and risky and insanely good, and it's theirs. He finishes Cam off with his mouth, letting him practically ride his face as he sprawls bonelessly on the bed.

They don't talk more about the future after they're done. They touch and wash the comforter and make out against the dryer in their skivvies. They watch TV, talk about everything and nothing until they end up back in Sean's bed among warm, fresh-smelling sheets. Cam decides he wants to give Sean's technique a try, and he pins Sean gently beneath him and grinds between Sean's ass cheeks until he spills over Sean's back with a cry.

Sean doesn't complain about the new mess when Cam turns him over; he's too happy to feel Cam's mouth around him. He's too tired and selfish and lost in his sin to care about anything but the pleasure and release and clarity. This is one of the good bits. Stolen, maybe, but good.

Two hours later, as Sean lies alone in bed, stuck in an endless loop of 'what ifs' and 'I can't do that,' he wants that peace back. Cam mentioned something, not tonight, a week or more ago, about Kayla not liking the windows open at night. Sean can't remember if she doesn't like the noise or thought it was a waste of energy with the AC on, or if she was worried some robber was gonna break in.

All he remembers is that Cam was sad about it, and that's why Sean's window is open now. A gentle breeze, carrying the warmth of the last day of summer, jostles the curtains and touches his cheek as softly as Cam did hours ago. Sean licks his lips, still tasting Cam there, and wonders if he's asleep too. Kayla will be home in an hour, but as far as Sean knows, Cam never waits up for her. Sean savors the wind and listens to the crickets and wonders if Cam is listening too.

cameron

"Are you sure you don't want me to do this? You still look like you're feeling crappy." Cameron looks up from his complete lack of coffee and squints at Kayla.

"It's fine. I want to." He does still feel unwell, but not as badly as last night. Or as he had said that he felt last night, in order to excuse himself from conjugal duties. It wasn't as if Cameron could say he couldn't get hard because he was too upset by the thought of Sean leaving. He couldn't even say that he was jealous of how much time Kayla got with Sean on her day off. That's the reason he's driving Sean to Farnell Salvage today.

"Okay, but both of you take it easy." Cameron looks up. Sean has rejoined them in the kitchen, pulling on a flannel shirt over his dark tee.

"I'll keep him out of trouble," Sean says with a smile to Kayla.

Sean looks less cocky when he's in the car with Cam. It's early still, and Sean doesn't say anything when they hit the drive-thru and Cam orders them two large coffees and pastries.

"Are you sure about getting there this early?" Cam asks as they pull away.

"Yeah, I wanna settle this bullshit before I talk to Danny, and you gotta get to your thing."

Cam nods. They head down a back road that takes them into the twilight areas between the suburbs and the country. Everything is rundown, even the giant "Christ Died to Save Sinners!" billboard. The "Hell is REAL!" on the opposite side has been graffitied to say: "Help isn't real." Cam believes both.

Farnell Salvage is one of those places the world changed around, like a boulder in a stream. Beyond the rusted gate, the sun-bleached buildings at the center sit like more wrecks among the dried husks of cars arranged in teetering columns and piles.

"This place sure went to shit since I was six," Sean murmurs as Cam parks in front of a weathered house that might have been green the last time it was painted.

"Is there an office?" Cam asks. There's a garage next to the house with empty bays and tools, but no one's inside.

"Best I remember, Bill did all his business out of his living room. His wife made a fuss about it. Guess we'd better knock."

They head to the front door of the house. Cam notes a ramp in place of stairs, which he knows Sean appreciates. A large pit bull waits by the door on a chain, napping in the sun and barely stirring when they approach, and Cam bends to scratch behind her ears as Sean knocks. They wait in silence for thirty seconds before Sean tries again. "Bill? It's Sean Lockwood. We talked on Thursday?" Sean calls, pounding harder.

"Maybe he's not home?" Cam suggests just as the door swings open.

"What?" It takes a second for Cam's eyes to adjust downward from where he expected to see Bill Farnell. The bearded man is seated in a wheelchair, glowering. Most of his hair is gray and coarse, but his hazel eyes are still clear and sharp.

"Good morning," Cam says cautiously, and he can *feel* Sean roll his eyes.

"Ain't nothing good about it," Bill growls. "Whadaya want?"

"My damn car," Sean snaps.

"Guess Tamara wasn't lyin' about you being a stubborn sunuvabitch." Bill's eyes fall on Cam and narrow. "Who's this? Your parole officer?"

"A friend," Sean replies. Bill seems unconvinced. Cam looks past him to the messy hall decorated with peeling wallpaper and stacks of books, boxes, and bottles. "Quit stalling. Where is she?"

"In back." Bill sighs, wheeling himself over the threshold and down the ramp. "Fair warnin', it ain't pretty." The dog perks up as Bill moves close, whining and wagging her stump of a tail. "You think you're getting a scratch for letting them in?" Bill asks, even as he knuckles between the animal's ears. "Useless."

They follow Bill as he rolls determinedly over the gravel to the back of the garage building, where they round a corner and a battered red car comes into view.

"Goddamn, what'd he do to you?" Sean hisses and rushes to the car like it's a wounded friend.

Cam has never seen 'her' before, but he can understand Sean's distress. The car is decimated, every window and light smashed, the chrome fenders hanging on by threads. The driver's side is concave where the truck hit, and the tires are deflated too. It's like the thing was picked up by a giant, crushed, and thrown aside. Sean wrenches open the hood with great effort and groans at the sight. Cameron doesn't know much about cars, but he's fairly sure the hoses shouldn't be torn and sticking up like that.

"Fuck," Sean exhales.

"Like I said, not pretty. Barely enough in good condition to sell for parts," Bill says.

Sean gives him a murderous look. "Then why the hell did you buy her?"

"'Cause an asshole mechanic I used to know had a real pretty Bel Air that this piece of crap reminded me of," Bill spits right back, and Sean bristles. "Didn't think I'd be getting the actual same car."

"How much do you want for her?" Sean demands, chin high.

"How much you got?"

Cam is intrigued by the lack of hesitancy in the exchange. Sean levels a look at Bill as he grabs a crowbar from a dusty workbench and wedges it into the trunk. It comes open easily, too easily for Sean's taste if Cam can judge by his expression. Sean's frown only deepens as he rummages through the trunk with increasing urgency. "Where the hell is my stuff?"

"You mean all the crap I pulled a muscle cleaning out?" Bill asks, smug as can be. "In a box in the bay. I don't think you'll be paying for this girl with some ratty jeans and old pictures."

"What about an envelope? Big. Full of—" Sean stops himself as Bill slowly shakes his head. "God fucking damnit." Sean turns and gives the airless back tire a vicious kick, then hisses in pain.

"I'll pay for it. Whatever you paid at auction," Cam says. Sean and Bill turn to him, equal amounts of shock on their faces.

"Cam, no."

"This is *your* car. I know how much it – she – means to you," Cam argues. It's only logical.

"What the hell do you want with her anyway?" Bill asks, dubious. "You and your *friend* here gonna fix her up?"

"She's all I've got of my family, okay?" Sean snaps. "So yeah. I kept her running fine for the last few years. I can fix her." Sean turns to Cam. "You do not have to pay for this, Cam, I swear."

"Your daddy teach you the trade?" They look back at Bill, who has a discerning look on his face. "Or do you actually know what you're doing?"

"I ain't certified or nothing, but yeah, I know my way around," Sean says, proud and defiant as Bill sizes him up.

"Engine work ain't body work, boy. You know anything about that?"

"I can fucking *learn*," Sean snarls.

"And I guess you're gonna pay for this on-the-job training?" Bill says, looking at Cam.

"If I need to," Cam replies, utterly confused.

"I ain't gonna let you throw money at some kid who may or may not know what he's doing," Bill says and presses on as Sean opens his mouth to protest. "So one you can pay for the car and the parts *if and when* this genius fixes her up."

"What?" Sean says, blinking at the grizzled man. "Here?"

"You think Mr. Sensible Corolla has the shit you need for a job like this? Yes. You can use the tools around here, try not to get in the way."

"What?" Sean repeats, looking to Cam for guidance that he can't give.

"Did I stutter? Come weekdays, I don't care how you get here, but you gotta bring your own damn food. No drugs. I don't care if you smoke. And you better be ready to help me with real jobs if they come in." Bill's already started rolling back to the house, waving Cam and Sean away. "Your shit's in the bay right by the door. It ain't locked."

"Wait! Why the hell are you doing this?" Sean yells, arms raised in confusion.

"What is he even doing?" Cam asks under his breath.

"'Cause when your dad wasn't on the bottle, he was a good man, and I need a half-decent mechanic around to help when my so-called employee is too stoned to sell my stuff on the internet," Bill calls back over his shoulder as he mounts the ramp back up to his house. "Now get off my property or I'll set the hound on ya."

Bill slams the door, and the dog whines.

"Did that man just... hire you?" Cam asks.

"I have no idea," Sean mutters and turns to Cam. "But it's a good thing, right?"

"I think?" Cam looks back towards the garage. Sean may have his car back, but he has to fix it himself. He doesn't have the money he stored there, and that will put a dent in Sean's plans to leave. So would having something resembling a job in St. Louis. Still, it's a change, and it leaves Cam unsettled.

"Guess I'll see what Danny thinks. Still pissed about that money." Sean kicks at the dirt as they head back to the Corolla. "Although..."

"What?"

"Don't know if it woulda felt right, you know? Paying you and Bill back with money I got from *that*."

"You did what you had to do to survive," Cam says automatically. He's never thought less of Sean because of his past or profession, but he's not sure Sean believes him when he says it.

"Still," Sean shrugs as he buckles in. "Sorta like blood money. Or I guess since it wasn't blood, in this case it was—"

"*Please* do not say what you're about to say."

Sean's face breaks into a brilliant grin, and warm laughter bubbles behind it. "You thought it too."

Cam rolls his eyes and attempts to suppress his smile. He fails, of course. He fails at most attempts at control around Sean, but finds that lately he doesn't mind.

The drive downtown after he drops Sean off – with instructions to tell Danny hello when they speak – is even more depressing than usual. Maybe it's the approach of fall. The few trees that dot the streets have started to change, removing the last traces of verdant life from the landscape. The people seem colder. Even the air feels empty and foreboding as Cam gets out of his car and trudges into the mission.

Lee waves to him, and he joins her in a corner with Drew and another man he doesn't recognize.

"…are you saying you don't support the latest measure from the church to protect children, or just disagree on certain points?" The stranger is asking in a dangerous tone.

"I don't think kicking kids out of sports or firing teachers is a good message to send to kids, or anyone," Drew answers, more forceful than Cameron has ever seen him. "The church should be welcoming and—"

"The *church* must uphold and promote the revealed word and will of God in the world," the man snaps back. Cameron doesn't know what they're talking about, but the tone makes his skin crawl.

"I think we'll have to disagree on that," Drew says with a firmness that Cameron would never have suspected.

"We're here to help the poor anyway, not debate policy," Lee interjects, clearly uncomfortable as well. "Good to see you, Cameron."

"You too," he says before Lee surprises him with a stiff hug.

"Mr. Steward. My cousin has told me quite a lot about you," the stranger says, eyes like flint as they meet Cameron's. They don't have a shred of the kindness that Lee's always carry.

"Lee has mentioned you as well. I didn't think you were moving to St. Louis so soon," Cameron says, shaking the cousin's hand.

"I'm not fully moved, but I wanted to take some time to see what sort of ministry opportunities there are here. Lee spoke highly of… this." He waves at the mission around him. "I'll be here full-time in a few weeks."

"I'm glad you're taking an interest. We do good work, I hope,"
Cameron says. It doesn't seem like he's very impressed. "I'm very sorry,
but I can't recall your name."

"It's alright. My name is Jeremiah."

20

FAITHFULLY

sean

"FEELS LIKE THE FIRST day of school," Sean says from the passenger seat of the Corolla. He doesn't mention that the last time he got dropped off at school, his dad had been so hungover he missed the turn and forgot to give Sean money for lunch. "Paper bag lunch and everything."

Cam squints dubiously at Bill's house through the windshield. "Are you sure about this?"

"I dunno, man. He said to show up. I can at least get an idea what kind of work she needs. Maybe start on the engine."

"Call if you need me to come earlier."

"Or I can take the damn bus like a normal person."

"That's a long walk."

"I'll be fine." He's not sure that's true, but since Kayla and Cam are squares who won't let him borrow a car until he's 'legally allowed to drive it,' they're stuck carpooling. "See you this afternoon."

"Good luck," Cam says with too much seriousness.

Sean considers leaning over the gearshift and kissing the idiot, but they're not like that. Kayla's the one who gets to kiss Cam goodbye. Not Sean. He settles for squeezing Cam's hand. It's soft; intimate in its own way, and enough of a boost to get him out the door.

He doesn't walk up the ramp until Cam drives out of sight. Being here brings back memories of a life that's long gone. Like the pictures at the bottom of the box of his things that Sean hasn't got the balls to look at yet. Faded images of the dead and the lost. Bill's whole property has the same feel, like a mausoleum. Sean doesn't want to disturb anything, so he takes his time, pausing to pet the dog and look up at the overcast sky.

"You gonna lollygag out there or come in?"

Sean spins to see Bill at the open front door. The dog jumps up, wagging her whole body at the sight of him. "I'm invited in this time?"

Bill makes a harrumphing noise that Sean takes as a yes and wheels away down the hall. Sean gives the dog one more pat before following inside. The windows are all either dirty or covered, so not much light gets in, but the state of the place is still evident. It's the kind of messy that has a purpose, with some scheme to the piles of books, junk, and papers on every surface that only makes sense to Bill. The number of empty whiskey bottles is troubling, but they complement the various car parts strewn about.

"This place went to shit," Sean says as he looks around. Bill glares at him from the desk that takes up half of the living room.

"Don't mean to offend your delicate sensibilities, Emily Post."

"Last I remember, you had a wife," Sean says, cutting right to it.

"Last you remember, I had two working legs too," Bill snarls back. Sean keeps staring Bill down, waiting for him to confirm what he already guesses. "Lost both the same day. Not that it's any of your damn business."

"What happened?" Sean asks and gets another glare for his trouble.

"Drunk driver. No need to comment on the irony."

"Sorry."

Bill shrugs. He's heard it all before, Sean's sure. "What happened to you?" Bill indicates the lower half of Sean. He'd thought he was doing a decent job hiding the limp. Maybe not so much. "Guessin' you were in that hunk of junk when she got pretzeled."

"By an angry asshole who was stone sober and real mad," Sean confesses.

"He angry about this?" Bill pulls open a creaky desk drawer and deposits a thick and very familiar envelope on the desk. Sean feels the floor go out from under him.

"Shit. Why didn't you—"

"Didn't want Mr. Sensible Corolla seeing this if it'd get you in deeper trouble than you already are." Bill opens the envelope and runs a thumb over the stack of cash. "No law-abiding citizen hides cash like this."

"It's not drug money," Sean says before he can think, and Bill gives him a look. "You ain't gonna believe me if I say I stole it, are you?"

"Not after what Tamara told me."

Sean would take a moment to think about what the shame he feels about his past means, since it's a new sort of feeling, but he doesn't have that sort of time. "So I hustled. I did what I had to."

"Does your boyfriend know?"

"Cam?" Sean panics more on Cam's behalf than his own. "Cam's married."

"Don't bullshit a bullshitter, boy."

Sean tenses and glowers at the old man. "How the hell do you think Cam and I met?"

To Sean's shock, Bill laughs. It's quick, and the sound is as decrepit and dark as his house, but it's real. "Always those quiet types."

"Please don't tell anyone."

"Who the hell would I blab to? I don't give a rat's ass where your dicks have been – or continue to be."

Are they that obvious? Sean wonders, amazed. He keeps finding new things to freak out about. "Like I said, Cam's married to a nice lady and I—" Sean sighs. He doesn't know what to say, so he flops into a dusty armchair. "I dunno. It's all fucked."

"Is giving you this gonna make things better or worse?" Bill gestures to the cash.

"Worse, probably."

"I'll hold on to it for now. See how much fixing up your ride costs me, then we can renegotiate." Sean nods, glad the money won't be burning a hole in his pocket. He looks around again, trying to make out the outlines of the same room in his memory. There was sunshine coming through the windows then, and Dad had asked for a second slice of pecan pie from Bill's wife and smiled.

"Jesus, sometimes I wonder what my dad would say if he knew how I got by."

"Can't imagine that would be pretty," Bill replies. "Jeff was never a fan of moral gray areas, except when they applied to him. He ain't around anymore?"

"I don't know," Sean answers. He pulls the Bel Air's keys from his pocket and runs his fingertip over the familiar grooves. "Two years ago, he bailed on me. Came back here to wait because I didn't know where to look or if he wanted to be found."

"What about your little brother? Danny?"

"Foster care in Ohio. Gonna try to get up there if I can." Sean presses the rough edge of the key into his thumb until it smarts. "But I dunno. I got a better support system down here or whatever."

"Well, if you can tell your ass from tailpipe, and fix up that girl well enough, I'll see what I can do for you here." Bill returns Sean's money to a drawer and pulls a legal pad from a pile.

"Why?"

"Chad – who you'll meet once he returns to this plane of existence from whatever he gets up to on the weekend – is leaving in a few months. I'll need a new idiot to help me reach the high shelves."

"No, why me? I remember my dad from back then too. He wasn't the sort of guy I'd like enough to give his kid a job."

Bill shrugs. "Jesus loved the cripples and whores, figured we all gotta stick together. No one else is gonna watch out for us."

"Hey, I'm getting better. On both fronts." Bill waves Sean off with the pad of paper.

"You'll need this. Figure out what you need and start checking the inventory. I got work to do. And fill up Taylor's water bowl. If you don't mind company and drool on your pants, you can let her off the chain."

Sean blinks. "Taylor? As in Swift?"

"Named after the greatest artist of our generation, you got a problem with it?"

Sean shakes his head. He's starting to like Bill.

cameron

"Okay, people, huddle up."

Cameron and Lee look up from their sandwich station to see Drew standing alone on the scuffed linoleum of the basement floor. Hesitantly, they wipe their hands and join him, which is enough of a signal for others to follow suit.

"Great, thank you," Drew says. He tries to clap his hands together and fails thanks to the pens and index cards he's holding. "So, today I have a new assignment for you."

"Another?" Isaacs rumbles from the outskirts of the circle, arms crossed.

"Yes. Another. And, spoiler, there'll be one next week too," Drew replies. Both Isaacs and Jeremiah objected vocally to last week's homework of learning the names and stories of at least four people on their rounds. Cameron appreciated Drew encouraging more involvement, but both Isaacs and Lee's cousin expressed quiet outrage that the goal was to get to know the poor, not minister to them. Cameron is relieved he's returned to Chicago to finish up his affairs. "What I'd like is for you to speak to the people you meet, hopefully some of the ones you contacted last week, and ask specifically what they need the most."

"It's always socks and underwear," Lee answers bluntly, but takes a card.

"Who is going to pay for that?" Isaacs asks, voice dripping with doubt.

"I assumed you all were open to making some contributions," Drew says, shaky. "Sandwiches are nice but, uh, remember what Jesus said about rich guys and camels, and sewing supplies."

"The eye of a needle was actually a small door in a city gate, but his point that wealth shouldn't be hoarded is still clear," Cam states and gets several affronted looks. He sighs. "Or we could do a fundraiser to pay for it. Spread the cost among the congregation. Maybe at the fall harvest gathering in a few weeks."

"That is a great idea! Halloween is perfect timing." Drew crows, and Cameron knows in his soul that he'll be stuck organizing it. "So with that in mind, everyone take some cards and let's get to work." Of course, getting to work means that Drew joins Cameron and Lee with an expectant smile minutes later. "Great work, Cam. Eron. Thank you."

"Cam is fine," he sighs as he hands Drew some baggies. "Don't call it Halloween, by the way."

"Seriously?" Drew balks. "Because it's pagan?"

"It's Satanic," Lee corrects, but there's no conviction in it, much to Cam's surprise. "Or that's the understanding in our community."

"According to folks like your cousin?" Drew mutters, and Lee gives him an arch look. "Sorry. Jeremiah just really—"

"He comes on strong," Cameron finishes for him.

"He does. I'm sorry," Lee says. "We don't agree on many things. I actually don't think Halloween is dangerous."

"What about me? You know he wrote a letter of concern to Osborn," Drew shoots back, and Lee shakes her head. "Didn't think I was taking a hard enough stance on *deviancy*. Friggin' douchebag, telling people they're *abominations*." Drew takes a tense breath. "Sorry. I know you guys probably think he's not wrong, and I get it if you want to report me too, but I don't think he's the model Christian."

"He had a friend in college," Lee says, stiffly, her eyes downcast. "Their name was Kevin. Then she changed it - and other things about herself. She was... well, it ended badly. He thinks he's saving people from a fate like hers."

Cameron shivers at the thought. That's the kind of horror story about certain 'lifestyles' he hears all the time from his family and from the pulpit. It's somewhat amazing that Drew looks appalled and isn't giving the knowing nod others might.

"That's awful, and I'm sorry for his friend. Maybe if she'd had less bigoted people around or someone saying she wasn't an affront to God, it could have been better," Drew says.

"Do you really think that?" Lee asks, tilting her head curiously at Drew.

"*Yes.*"

Cam is quiet, glancing to where Isaacs lurks across the room. He knew Drew was progressive, but not like this, and he feels a target forming on his back by association. What if someone – that ever-present *someone* – hears this conversation? The thought sends acid surging into Cameron's throat, searing and sour. How would people look at him if they knew that two nights ago, he spent an obscene amount of time worshiping another man's naked body in several rooms of the house he shares with his wife? Or that the next night he failed to copulate with said wife because he's upset his lover is leaving.

He keeps things detached and professional as he works with Lee and Drew. They separate at the camp, as Cameron makes his weekly check with Lyle, who's back in his old spot. He, like most of the people Cameron talks to, asks for a new tent and sleeping bag for the coming winter, as well as socks.

"How's Sean doin'?" Lyle asks, voice steady for once.

"He's well," Cameron replies, smiling reflexively.

"Your little cocksucking friend still up and kicking?" A man across the way asks with a grimy sneer, and Cameron freezes. "Thought some good Samaritan fucked him up."

"Shut up, you don't know what you're talking about, private," Lyle spits. He looks back at Cameron apologetically. "Don't worry. That ain't Sean. It was some other kid. Came in here all bloody and moaning about some fucker callin' him a fag. I gave him one of your sandwiches. Straightened him right up."

"That was very kind of you, Lyle," Cameron says slowly.

"You don't need to worry. Sean does some stupid things, but he knows his daddy would kill him if he sold himself."

Cameron nods, his insides roiling.

"He's a good boy."

"He is." Lyle smiles, and Cameron retreats too quickly, avoiding the eyes of the rest of the camp. He doesn't want to get sick here.

"Everything okay?"

Cameron turns to see Drew looking worried and unhelpful. "It's fine," Cameron says, unconvincing.

"Are you sure? Because, if you need to talk, I'm here."

Cameron considers it. He doesn't know what to do, and everything about what Drew has said and done since they've met makes him think this man might actually show understanding. But what would be the use of understanding from someone so far from God?

"It's fine. I'm fine," he repeats. He turns and starts the walk back to the mission. He's not sure if Lee and Drew are following, and he can't care.

Tomorrow is October. He can feel the chill of it creeping into the air, the threat of rain like the world holding its breath before the storm begins.

sean

"I got a pie for dessert."

Sean looks up at Kayla from where he's distributing produce in the fridge. "An entire pie?"

Kayla's smile looks forced, like the pie is an apology for something Sean doesn't know about yet. "I figure I owe you since you're making dinner."

"You bought the food, I think that evens out."

"Maybe I wanted to suck up to you."

Sean turns. "Why?"

"Did you tell Cam your plans?" Kayla crosses her arms and leans on the counter. It makes her look small and vulnerable.

"Uh, yeah. Did he say something?"

"No, but I know you keep talking about when you're going to leave, but—"

This is the conversation he's been dreading. Kayla wants to know when he's going to book it. "Once I get some cash I'll—"

"I think you should make a firm plan to stay through the holidays. At least," Kayala says firmly, and Sean's brain melts.

"*What?*"

"I know you want to get moving, but you have this new thing with Mr. Farnell, and we won't be able to get your license for a few weeks." Kayla shakes her head. "You shouldn't be alone somewhere strange at the holidays. It's not right."

Sean can only stare. That's at least three more months in this house with Cam right there, and that might kill both of them. "Kayla…"

"We need you here." Kayla looks away when she says it, so it makes even less sense.

"You what?"

"Things are better with you here. It's more of a home and… It's better." Sean wants to laugh because it's not like he's actively involved in Kayla's husband cheating on her under her nose or anything.

"I gotta think about it," Sean says dumbly.

"Of course." Kayla looks pleased, like she's already got a yes. Before Sean can make more weak-ass arguments, the garage door rumbles open. Cam enters a moment later, the same grim expression as usual on his face. Unlike usual, it doesn't lift when he sees Sean.

"Hey, babe, we were just talking about you," Kayla says with a grin.

"Why?"

"Wondering where you were," Sean says, picking up the lie. "Bit late for you to get home."

"We had a longer debrief than usual," Cam sighs, shoulders heavy. "I've been press-ganged into helping organize a fundraiser for the mission."

"Let me guess, you had a bright idea and ended up doing all the work to make it happen?" Sean tries, and Cam finally cracks a tired smile. "Knew it."

"Do you want to help?" Cam asks. "We have lists of supplies to focus on, but your input would be helpful."

"Sure. I gotta look at your wife's stupid car first. Again."

"It's *fine*," Kayla groans

"You said the check engine light has been on for five days," Sean argues.

"When was the last time you got an oil change?" Cam adds.

"I don't know, Easter?"

Sean grimaces. "Not *too* bad."

"Last year."

"And they won't let *me* drive a car." Sean shakes his head. "Come on, Cam."

"Why me?" Cam asks, squinting.

"Because this is what men do. We go into the garage, make noise, and fix things. Move it." Kayla's giggle doesn't cover up Cam's powerful sigh.

"See, you're indispensable," Kayla smiles and squeezes his shoulder as he passes by her. Kayla's hand is warm and feels *wrong*.

Sean waits until he's out of the house, the garage door closed behind them, to touch Cam to balance it out. Just a brush of his hand on the small of Cam's back. It's grounding, calming. Cool water on a hot day.

"Everything else okay?" Sean asks as Cam looks fondly in his direction. "No problems downtown?"

"Not really. Anything interesting here while I was gone?"

"Not really."

cameron

"So what's with the new schedule?"

Cameron looks up from putting on his coat to see Flor staring at him, her dark eyes (lined in vivid blue shadow) calculating. "I don't know what you mean."

"You're not so Johnny on the dot lately, and you're actually leaving *early* today." Flor drums her long, pointed nails on her desk. They have little jewels and skulls on them today.

"What's wrong with that? You're leaving early."

"I'm a shitty employee, and you know that." Flor puts on her jacket with a smirk and follows Cameron out the door.

"Sometimes I like to get out early. That's my business."

"You're up and down so much lately, I'm worried," Flor presses on. "What's tying you in knots? Tu familia culera or your uptight wife? Or are things getting weird with the house guest?"

"How many times do I have to tell people I'm fine before they believe me?" Cameron growls and pushes out the door into the October air.

"Saying something over and over again doesn't make it true!" Flor snaps as she rushes after him. "Cam, I'm your friend. I just want to help."

"I assure you it's under control."

"Are you sure?" Flor asks, low and doubtful. "If you need me, I'm—"

"Here if I want to talk. Yes. Join the line." Cameron scowls as he gets in the car and scowls the entire ride home. The sight of the empty garage pops the anger pressing in Cameron's chest like a balloon.

It's Thursday. He left work early because he was coming home to Sean. Walking into his house from a day at work used to feel like moving from one prison to another. Not now. Not when he walks into the smell of spices and the sound of rock and roll coming from the tiny speakers of Sean's laptop. Sean's swaying and singing along to 'Faithfully' by Journey as he stirs a skillet, and it makes Cam so happy for one incandescent second that tears spring to his eyes.

Home. He's home.

He breathes and gets a hold of himself, laughing as Sean leans back to howl the crescendo of the song, then jumps when he sees Cam there.

"Jesus, Cam! That's creepy."

"I didn't know you could sing," Cam replies. "You have a nice voice."

"Usually need a few beers in me to really get going." Sean shrugs and turns his concentration to the food. Maybe the blush on his cheeks is from the heat of the stove, but Cam doubts it.

Cam hangs his coat, drifts into Sean's space, and makes a show of looking over Sean's shoulder into the skillet of sausage and peppers before pressing a soft kiss to the back of Sean's neck. "I like listening to you."

He feels Sean shiver as he whispers in his ear, his lips barely grazing the lobe as he does. "Definitely creepy."

"This looks good." Cam leans against Sean before grabbing a slice of browning sausage from the pan and popping it into his mouth over Sean's protests.

"It's chicken sausage, which is stupid because sausage should be pig, but it's still pretty tasty. Hey!" Sean swats at Cam's hand with his spoon. "Give me two minutes and I'll have it on an actual plate for you! Go get us drinks or something, you barbarian."

"You just called chicken sausage stupid, and *I'm* the barbarian?"

"Shut up or I don't feed you at all."

Dinner is easy. Talking. Laughing. Just being together. They talk about Sean's second week at Bill's. He's made decent progress on repairing the Bel Air's motor and thinks she might even start sometime soon. He had to find or order new parts, and somehow that turned into doing a full inventory check for Bill with the help of the other 'employee' at Farnell Salvage, a constantly high computer whiz named Chad.

"It sounds like you're getting back enough strength to start on the body soon," Cam says, poking at the few remaining bits of rice on his plate.

"Yeah, soon I won't need to carpool. If everything goes okay at the DMV tomorrow."

"I like driving you," Cam says quietly to his plate.

"Yet you still keep saying no to pulling over and fooling around."

Cam's cheeks heat. "I only say no because we would never make it to work if I did, and that would be unproductive in the long term."

"So, speaking of, uh, terms. Kayla asked me to stay through the holidays."

"*What?*" Cam's glad he wasn't eating because he would have probably choked.

"Okay, guess she didn't clear that with you." Sean shakes his head and blows out a breath. "Great communication you two got going."

"When did she suggest this?" Cam asks, dumbfounded.

"Saturday?" Sean grimaces, shoulders high and voice unsteady. "Don't be pissed! I wanted to talk about it with you alone. When we had time. Also, Bill's got my money. I've been trying to figure out when to tell you that too."

"Are you going to use it?" Cam tries to keep his mind from racing, but he *can't*. He feels like he's on a rollercoaster, losing Sean and getting him back over and over in his mind.

"I dunno, man. I told you, it feels wrong." Sean drops his head into his hands. "I don't know what to do. This whole thing is so far past complicated I can't even see straight."

"Is it?"

"What?" Sean looks up at him.

"Is it complicated? You have money and several good reasons to leave town."

"I got several good reasons to stay too," Sean replies, something offended and hurt in his eyes. "And I ain't talking about the job or Kayla asking me to."

"Are you asking what I want?" That doesn't make sense. Sean has no obligation to make any choices based on Cam's happiness.

"Of course I am, dillweed. You're sorta complication number one."

Cam looks at his plate in shame. "I don't mean to be."

"Too bad. I wanna know what you want me to do." Cam shakes his head. Sean climbs off his stool at the counter and crosses the few inches that separate them, forcing Cam to turn and look at him as he wedges himself between Cam's legs. "I know you've got an opinion."

"It would be unfair of me to complicate things more," Cam whispers tightly.

"What the hell does that mean?" Sean's eyes are bright, searching his.

"Sean, you know I want you to stay. Here. As long as possible, but that's not what's best. For anyone."

"Workin' fine so far," Sean says, running a knuckle up Cam's shirt, grazing the buttons one by one. "I don't see why you're so afraid of having what you want."

"You know exactly why."

Sean nudges Cam's head up and kisses him, molasses-slow and sweet. It's an effective way of derailing the discussion and avoiding a fight, so Cam is happy to let it happen. Sean moves him, positioning him so that the counter digs into Cam's back as Sean presses against him, the granite cold through his shirt. Sean is warm though, stoking an answering heat in Cam that he's been fighting down since the last time they touched.

"Your room," Cam breathes, and Sean pulls back from him with a nod. It's a simple thing, following Sean into the privacy of his room, kissing every second they can while divesting each other of clothes. It's a routine by now: the door shutting behind them, the soft sound of someone, Sean this time, sinking to their knees. But every time it's still heaven; still intoxicating and hot and *his*.

"Hey there," Sean purrs, and Cam honestly doesn't know if he's speaking to him or some specific part of Cam's anatomy. The kisses on his thighs and the pleased noise Sean makes as he nuzzles Cam's erection would point to the latter. Cam makes an inarticulate noise – something between a 'yes' and a groan – as Sean takes him into his mouth and hand. He's slow and teasing, but the diligent attention of Sean's tongue has Cam panting and his legs shaking in minutes.

"Get up. I – bed," Cam pants. Sean jumps to comply. They practically fall to the mattress, Sean making a strangled sound as Cam ruts on top of him.

"Are you alright?" Cam demands, springing back and taking his weight off the bewildered man below him.

"Hell yes. That was a happy noise." Sean looks down at Cam's hand on his hip. "Oh, *that*. I think I'm good." Sean experimentally pulls Cam back down, wrapping one leg behind Cam's thigh. "I think I'm very good." Sean kisses his throat as they grind together.

"Can we—" Cam starts to ask it before he can even think, the thought of being inside Sean again wiping out every last trace of caution.

"Hell yeah," Sean says before Cam can apologize. "Finally get to use your birthday present like the Lord intended."

"Let's not bring him into this, please," Cam murmurs, kissing Sean's side as he leans over to retrieve the lube from the nightstand.

"Fine. Let's bring you into—"

He kisses Sean to shut him up, but he laughs anyway. This is different, not only from the last time they fucked, but from every time before. There's warmth behind it, a bubbling sense of joy that's both alien and welcoming. They snicker when they get caught in the covers, and the sound Sean makes when Cam first teases his hole with a lubed finger is different, real and raw, not a hint of performance. Sean arches back with his eyes fluttering closed, throat working, and sweat on his brow; utterly vulnerable. Sean's been with more people than he can count, but this? Only Cam gets to see *this*.

"God, I missed you," Sean says, voice breaking, as Cam slides a finger deeper past the tight ring of muscle.

"You're tense," Cam whispers, resting his forehead against Sean's.

"So relax me."

Cam obeys, licking at Sean's collarbone, then down to his nipple. Sean whimpers at the attention, and Cam pumps inside him, until his tension starts to uncoil. Only then does he add one more finger, savoring Sean's sigh as he does. It's easier from there. He works Sean open, teasing until neither of them can wait any longer.

"Cam, please," Sean breathes, all pretense of bravado gone, his eyes half-lidded and dark. "Please."

"Are you sure?"

"Yes. We're clear. Come on." Cam withdraws his fingers and fumbles for the lube, surprised to find his hands shaking. "Hey." Sean sets a hand on his face. "Are *you* okay?"

"Yes. I just never thought…" Something tightens in his chest that he wants to ignore. "Never thought I'd have this again."

"It's all yours," Sean smiles.

Cam takes a steadying breath and slicks himself up. It's colder without the condom, slippery and smooth. He's so caught off guard by the sensation that Sean's hand joining his is a surprise. It's welcome, a familiar echo of their first times together as Sean guides him.

It's not the same at all when he pushes into Sean. Surrounded by tight, gripping heat with nothing between them, Cam moans as he slides home. There's nothing but this: Sean beneath him and around him, kissing him as Cam starts to move. Breath and the rustle of sheets fill the silence, the scent of sweat tinging the air. Sean keens when Cam gets a hand on his cock and jerks him in time with his thrusts, keeping the rhythm steady even as the pleasure begins to crest inside him. He's unhurried, falling apart along with Sean in slow motion, like ice around them steadily melting away. He knows Sean's signals, the catch in his breath, and the tension in his thighs when he's close. Only then does Cam speed up, chasing that pinnacle along with the lover beneath him.

Sean comes, spilling over Cam's fist with his mouth in a silent O. Cam follows him seconds later, hips stuttering as the release bursts inside him and the lights of a supernova dance behind his eyes.

He returns to reality to see Sean smiling up at him. "Happy birthday," Sean murmurs with a hand through Cam's hair.

Cam laughs as he pulls back. "I'll be right back." His legs are wobbly, but the walk to the bathroom and back with a wet cloth isn't too hard. Sean takes it gratefully, cleaning up then tossing the washcloth back over Cam and through the bathroom door where it lands with a splat on the tile. "Very sanitary. Please don't slip on that and break anything else. I like having you in one piece."

"No guarantees," Sean smirks as they settle under the sheets. Sean props himself up on one elbow and regards Cam thoughtfully. "So. Real talk. Why do you hate your birthday?"

"*That's* what you want to talk about?"

"Better than the weather."

Cam sighs and looks at the ceiling, the afterglow still warm around him. He doesn't want to drive it away talking about this, but maybe it's the only time and place he can. "You won't like it."

"Did your nutso family do something back in the day? Or does the church say birthdays are evil?" Sean looks so smug and satisfied with himself that it's comical.

"Nothing like that. I…" Cam shakes his head. "Each birthday is a reminder I'm one year closer to death."

"Holy shit, morbid much?"

"I told you you wouldn't like it."

He turns his head on the pillow to see Sean staring at him, trying to figure him out. "It makes me think of how much time I've wasted and how little time I have before I go…" The words dry in his throat, fear as old as memory whispering inside him.

"To hell," Sean finishes for him. Cam shivers and nods, trying not to imagine the fire or void that awaits. "You really think you're headed that way?"

"I'm a sinner. I haven't had the strength to change or resist."

"I thought the whole Jesus gig was that if you accept him or whatever, you're saved," Sean asks innocently. "Don't you get last rites or something?"

"Wrong church," Cam sighs. "It can't be that easy. God's laws have to matter, don't they?"

"Like the love thy neighbor thing, not stupid ones about where you stick your junk." Cam shakes his head. He's had this debate with himself so many times. "Hey. Look at me." Sean palms his cheek, forcing Cam to meet his eyes.

"I know you don't think I need to be fixed, but–"

"Not just that. Listen," Sean's green eyes are alight with conviction. "I don't even know if there *is* a God, but if he'd send you to hell for living the way he made you, he's a fucking asshole."

Cam laughs at the same time tears sting his eyes. "*God* is an asshole?" he asks, covering the hand of the impossible man next to him with his own.

"Fucking yes if he sends good people downstairs because of who they fuck or how they pray or whatever."

I love you.

The thought comes so clearly and with such certainty that Cam nearly says it aloud. He keeps it inside, thanks to some shred of self-preservation and reason, as a breath that could have held the secret whispers from his lips. It's not a revelation. He knows that. It's been there, steady and true, for a very long time. He'd just been too much of a fool to see his feelings for what they were; too caught up in the tangles of his other sins. He loves Sean, entirely and unquestioningly. It changes very little, to know it, but it's important even so.

"It still scares me," Cam says softly, turning on his side to curl closer to Sean.

"It's okay to be scared. Everyone's afraid of dying."

"I'm less afraid when I'm with you." It's not the same as admitting love, but it's close. Sean knows it means more, if the gentle look in his eyes is any indication, or his tender, seeking kiss.

"Me too," Sean says when they part, barely above a whisper.

"I don't want you to leave," Cam blurts out. "I know I have no right to ask you, but I want you to stay. Please stay. As long as you can."

"Cam, I…"

"You don't have to answer now. Just take it into consideration when you decide." He feels himself retreating, and Sean stops him, kissing him again and holding him close. It's a comforting kiss, not seeking to build into something more. Knowing there's love behind it, at least on one side, should make it feel like less of a sin, Cam thinks, but the change is negligible. It always felt like this: something gentle. Something good.

Something holy.

sean

Sean says yes the next morning.

It's simple. Muttered through a kiss over their morning coffee, like none of it is a crime. It was impossible to consider when Kayla asked. Unthinkable even. Cam though… Cam he can't say no to. The same way Cam can't say no to him when he presses their lips together with Kayla asleep upstairs. It's a cycle of addiction and bad decisions now, and even though Sean can see it, he won't pull away. He's never been good at self-denial, and that's a problem for next year's Sean. Right now, he can make Cam happy. He can make Kayla happy. And hell, *he's* happy when he's with Cam too, in his way. That sad, aching sort of happy that hurts as much as it helps.

God gives him two weeks of happy. Of peace and routine. Days under the Bel Air's hood and sneaking swigs of Bill's liquor. Dinners and *Serial Monsters*. Walks with Wanda and a brand new driver's license that he doesn't use much because he likes the ride with Cam, for the company and conversations, and for the kisses they start to sneak before they turn past Bill's gate. It's a taste of the heat when Cam is with him, hot and fierce, on those stolen nights together, once a week. Two weeks of something like normal, like the eye of a storm.

The call comes an hour after Cam leaves on a Friday in late October. Kayla's still asleep, and Sean's heart stops when he sees an Ohio is the source.

"Hello?"

"Hello, Mr. Lockwood?"

"Yeah?" He doesn't recognize the voice.

"This is Anthony Gardner, I'm your brother Danny's social worker."

"Is he okay?" Fear rushes through Sean, more intense than anything he's ever felt. If something happened to Danny and he wasn't there…

"I'm fine, Sean." Sean starts at the sound of Danny's voice.

"Danny, what's going on?"

"I don't know. Anthony took me out of school and said he needed to talk to both of us," Danny says. It sounds like they're on a speaker phone together somewhere.

"I'm very sorry to do this in this way, but I wanted to tell you both at the same time. I've just been in touch with law enforcement in Iowa. They've identified a body as your father. He's dead."

21

sunsets

cameron

CAMERON'S HEART IS RACING when he parks at home. Kayla's text had been cryptic at best: "canceling date tonight, come home early if you can." He tells himself that if he and Sean had been discovered, Kayla would be less casual, but he's still on the edge of being violently sick as he enters the house. Kayla jumps up from her spot in front of her easel when he comes in. She's painting, which means she's emotional, but she doesn't look angry or hurt.

"What's going on?" Cameron asks as Kayla wipes her hands.

"It's Sean. He… It's his information to share with you." This does nothing to calm Cameron down. "He's out in the back."

It's not summer anymore, and all the leaves are either on the ground or fading. There's a chill in the air when Cam steps onto the porch that makes him glad that his coat is still on. Sean isn't wearing a jacket, only a flannel over-shirt. He's sitting on his favorite lounger at the edge of the porch, back to Cam, shoulders hunched, and eyes fixed on the overcast sky.

"Sean?"

Sean doesn't move as Cam pulls a chair beside him. "Hey, Cam. What're you doing home?"

"Kayla said I should come home early. She didn't tell me—"

"My dad's dead."

Cam doesn't know what he was expecting, but it wasn't that. "Sean, I'm sorry."

"Why're you sorry? You never met him." Sean's voice is brittle, a complete contrast to the warm tones Cam enjoyed last night when they were tangled in bed.

"I'm still sorry for you," Cam tries again. Sean still won't look at him.

"What? For my *loss*? The bastard's been dead to me for two years."

"That doesn't mean you stop caring."

Finally, he turns to Cam, but it's a glare. "Lay off, Cam, I don't need therapy. You're worse than Kayla."

"Kayla's been through this; she might have insight." He remembers Kayla's bursts of anger after her adoptive father's death, the way she shut everyone out for days. The loss of her mother had been worse and easier. The grief had been more familiar, yet more profound for the space the loss left in both their lives.

"Yeah, yeah. Insight. She tried to tell me he was in a better fucking place. That he was at *peace*." Sean snarls the word and looks back at the clouds.

"Most people find that comforting."

"Then they're idiots." Cam waits as Sean flexes his hands and breathes. "Your people don't believe my dad's at peace. He wasn't saved, remember? He didn't deserve to be. My dad died in a truck stop bathroom in Iowa. He was dead for hours before a damn janitor found him and called the cops. The needle was still in his arm, so that made the cause of death pretty easy to figure out."

"You never said anything about drugs."

"Yeah, well, guess he took going off the rails pretty serious." Sean shakes his head, the unshed tears in his eyes catching the evening light. "He died alone, shoving poison in his veins at the end of a life full of booze and bad decisions. There ain't no peace for people like him."

"I'm sorry," Cam repeats. This time, it isn't an automatic platitude; it's sincere regret for the pain that radiates from Sean. For a long while, there's no sound but the crickets and the distant murmur of traffic.

"He died alone," Sean whispers.

Cam doesn't know what to say to that. There's nothing that can make it better, and maybe that's the point. He can't erase this grief. All he can do is be present, watching helplessly as someone he loves suffers.

They sit together in silence as the sun sets, the chill rising as the sky deepens from pink to navy. Eventually, the door opens, and Kayla approaches behind them.

"I got dinner from the Thai place," she says softly. "Including the sticky rice."

"Thanks, I…" Sean starts and then bites his lip, looking at Cam. He sees the moment Sean's mask settles back on him, a smirk on his face that doesn't reach his eyes. "We sure that won't kill this one?"

"I asked them to make it mild," Kayla says. "And he's been doing okay." Cam's stomach has indeed been calm lately, something he attributes entirely to Sean, rather than his diet. Kayla doesn't need to know that.

"I'll be fine, come on," Cam says.

Dinner is quiet. Kayla asks about work, and Cam's answer bores even him. Kayla saves them from lingering on the topic by asking how the new season of *Serial Monsters* is. Luckily, they'd found some time last night to get out of bed and actually watch it, wrapped naked in Sean's sheets on the couch. It had been exceedingly pleasant, though the plotline involving a vampire king getting his PR manager pregnant was incredibly tiresome.

After dinner, they watch *Casablanca,* and Cameron spends most of the film stealing glances at Sean. His eyes remain fixed on the screen, but unfocused. Sean excuses himself quietly after, no different than any other night. Cam wishes he could follow Sean to his bed, hold him, and wake up next to him. Also, the same as other nights, but tonight the feeling is more pronounced.

"Hon?"

Cam looks up. He didn't even notice going upstairs into their room. Kayla is staring at him, her shirt off, and her eyes expectant as if she just asked a question. "I'm sorry. What?"

"I was saying I hope Sean is okay. What he's going through is pretty complicated."

"Oh. Yes. I can't imagine— Actually, I can." Cam shakes his head. "If my father were found dead, I think I would feel anger and guilt as well."

"You think he feels guilty?" Kayla asks, pulling off her jeans and tossing them into the hamper.

"Sean takes responsibility for everyone." Cam shrugs and heads to the bathroom to get ready for bed. He's not really tired, but he has a book to read, or he might watch the news if he feels particularly masochistic. He turns while brushing his teeth to see Kayla leaning against the bathroom door, changed into her sleep clothes.

"I think I'm gonna go to sleep, unless you want to..." Kayla raises her eyebrows and looks Cameron over. It takes him far too long to realize she means sex.

"Not tonight, if that's alright."

Kayla smiles, but doesn't move to her sink. Instead, she comes to Cameron, snakes her arms around his middle, and presses herself to his back. "Thinking about Sean's father – or when I have a bad case at work – just makes me so grateful for you."

"I'm not going to die, Kay," Cam mutters, skin crawling a bit. "Not tonight at least."

Kayla squeezes him tighter. "I don't know what I'd do without you, babe. Without us as a family."

"I know," Cameron whispers. It's all he can get out past the surge of guilt. He thinks about how he'd feel if Kayla were dead, and the first impulse is that he'd feel free, which is utterly horrible. She deserves a husband who doesn't think such awful things, but she loves him, and love is rarely logical. If it were, he certainly wouldn't have chosen to love a man with whom he has no future. He turns in Kayla's arms and kisses her forehead. "Let's get to bed."

He doesn't read. He watches mindless TV while Kayla falls asleep on him before rolling over. He turns off the screen to stare at the ceiling and go through his usual catalog of dread. It hasn't been as bad lately, but it's in full force tonight. Thoughts of death, of hell, God's judgment, and Sean's pain. Praying to God to save Sean. Memories of the night before and how he cried out as he came buried deep in Sean, such a contrast to the silence now.

At 12:04, his phone buzzes on his nightstand. It's a text. From Sean.

> **u awake?**

>> Yes.

>> Do you want to talk?

The little dots that indicate Sean is typing remain for a minute, long enough for Cam to get nervous before his phone buzzes again.

> **No**

Cam exhales. More words appear.

> **just wanted to know if you were there**

> **you know what I mean**

Cam smiles sadly at his phone.

>> I do.

>> I'm here.

sean

It takes Sean a second to realize the car has stopped. A second more to process that Cam's staring at him. He needs more coffee. He'll grab a mug of Bill's sludge before heading out to the yard. He has to check the paint job and buff up the chrome on the Bel Air if he can stand to look at her. Then Bill wanted him to take a look at an old Charger to see if it was worth restoring or should be gutted. Then he has to find Chad about the… what was it?

"Sean."

He looks up. Cam is still there. Right. He's still in Cam's car. They're parked on the dirt drive outside the main gate. Last time they were here, he got a hand job. Or was it Cam? Someone came, and they had a scare about staining the upholstery.

"*Sean.*"

Fuck.

"Sorry. I was…" He waves at his head like it explains everything. "Didn't sleep well." He hasn't really slept more than an hour at a stretch for the last three nights, but Cam doesn't need to know that.

"Are you sure you don't want to take the day off? You don't seem fully present."

"Like another day sitting on my ass is gonna make a difference."

"You've hardly been sitting on your ass."

"You'd know, you keep a good watch on it," Sean leers at Cam and gets a deepened frown in return. Cam isn't wrong. Sean threw himself into being useful all weekend. He fixed Wanda's gutters and oven, trimmed her trees and Kayla's roses, and made enough food for a week. Literally. Everyone has perfect little lunches to take to work, and Sean still wanted to set something on fire.

"Sean, please. Are you okay?"

No. Cam is gonna try and talk again, and Sean can't do that. Nothing has changed, and no matter what his smartass teenage brother says, getting his feelings out is not something he needs. It's not like Danny knows, since he doesn't even *care.* The kid wanted to talk about school and his fall dance, and not the fact that their dad wouldn't even have a funeral.

"I'm fine, how much do I have to say it?" Sean snaps.

"You know I said that to a friend recently," Cam says with a scowl." She, knowing that I was lying, said that saying something enough times doesn't make it real."

"Doing something until it's real is like your entire life philosophy," Sean shoots back, and Cam purses his lips in a thin line of anger and hurt. Good. "Did you stop us here for a chat or something else?"

"What?" Cam looks scandalized, which is frankly hysterical given the various ways Sean's learned to twist himself around a Toyota gear shift in the last weeks.

"What do you want? Hand or mouth?"

"I don't – I don't want anything," Cam says, the lines deepening between his brow. "I wanted to check on you."

"And I said I'm—" Cam glares at him. "*Good.* I'm cool and I don't need to be babied. So either you let me be useful to your closeted ass or I can go to work."

Cam stares at him, something inscrutable in his eyes. "Go to work, Sean. I'll see you later."

"Whatever."

Sean doesn't look back the whole time it takes to walk to Bill's door. Taylor whines at not getting her usual five minutes of scratches, and Sean stashes his stupid lunch in Bill's fridge and doesn't make any threat about buying Bill non-liquid food before slamming the fridge door. The old man is at his desk as usual.

"What crawled up your ass and died, princess?" Bill asks without looking up from his ancient laptop and the pile of papers next to it that only he understands.

"Shut up." Sean stomps towards the door.

"Oh, I'm sorry, was that offensive?"

"You need me to do anything before I start? Within limits. I ain't chasing another raccoon out of your basement."

Bill narrows his eyes. "I'm fine. Your supervisor ain't coming in today, so you're on your own with the Charger. I got some orders need goin' over while Chad's on the dark side of the moon."

"On it."

The door bangs shut on loose hinges behind Sean. Bill's house is falling apart worse than him, and it suddenly makes Sean furious. So he finds Bill's ancient toolbox first and fixes the door, then pounds a few fresh nails into the deck and fixes the loose board on the stairs. His phone keeps buzzing, so he leaves it on the deck.

He spends an hour with the Charger, then two more deciphering Chad's notes and scouring the yard for the parts on order. It's one of those rare, sunny October days where it's summer-warm but the light isn't quite the same. Sean sweats among the rusted skeletons of cars, piling parts into a cardboard box. It's monotonous, hard work, but wrenching the guts out from under creaking hoods feels as good as swinging a hammer. He avoids looking at the Bel Air the same way he pushed the box of pictures and shit from her trunk under his bed. He felt it in the room like a physical thing the last few nights, waiting for him. Today, Dad's old car feels the same: another ghost to run from.

A box of carburetors slipping off the rusted hood of a Pinto with a dull clatter jolts Sean from his thoughts. He stares at the mess, metal and wire smashed in the gravel. An hour's work lost because he was stuck in his own idiot head.

Knew you were useless.

Suddenly, the mess is a bowl of spaghetti shattered on the floor, and Dad is yelling, and Danny is screaming because he's hungry. Dad spent hard-earned money on that damn dinner, and Sean ruined it like he ruined the job the week before, when he ran when he should have been on the lookout for cops and…

What fucking use are you?

The crash of the Pinto's window shattering under Sean's fist echoes through the yard. He looks down at his hand, red blood from his knuckles glistening vividly in the sun. It doesn't hurt yet. It's that moment of shock before the pain really hits, and all Sean can think is how bright his blood looks in the autumn light.

Taylor barks in the distance, and the pain shoots up Sean's arm like a shock. "Goddamnit."

"Glad you took it out on that piece of shit instead of your own ride." Sean looks up to see Bill, eyes glinting under his bushy brows. "You want a crowbar for the rest?"

"Sorry. I'll pay for it," Sean mutters, trying to hide his hand.

"It's a damn Pinto, you can do whatever you like to it. Set it on fire if it'll help you work through the grief or whatever. Can't think of a better way to honor the memory of a bastard like Jeff."

"How'd you—"

"Your man called. Said you weren't answering his texts and wanted to check that you were still alive."

Sean scrubs his face, and it makes his injured hand smart. "Jesus, Cam."

"Before you get your panties in a twist, I asked what was up with you, and he spilled. Sorry to hear it."

The 'sorry' makes Sean's blood boil. If he has to hear that word again, he's gonna start punching more windows. "You said it yourself. He was a bastard."

Bill shrugs. "Come on inside, let's get you patched up." He rolls away before Sean can protest, not paying Sean a second glance until they're back in the house. "First aid kit's in the bathroom."

"I can do this myself," Sean protests when he joins Bill in the main room with the ancient plastic box of bandages, swabs, and ointment. Looks like military surplus.

"I was a field medic. I know what I'm doing better than you."

"You were in the service?"

"Marines. Paid my way through college." Bill reaches into a cupboard and pulls out a bottle of whiskey, pops the cap, and hands it to Sean. "It's medicinal."

"Guess I'm off the clock." Sean takes a swig that hits him like a truck. "Jesus."

"Don't tell me you can't hold your liquor after all your clean living." Bill yanks Sean towards him, forcing him to sit and send up a puff of dust from the couch. He examines Sean's knuckles. "These ain't deep, you'll live."

"Hallelujah." Sean hisses as Bill dabs alcohol on the cuts, then takes another swig of the rotgut. "Cam tell you anything else?"

"Nope. Very respectful."

"Always a gentleman, that one."

"He's real worried about you though." Bill places a bandage on the worst of the cuts, eyes intent on his task and hands steady. "He didn't say so, but you can tell with those sincere types."

"Told him not to, I'm—"

"You ain't fine, boy." Sean looks up to see Bill's eyes boring into him. "A piece of your life just got yanked away without a damn warning. You're angry and you're hurting and you're acting a fool, but you ain't *fine*."

Sean stares at him, the whiskey slowly working through his veins. It's nice, so he takes another sip, then offers the bottle to Bill. He takes a pull without blinking, and Sean wonders how bad his liver is. "You should drink less."

"We're drinking to the dead; this don't count." Bill sets down the bottle anyway. "I know how you're feeling—"

"No, you—"

"My daddy was a mean drunk too."

Sean's mouth snaps closed. He thought Bill was talking about his wife.

"But unlike yours, he wasn't even decent when he was sober. He smacked my mom and me no matter what, just hit harder when he was on the bottle. He put a shotgun in his mouth when I was fourteen."

"Holy shit, I'm…" Sean stops himself before he says sorry. This isn't that kind of story.

"I found him. Out in the woodshed," Bill goes eyes, eyes clouding with memory. "And do you know what I felt? The feeling that was bigger than all the anger and hurt and fear? The thing you probably felt too when you heard?"

Sean takes a deep breath. This isn't a rhetorical question, but it feels so wrong to say it out loud. "Relieved."

"Damn right."

"I shouldn't feel happy that my father is dead," Sean protests, itching for more whiskey.

"Relief ain't the same as happy. And there ain't no should or shouldn't in this."

"Fuck, yes, there is!" Sean shouts, the words bouncing against the faded wallpaper. "I'm not a damn robot like Danny! I can't say I saw it coming and move on. I should be mourning or some bullshit, and I—"

"No one's sayin' you're not, son. I'm sayin' that it ain't *all* grief," Bill cuts in, gentler than Sean would expect from him. "That part'll come. Believe me. It'll come. Then it'll go. Then come back again."

Sean sinks back into the couch, and it creaks under his weight. "When do I stop blaming myself?"

Bill gives a hollow laugh and picks the bottle back up. "I'll let you know." He takes a long swig, and Sean wonders if he's seeing his wife's face when he closes his eyes to savor it. "Not that you're gonna listen, but it wasn't your fault."

"Thanks for saying it anyway."

Bil shakes his head and fingers the bottle in his hand. "Some people – they get broken. Or they're born that way, I dunno. But they spend their whole lives trying to find that somethin' that'll make 'em forget the pain. Or end it. Usually the same thing."

The image that Sean can't get out of his head for more than a few seconds comes back: his dad, dead on some dirty tile, eyes glassy, mouth slack. Needle in his arm. He pushes the thought away and grabs the bottle from Bill and tosses it so it shatters in the sink.

"What the hell was that for?" Bill squawks.

"I don't wanna see you chasing peace till it kills you either," Sean declares because, to his shock, it's true. "Like I said, you drink too much."

"Excuse me, this little chat was about setting you straight, not my issues."

For the first time in days, Sean smiles. "Ain't nothing straight about me, old man, thought you knew that."

"Moron," Bill grumbles. Sean shrugs. Maybe it's the booze, maybe it's the words, but he feels a little less like shit. "Now you're gonna have to get sober before you drive home."

"One of us is," Sean counters.

Bill wheels to his desk and fetches a few papers, then hands them to Sean. "No, you are." Sean has to blink a few times to understand what he's looking at. "Title to your ride. Registration too. All in your name."

Sean feels like an idiot that this, of all things in the last few days, hits him enough that the tears that have been trapped finally escape. "Bill…"

"She's all fixed up, and she's yours. I'm just hoping you don't use her to make a run for it. I've still got work for you, if you need it. You gotta fill out the shit at the bottom of the pile to make it all official."

"I won't," Sean says quietly, pushing moisture from his cheeks. "I mean, I won't bail."

"Good. Danny may be far off, but you got family here too now."

Sean wants to laugh at that, but it doesn't make it out of his throat. "Thanks, old man."

"Don't get too excited. This means I can officially fire your ass next time you bust a bottle of my liquor."

Sean shakes his head, overcome, because he knows Bill won't.

cameron

Cameron has to rub his eyes when he pulls up to his house, because the sight of a red car the size of a boat in front is so unexpected. But, no. It's really there, parked right on the street so conspicuously, he can see the letter from the homeowner's association right now.

Kayla's car isn't in the garage, which is odd for so late in the day, and the house is quiet when Cameron walks in. He checks his phone, and sure enough, there's a text from Kayla that must have come while he was driving.

> **Home late. Big accident on interstate. All hands on deck.**

> **Take all the time you need. We're fine here.**

He stows his phone and looks around. The porch is empty, but the door to Sean's room is ajar. Cameron still knocks gently before pushing it open.

Sean is seated on the edge of his bed, a cardboard box open in front of him, holding some pictures in his hand. "Hey."

"Hey."

"Kayla's going to be late. Are you hungry?"

"Not really." Sean finally looks up over his shoulder at Cam. "You gonna come in?"

"Are you done being a jackass?"

Sean rolls his eyes and scoots over on the bed, which means yes. Cam takes his place next to Sean, close enough that their legs brush and he can see the faded photographs in Sean's hand. "Sorry. For... you know," Sean mutters.

"You're grieving. It's okay." Cam nudges Sean's shoulder with his. "You got your car back."

"Don't worry, I already promised Bill I'm not gonna fuck off."

"Good." The burn in Cam's chest ebbs as he examines the picture Sean's holding, his thumb running absently over the edge. It's a family: A husband with dark hair and a wide grin next to a beautiful blonde wife. Between them is a young boy with a familiar smile holding a fat infant. "How old were you there?"

"Eight. And three quarters."

"Your hair was blonder then." He sees Sean's mouth tick upwards from the corner of his eye. "Like your mother's."

"Yeah."

"She was beautiful."

"She really was." Sean gives the slightest sniffle, which Cam courteously ignores. "When she died, I asked Dad where she went. She believed in it. Heaven and stuff. Talked about angels and saints and prayed to Mother Mary for peace and to protect us. Especially when Dad was drinking. I thought he'd tell me she was in that better place, but… That was the only time I ever saw him cry. Fucked with me more than anything else, seeing him break, knowing she was gone. Don't think he ever got better. I know I didn't."

It's sunset, and Sean hasn't turned the lights on, but the window is open. The room is suffused with fading golden light that takes the edge off the silence.

"I don't remember what my father looked like," Cam says, leaning closer to Sean.

"You don't have pictures?"

"Mom made them disappear, and I was too young to save any. I only have a vague notion of his appearance. Apparently somewhat like me, but not quite."

"Would you want to know? If he were dead?"

Cam has to think about that for a while. "I don't know. I used to think about that. Years ago. Usually, it would hurt more to imagine him with a whole other life. Some other family he chose over us. Kids. A nice wife."

"Or a husband."

Cam smiles at that. "The thought has crossed my mind that he left because he was… like me."

"That still ain't an excuse for abandoning your family."

"I know." Cam doesn't say that he wishes it were. He doesn't need to. "I wanted to believe he was taken, not that he chose to leave. Made missing him make more sense."

"Yeah. I feel that."

"Do you miss him?" Cam feels bad for never asking before.

"It's weird, knowing he's gone. Nothing about my stupid life has changed. I'm still pissed at him for all the shit he did. But I've missed my dad for a long time. Not the guy that ditched me or hit me, but the guy he was. The guy in these pictures died the same day as mom and now—"

"He's really gone and never coming home."

Sean nods, eyes slipping closed, and the first tears Cam has seen slipping down his cheek. "Fuck, man, I don't even know why I *care*. All I can think is that I don't even remember the last thing I said to him."

Cam doesn't think he's supposed to talk here, even if he knew what to say. So he takes Sean's hand and squeezes it tight. He doesn't remember it being like this with Kayla when she lost her parents. There were more tears. More prayers and words of comfort that they were safe in the arms of the Lord. Neither seems appropriate now.

When Sean tilts his head up and kisses him, that does feel right. It shouldn't. It's a terrible angle, and Sean is moist in all the wrong ways, but he can feel how Sean relaxes, the way something uncoils in him, and he melts into Cam when he wraps his arms around him.

Cam draws back and looks at Sean in the amber light. "You don't have to do anything for me, if that's what you're trying right now."

"It's not. This is for me." It's good to hear that aloud. Still, Cam hesitates, trying to read all he can from Sean's eyes as he runs a thumb over his cheek. "You're less scared with me. I hurt less with you."

Cam could tell him, he thinks. Tell him right now that he loves him. But it's not the moment for that. It never will be. It makes life too much of a tragedy to confess it, and Sean would take it as another burden. Another job to do and fulfill. Cam doesn't want that. He doesn't need Sean to know. All he can or should do is love him. So he kisses him softly without any expectation, until it's dark and someone's stomach rumbles with hunger.

"Come on," Cam says. "I'll make you a sandwich."

22

Harvest

sean

SEAN WAVES TO BILL as the Bel Air door closes with a satisfying creak. Settling into the worn leather is more comforting than slipping on his old coat or lying down in bed after a long day – mainly because his favorite coat is torn to shreds and stained with blood now, and his bed isn't really his. The point stands; nothing feels more like coming home. Well, almost nothing. Kissing Cam for the first time after days feels pretty damn good too.

He gets to do that tonight. The promise of it makes him smile like an idiot, but screw it, no one but God can see. For the first time in nearly a week, he doesn't feel like pounded shit. He put in a good day's work, and the weather is decent. He gets to drive home in *his* car. Some things are good.

Sean rolls down the window and enjoys the air as he drives home among the autumn leaves. It's still nice this time of year, before everything goes pale and barren with winter. He wonders idly what he can do for dinner. They still have the makings of some fancy salad thing Kayla was going to foist on Cam's family on Tuesday, but that torture got postponed because someone's kid was puking. Do they have chicken? He knows they have onions…

Sean's meal planning is cut short when he sees an unfamiliar Buick taking up his regular space. Sean pulls into the driveway instead and gets out to investigate – then freezes as the Buick door opens. Shit.

"Susan? I mean, Mrs. Steward?" Sean asks in horror as Cam's mother approaches, sizing up the Bel Air.

"No Mrs. Steward, Sean. Unless you'd like me to call you Mr. Lockwood."

"Please no."

"Then Susan is fine. Quite the machine you have here. This is the car you were living in?" She manages to make that sound like an insult and pity at the same time.

"Yeah. Home sweet home," Sean replies, summoning up every ounce of bravado to smile at her.

She smirks back. "Well, are you going to show me in? I seem to have misplaced my key."

"Uh, Cam isn't here yet..." Susan stares him down, since that much is obvious. "He didn't mention you'd be coming."

"Since we missed family night on Tuesday, I thought it would be nice to have it here tonight. It makes me so sad thinking about Cam sitting at home all alone while Kayla works into the wee hours."

"He's not home alone. He has me." Sean probably shouldn't say that, but judging by how Susan is already walking to the door, she doesn't care.

"Will you grab that bag from the back for me?" Susan calls, and Sean suppresses an eyeroll before obeying.

"So, is it just you?" Sean asks as he meets Susan at the door and digs for his keys while trying to keep her bag of groceries from falling.

"Oh no, Vincent and Luke will be joining us. It's been too long since I've had an evening with just me and my boys." Yeah. Sean is *not* invited.

"That oughta be nice. For everyone." Susan neither waits for Sean to follow her nor thanks him when he deposits the bag in the kitchen; she just starts unpacking like Sean isn't there. "I'm gonna go, uh, wash up." Sean ducks into his room and has his phone out with Cam dialed in no time.

"Sean?" Cam answers, concern in his voice. "Are you—"

"No. Red alert. Your *mom* is here for a surprise family dinner. Statler and Waldorf are on their way too."

"*What?*"

"Exactly."

"Shit."

"I'll try to keep her entertained or whatever, but…" Sean hears the sound of the fridge opening and cringes. He knows it's not *his* house, but he's been here longer than anywhere in the last few years, and he's territorial.

"I'm already in the car. I'll be there soon."

Sean glances at the time. "You left early."

"I *was* excited to get home."

Sean smiles despite himself. "Drive fast anyway."

"I will."

Sean washes the lingering grease from under his fingernails and changes into a clean shirt before returning to the kitchen to find Susan rummaging through the pantry.

"Can I help?" Sean asks, summoning his charm.

Susan finally looks up at him, eyes narrow. "Do you do a lot of cooking, Sean?"

Jesus, with that tone, might as well be asking if he likes it up the ass. Same answer either, at least. "Yeah, I do. I've been taking care of dinner a few nights a week lately. Gotta earn my keep somehow, right?"

"Somehow," Susan smirks. God, Sean hates these suburban ladies who can insult you to your face and make it sound like idle chit-chat.

"Saw you got some steak. I can go clean up the grill and get it hot." Sean grits out, determined to kill her with kindness.

"I was just going to broil them, thank you though." Sean looks over to the four (of course) steaks she has out and shakes his head. They're cheap cuts that will turn to shoe leather under a broiler.

"Can I get you something to drink then?"

"I was under the impression Kayla didn't allow alcohol in the house, due to the effect drink had on her father."

"I meant, like, tea."

Another pitying, annoyed look. "Sean, you're very polite, but one guest doesn't need to play host to another. I'm fine on my own if you'd like to go do whatever it is you usually do these evenings."

"I *usually* make dinner for Cam and hang out with him," he says, trying not to make it sound too intimate.

"Hm. I can't imagine you have much to talk about. Your backgrounds are so different, bless your heart."

Bless your heart. It's the cruelest and most devastating thing a woman from the South or anywhere adjacent can say, and she knows Sean knows it.

"Sometimes talking to someone of a different background is a good way to learn things. Expand your mind and such," Sean says with a tight smile. "We've got more in common than you'd think." He keeps the 'including how much we love dick' to himself.

"I do hope that he's continued sharing the gospel with you," Susan says, fixing Sean with her full attention. "Especially since your recent tragedy."

"My what?"

"Your father. Kayla told me on Sunday, when I asked why you still hadn't joined us at services."

"Services? I'm invited?" He tries not to laugh as he imagines getting hit by lightning the moment he walks in.

"Love of the Lord is what brought you into Cameron and Kayla's life, isn't it?" Susan says, and Sean's really proud of not laughing then. "Showing your devotion and joining the flock is the next step in the Lord's plan for you. It's only right."

"I don't know. I feel like I've already caused enough of a stir just being here." This is now the way Sean wanted to be screwed tonight.

"That's true." At least she doesn't sugarcoat things. "I lost a parent when I was close to your age. It was hard. I felt like there was no justice in the world when so many bad people kept on living, and she… Well, it's in the past. The church helped me. Even if I just felt less alone in my grief. It could help you too."

For one long, strange moment, Sean feels like Susan Steward is looking at him like another person in pain that she can relate to. It throws Sean off balance completely.

"Uh… I'll think about it."

"Good. I am very sorry for your loss." Those familiar, awful words snap Sean out of his stupor just in time for the doorbell. "I didn't hear that awful truck, so that must be Vincent."

"I'll go let him in." Sean's not sure if he's jumping into the fire or the frying pan. He opens the door to see not one but two Steward men waiting. Fire it is.

"Hi. Guys. Your mom is in the kitchen," Sean says, feeling sized up by both men. He does look a lot better than since they last saw him. "Cam is on his way."

"Mom's cooking? Great." Luke gives Vince a dubious look. "Maybe we got lost on the way here?"

"That bad?" Sean grimaces.

"Mom's a literal cook," Vince replies. "Mashed potatoes are just mashed potatoes. That's it."

"No butter?" Sean asks in horror

"Not even *salt*," Luke replies.

"Holy crap."

"Hey," Vince says, elbowing his brother. "Remember the time she put a canned ham in the oven *in the can?*"

"Or the pot roast that was just a roast in a pot with nothing else?" Luke adds, laughing.

"I can hear all of you. I'm not that old," Susan calls.

"How bad do you think she'll take it if I try to take over?" Sean asks under his breath.

"Don't risk it. Anyway, leaves room for dessert." Vince holds up a store-bought cake and smiles.

"And these," Luke says as he pushes a six-pack of beer into Sean's hands and heads inside, his brother following.

Sean looks out the door just in time to see the blessed sight of Cam's Corolla pulling up. "Thank God." Cam meets Sean's eyes with an apologetic frown the second he's out of the car. "Dude, you almost missed the party," Sean calls as Cam strides to the door.

"I am so sorry," Cam exhales. "She didn't say anything."

"It's fine. We'll talk after." Cam gives Sean *a look*. Who knows when after will be.

"Cameron, how many times am I going to have to tell your wife to buy you a new coat. That thing is ancient," Susan says as Sean and Cam return to the kitchen.

"He needs a damn pair of jeans before you get a new coat," Sean says before he can check himself and gets a withering glare from Susan. "You know, I'm just gonna go."

"No, please stay," Cam says instantly, which makes Sean feel a bit better. Especially when Susan says, "If that's what you feel is best," at the same time.

"Heck no, Sean, you're staying here. We'll make room for you," Vince says cheerfully.

"You can even have my steak," Luke adds with a shit-eating grin.

"Are you sure I can't help cook?" Sean offers one more time.

"Nah, come over and have a beer," Vince says.

"Sure," Sean says. Luke passes out warm cans of Heineken, and Sean's surprised to see Cam take one.

"So, Sean, how is the job search going?" Vince asks, clapping Sean on the shoulder in that overly-familiar, dad way. "If you're still in the market, we have an opening at the station in janitorial. It's rough, but it's a good start for a fellow like you."

Sean's not sure what kind of fellow Vince thinks he is. Nothing he could be thinking would be as bad as the truth, so he has no right to be offended. "Thanks, but I got a gig. Salvage yard, not too far off."

"Sean restored his own car. The one outside," Cam says with a proud smile.

"The Bel Air?" Luke asks, eyebrows high. "I was saying to Vince what a gorgeous car that was. Nice job."

Sean braces himself for the backhanded compliment or snide addition, but it doesn't come. "Thanks. I'm doing a few classes online to learn more about restoration and sh-stuff. Brushing up on the mechanic stuff too."

"I hear you have to practically be an engineer to work on the new cars, all computers," Vince says, and again, it's not mean. Just personable.

Sean nods enthusiastically. "Yeah. Lucky for me, Bill – the guy I'm working for – he only gets the old stuff so far, but I do want to learn the new technology."

"Another reason the classic cars are better," Luke says. "I don't want to worry about my car getting malware along with a flat tire."

"Hey," Vince nudges Cam. "Do you remember our first car?"

"Very fondly," Cam says with that warm smile Sean sees so rarely. "I think my shoulder is still recovering from using that gear shift."

"Wait, whose car was it?" Sean asks the brothers.

"Everyone's," Luke replies. "Where the heck did you find it, Vince? Some farmer had it for sale in his front yard, right?"

"Yup. For $600. This busted up old Ford truck," Vince grins.

"It had a family of raccoons living in the bed," Cam tells Sean.

"Hey, you wanted pets," Luke says.

"And I, enterprising teen that I was, thought it would be a great investment," Vince goes on.

"I don't hear any of you mentioning how furious I was," Susan calls from the kitchen, and the Steward men all smile and laugh.

"I drove that thing for a few years until Luke needed it, then Cam took the reins at the end."

"That thing could barely get me to school at that point," Cam remarks with the same fondness.

"Better than walking in the snow," Vince says.

"None of us ever had to worry about ladies making any untoward advances when we were driving *that* thing," Luke adds, and Sean smiles.

"Yeah, not sexy like your girl out there, Sean. Where'd you get her anyway?" Vince asks, looking over and taking a sip of beer.

Sean looks down, weirdly shy about being included in the conversation. "Uh, she was my dad's. He left her to me."

"Good to still have a piece of him, huh?" Luke says, and Sean's pretty sure it's sincere.

"Yeah. Yeah, it is," Sean replies quietly.

They chat about cars (everyone gives Cam a hard time for not buying American) and other inconsequential things until they're summoned to the table. Susan takes her place at the head, and Vince and Luke naturally fall into place together on one side, with Cam and Sean on the other. As promised, Luke donates his steak to Sean. It hits his plate with a disheartening clang, and Sean picks up his fork to give it a poke before Cam kicks him under the table. He looks up to see everyone's head bowed and hands clasped. He copies the posture as Susan takes a deep breath.

"Lord, thank you for this food and this company," Susan prays. "Thank you for this day when those we love are safe and whole. Please continue to give us patience, wisdom, and peace, through you and your son, Jesus Christ. Amen."

"Amen," everyone echoes, including Sean. The word feels alien on his tongue, but if he's gonna get to church with the fam, he might as well get used to it.

"So, how is Courtney? The first trimester is always the hardest," Susan asks as most of them start to saw their steaks. Cam slathers his in A1 first.

"She's well," Vince replies, and Sean starts to tune out the conversation. He finally gets a piece of meat cut and, yep, shoe leather. It takes him so long to chew that his jaw is sore when he finally swallows.

"...we're going to wait and be surprised on the gender," Vince is replying to Cam as Sean looks for the steak sauce.

"Are you sure? What if you don't have the correct clothes?" Susan asks in concern.

"We have plenty of baby clothes left from Meghan," Vince laughs.

"But they're *girls'* clothes," Susan argues.

"They're baby clothes, mother," Cam says.

"I don't want my possible grandson getting confused. That sort of thing can do lasting damage, you know."

Sean feels Cam tense beside him. He really wants to rub a soothing hand on his thigh, but that's not a good idea.

"We've got Jake's stuff in a box somewhere if that's the case," Luke offers.

"Guess we were both hoarding the baby clothes for this one, huh?" Vince smiles at Cam. "When are you two gonna get on that?"

If Cam was tense before, he pretty much turns to stone at that point. Sean casts him a look and finds him intent on his 'steak.'

"That's what I keep asking," Susan says, swallowing a dainty mouthful. "I imagine you don't want to add anyone else to your home while it's so crowded."

Sean grips his utensils tighter and stabs at the crime against cow-manity on his plate.

"We're certainly not ready now," Cam says. Sean wonders if Cam's family can hear the defensiveness in his voice. Cam straightens up minutely and looks directly at his mother. "We may never be ready."

"No one is ever truly ready for a child," Susan replies, simperingly sweet.

"Mother, I'm saying—"

"I know what you're saying, Cameron," Susan snaps, her voice suddenly cold. "But I also know you'll come to your senses eventually. Be fruitful and multiply. That's what God asks of us; it's very simple."

"We need to raise good children to fight the evils in this world," Luke agrees. "Especially with parents out there letting their kids grow up as homos or transwhatevers."

"Luke, please. Language," Susan sighs. "Though your point is well taken."

"I dunno, I can think of worse ways for kids to grow up," Sean says darkly. He's sure Cam is going to bust an ulcer if he keeps talking, but he's so damn furious he wants to beat Susan over the head with her shitty steak.

"Yeah, as democrats!" Luke guffaws. Susan and Vince both laugh politely. Cam deflates.

Sean keeps his mouth shut for the rest of the meal unless he's addressed, which doesn't happen much with Susan leading the conversation. It's a weird mix of normal chatter, brotherly ribbing, and blatant bigotry and misinformation that leaves Sean's head spinning. Everyone is finished pretty quickly, bits of meat tucked discreetly under vegetables to make it look like more has been consumed. Sean's the first to rise and take his and Cam's plates to the sink.

"Sean, you don't need to do that," Susan says, managing to sound polite and offended at the same time.

"No worries. Whoever cooked doesn't have to do dishes, it's like the 11th commandment," Sean says, and the joke lands like a stone. "You talk to your kids."

Susan nods, and she, Vince, and Luke retire to the couch as Cam gathers the rest of the plates for Sean.

"Thank you," Cam says quietly as Sean starts the water.

"It's no problem, Cam."

Cam catches his elbow, and Sean looks up into earnest blue eyes. "*Thank you*, Sean."

Sean nods. He doesn't want to say anything, not right now. He takes his time in the kitchen, first with the dishes and then making coffee, one cup at a time for him, Vince, and Cam. Luke and Susan turn it down, and Sean wonders if that's a religious thing until Luke explains he has to be up early, and Susan mentions a delicate stomach. Must be where Cam gets it. Sean and Cam, for their part, don't care about their stupid stomachs and intend to be up very late. The cake Vince brought is dry and too sweet, but Sean still puts back a huge slice because it's at least edible.

"Really, Sean?" Vince exclaims, and Sean looks up in panic from moving the crumbs on his plate, seeking Cam's help.

"I'm also glad you're interested in services, finally," Cam says slowly. Susan must have spilled that. Great.

"Your mom's really persuasive," Sean smiles back.

"Cameron says you've been helping with the planning for his little fundraiser at the carnival afterwards," Luke says.

"Just giving him ideas, mostly," Sean replies. "Should be a fun Halloween party."

"It's not a Halloween party, it's a harvest festival," Susan corrects as if he just suggested something heinous.

"Halloween is a pagan orgy that spreads the teachings of Satan to children. *This* is a celebration of family and the season," Luke adds.

Sean so wants to argue, but he's too tired and not suicidal. "As long as there's candy."

"It'll be great to see you around the congregation more," Vince says.

"I'm excited," Sean lies. Cam looks about as dubious as Sean feels, but nods along.

It feels like forever until Susan rises. "Well, I do think it's about time to get home. Most of us have busy days tomorrow." She gives Sean a glance with that one, and he has to fight not to roll his eyes.

"We *all* have busy days tomorrow," Cam says as he guides his family to the front door. His brothers pull him into manly, back-slapping hugs, then shake Sean's hand while Susan kisses Cam on the cheek.

"See you on Sunday, Sean," Susan says before heading out the door, like a threat.

The second Cam has the door locked behind his family, Sean slouches against the wall, sighing and rubbing his eyes. "Jesus fucking Ch—"

Cam cuts him off with a ferocious kiss. Sean melts, eyes falling closed again and letting Cam press him against the wall. Right when Sean's head starts spinning, Cam pulls back, resting against Sean and panting.

"Sorry, I just needed to—"

"Hey, you can spite kiss me all you want," Sean smiles, and Cam lets out a shaky laugh. "Just promise to spite fuck me too."

"Done."

Cam doesn't go easy on him, and that's fine. It reminds Sean of the desperation of the first times they were together, and he understands it more now. It's not just about want. It's rebellion. It's taking something – *one* thing – because Cam has nothing else. Sean probably shouldn't like that, but it makes him feel important to mean so much to someone – to Cam. Sean's the only one he's willing to rebel for, the only one

Cam wants to steal and take and hide. He'd never do this with anyone else. Sure, he gets horizontal with Kayla, but he never fucks her so hard the bed shakes, and he could never do this with another man. Sean can't even imagine that. He can't imagine *himself* with anyone else like this either. That's kind of insane, but he'll blame the mind-bending orgasm.

Cam collapses beside Sean on the bed, panting, beautiful, and wrecked. Sean grabs someone's pants to scrub the come off his stomach because this is too good to leave.

"Your family should come for dinner more often." Cam chuckles, eyes bright as he watches Sean from the pillow. "Thanksgiving's gonna be amazing. For me at least."

"God, that dinner was awful," Cam groans, raking his fingers through his hair.

"You know what's weird? It wasn't *all* awful." Cam looks at him curiously. "Like, half the time, they were decent humans. The way y'all were talking reminded me of Danny so much."

Cam gives him a sad smile. "You miss him."

"Like hell." Sean moves closer to Cam so that they're touching more. It would be considered snuggling by some, but Sean's okay with that.

Cam runs his hand through Sean's hair. "Sometimes I wish they would be terrible all the time. It would make it easier. I can't believe she convinced you to come to church."

"Yeah, well, I can help with your not-Halloween party thing after, it'll be fun. Or something."

"Or something. I have to warn you; our pastor is—"

"Boring?"

"An asshole."

Sean laughs, trailing his knuckles over Cam's biceps. "Sounds like that's going around in the congregation."

"It didn't used to be this way," Cam says, touching Sean's back, exploring and soft. "The pastor when I was younger was wonderful. He made me feel like God was there when no one else was. He knew my father, and he was the only one who would really talk about him when I asked. He always knew the right things to say about God's wisdom and forgiveness and plans. He made me feel better. Ted Osborn just makes me remember what a sinner I am."

"You're not a sinner," Sean says automatically, and Cam gives him an indulgent 'thanks for lying' look. "And at least old Ted sounds better than the fucko who beat me up." Sean shudders at the memory. It wasn't the pain that scared him most, but the unquestionable hatred in Jeremiah's eyes.

"That's a low bar." Cam grimaces. "The last time I saw our old pastor was at my wedding. He did it especially for Kayla and me since he was already retired. He told me my father would have been happy. I think he was lying."

Sean's heart breaks, thinking of Cam on that day. He doesn't need to ask about the wedding night; he knows it was a disaster. He wishes Cam's dad had been there to tell him not to do it.

"Speaking of daddy issues, when are we gonna listen to those records?"

Cam raises an interested eyebrow and looks over at the clock that recently made its way into Sean's room. "It's getting late."

"Not like we're going anywhere. And we had coffee."

Cam looks back at him and smiles, indulgent. "Okay. Come on."

They slip their boxers back on, and Cam leads them out of the room and to the staircase. Sean hesitates before mounting the stairs. It feels like crossing some final boundary, but it's the only way to follow Cam, so he keeps moving. The upstairs hall is smaller than Sean would have thought, but he figures that since the great room takes up two floors of space, that reduces what's left upstairs. There's a set of double doors he assumes lead to the bedroom, three normal doors, and a narrow linen closet.

"This one," Cam says, beckoning Sean away from the bedroom. "That's the second guest room we don't use, and this was supposed to be another office. We never got around to organizing it." Cam opens the door to the not-office and reveals a jumble of boxes and old furniture. "Most of this was from my first apartment. Kayla wanted nicer things, but I'm sentimental."

"Hoarder," Sean whispers, and Cam swats him gently.

"Here." Cam moves a few boxes to reveal one that looks older than the rest and kneels to open it. Sean joins him on the floor and pulls out the first album carefully.

"Bob Seger. Nice." It's actually sort of hard to make out all the details of the cover, besides Seger's epic mustache, since they haven't bothered to turn on the light. Cam pulls out *Sergeant Pepper's* then *Leftoverture* by Kansas. They thumb through dozens of albums, the scent of old paper and wax in the air. "Oh yes..."

"What?"

Sean grins as he pulls his prize from the box. He'd know Zepp II anywhere. "Go find your record player."

"It's over here." Cam clatters around until he has the player set up on the floor near them. Sean delicately removes the record from the sleeve and paper sheath and sets it on the turntable. It's been forever since he's played a record, but setting down the needle is still easy, and it's so satisfying when the first chords of "Whole Lotta Love" fill the room.

"You know this band?"

"You *don't?*" Sean balks.

"The voice sounds familiar."

"It's Zeppelin, man, come on." Cam shrugs. "Your dad was much cooler than you."

"Probably."

Sean settles back on the carpet. The music takes him back years, to the record player at their old house, to cassettes on long drives, even to Frankie Pennington's basement in high school. Sean grins at the memory and nudges Cam with his shoulder. "This is prime make-out music, you know."

"Is it now?"

"Hell yeah. When I was in high school, I'd put this on; Second base by the 5th track. Never fails."

"Our high school experiences were very different."

"Yeah, well, you graduated, so that's a given."

Cam gives a crooked smile. "I wish I'd known you. Back then."

"I was like ten when you were in high school, creep."

"You know what I mean," Cam says, butting Sean with his shoulder. His bare skin is cool and smooth, and Sean doesn't ever want the contact to stop, so he leans on Cam to prolong it. The song ends and fades into "What Is and What Should Never Be."

"Yeah. I know."

"I wish things were different," Cam whispers as Sean rests his head on his shoulder.

"Me too."

It's a weird thing to think about. Meeting Cam in some other life, where they weren't broken and screwed over by fate. Would they still be them, though, if they hadn't been put through God's ringer? Who's to say their lives in some other universe wouldn't be even more fucked up?

It could be worse, maybe, Sean thinks. They could never have met and or never have kissed, or left too much unsaid, but there are so many ways it could be better. They could be out and open and just together. Really together. That's a thing Sean's never even considered with anyone, especially with Cam, but the idea is suddenly so real it steals the air from his lungs.

"Are you alright?" Cam asks. Sean must have made some sort of sound that he didn't notice.

"Yeah, I'm fine just. The music just makes me think about stuff."

"Stuff?"

"Just, you and me, and if we could..." Sean swallows. They can't. "And, you know, my dad and shit. He loved this song." It's a good cover. Not really a lie because he *is* thinking about his dad. And Cam's dad and their moms and Danny and Kayla and all the people that they love and Cam's asshole God and everyone who makes being with Cam the stuff of dreams. It's a good dream, though.

"Can I do anything?" Cam never wants him to hurt. He always tries to make it better.

"Yeah, time for that make-out session."

Cam smiles, eyes glinting in the orange light from the streetlamp outside. "Alright."

Kissing Cam doesn't make it easier to keep the dream away, but it makes it hurt less to dream it, and that's good enough. Sean loves the way Cam kisses him, and for a little while, he decides to let go. There in the dark, with ghosts of the past and impossible futures hovering around them, he lets himself want it. Want everything. He kisses Cam and imagines a life they can't ever have, and he wants it more than anything.

cameron

Cam drifts in vague dreams. Sean is there, wearing a suit. He looks wonderful. And Cam is his. Just his. They're free and together, and it's fantastic and bright, and holding him feels better than anything in the world. There's also a large rhododendron trying to eat one of their neighbors, but it's not of import.

He's kissing Sean, holding him close and drinking in his heat as he ruts against him. Sean is suddenly not in a suit and in Cam's bed, sliding a delicate hand up his thigh. His hand shifts into a bird's claw. That should be disturbing, but he straddles Cameron and pulls his sleep pants down and coaxes him to full hardness. Soft thighs bracket his legs, and Cameron groans.

"Does that feel good?"

Cameron's eyes flutter open to see Kayla above him, framed in the early morning light, long hair tumbling over bare breasts, eyes hooded as she strokes him. "Kayla, wait."

"You started it. Let's have some fun," Kayla says with a grin, nails grazing too-sensitive skin and making Cameron tremble with revulsion. This is not what he wants, not what he was dreaming of, and it's all wrong. The whiplash of going from the imaginary paradise to this is too much.

"Kayla, I—"

"Come on, babe, doesn't it feel good?" she asks, her voice thin.

Cameron's mind and body crash into sync, his erection flagging. "I'm sorry."

"Here, touch me." Kayla grabs Cameron's hands and forces him to grab her breasts and knead them. "Better?"

"No."

The word falls out of his mouth unbidden, and Kayla stills, her face filling with confusion and hurt. "What?"

Cameron's pulse pounds, his gut burning. "This isn't— Please get off."

"Cameron."

"I don't want to do this." Cameron struggles away, chest tightening and head spinning.

"I can do something different!" Kayla says, desperate. "I can turn around or whatever you need to pretend to make it better."

"No. No more pretending. I can't..." He's worried he's going to be sick before the words make it out.

"You can. I know you can." She sounds like she might cry, and Cameron doesn't care.

"No. I can't. Kayla, I can't do this anymore, I'm—"

"Stop!" Cameron recoils at the force in her voice. She shakes her head. "I'm sorry for surprising you. We have things to do today. Go for your run. I need to shower."

"No, I want to talk. If we don't do this now..." He doesn't think he'll be as brave or foolish in an hour, or even a few minutes. He's not even sure what he wants to say, but a lifetime of secrets is suddenly too much to keep in anymore.

"We're going to be late. We can talk later," Kayla declares and retreats to the bathroom.

Cameron pulls on his running clothes in a fog and heads out the door into the chill October morning. Their entire married life has been a series of avoided conversations and willful ignorance. And it can't go on.

He runs hard and fast, trying to drown out the cacophony of thoughts until his lungs are burning. He doesn't know what broke or why. Maybe it was the violation, maybe it was the dream. Maybe it was all the things

Sean and he almost said alone with those records. Maybe it's everything. Every day lately, it's harder, harder to not look at Sean, to not want to grab him, run away, and never look back. Everyone would be fine without him. And then they could… What? Date? Does Sean want that?

Cameron nearly stumbles off the sidewalk. He doesn't know if Sean wants that. He's never asked, only guessed and assumed. He has to talk this through with Sean. He'll know what to do. After church, they'll find some time and figure it out. Somehow.

He manages to avoid Sean and Kayla when he gets home, showers, and dresses for church. His mind is slightly clearer when he gets back downstairs to find his wife and his lover chatting quietly over plates of eggs. Sean has on a button-down with dark jeans, his attempt at Sunday best.

"Do you need to bring anything for the carnival?" Kayla asks brightly.

"No, Drew and Lee are in charge of supplies. I'm on set up," Cam mutters.

"Hope supplies include candy," Sean says.

"You're literally eating right now," Kayla laughs.

"But not *candy*," Sean grins. "Cam, you want some grub?"

"No, I'm not hungry."

"Suit yourself," Sean says. Kayla opens her mouth, then closes it, likely rethinking telling him he should eat.

The drive to church is quiet and more than a little awkward. It makes no sense for Sean to sit in the back, since he's so much taller than Kayla, but it would also be wrong for Kayla to give up her place. It's not a long ride, thankfully, and soon they pull into the tree-lined lot. Sean smiles at the church as they get out. Cameron has no illusions about the building's aesthetic appeal. It's mid-century modern, angular, and covered in windows. The white cross on the top is too big for the building, and it falls off every few years when they get a big storm, but they never change it.

"Are you sure about this?" Cameron asks Sean as they watch people begin to file in.

"Yeah, it'll be fine," Sean says unconvincingly. "New adventure or whatever."

He watches Sean brace himself as they head inside. Susan greets them warmly when they reach their row, and Courtney manages not to glare daggers at Sean, so it's successful. The pew feels more stiff and uncomfortable than usual with Sean beside him on the aisle. The congregants take their seats, and Cameron keeps his eyes resolutely forward.

"Good morning, everyone," Osborn says, stepping to the pulpit. "I hope you're all feeling seasonal today. Now you'll note I say seasonal. Not 'spooky' or 'in the holiday spirit.' I made a choice there. And that's what I want to talk to you about today: choices."

Next to him, Cameron feels Sean shudder, but he keeps his eyes forward.

"Every day we face choices. Some are simple, like whether you reject a so-called holiday devoted to occultism and indulgence and choose the way of the Lord. When you find a wallet on the street with money in it. You know to do the Christian thing in those situations. But what about others? What about those little lies you tell each day? 'No one will know if I break the speed limit.' 'It's a secret ballot, I can vote however I like.' 'No one saw me looking at that attractive woman.'" Osborn sends a simpering smile to the front row that's frankly disturbing.

"But God knows. God *knows*. That's why you must make the right choices. God knows how you hurt others, even when they don't know it was you. God knows when, by inaction, you allow evil to flourish. God knows your hearts and sins. That is the truth of choice – you always have it, but there is only one right choice in the eyes of the Lord."

And Cameron can only seem to make the wrong ones.

Eventually, the sermon ends, and Don Boyle, the city council candidate, takes the pulpit to speak in place of testimony from parishioners. He goes on for too long about supporting families and law enforcement and small business, and American values. After a while, he drops the façade. Get the homeless off the street and the immigrants back where they came from, then send the gays and the transexuals to therapy for a cure. Cameron wants to vomit the whole time.

After that, the choir performs, and Cameron notices Sean cringing at that more than anything else. Community announcements, and then it's time for reading from scripture.

"Before we read, Mr. Barons would like me to remind the volunteers setting up for the harvest party that they are needed now," Osborn says, and doesn't sound happy about it.

"That's my cue," Cameron sighs. He's very careful not to touch Sean as he exits the pew. He wonders what Sean will think of Corinthians, but he's relieved to get away.

Lee greets Cameron with a stiff smile when he makes it down to the large basement. He's glad to see a friendly face. Less so to see Jeremiah beside her.

"So, what can I do?" Cameron asks.

"Mr. Barons is handing out tasks," Jeremiah says and manages to make it a sneer.

"Help me set up the fishing and photo booth. It won't take too long," Lee says. "Jeremiah is moving hay bales."

"Did Luke donate those?" Cameron asks.

"Yes. Very good man, your brother," Jeremiah says in that low, dangerous way that communicates exactly what aspects of Luke he admires. "It's good to have righteous people in your family." He glances at Lee, and Cameron's hackles rise.

"Come on, Cameron," Lee says, tugging him away before he can comment. When they're out of earshot, Cameron sighs and relaxes incrementally. "Don't worry about Jeremiah, he's just mad that I told him *again* I have no intention of marrying a nice man and settling down."

Cameron turns to Lee. She's never said anything so openly before. "That's a good plan." He starts working on the photo booth setup. He can't recommend married life very highly; then again, he's not even sure if what he has is a real marriage. Not the way it's supposed to be, at least. The flagrant adultery is a main factor.

"Cameron, are *you* alright?" Lee asks after ten minutes of setting up backgrounds and a painted board for the fishing game.

"No," he answers, utterly tired of lying.

"What's wrong?"

Cameron kneels, avoiding her eyes to organize a bucket of fishing poles with clothespins on the end. "It's Kayla and me—"

"Can I help finish up?" They both spin at the sound of Jeremiah's voice. He looks suspicious, but maybe Camerone is imagining it.

"No, we're done," Lee says. "And I think they're finished upstairs. People should be coming in soon."

"Good," Jeremiah says. "This party is a good start for helping the community move away from the devil's so-called holiday. Maybe next year we'll be able to do a full hell house."

"A what?" Cameron asks.

"No. They're horrible," Lee says with surprising force. "Haunted houses with rooms depicting different ways to hell to frighten people."

"Abortionists torn apart like the children they kill. Sodomites wasting away from AIDS. Transgenders preying on children in bathrooms. You know the drill." Jeremiah smiles. "They're effective."

"It sounds appalling," Cameron says, as his eyes flit to the first people coming down the stairs.

"It's the kind of thing this town needs," Jeremiah replies. "There's already far too liberal an attitude creeping in here from that god-forsaken city."

"I doubt that," Cameron replies. Jeremiah sneers and looks like he's about to argue, but Cameron sees a familiar flash of blonde hair approaching, with Sean looming behind. "Jeremiah, let me introduce my wife and our friend."

Jeremiah turns to Kayla first. "Hello, I'm Kayla Steward," she says with a bright smile that the man doesn't deserve.

"Jeremiah Fowler," Jeremiah shakes Kayla's hand, then turns to Sean.

Cameron's heart drops. In all the time he's known Sean, he's never seen him look so afraid.

23

confession

sean

SHIT.

This is bad. This is scary bad. Sean came ready to deal with assholes and bigots today, but not the one who *nearly killed him*. Sean meets Jeremiah's icy eyes and sees a spark of recognition.

Shit shit shit. *Fuck.*

"This is Sean," Kayla says before Sean can stop her. "He's staying with us temporarily."

"The homeless man?" Jeremiah says, low and thoughtful. Great, Jeremiah, like fucking *everyone*, knows what the deal is.

"Cam and I met downtown," Sean says carefully. He feels like he might throw up, but he can't let Jeremiah think or guess that Cam was a client. "Bonded over sandwiches. Cam and Kayla here took me in after I hit a bad patch."

"A bad patch?" Jeremiah repeats.

Sean can see Cam watching him from the corner of his eye. Cam knows Sean isn't okay because he knows Sean. Sean does not deserve him, but he's the only reason Sean feels even a sliver of safety right now. "Yeah, some asshole beat the crap out of me and hit me with an ugly truck."

"You mean almost killed you," Cam adds.

"It was awful," Kayla agrees, and Sean refuses to break eye contact with Jeremiah.

"Yeah, it was. Can't imagine what's wrong with a person that they'd wanna hurt another human like that," Sean says, dire and steady, and Jeremiah narrows his eyes. If Jeremiah recognizes him, Sean wants him to know it goes both ways. Somehow, he thinks that Jeremiah wouldn't want the respectable folk to know about his extracurricular activities. Even this crowd would think that was too far. Well, most of them.

"That brought you into these good people's home. So strange how the Lord works sometimes." Jeremiah replies, smirking. "I hope that you're taking this opportunity as a blessing. To find peace in Christ." The good news has never sounded more like a threat.

"You know, I think I left my phone upstairs, I gotta…" Sean turns and walks away. He needs air. He needs to figure this out. Cam says something behind him that he can't make out as his feet take him up the stairs and straight out the door. There's nowhere to go from there, since Kayla and Cam are his damn ride. He hangs a left and trudges through the bushes to get to the back of the building, then collapses against the rough beige siding.

"Fucking hell." He pulls out his phone. At least he can text Cam and give him a heads-up.

"Um, are you okay?"

"Jesus Christ!" Sean exclaims as he jumps and spins to the source of the voice. It's a short man with a raggedy beard and too many layers who looks as spooked as Sean.

"Sorry! You looked like you were having a shitty day too! And you know, also hiding," the guy says. "Didn't mean to scare you."

"It's okay, man." Sean deflates. "I didn't mean to take the Lord's name in vain or whatever."

"It's fine. Great actually. Don't hear it enough." The guy pulls a silver flask out of his jacket and takes a swig, then offers it to Sean with a slightly shaky hand. "You want some?"

"Hell yeah." Sean takes a deep drink from the flask. It's cheap vodka that burns all the way down, but, man, it's a relief. "Thanks," Sean says as he hands back the flask. The guy takes it, then offers his hand to Sean.

"I'm Drew, by the way. Barons."

"Drew as in the *pastor*?" Sean balks as he shakes his hand.

"*Assistant* pastor?" Drew squeaks back, and Sean huffs.

"Do you offer your congregation drinks very often?"

"I'm pretty sure I'd remember if you were part of the congregation. Unless you're new. In which case; crap."

"I'm just here with some friends. I'm Sean," he says, letting go of Drew's hand.

Drew's eyes go wide. "Sean? Like Cam's Sean?"

"Does everyone here know who I am?" He doesn't even want to know what a pastor (assistant or otherwise) thinks of him on top of everything else.

"No!" Drew yelps. "Well. Yes. Probably. But, like, I just know 'cause Cam has talked about you. He's a really good guy, Cam."

Sean can't help but smile at that. "Best guy I know."

"It's really great to finally meet you," Drew says, sticking out his hand again. "Shit. Did that already."

"So, why're you out here?" Sean asks as Drew draws back into himself, reminding Sean of some sort of neurotic armadillo. "Shouldn't you be managing your harvest shindig instead of hiding in the bushes drinking with a stranger?"

Drew takes another drink and automatically passes the flask to Sean. "Come on, would you rather be out here or stuck in the basement with a bunch of bigots that want you fired?"

"Dude, no arguments here. That crowd, man; even the nice ones are jerks half the time and the not so nice ones..." Sean lets out a whistle, a twinge in his bones from old wounds. He takes a swig of vodka. It doesn't help.

"And like, I'm trying. I really am! But there's only so much I can do before I'm hitting my head against a wall. They've been taught so many lies about the Bible and history, and they believe such stupid bullshit, it's horrifying. There are good people in there, but they're scared of the assholes like Osborn and Isaacs, and fuckers like Jeremiah."

"Jeremiah?" Sean echoes, queasily reminded of why he's out here.

"Yeah. Total tool. I think he wants my job," Drew sighs, grabs the flask from Sean, and takes another drink.

"Sounds like you don't want this job." Sean wonders if it's worth it to tell Drew what a psychopath Jeremiah really is, but that involves revealing things about himself he's really not ready for a man of God to know.

"I dunno. I didn't want it when I got it, but I feel like I'm responsible for people now, you know?"

"No."

"Maybe, like, God needs me here," Drew goes on, half-breathless. "There's gotta be some balance. Someone has to speak for the oppressed people, the ones Jesus *actually* cared for, or nothing's ever gonna change."

"How did you even end up here?" Sean asks. In his hoodie and scuffed Converse, Drew certainly doesn't look like the rest of the congregation.

"My ex thought that the church was a joke. Or maybe God was the joke. I'm not sure. Hated that I went to seminary. So last time we broke up—"

"Last time?"

"Dude, it's a whole messy story. But he thought it would be *so funny* to get me a gig working in Hicksville, Missouri, with a bunch of family values nuts. Really show me what the God I want to serve gets used for."

"He what?" Sean can't process any of this. "*How?*"

"He works for a porn company. Knows exactly how much naughty schoolgirl content Ted Osborn enjoys, among other things."

Sean cringes with his entire body. "Ew. I don't wanna think about that."

"Right?!" Drew's eyes are wide and slightly unhinged. "I have to have that image in my head every time I see him. Not great for a productive working relationship."

"Wait, wait, go back to the part about your ex." Sean's sure he hallucinated. "You said... he?"

"Oh. Yeah." Drew digs his hands into his pockets.

"You're gay?"

Drew shrugs, his cheeks slightly red, but otherwise he looks unfreaked. "Bi. But, yeah. I'm queer."

Sean stares at Drew like he just told him he was a unicorn. "Shit," Sean whispers.

"Don't tell anyone. I know that's unfair to put on you, but obviously, it wouldn't be great if that got out. Which sucks."

"Why the hell did you tell me?" Sean demands. Most of his clients spent half the time Sean had their dicks in his mouth saying how straight they were, so he has no idea why this rando would confide in him if it might cost him his job.

"Oh, I, uh, lust figured that since you also were, I mean, are—"

"I never said *I* was queer." It's been a whirlwind conversation, but Sean's pretty sure he'd remember dropping *that* bomb.

"Fuck." Now Drew looks scared.

"How'd you know?" Sean advances on the much smaller man, who raises his hands, cowering.

"It was Kayla!" Drew yelps, bracing himself.

"What?" Sean's heart falls so fast that it possibly reaches the earth's core. "Kayla?"

"She didn't *know* know, okay? She just had suspicions, and there's the way Cam was acting and I do have some gaydar, okay?" He's covering, and it's only making this worse.

"You cannot tell anyone," Sean growls.

"I won't! I—"

Sean grabs Drew by the collars and practically lifts him off the ground. "You cannot tell *anyone*."

"Okay! Chill, man! I don't out people!" Drew squeals, and Sean drops him. "Especially around here. Christ."

"I can't do that to Cam," Sean says, catching his breath. That brings the reason he was out here right back to his mind. "Shit."

"What?"

"Can you do me a big goddamn favor?"

"Are you gonna strangle me again?"

Sean gives Drew a glare that he's free to interpret anyway he likes. "That Jeremiah asshole makes me hella uncomfortable. That's why I came out here."

"Feel you there."

Sean almost feels back for asking this. "Can you go down there and keep him away from me? And Cam and Kayla."

Drew looks at him thoughtfully. "You really care about Cam, don't you? Kayla too?"

"Yeah," Sean answers without hesitation, even though the way he cares for them is very different. "They're good people."

"Okay. I'll keep Jeremiah busy. And if *you* ever want to talk…" Sean purses his lips, and Drew flinches. "Too much. Okay. I'm gonna go back in now. Thanks. See you. Uh, God bless."

Sean collapses against the church wall. Fuck, Sean *does* want to talk to someone. He wants to call Danny or bitch at Bill, but neither of them would understand this. No one would console him or tell him it's going to be okay, because it's not. They'd tell him to do the right thing and get the hell out of Cam's life right now.

Sean's phone starts buzzing as he opens his texts, Cam's name and the dorky picture Sean snuck of him filling the screen.

"Cam—"

"Are you alright?"

"I'm fine." He can hear Cam glaring. "Ish. I just needed a second."

"Why are you frightened of Jeremiah?" Jesus, the guy is perceptive.

"Are you around him right now? Did he say anything?"

"Where are you? What's going on?"

"I'm around back. I'll meet you at the front, okay?" He knows it's stupid to be alone with Cam here, but he can't say this over the phone.

"Fine." Cam hangs up without ceremony.

Sean makes his way out of the hiding spot. It must be a regular hangout because there are cigarette butts ground into the dirt. Man,

what he wouldn't give for a smoke right now. Or a joint. The vodka
barely took the edge off, and he's already missing Drew's flask.

"Sean," Cam calls, exiting the church as Sean comes around the
corner.

"I'm fine," Sean says as Cam rushes to him. He's sure he doesn't look
fine, but it's brave face time. "It's Jeremiah."

"How do you know him?" Cam's face falls. "Was he a…" Cam can't
say john, or even client, where people might hear.

"No! I mean, he was gonna be, I thought. Until he beat the shit out
of me."

"*What?*"

Why does Sean feel like he's confessing the crime here? "He was the
one, Cam, who messed me up."

Cam turns back to the door with *murder* in his face.

"Cam, no!" Sean cries, grabbing him by the arm and pulling him
back. "We cannot make a scene. We gotta, I don't know, make a plan."

"A plan? For dealing with the man that *nearly killed you* in the name
of God," Cam growls, struggling against Sean. "He deserves to be
punished."

"The man that could out me and *you* to the whole goddamn congregation if we're not careful!" Sean hisses.

Cam turns to Sean, looking stricken. God, had he not even thought
of that before barreling off to go medieval on the guy? "Fine. What sort
of plan do you have in mind?"

"I don't know!" Sean exclaims as a woman in a sweater set walks by,
giving them the stink eye. "We can head it off at the pass maybe? I could
tell Kayla something?"

"I don't think so," Cam pants. "Kayla. This morning. I tried to talk
to her. After she… never mind why, but I almost told her."

"About *us?*"

"About me." Cam looks ill, and Sean doesn't know if he's freaked out
or amazed. "That I'm… Jesus, I can't even say it to you and you *know*."

"Maybe she already knows." Cam looks up at Sean with an expression
that's more realization than surprise. "Listen, that's the other thing. I

ran into Drew, we got talking, and he knew I was queer because of something *Kayla* said to him."

"We need to talk to her," Cam says with the same enthusiasm one might have about having to go to a grandparent's funeral.

"Seriously?"

"If you're alright with it."

Sean doesn't get why that matters. "With Jeremiah around and her knowing something, I don't think *I* have much of a choice. But you—"

"We always have a choice," Cam says with a bitter, half-smile. "Didn't you listen to the sermon?"

"Then, I chose whatever you need." Cam gives him a look Sean's not accustomed to seeing outside of Thursday nights. It's warm and intimate and too much for such a public setting. "What do you need, Cam?"

"I don't know," Cam whispers. "I don't know. I hate hurting her, and I know I am, but if this gets out, I'll lose my family. My job. My friends. So will she, and she doesn't deserve that."

"Neither do you," Sean says, tender and fervent.

"I deserve to suffer. I've lied and betrayed her. I've used her, and you. I've defied God again and again." Cam looks up towards where the church's white cross stands out against the grey sky. "I deserve all of this. I should tell her. But if she leaves me..."

"Do you want her to leave you?" Sean can't even contemplate that: Cam being free. Cam choosing him. It's impossible. "Do you want to leave her?"

Cam looks back at the sky and the church and shudders. "I don't know. We'll tell her what Jeremiah knows, ask her what she thinks she knows, and go from there." It's another cop out, but Sean can't blame him. He has nothing to offer Cam. He has nothing to offer anyone.

"Okay. I've got your back, whatever happens." Sean's surprised that the words come out of his mouth, even though they're true. Whatever Cam wants, he'll do, be it lying or leaving. It's the sort of thing you're supposed to do when you care about someone.

"We should get back in. You don't think Jeremiah will—"

JESSICA MASON

"Nah, Drew's running interference." Cam raises an eyebrow at that. "We bonded. And seriously, I know you have thoughts and feelings and whatever about God and being—" He stops himself. It's Cam's choice to say it first, not his. "You know. He might be helpful."

"Why do you say that? What did you two talk about?"

Sean's not sure if, given everything, he has any right to out Drew, even to Cam. "Just talk to him."

"Fine. Let's get back inside," Cam grumbles, and Sean follows him back into the church and down to the basement.

cameron

The drive home is only slightly worse than the carnival. Cameron spent the whole time looking over his shoulder, worried about Sean yet wary of speaking to him too much or at all. He'd let Kayla take the lead and guide him through the crowd, careful to dodge Isaacs and Osborn and Jeremiah and Luke and his mother and family. Pretty much everyone. He's exhausted and worn, but ready to get home and make it so much worse. Better to pull the bandage off quickly.

No one talks when they get out of the car. Oddly, Kayla checks her phone and sends a text, pointedly avoiding Cameron's eyes when they get inside.

"Kayla, we still need to talk," Cameron begins.

"Tomorrow," Kayla sighs. "More important things are happening today."

"Um," Sean says. "I don't think this can wait."

"Of course it can." Kayla's false confidence and smile are paper-thin, and it hurts to see her trying so hard to keep them up.

"Kay, we can't keep avoiding this," Cameron says gently. Kayla retreats into the kitchen, placing the counter between her and the two men as if it might protect her.

"There's nothing to avoid, babe." She glances uneasily at Sean. "You had a bad morning, but it's all okay. We can talk in private later."

"Kayla, this is about me, okay? Something I haven't told you," Sean says, and Kayla gives him a bewildered look.

"Alright, go ahead." There's a challenge in her voice that's disconcerting.

"That guy at church, Jeremiah. Lee's cousin. You probably noticed he freaked me out," Sean begins, and Kayla nods. "It's because I know him. He's the one who put me in the hospital."

"*What?*" Kayla seems genuinely confused now.

"Guess he was in town visiting and…" Sean visibly braces himself, as if he's saying goodbye to the person Kayla thought he was. "His idea of a good time was looking for people like me to educate."

"People like you," Kayla repeats slowly.

"Men who have sex with men." Sean straightens his spine, visibly pushing away his shame, and Cameron feels a strange ripple of pride. "For money."

There it is. Cameron watches Kayla's face and waits for her anger, or her suspicion, or hurt, but there's only contemplation. "Did you and Jeremiah—"

"*No.* It was a con. On his part. He got me alone and he beat the shit out of me in the name of God or some bullshit." The look of horror on Kayla's face is encouraging. "But, at the church, I'm pretty sure he recognized me. I wanted to tell you before he did. That's what I used to do for money."

"You're a prostitute," Kayla says carefully, her eyes unfocused. "You get paid to have sex with men."

"I—" Cameron thinks Sean is going to correct her tense, but Kayla cuts him off with a high, hysterical laugh. "Not really the reaction I was expecting."

"Kayla?" Cameron asks, completely thrown as Kayla continues to laugh. She smiles and turns to Cameron.

"He's not really homosexual. You pay him! For sex. It's just sex." Kayla rushes to Cameron and hugs him tightly. "This makes so much more sense! Oh my God, you paid him. It's not *real.*"

"What are you talking about?" Cameron looks down at Kayla's face. There are tears in her eyes, but she's smiling.

"You and Sean. I was worried you had feelings for him, but it's not like that." Cameron can't understand this. How is she happy about this?

"So you know?" Sean asks before Cameron can. "About me and... us?"

Kayla scowls at Sean. "I'm not an idiot. I know my husband has certain impulses. Why do you think I let you stay here?"

"*Let* him?" Cameron echoes, completely lost.

"I thought you didn't want me to die on the street," Sean balks.

"Sean, I didn't. I do care about you and like you. I want to help you, but the most important thing will always be my family." Kayla turns back to Cameron. "Babe, this was always for you. So you can get better. So we can help you."

Cameron needs to sit down. He feels ill and dizzy, too many emotions swirling inside him to bear.

"What do you mean, help?" Sean asks, his voice low and threatening as Cameron gropes for a kitchen chair.

"Cam is sick and confused. He needs to learn to enjoy doing things the way God intends," Kayla says. It sounds rehearsed but completely sincere.

"The way... are you insane?!" Sean yells, and Kayla's eyes fill with cold fire.

"Why else do you think I would allow my husband to fornicate with you if it wasn't for his own good? Do you know how hard it's been for me? Knowing what you two do when I'm gone." She shudders. "But he was getting better, he was doing what God wanted him to do with pleasure. You started before the accident, didn't you? The first time things changed."

"Did you know then?" Cam asks numbly, mind jumping across the timeline of the last few months.

"I had my suspicions and worries, but I didn't know until he came into the hospital. The moment I saw you two in the same room, I feared the worst," Kayla confesses, old pain in her face. "But I knew for sure thanks to Dawn. She saw you when Sean was there. Saw you kiss him."

Sean winces and shakes his head. "Damn it."

"It's alright. It was worth it because it gave me a way to help you and *you changed*. You can keep changing." Kayla's eyes are wide and beseeching as she sits and covers Cameron's hand with hers. He recoils, darting his hand back. "I know it's difficult, but with prayer and counseling, and other help, we can keep curing you."

"Cam is not sick!" Sean bellows so fiercely that Kayla jumps. "How can you say that? For fuck's sake you're a *doctor!*"

Kayla straightens and shakes her head. "You don't have an objective view of the situation, Sean. You're confused too. I can't imagine the horrible things you've done to survive, but God will forgive you. He can help you too."

"Don't give me any of that Christ saves crap! I'm not some victim. I have sex with men because I like it," Sean spits.

"You like condemning your soul? You chose to be homosexual because you enjoy it?" Kayla says it like he's choosing to lose a limb.

"Sean is bisexual," Cameron says quietly, and both of them turn to look at him.

"That's not even a real thing," Kayla replies, cool and stiff, waving Sean off as she sets her focus back on Cameron. "There is one natural order ordained by God. Cameron, I love you, and I want to help you enjoy it and thrive in it."

"By letting us screw around behind your back so he could get it up for some at-home conversion therapy?" Sean barks. "That is fucked up and horrible, and you know it!"

"Don't you dare try to act innocent and offended here!" Kayla yells, rising again. "*You* lied to me from the moment we met. You put my husband and me at risk and helped him to break a vow he made to me before God. Just because you're paid to do it doesn't mean it's not wrong."

Sean's mouth hardens to a thin, defiant line. "Cam hasn't paid me for a long time," he says, voice cold with fury.

"That's very unfair of him, after all, you are providing a service," Kayla spits back, and Cameron finally snaps. He slams his hand on the table, and Kayla jumps.

"That is not what it was," Cameron growls. "Not what it *is*. Sean and I, we—"

"No. Stop," Kayla snaps. "Don't act like what you two do is real or comparable to *us*. You did it for the sex. It's *only* sex, and it's not even real sex. I know your heart is still in our marriage, or you would have been honest and left. That's the only way I was able to endure that humiliation."

"Kayla, this isn't you," Cameron says in horror. "You're not cruel like this."

"Me?" Kayla barks out a sour laugh. "I'm cruel? I'm not the one who *cheated*. You lied to me and betrayed me for *months*! Do you think this was easy? All those nights away, trying to do my job and help people while I *knew* what you were doing. The only thing that kept me from going insane was seeing how it made you better; how it made you happy with me. My prayers were answered, and all I had to do was endure long enough for you to learn."

"I got some bad news for you, bitch," Sean says, and Cameron looks up. Sean's face is stony and resolved. "Cam ain't gonna change, and I sure as *hell* won't be a part of it anymore."

"Well, you two won't be fornicating anymore, but that was going to change tonight anyway," Kayla replies, confusingly. "But you help just by being close by. You inspire his lust, and that needs an outlet. Eventually, he'll come around and see what a family can offer."

"No. I won't," Cameron protests, and looks to Sean.

"See, this is why you have to stay here, Sean," Kayla says, her attention drifting back to her phone as it buzzes with a text. She looks back at Cameron and shakes her head as if he's a stubborn child. "He's not ready, and if you leave, so will he. If that happens, everyone loses. Jobs, homes, families, reputations. We can't have that."

Cameron hears the words like the clanging of prison bars, but he *can't* do this. This is not what was supposed to happen tonight. It's only now that he realizes what he hoped for.

"I don't give a rat's ass about your jobs, or any of this. I'm leaving," Sean says. "Cam, you can come along or not, but I'm not staying here."

"Don't be rash. Either of you," Kayla says before Cam can ask what that means and if Sean truly wants him to come. "I need you to take a few moments to compose yourselves. Calm down and think about the consequences. I know we're all emotional—"

"Calm down? Are you *high?*" Sean balks.

"I wish you hadn't insisted on doing this *today*. Things were going to change anyway, but now you've gone and made it awkward."

Sean throws up his hands and turns away, stalking into his room, presumably to get his things. He's really leaving.

"Kayla, I think things are far beyond awkward," Cameron says, numbly. "Is my suitcase still in my office?" For the first time, Kayla looks truly worried, and it gives Cameron a horrible sense of satisfaction.

"Babe…"

"I'll go look." He walks to the office in a daze and stares at his desk. Wedding pictures. Family portraits. A framed passage of scripture. Jeremiah.

"For I know the plans I have for you," declares the LORD, *"plans to prosper you and not to harm you, plans to give you hope and a future."*

He bats it onto the floor, and it lands with a dull thud, unbroken.

The sound of the doorbell shocks Cameron from his stupor. He has no idea who could be there. Maybe confused trick-or-treaters. He considers not answering until the bell rings again, accompanied by an insistent knock. Kayla lingers in the hall when Cameron exits the office, waiting as he opens the door.

He doesn't recognize the man or the teenager on his front step. They look nervous and tired in the weak light from inside.

"Can I help you?" Cameron asks. The adult opens his mouth, but a crash from behind Cameron in the hall cuts him off. He turns to see

Sean, a box at his feet. His jaw is slack and his face pale, like he's seen a ghost.

"Danny?"

24

Reunion

sean

"SEAN?" DANNY'S FACE BREAKS into a smile, and Sean's heart starts beating again. He approaches carefully, like walking to a mirage, as Danny looks up at the guy he's with. "Holy crap, Anthony, why didn't you tell me?"

"We didn't want to get you too excited in case something went wrong," Gardner says gently.

Sean stops next to Cam in the doorway, all his anger and disgust forgotten as he stares at his brother. It's pure reflex to ruffle his hair. "When'd you get so tall, kid?" Sean asks, voice shaky and thick.

"When did you get so old?"

They break at the same time. Danny drops his bag and tackles Sean into a hug that makes his ribs smart, and Sean crushes him right back. He can't help the tears. Half of him has been missing and suddenly it's back; a phantom limb returned.

"God, it's good to see you, short stuff," Sean murmurs into the kid's hair before finally letting go. He roughly pushes the tears from his eyes and looks at Gardner. He's not the way Sean imagined him at all. He'd been thinking of someone bookish and small, but this guy is actually pretty built, and he looks like he might be Native American. He has long black hair pulled back and thoughtful eyes. "What the hell are you doing here?"

Gardner looks slightly worried, glancing over Sean's shoulder to either Cam or Kayla. "This is Danny's new foster placement."

"*What?*" Sean's mind races back to reality. "How?"

"It wasn't easy," Gardner says with a kind, if thin, smile. "We had to rush the interstate compact and certification for the Stewards, and waive the home study. But I was willing to do a favor for Kayla and to get Danny here."

"You…" Sean turns to Kayla, keeping a hand on Danny to steady himself. That means Kayla's been planning this for a long time. Working behind his back, all part of her plan to keep him here and use him. "You didn't tell me," he says, looking between Kayla and Cam. The slight twitch of Cam's head and the look of shock on his face are all Sean needs to know that he had no part in this.

"We also didn't want to get your hopes up," Kayla says. "Come on in. No reason to stand out there in the cold."

Sean picks up Danny's bag and leads him in, a hand on his arm. He knows he's probably being clingy, but he's convinced Danny's going to disappear any second. Touching him is better than punching Kayla in the goddamn face anyway. The front hall feels too crowded with four adults and a gangly teen in it, but Sean's not sure about what to do next.

"Introductions first, I guess," Gardner says. "I'm Anthony Gardner. Danny, this is Kayla Steward. She was Kayla Miller when we met. We're actually old friends."

Danny cautiously shakes Kayla's hand, then looks at Cam. He's as shell-shocked as Sean. "Danny, this is Cam, Kayla's better half," Sean says pointedly.

"Hello, Danny. It's very good to finally meet you in person." Cam offers his hand, but Danny pulls him into a hug instead. It's brief, but it makes something crack in Sean's heart.

"It's really great to meet you, Cam. Someone Sean likes this much must be pretty great," Danny says quietly, smiling at Cam. Cam doesn't seem to know what to say, and neither does Sean. Danny turns and smiles at Kayla too. "You also, I guess. I, uh, can't believe this." Kayla looks nervous and queasy, and Sean's fine with that.

"It'll take some getting used to," Sean breathes.

Danny drifts towards the great room and kitchen, craning his neck to look at the high ceilings. "Wow, you weren't kidding," Danny says with a grin as he looks around.

"Nicer than the Weaver place?" Sean asks.

"They had plastic on their living room furniture," Danny replies with a shudder.

"You can see everything here, except the office behind you, in the front," Kayla says, cheerful and easy, like the last thirty minutes didn't happen. "Oh, and Sean's room is over there by the kitchen. Danny, you'll be in the other guest room, upstairs."

"Unless you wanna swap," Sean offers.

"I don't want to make you move," Danny mutters and looks back at Sean. "I can't believe this. I saw the car out front, but even then... Holy crap." Danny grins, wide and innocent, and Sean thinks he might cry again, goddamnit. "I was so pissed about moving again, but... wow."

"So is this permanent?" Sean asks, turning to Gardner, who gives Danny a nervous look.

"Usually this isn't the sort of thing we discuss with wards present," Gardner says.

"I'm gonna hear it from whatever lawyer you stick me with," Danny argues. "Come on, Anthony."

"Fine," Gardner sighs. "Danny, you're smart and mature enough to understand this anyway. The answer is: we have to see."

Sean doesn't like the sound of that, and it ties his stomach in new knots. "You mean he might have to go back?" he asks.

"No," Gardner replies. "The judge in Ohio agrees that St. Louis is a better place for Danny, and we're transferring the case and jurisdiction here, but we won't make a decision on custody and long-term place-ment for about thirty days. We'll have a hearing in the juvenile court at that time. I'll stay and supervise until then. I'm subbing in at the local child welfare office so I can also help them with some ICWA cases."

"So, uh…" Sean can't comprehend this. It's not possible. Danny's looking at him like he's thinking the same thing.

"If you're in a stable, suitable residence and employed, custody would go to you, Mr. Lockwood," Garner says, like it's not a miracle.

"Really!?" Danny yelps, turning to Sean with a grin.

"Holy—" Sean bites back the profanity. How is this happening?

"Now, there will be interviews and background checks. Drug test too. We want to be thorough. Given your previous situation, we're cautious. You'll be assigned a juvenile court lawyer, who can explain things," Gardner goes on.

"Great. I love lawyers," Sean grumbles, and Danny elbows him in the stomach.

"Let's not get ahead of ourselves. Kayla, can you show me where he'll be staying?" Gardner asks, all formality and politeness.

"Of course," Kayla says and leads Gardner upstairs after he grabs Danny's bags.

"Danny." The brothers look up to where Cam is standing by the kitchen. "I want you to know that we are very happy that you're here, no matter how or why, or what happens."

Danny looks confused, but Sean wishes more than anything that he could hug Cam and tell him it's okay.

"Thanks, Cam," Sean says. "Danny, this is the best guy… person, whatever, I've ever met. No competition. I'm really glad to have you both in the same place."

"Me too," Danny smiles. Sean pulls him into another hug, much briefer, but still tight. He looks over Danny's head at Cam. He's not trying to hide the pain and worry in his eyes, and Sean can't stand it.

"So, uh," Sean stammers, pulling back and looking at Danny again. "You're too skinny and we ain't had dinner. What do you want? If you say vegetables, so help me, I will send you back right now."

"I haven't had pizza in a while," Danny says with a dopey shrug.

"What do you want on it? I'll order," Cam says, pulling out his phone.

"Someone I know insists pepperoni and pineapple is the best pizza," Danny replies, and Sean smiles.

"You remembered," Sean says. "You sure you don't want your mushroom and black olives abomination?"

"Also green peppers and sausage," Danny grins.

"I'll get one of each," Cam says, indulgent.

"What about Kayla?" Danny asks, all innocence and ignorance about what he walked into.

"She'll be fine," Cam says and heads off to make the order in a quiet corner.

Sean opens his mouth to ask Danny something, but he can't even think of a good question. *How was the trip, and also the last few years of your life that I bailed on to suck cock and nearly get killed?*

"Well, it looks good up there," Gardner says as he descends the stairs with Kayla behind. "I'll be back in the morning around seven to get you to the school and all signed up."

"I'll come too," Sean interjects, and everyone looks at him. "Bill won't mind if I'm late. I wanna be involved and stuff."

"That sounds great," Kayla smiles, and Sean keeps his cringe to himself.

"It is. I'm glad you're so enthusiastic. I'm sure this is a shock," Gardner replies.

"It's fine," Sean says as Cam hangs up and comes over beside him and Danny.

"I should get going," Gardner says. "Unless you need anything, Danny?"

"I think I'll be okay," Danny says with a bright look at Sean that tears his heart out.

"Are you sure you don't want to stay for dinner?" Kayla asks. She looks justifiably nervous, and Sean takes some small amount of satisfaction in her discomfort. "We were going to have—"

"We ordered pizza already," Cam interrupts, and Kayla's smile falters. He gives Kayla a look of quiet defiance that makes Sean want to pump his fist in the air. "Danny's request."

"Anthony's a vegetarian," Danny says, maybe noticing the tension.

"And I have to go get checked in at my hotel," Gardner says politely. "It was nice to meet you, Sean. Cameron. Great to see you, Kayla. See you tomorrow, Danny."

Kayla walks Gardner out and returns awkwardly to the kitchen. Sean decides he can't look at her and turns to Danny. "Let's go up and get you unpacked, you can tell me about whatever boring ass podcasts you listened to on your trip."

"I'll help," Cam says, before looking at Sean. "If that's alright. I like podcasts."

"Sure," Sean says. They can't talk, but at least he can save Cam from being alone with the woman who thinks he can be trained to stop being queer like a dog that keeps peeing on the couch. He doesn't look back at her as they climb the stairs.

"See, Cam likes them. Not boring," Danny says as he follows Sean up the stairs. "And this one we listened to was super cool! This is a whole deep dive into the Medieval monarchies. Did you know Saint Louis – literally the guy they named the city after –was a French King?"

"When did you turn sixty?" Sean sighs. He glares at Kayla and Cam's door as he walks by, but pushes his rage down and focuses on Danny and Cam nearby. He can yell more later.

Later takes a long time to get there. They eat dinner and make awkward conversation, with Sean talking over Kayla, or Cam ignoring her each time she says something about what he should eat or drink. Danny doesn't notice. He talks a mile a minute about school and his hopes for the new place. He doesn't mention many friends at his old school, which sucks in some ways and isn't so bad in others. Sean knows what it's like moving again and again, and he hopes this is the last time Danny has to do this. Maybe that's why he's so enthusiastic.

After dinner, they end up in the office on the laptop, looking at the school website. It's nice, and they've got a track team. It turns out Cam did track in high school and he and Danny get talking about it and how to train. Sean makes bad jokes about shotput, and it's nice until Kayla knocks on the door to remind them it's getting late. Sean resists telling her to go fuck herself because Danny started yawning fifteen minutes before. Sean won't say it, but he's tired too. He's pretty sure he won't sleep, but he's exhausted from a full day of getting his world flipped over and over, like he's some empty can God's kicking down the street.

"I'll go up with you," Sean says, pointedly avoiding Kayla's eyes as he and Danny walk past her.

"You don't need to tuck me into bed," Danny grumbles, but there's no conviction behind it.

Danny's new room is crisp and clean and boring, like Sean's room and the rest of the house. Danny has the same view of the garden as Sean, but a smaller bed.

"Kinda feels like a hotel," Danny says as he looks around.

"I'd have killed for a hotel this nice," Sean mutters.

Danny looks instantly cowed. "I'm sorry. I wasn't thinking."

"We've both had a shitty time of it for the last few years."

"Yeah, but you…"

"It ain't a competition." Danny stares at him, and Sean does the same back, trying to familiarize himself with the way Danny's face has changed and stayed the same. Is he shaving yet? God, probably. And Sean wasn't there to teach him. He doesn't even know who was. He doesn't know if he's had a first crush or if he still hates licorice or what he'd think if he knew his brother was queer or… Danny's face is blurry all of a sudden. Crap, he hates crying. He'd gone a good long while without this nonsense before he started caring about shit, like an idiot.

"Sean, are you okay?"

"Danny. I'm so sorry," Sean says before he can think better, and Danny looks away, like he doesn't want to hear. "No, really. I am. I shouldn't have gone with Dad. I shouldn't have left. I should have been there for you. I screwed up and I failed you and I am so, so sorry."

"Sean, it's okay." Sean rolls his eyes as he wipes away his stupid tears. "I mean, it's not. It was crappy. For everyone. It's extra crappy that Dad's gone, but this is where we are now."

"Yeah, we're here because…" Sean stops himself. He sure as hell can't explain to Danny that he's part of some screwed up hostage throuple situation to fix someone that isn't broken. "It doesn't matter. I *swear* I won't fail you again."

"I know you won't," Danny says. Sean crosses the room to give his brother one more hug, just in case he wakes up and this is all a dream.

"Get some sleep. Big day tomorrow."

"You too."

Sean closes the door behind him and walks into the hall where Cam is waiting. He nods towards the closed door of their bedroom. "She in there?"

"Yes," Cam replies. "The doors are pretty thick if you feel like yelling."

"Thanks." He doesn't plan on yelling, but it's a good tip.

Kayla jumps from the bed when Sean walks through the door. She's not in pajamas yet, but she still looks vulnerable and small, her face wrought with worry. He finally made it into Cam's bedroom, and it's... nothing. Big bed, family pictures by the TV. Kayla's paintings and framed scripture on the walls next to a cross. "Sean? Cam isn't..."

"Oh, he's right here," Sean says as Cam comes in behind him and quietly shuts the door. It feels nice to have back-up. "But I want to talk to you."

"I don't think there's much to talk about," Kayla stammers. She's not good at this, not used to being hated and wrong. Too fucking bad.

"Yes, there is," Sean snarls. "You know what? I was mad before, but I could have gotten over it because no matter your reasons, you've done good shit for me, and God knows I was pretty bad about showing my gratitude. Hell, getting used and thrown away is par for the course for me. But bringing Danny into this? That is low."

"I brought him here because it was best for him and for you to stay here. Aren't you happy to have him back?" Kayla asks back, bracing herself against Sean's furious voice.

"That is beside the point," Cam rumbles from behind Sean.

"You dragged a kid into your sick scheme; my *brother*," Sean growls, fists tight. "Fucking with us is one level of screwed up, but this? Maybe you did finally convert me because I want to believe in hell just to think that you're going there."

Kayla's mouth is a thin line of anger, her posture stiff and defiant. "I want to help Danny. I want to help both of you. I do care about you. I know you don't understand it or believe me right now, but eventually—"

"I don't want to hear it. Fuck you," Sean spits the words, and Kayla flinches, but her expression doesn't falter.

"Are you done?" Kayla asks.

"Unless Cam has something to say," Sean replies.

"He doesn't," Kayla says, and Sean's anger starts to rise again. "I want to be clear, what happens from now on."

"That'll be a nice change," Sean sneers.

"Don't start," Kayla scoffs. "You will stay in this house. I am completely sincere about helping you get full custody of Danny when this is over. That has *always* been what I wanted, but you will have to meet the state's standards and behave while you are here." Sean opens his mouth to tell Kayla to go fuck herself again, but she raises a silencing finger. "As you said, he's a child. You should moderate your behavior appropriately. We don't want him or Anthony getting the *wrong idea* about you and ruining things."

Sean's mouth hangs open in horror. It's Cam who speaks. "So you don't have a problem with a bisexual man raising Danny, you'd just use his sexuality and his past to keep him in check?"

"You know the court won't let Danny be with Sean if they find out about you two, or his past," Kayla replies. "And so you know, it was always the plan for this to be the time for Cam to stop his activities and redirect."

"What is wrong with you?" Sean demands, ready to puke half a pizza on Kayla's pristine white carpets. "You did a fucking abortion. Where do you get off with this Westboro bullshit?"

"It's not like that," Kayla protests, her composure faltering.

"The hell it's not." Sean has to look away from her, or he really is going to start screaming.

"Stop telling yourself this is alright," Cam adds.

"Isn't that what you two did?" Kayla shoots back. "Told yourselves it was okay? That the things you did in the dark weren't real? You knew it was wrong, and you kept going. What I'm doing is trying to redirect things to save the marriage you were fine with destroying before running away?"

"I wasn't going to—" Sean stops and looks at Cam. He looks as bad as he did before. Sick and shocked and pale.

"You were going to leave, right?" Kayla asks. "Go be with Danny and never look back? This is better. Everyone's eyes are just open now. Getting what we *all* want can be as easy or hard as you make it."

Sean can't take any more. He pushes past Cam and out of the room. He knows Cam isn't following, because frankly, he shouldn't. If it weren't for Danny in the room upstairs, he would be out the door with this godforsaken place in his rearview, but he's trapped.

Kayla's made him into more of a whore than he ever chose to be before. He's there to be an object and make Cam feel something she can steal. Sean hates it because it's crazy and because he doesn't want Cam to break and play along.

He shuts his door and sits heavily on the bed, his head falling into his hands. How did this day turn into this? What the hell is he supposed to do? He's gotta be there for Danny, but he can't let this happen to Cam... can he? He doesn't know what to do or who to talk to. He wishes a God were listening, because he can't think of anyone else who could help.

cameron

Cameron spends an hour cleaning the spare room. He moves the boxes off his ancient, sunken couch and uncovers his old desk and nightstand. It's mindless work, lots of heavy lifting and moving. His back hurts, but the room is in much better order when a knock finally comes at the door.

He's more than a little surprised to see Danny Lockwood standing in the hall.

"Hey, Cam. I mean Cameron." Danny is wearing an old tee and sweats, but he doesn't look like he's been asleep.

"Cam, please. Was I keeping you up?"

"No. I mean, I could hear you, but not really. I just wanted to say—" Danny bites his lip and looks up at Cam from under his floppy bangs. Sean may have a point about him needing a haircut. "Thank you. Again. I know it's stressful having a stranger here."

"You're not a stranger, Danny." Some of the tension eases from Danny's shoulders.

"And thank you for saving Sean." Cam starts to object, but the utter sincerity in Danny's face stops him. "I know Kayla helped and that he did a lot too, but I don't think he would have done any of this if it wasn't for you. For all I know, he'd be dead. Things were bad, but thanks to you, we might be a family again and just... Thank you."

"You're welcome," Cam says, humbled and amazed. He never thought of it that way. He'd always thought of Sean as saving him.

"Um, what were you doing in there?" Danny asks, awkwardly peeking around Cam into the reorganized room.

"Oh. I was trying to find this old desk. I thought you might need it."

A smile spreads over Danny's face. He shares Sean's sharp features and dazzling smile, but it's the warmth in his eyes that's really the same, and the sheer heartbreaking wonder that someone would show him kindness. Cam knows one thing for certain: he'll do anything to make sure this boy and Sean have a better life as a family.

"We should both be in bed," Cam says.

"Sure. Uh. See you in the morning. Cam."

"Goodnight, Danny."

Cameron walks into his bedroom in the same stupor he's been in all night. He's certain the shock will wear off eventually, and he'll move on to anger or grief or bargaining, but he'd rather it not be tonight. He's tired and he needs an antacid. Maybe he'll take a sleeping pill too.

"What are you doing?" Kayla asks him from the bed. He had hoped she was asleep.

"Getting some pills and brushing my teeth. I'll change downstairs."

"Downstairs?" He doesn't understand why she's surprised, but if there's anything he learned today, it's that he doesn't understand at all how her mind works.

"You can't honestly expect me to sleep here."

"I'm not going to do anything inappropriate, babe, come on." Kayla rises from the bed, and Cam takes an automatic step back.

"Like this morning?" It seems like a week ago already, but now the memory makes his skin crawl.

"You said his name," Kayla whispers, picking at her nails. "In your sleep. And you were... You know."

Cam wants to say something snide about how if she can't even talk properly about sex, she shouldn't be telling him how to have it or forcing it on him. But for the first time, he notices her eyes are red from crying, and he imagines what it must be like to hear your spouse say another's name in their dreams. "Have I done that before?"

Kayla sniffles and nods. "A few times. Never quite so clear."

"Before you met him?"

Kayla nods again. Before she even knew what he looked like or if he was even real, she had to hear Sean's name. "I thought it was another infatuation, but then when he came in. The way you..." Kayla swallows thickly. "You never looked at me like that. Dawn saw it too. She called me while I was home alone freaking out and she told me you kissed him."

"On the forehead," Cameron corrects numbly.

"I spent the whole night praying and trying to convince myself it wasn't like that. I even called you, like an idiot." Cameron squints at her. He doesn't remember that, but he does remember her being alone with his phone the morning after. "Do you have any idea how lonely that is? How lonely I've been with you right there beside me? But I calmed down and tried to be reasonable and I—"

"Figured you could pretend to care about Sean, invite him into our house, and use him to fix me," Cameron finishes for her.

"I do care about Sean, but I want you to be happy again. I want to save you," Kayla protests. "I saw a way to make you happy, and it was working. It is working."

"Kayla…"

"You can't leave. I won't let you give up on us," Kayla goes on, her voice thick with tears. "You have to stay now or you won't only ruin things for everyone."

Cameron closes his eyes, all that anger and grief threatening to burst out in a torrent. He holds it back, but just barely.

"I'm still going to sleep downstairs."

"You *can't*."

"I meant on the couch," he sighs.

"What if Danny sees that?" It sounds completely rational. Because it is. For Danny to stay here, they all have to keep up the charade that this is a normal, functional family.

"Then I'll be in the spare room."

"If he—"

"I'll set an alarm."

Cam grabs his clothes and toiletries without another word and dumps them in the spare room. He makes it fifteen minutes before he pads down the stairs to lurk at Sean's door. He shouldn't knock. He shouldn't think of sleeping on the couch despite Kayla's warning. Or in Sean's room. He thinks it anyway. He knocks.

"Cam?" Sean asks as he opens the door. It's a strange mirror to how he found Kayla. He looks like he's been crying too, but in this case, all Cam wants to do is comfort him.

"I'm sorry." The words tumble out before he can think. "I didn't know. I didn't think she'd ever—"

Sean pulls him into his room, shutting the door behind them and wrapping Cam in his arms. "It's okay," Sean whispers against Cam's hair.

"No, it's not." Cam pulls back and looks at Sean. There's barely any light in the room, just the glow of the clock and the dim orange streetlights through the open window. He can still see Sean as clearly as if it were midday, his mind filling in the shadows with freckled skin and green eyes. Kissing him is stupid, but he does it anyway. He needs this, needs Sean. For the first time in hours, he can breathe. Sean kisses him back with the same desperation, cradling his face in his rough hands before pushing him back.

"We can't," Sean breathes, even as his thumbs trace Cam's jaw.

"Why?" Cam asks, despite knowing. "She knows, and I am not going back to our room. Ever." They kiss again, and Cam doesn't know who started, but again it's Sean who stops it.

"Danny. We can't because of Danny." Sean says it with a fervor that makes Cam think he's convincing himself as much as Cam. "If we step out of line, I could lose him again, and, Cam, I can't. I can't do that."

Finally, inevitably, the dam inside him breaks. He grips Sean tighter, as if holding him tight enough will mean he won't slip away. He refuses to weep, so it all stays inside that searing pit in his chest, tearing him apart. "So that's it? It's over? She wins."

Sean winces and breathes deep. "Come on, don't think that way. You were never gonna leave, right? We were never gonna be anything more."

Cam wants to argue, wants to say that they could be. A few hours ago, he was ready to walk out the door and follow Sean into the unknown. But Sean never wanted that; that's clear now. Just like it was clear before. Now he can't walk away without ruining Sean and Danny's lives.

"You're right. I guess she was too. This isn't real." Sean doesn't need to know it was real for Cam. He doesn't need to hurt anymore.

"I'm sorry, Cam. It was nice while it lasted."

Cam doesn't want to hear that, doesn't want to think about endings or that he'll spend the night wondering what this all means for his damned soul. So he kisses Sean one more time and tries not to think that it's the last. Sean kisses him like it's real, and it hurts more than anything.

He pulls back and doesn't say anything else. He can't. He walks through the dark, silent house and up the stairs. He doesn't hesitate in the hall.

He sleeps in the spare room.

sean

Sean wonders if Bill has a bottle of something stored in one of the old cars in the yard. The house is cleared out, except for beer, but he hopes there's something squirreled away because he needs a drink like never before.

He can't find anything, of course. Which is good. Getting blind drunk is not ideal when you've got a social worker looking over your shoulder. At least being out among the rusted corpses of Impalas and Continentals is comforting. This is the sort of place he belongs: as gray as the clouds above, full of jagged edges and forgotten things.

He'd felt like a goddamn alien in the pristine halls of Sunrise High, like there was practically a neon sign above him flashing "drop out" and "homeless cocksucker." It reminded him too much of Cam and Kayla's house: bright and clean and colorless. A place he'll never, ever belong.

Danny wasn't bothered by it. He was too distracted by wide-eyed awe at the track and computer lab. Gardner took the lead, talking up how smart Danny is and assuring the vice principal that Danny could keep up in the honors classes and that he had perfect attendance at his old place. It hadn't taken very long to get him signed up, but Sean felt like he was buying a house or something when they added his name as an emergency contact. He made sure Cam was on there too. Eventually, Danny went to his first class, and Sean was done. He's glad to be at Bill's now, but not alone with his thoughts.

Sean sniffs the air, catching a familiar skunky aroma right before Chad comes around a corner.

"The boss man wants to see ya," Chad says before stumbling back when he gets a look at Sean. "Whoa, man, you okay?"

"Do I look that bad?" Sean barely slept, tossing and turning until three am as he went over that last conversation with Cam in his head, and everything that led up to it. He kept telling himself it was better to end it: he has to think of Danny, and that shouldn't feel like reattaching one arm only to saw off the other.

"You look like shit, and man, your aura. You got some bad mojo going," Chad wheezes.

"Thanks," Sean says, scrubbing a hand over his face. "Bill say what he wanted?"

"He said, 'tell that fool to stop sulking and get his ass in here and review these orders,'" Chad replies with a grin.

"Great." Sean trudges back up to the house where Taylor rests by the door in a tire lined with an old blanket. She sniffs happily at Sean, and he smiles despite himself. Danny would like her. He always wanted a dog.

"So I just got an interesting call," Bill drawls before Sean can even get the door closed. "Some social worker checking in to verify your employment. I assume that has something to do with you bein' late this morning."

"Yeah, I was gonna explain—"

"Danny's back." Bill finishes for him. "I got that. You mind explaining to me how? And why?"

Sean collapses into the worn armchair across from Bill and kneads his temples. "It's a long, fucked up story."

"Do I look like I got anywhere else to be? Talk."

Sean stares at Bill. Well, he wanted someone to talk to.

"I told you I met Cam on the street…"

The words tumble out like an avalanche. He tells Bill the whole thing. Meeting Cam. The sex. Jeremiah. Moving in with Cam and Kayla. The other sex. Danny. Everything. It takes nearly thirty minutes to get it all out, and Bill listens to it all without a flinch or frown.

"So I told Cam it was over, and today I took Danny to school and here I am."

Bill rolls to the kitchen, opens the fridge, and grabs two beers. He returns to Sean and pries the cap off one before handing it to him.

"I shouldn't—"

"Boy, you need it."

Sean takes the beer without further protest, draining the neck in one swig. It's sour and not cold enough, but it eases his nerves with sheer familiarity. "So. That's the story. Turns out I've been living with a psychotic bitch and now I'm stuck there for another month at least, and I'm not even getting laid anymore."

"Could be worse," Bill says with a shrug and opens his own beer. "At least you got Danny."

"Yeah, in the shittiest possible way," Sean scoffs as Bill takes a drink. "You know what's the worst part? I *liked* Kayla. I thought she was nice, and I felt like shit going behind her back after all she did for me. I don't get how I missed that she was crazy."

"Now you know that ain't true," Bill grumbles, and Sean raises an eyebrow.

"Did you not hear the part where she wants to screw Cam straight and use me as some fantasy to do it?"

"And that's backward and stupid, for sure, but this Kayla, she ain't crazy." Sean takes another long sip of beer and waits for Bill to explain. "You just wish she was crazy because crazy is easy. Crazy, you can write off; it ain't real. Because when normal, rational people do twisted crap, that's a lot harder to take. Especially when they have a reason. And she's got the worst one in history."

"What the hell are you talking about?"

"Love, ya idiot. Some of the worst things in the world been done 'cause of *love*." Bill spits out, and Sean stares at him.

"What she's trying to do isn't something you do to someone you love," Sean argues. "It's selfish and cruel and manipulative—"

"You don't think love can make people do awful things? The worst things when they want to make someone love 'em back who don't feel the same way. Add in loneliness and a little religion, and there's the recipe for disaster right there. It ain't the good sorta love, but it's love." Bill raises his bottle in a mock toast. "Ain't it grand."

"Never knew you were such a romantic."

"Love can drive you to the darkest places if you ain't careful." Bill looks out the window towards a tower of wrecked cars. "My Linda. When I lost her – and lost my legs – I thought long and hard about pulling out my .45 and joining her. Only reason I didn't do it was fear that maybe I wouldn't see her. Figured living with her memory was better than, well, other options."

Sean stares silently at his friend, heart breaking a little bit. "Bill, I didn't know."

"Course you didn't, I ain't ever told anyone." Bill shakes off the moment and looks back at Sean. "All I'm sayin' is you can't pretend you don't know why she's doing this. Hell, don't tell me there's not a whole mess of cruel, thoughtless things you'd do if it was for Danny."

"That's different, Danny's family."

"What about the mountain of stupid you've climbed to be with Cam, and not even keep him?"

"I'm not—" Sean's voice cuts out the same second Bill's eyebrows go high. His heart stops too. Then it sort of explodes. Or something like that. Something painful and stupid and pointless like the love he didn't even know was there. "Oh crap."

"Maybe you are dumber than I thought."

"Never been in love before, I guess," Sean whispers. "Bill, what the hell do I do?"

"What do you mean *do*?"

"I told him it was over! I… fuck!"

"Ain't nothing to do, boy. You buckle down and carry on. Keep working to get Danny back."

"But—"

"Didn't you say he's never leavin' and you've been halfway out the door for a month? That *he* said it wasn't real?" Sean cringes at his own words and the memory of Cam's. He was stoic and cold like always. Because of course he'd never feel the same, because Kayla and Bill and, fuck, Sean himself, were right. It wasn't real. Sean is good for a fuck, but he's not the kind of person that someone like Cam could love.

He's just the kind of idiot that falls stupidly in love with the one guy he's never gonna be with and realizes it too damn late.

25

Halloween

cameron

"Trick or treat – oh my God, are you okay?"

Cameron raises his head from where it was cradled in his hands. He wasn't sleeping. Just resting his eyes for… a while. The clock says it's nearly noon. Damn. He turns to Flor and sighs. "I'm horrible. But it will pass. Probably. Why is your hair like that? And your nose." She's wearing pointy buns, and her face has lines on it.

"I'm a cat, you dork. It's Halloween."

"Oh. I lost track."

Cameron can't be blamed. He was always pressured to ignore the holiday, despite the number of children in their neighborhood who had to be turned away from their door, disappointed. He also can't be blamed for not knowing what day it is since yesterday, which he's reasonably sure was a Monday, lasted an eternity. Work and pretending to be a functional family were awkward and draining, as was the long night on the lumpy couch in the spare room. He'd spent hours contemplating his life and soul and begging God for help before sleep finally came.

"What have you got there?" Cameron asks, peering at the bowl in Flor's hands.

"The kids today call it candy. Though you could use some."

Cameron grabs a small Milky Way and tears off the wrapper. The first taste bursts with caramel and chocolate, and he almost groans. He's barely eaten the last few days, thanks to his stomach and the fact that his life's a disaster. It makes the candy taste better. He takes another – a Butterfinger this time – and inhales it. After the third, he looks up to see Flor staring. "I'm hungry."

"You want me to leave the bowl?"

"Yes, please."

"You're gonna ruin your appetite for your mom's awesome cooking."

"Damn it." The last thing he wants to deal with tonight is a family dinner with Kayla beside him, pretending everything is fine, while Sean and Danny sit at home with the porch lights off, wondering why they can't give out candy. Cameron shoves another fun-size in his mouth.

"What the hell is going on with you?" Flor demands,

He glares up, chewing petulantly. "Nothing."

"Does it have something to do with the hospital lawyer wanting to see us?"

"What?" Cameron spins to look at his email inbox.

"She just called, don't freak. She said it was some accounting hiccup. It'll be fine. Abby is cool."

"Abigail Beecher could kill someone with her shoe and smile through it." Does she know something about him? Or Sean? About what he said to Isaacs to fix Sean's bills, so Kayla's patient would be punished. He doesn't want to – no, he *can't* deal with this today. As if on cue, his phone buzzes with a text alert. He makes the mistake of looking in the hope that it's from Sean, but it's Kayla.

> **Switching Thursday shift to tonight to cover in case things get crazy. I let your mom know to still expect you. I'll be home by eleven at the latest.**

He wants to throw his phone across the room or text back something snide about whether he should ever bother making his own schedule ever again. Instead, he looks up at Flor. "Does Miss Beecher want to see me today?"

"No, just when you're free."

"Good. I'm going home."

Cameron gets up and grabs his coat before his resolve fails. Lee and Nate both give him shocked looks as he grabs one more handful of candy before he leaves.

He's not sure how he ends up at the grocery store with a cart full of over-priced candy and pumpkins. He never tried to buy beer as a young person or sneak out of the house, but he wonders if it felt the same as this.

"Kinda late for shopping."

Cameron turns to the voice behind him. Somehow, it feels appropriate to see Drew here. God doesn't let him get away with anything. "Are you going to lecture me about spreading Satan to children?" Cameron asks flatly.

"What? No! That's Ted's stupid thing. I was just saying hi." Drew moves his own basket behind his back, but not before Cameron catches sight of wine and several boxes of macaroni and cheese. It reminds him vividly of the last time he ran into Drew in the store, when he had been so shocked that Sean was coming to stay with them. After Kayla had spoken to him and told him something that made him suspect Sean's sexuality.

"Hi," Cameron says, acidly. "What did my wife tell you about Sean?"

Drew goes pale. "Fuck. Uh…" Drew stammers and sets down his basket with a clank of glass to raise his hands defensively. "Okay. She came to me in crisis, right? She said she thought her hus-*you* had feelings for a man who had come into the hospital and that she wanted to make things work."

"And?"

"And I told her to show compassion and understanding! I said to take this test as a blessing or an opportunity for positive change!" Drew squeals. "I was hungover, okay? I did *not* tell her to move Sean in!"

"But you knew that Sean and I."

"No! I mean, I had my suspicions, but I didn't *know*. I swear I'm not outing anyone." Drew looks nervously around the candy aisle and picks up his basket.

"I know," Cam sighs. "I'm just trying to understand how I got into this situation."

"I'm always around to talk," Drew offers sheepishly while shoving five bags of Twix into his basket.

"I don't think that would be helpful." It's not like it would change anything. Cam can't make a move without putting Danny and Sean's happiness at risk, and his soul is already damned. "I'll see you on Sunday," he says, adding a few more bags to the cart and waving at Drew.

"Always here if you need me!" Drew calls after him.

He throws himself into preparations at home, letting it clear his mind like running. The sound of the door at 3:30 makes him jump in confusion. Danny looks similarly bewildered to see Cameron when he walks inside.

"Whoa." Danny looks at the cauldron of candy by the door and the pumpkin Cameron is currently disemboweling. "I didn't think y'all did Halloween."

"We didn't, but I want to this year," Cameron says, wiping his hands.

"Because of me? I'm kinda old for Halloween."

"I get the sense you and Sean missed a lot of holidays. Call it making up for lost time."

Danny sets down his backpack with a cautious smile. "I get that. Can I help?"

"Please. I'm not very artistic. How was school?"

"Fine." Danny picks up a knife and settles in next to Cam. "The teachers have been pretty great about giving me what I need to catch up, so that's cool. I might go to the math club meeting later this week."

"I remember math club," Cam says as he starts sawing into his hollowed pumpkin. "Don't tell Sean that."

"He's a nerd too, don't let him fool you." Danny looks down, fiddling with the newspaper spread on the table and frowning. "At least, he used to be."

"Danny, are you okay?"

"I talked to him on the phone, but I didn't see him for years. I hardly knew what was happening in his life. I didn't even know he was homeless, and half the time now I feel like he's putting on a brave face for me and..." Danny takes a deep, steadying breath. "I don't know him."

"He's your brother," Cam says carefully. "Though I guess that doesn't count for much. Sometimes I feel like my brothers are strangers."

"It's not that he's a stranger," Danny muses as he starts cutting into his pumpkin. "It's more like I never see all of him, ya know? Like he's always showing me what he thinks I want to see?"

Cam smiles ruefully as he carves a triangular eye into this jack-o-lantern. "You're a very perceptive young man."

"Does he do that with you?"

If only he knew. "Sean doesn't think much of himself. Which is a shame, because he's truly a remarkable person. I think he feels like he's failed people – you, your parents – and so he gives up himself in order to be what people need. He'll do or say what he needs to help."

"You're pretty perceptive too," Danny says. "So how do I get him to trust me and, you know, think about himself for once?"

"If I knew how to do that, I would certainly tell you. As for trust, that takes time. It's a precious commodity."

"He trusts you," Danny says easily, and Cam stops carving.

"It's mutual," Cam says softly. "I trust him more than anyone."

"Except Kayla." Cam looks up to Danny's wide, expectant eyes.

It used to be true. They used to trust each other completely. And they had both been completely wrong to do so. "Marriage is different," Cam evades.

"Does she know you're home and halloweenifying the house?"

"She's working late tonight, but I'm sure she'll get a concerned phone call about our souls from someone in the homeowners association."

Danny smirks and gets back to carving. It's the first time Cam's had a long stretch alone with Danny, and it only confirms all the praise Sean's given him. He's smart and snarky like his brother, but in a different way; like the variation on a familiar tune in a different key.

Once the jack-o-lanterns are done, Danny helps Cam set them up outside and decorate the front porch until it's 'creepy but cool' in Danny's words. Then go inside to make sure the candy isn't poisoned, and Cam doesn't call his mother to let her know he's not coming to dinner.

sean

Sean wonders if he pulled up to the wrong house. There are pumpkins on the front porch, and the lights are orange and – are those cobwebs and fake skeletons? Maybe he slipped into an alternate reality. The idea sticks with him when he walks in to see Danny and Cam parked on the couch with Danny's algebra homework spread on the coffee table.

Coming home to people he loves looking happy and taken care of really shouldn't feel like someone ripping out his heart with their bare hands, but his life is weird, Sean figures.

"Someone wanna tell me why we're living in Halloweentown?" Sean asks, pushing his feelings down to be dealt with some other day or decade.

"I thought it would be nice. For Danny," Cam answers with a gummy smile.

"And you too. I saved you some Butterfingers!" Danny says, grinning as well.

"Any licorice?" Sean asks as he doffs his jacket.

"Ew. No."

Sean looks between Danny and Cam, who spoke simultaneously.

"See, Sean. Cam is a normal person who doesn't like dirt candy," Danny expounds.

"There are Twizzlers in the cauldron," Cam says with a shrug. "That's as close as you're getting."

"You got a…" Sean turns to see the absurdly large plastic cauldron of candy on the kitchen table just as the doorbell rings, and Danny jumps to answer it. He snatches the candy before Sean can touch it. "Hey!"

"Here." Cam passes Sean a small Butterfinger as Danny answers the door to a chorus of sweet voices crying "Trick or treat!"

"Thanks, Cam," Sean says as he takes the candy, smiling despite himself. "You two have fun?"

"Yes. It seems I have a weakness for Lockwoods," Cam says as Danny comes back.

"We're pretty charming," Sean grins. It makes Cam and Danny smile.

"I'm charming. You're just old," Danny teases.

"If Sean's old, that makes me ancient," Cam says with a shrug.

"No, dude, you're like, distinguished. Hey, did Sean, did you know Cam did math club in school too? I told you it was cool!"

"I thought we were going to keep that between us, Danny," Cam says, deep and serious.

"A distinguished nerd, awesome," Sean laughs. "Guess that beats a hippie nerd."

"I am not a hippie!"

"Your hair says otherwise, kid."

Danny rolls his eyes. "Well. I'm gonna do math club, so don't be a jerk about it."

"Danny." They both turn to Cam, whose voice is low and conspiratorial. "Don't tell your brother this, but I also was in the poetry club."

"Oh man, that *is* lame," Danny whispers.

The bell rings again, and this time it's Cam who answers. Sean cranes his head to watch him smile at a small dragon and a dalmatian in a fireman's hat. "Where's Kayla?" Sean asks.

"I guess she had to work late or something?" Danny answers with a shrug.

"She'll be home after ten," Cam adds as he returns, sounding extremely unhappy about it. "She switched shifts. She'll be here on Thursday night." Sean hopes Danny doesn't notice the sullen look that Cam gives him when he says that.

"And you ditched family dinner to celebrate the devil's holiday?" Sean asks, and Cam's frown turns into a smirk. He loves that Cam can be a little shit when he wants to be. As it turns out, he loves a lot of things about the nerd. "So, have you had any food today besides candy?" Cam shares a guilty look with Danny, and Sean gives a dramatic sigh. "How am I not surprised?"

Sean works on dinner while everyone takes turns answering the door. Danny eventually finishes his math homework, and they eat on the couch like savages once the trick-or-treating mobs have died down.

"Are there any Kit-Kats left?" Danny asks once the dinner plates are cleared. Sean throws him one from the cauldron, and Danny catches it with a smile.

"I can't believe you smack-talk licorice when you like stupid Kit-Kats," Sean grumbles as he plops on the couch between Danny and Cam, who's working on a tiny bag of M&Ms.

"Those are in no way comparable," Cam says, and Sean glares between the two of them. "Kit Kats are at least edible."

"How are you two already ganging up on me?" Sean says.

"Hey, do you remember the Kit-Kat cake?" Danny asks wistfully.

Cam squints at them as Sean laughs to himself. "What did that taste like?"

"Not cake," Sean replies, looking over at Danny. "What were you? Six going on seven?" Danny nods, and Sean looks back at Cam. "It was Danny's birthday, and we didn't have a cake for him. So I improvised. Layers of Kit Kats and, uh, some peanut butter, and I think mini marshmallows? Oh, and there was a banana in there too, so it was healthy. I had to take a five-finger discount for a week to get all the stuff."

"And pudding for frosting," Danny adds.

"It was *disgusting*," Sean goes on, shaking his head so he doesn't have to see the fond look on Cam's face.

"It was awesome," Danny says, quieter. "Sean always made my birthdays nice. Even when everything else was crappy."

"He seems to make a habit of that," Cam says. "He made steaks for mine. He's improved as a cook."

"I can make you a Kit-Kat cake next year," Sean says, and the warmth in Cam's face fades. Who even knows if they'll be allowed to speak next year.

"Twix, please," Cam still says after a beat of staring.

"You got it, poetry club," Sean replies with a wink.

"So what'd you *do* in poetry club?" Danny asks, oblivious. "Just read poems?"

"Worse than that, we wrote then." Cam's actually blushing, and it's adorable.

"*You* wrote poetry," Sean states, trying to wrap his mind around that.

"Don't tease," Cam mumbles.

"No, it's cool. Do you still have any?" Sean asks.

Cam shakes his head. "Someone got rid of my notebooks. I kept it up for a few years in college, but I wasn't as productive without people to support it." Sean stares at Cam, catching the air of regret around him. He imagines a life where Cam was never scared into the closet. Cam, as a poet, studying classics, eating pizza whenever. Happy, somewhere else.

"Did you ever write poems for Kayla? Like, when you were dating?" Danny asks, knocking Sean's thoughts off track.

"No," Cam mutters. "They weren't that kind of poems."

"I know a good one about a man from Nantucket," Sean pipes up and gets the groan from Danny he was hoping for, as well as the smile from Cam. The doorbell saves them all, and Sean retreats to hand out candy to a potato, a gremlin, and a monkey. "Danny, you got much more homework?" Sean asks when he's back.

"No, they're going easy on me to let me get the swing of it," Danny says. "We're actually in the poetry unit in English, maybe Cam can help me with that?"

"I'd love that, Danny," Cam says without missing a beat.

"Tonight?" Sean asks.

"Nah. I'm done for now," Danny says. "Can we watch a movie?"

"How about *Nightmare Before Christmas*? Get all the holidays in at once," Danny suggests.

"I've never seen it, that sounds great," Cam smiles.

They talk over half the movie, explaining jokes to Cam or reminiscing about their holidays as kids. It reminds Sean that Danny's never had a good Christmas, or Halloween, or birthday, Kit-Kat cake or not. He has a chance to give him that now; he already has one under his belt thanks to Cam. The thought of other holidays (or any part of being responsible for Danny) without Cam is terrifying though. Sean doesn't know how to do this. What if he can't keep Danny in the right school district or afford shit or…

"Sean?" He looks up to Cam. The credits are rolling, and his eyes are dark blue in the dim light.

"Sorry, zoned out," Sean says. "What?"

"We were asking if you wanted to watch something else," Cam explains.

"It's kinda late, you rebels," Sean replies just as the garage door rumbles open. "And the warden is back."

"Is she gonna be mad?" Danny asks, blessedly ignorant. Cam shrugs.

Kayla looks more confused than angry when she walks in. "Hey, guys?" Her eyes fall on Sean. "Did you and Danny—"

"It was me. Danny helped. I came home early and set it up," Cam says, quietly defiant in a way that makes Sean so goddamn proud.

"You came home? What about dinner with your mom?" Kayla asks.

"Slipped my mind," Cam says coolly. There's nothing Kayla can say right now without making Danny suspicious.

"Well. Uh. Had a crazy night at work. Lots of fights and this one patient—"

"I don't know if Danny needs to hear about that," Sean cuts her off.

"Yeah, I gotta get to bed," Danny agrees. "Night, everyone." Danny retreats, leaving the adults to quietly stare each other down.

"Sean, will you help me blow out the pumpkins?" Cam starts towards the door without waiting for a yes. Sean gives Kayla a shrug and follows. She looks hurt by all the cold shoulders, but Sean can't be bothered to care. When the candles are out, they stand in the quiet autumn night that smells of sweet decaying leaves and approaching rain, looking up at the sky.

"Do you really think the dead come back tonight?" Cam asks out of nowhere, and Sean turns to him.

"I hadn't really thought about it."

Cam keeps staring out into the darkness. The sky is surprisingly clear, a few dim stars visible in the black, but there's a chill in the air. Maybe it is ghosts, who knows. "I'd rather be a ghost. If I had a choice, between that and hell – or nothing – I'd choose to linger."

"I'm not letting you watch creepy movies anymore," Sean mutters. A light comes on above them, making it easier to see when Cam smiles at him. Sean can't stand the idea that someone whose smile can make him feel so blessed thinks he's bound for hell.

"Let's get inside," Cam says, easy, like he didn't just bring the mood down a hundred notches. Not that Kayla hadn't already accomplished that simply by coming home. Now Cam has to share a bed with her. He doesn't rush up the stairs though. He walks Sean to his bedroom door like he's saying goodbye at the end of a date.

"Guess you better get up to—"

"I've been sleeping in the spare room."

Sean doesn't know what to say to that. Why is all of this so fucked up? How can spending a few hours with Danny and Cam leave him so happy that he gets this time with them and so empty, thinking of the future?

Cam doesn't move or resist when Sean closes the distance between them and kisses him, gentle with regret. They don't touch, other than their lips; that would be too much. But it still makes Sean ache and tremble down to his bones. Cam looks as sad as before the kiss when Sean pulls away.

"You said it was over."

"I did," Sean whispers. "But tonight was nice and…" *I wanted to kiss you at least once, knowing I love you.* "I'm sorry."

"I didn't mind," Cam says, like a fucking saint. The martyred kind that end up tied to a tree and killed by arrows for their stupid faith. Stepping back is easier than words. It is over, for good now, and they both know it.

"G'night, Cam."

"Goodnight, Sean."

cameron

Cameron dresses for church – in a bit of painful irony – in the walk-in closet. He takes longer because he can hear Kayla moving in the bedroom.

The week was easy in terms of keeping his distance. It's not like they didn't speak – Cameron was polite as he could manage – he simply had nothing to say to her. At least there was no mention of date night. Saturday was harder, but Cameron managed to spend extra time at the mission and then ran errands with Danny and Sean, including a trip to the grocery store that provided the house with several foodstuffs that had been forbidden for years. It was satisfying to his soul to bring home bacon and beef because "Danny likes it." Kayla doesn't need to know how much his stomach has suffered all week.

Kayla is waiting for him when Cameron finally emerges into their room. He sighs and heads for the door, but Kayla jumps up to block his exit.

"I need to let Sean and Danny know we're ready to go," Cameron grumbles, and Kayla's brows knit.

"They're coming to church?"

"I assume you'd want them to. We wouldn't want people *getting ideas* after last week."

"Oh. I hoped we'd have some time alone to talk," Kayla frowns. There's the real reason Cameron is happy to bring Danny and Sean along: a buffer.

"There's nothing to talk about. Please let me through."

"Yes, there is." Kayla stops him with a hand on his chest, eyes plaintive. "Like when you're going to stop punishing me?"

"You think this is a punishment?" Cameron asks back, recoiling from the contact.

"You won't talk to me or look at me. I feel like I'm living alone."

"This is the only way I know how to survive in this house." He tries to leave again, but Kayla steps in front of him. She looks small, faded, and lonely.

"Babe, come on," Kayla pleads. "I know this isn't ideal, and believe me, this wasn't the plan. I *know* how hard it is to forgive someone when they've hurt you, but I'm trying to do that, and I just want you to try too. I did all of this for you, and I miss you."

Cameron waivers. He knows that sharing a home with someone you love and not being with them is the loneliest thing on earth. He made this mess, and he should suffer the consequences, but maybe he doesn't have to hurt someone more than he already has.

"We have to go," Cameron repeats quietly, and Kayla moves aside with a sigh.

He walks into the hall, shoulders heavy and tense. He can't even begin to think of what the future will be when Sean and Danny are gone and he's left alone with the same life he had before he knew them, only now with nowhere to hide and no moments of escape in sight.

The car ride with everyone is awkward and silent. They take seats in a rear pew and avoid talking to anyone before the sermon starts. Osborn is in rare form, launching into a litany of the disasters and tragedies from the last months. Cameron hopes it's a prelude to an appeal for Christian charity, that maybe Drew is organizing some sort of relief effort for the holidays.

"All of these horrors, all of this suffering, inflicted on our nation because, while good men continue to lead us towards our Lord, there are still too many who have turned from Christ and his commandments." Cameron sighs. It was worth hoping. "Though our leaders are fighting valiantly to return our country to the Christian ideals of our founders and purge us of evil, there are still those servants of the devil who seek to pull us all into the quagmire of sin. Fornication. Open borders. Sodomy. Feminism. Environmentalism. Child rape and murder. Socialism. All these forces weigh upon us every day, dragging us into hell! God sees and *weeps*."

"Is he serious?" Danny whispers under his breath to Sean. Sean shrugs, and Cameron feels a surge of embarrassment.

He's spent many years tuning Osborn out, doubtful, but accepting his version of The Lord. He always seemed generally correct, as far as Cameron could tell, because he agreed with everything Cameron had always been told, though with more focus on anger and judgment. Then again, Cameron always knew God was angry and was punishing him for his sins, time and again. He accepted it. Now, trying to listen like Danny would – or, like Sean would, especially after what Jeremiah did – makes his skin crawl. Not just from the usual shame for his sin, but for his complicity in such hate and perversion of the faith he loved.

"There is work to be done, my friends," Osborn goes on. "The word of God must be spread; the poison of sin must be sapped from this great nation. We must be cleansed! Ready your souls, reach out to those who need it. Do not let them walk so easily into hell."

"How long is this going to take?" Danny asks, and Sean shushes him. Cam smiles.

Things get better after the sermon. A few people stand up to testify; one about how God gave them strength through illness, and last week they were pronounced fully in remission, and another on how she was moved to donate an inheritance to a children's hospital. The final witness speaks of overcoming temptation, Cameron isn't sure what kind, but he notices Kayla glancing at him as the man testifies of finding strength in God to overcome his vice. It's a relief when the choir begins. The readings are boring, as usual, and finally Osborn turns to community announcements, urging everyone to vote *correctly* next Tuesday. Drew asks for more mission volunteers before his mic is turned off, and everyone files out to mingle.

Cameron hopes this part will go quickly so he can avoid Jeremiah (and strangling him). Like most, it's not a high hope.

"Cameron." He turns to the sharp voice. Of course, his mother is the first to find them, with Vince and Luke flanking her. "I've been trying to get in touch with you all week, and now you won't sit with your family. Where were you Tuesday?"

"Someone had to give out the candy," Cameron replies flatly. Luke looks nicely scandalized.

"You ditched family dinner for… Halloween?" Vince asks.

"Cam wanted to spend more time with Danny here," Kayla interjects. Vince and Luke's eyes go wide as they finally notice that Sean isn't alone. Susan remains implacable. "This is Sean's brother. He's staying with us."

"Hm. Fostering will be good for you," his mother remarks. "Took long enough."

"Nice to meet you too," Danny mumbles.

"Sorry for them," Luke says and steps forward to offer Danny a hand. "Luke Steward. This is my brother Vince. Mom is Susan. Our wives and rugrats are somewhere around."

"Glad you joined us, Danny," Susan says, watching as Danny shakes Luke's hand, wincing.

"So, uh, Cam says you own a radio station?" Danny asks uneasily.

"Nah, Vince here is the media mogul. I'm just around for the meat," Luke replies.

"Best steaks in the state," Osborn's voice comes from behind them, and Cameron cringes.

"Hello, Ted. Lovely sermon," Susan says with a smile to the pastor as he joins the group, and Cameron's discomfort grows.

Osborn's eyes fall on the Lockwoods. "New parishioners? Wait, you're the Steward's… what's the right word? Adoptee?" Osborn says.

"Let's go with friend," Sean replies, low and fed up.

"And you, young man?" Osborn asks, turning to Danny.

"I'm his brother," Danny says, a steel in his eyes that Cameron has never seen. "Do you really think hurricanes are caused by feminists?"

Osborn frowns, and the crowd around them goes quiet in shock. "It's slightly more complicated than that, young man," Osborn chuckles.

"Yeah, the science of global warming *is* complicated," Danny spits back. "But I'm fourteen and I get it and it doesn't have anything to do with God being mad at America because we have gay marriage or trans people or something else stupid."

"Young man, you shouldn't address your elders like that," Susan admonishes, looking horrified.

"He's only speaking his mind," Cam says and gets a glare. "Free speech is what makes us great, isn't it?" Danny gives him a crooked smile for that.

"Danny, these are adult topics," Kayla gently warns.

"If they're so adult, then you shouldn't be talking about them in church; probably scarring poor, confused kids," Danny snaps back.

"I think you may be the one confused, Daniel," Osborn says, eyes narrowed to suspicious slits.

Danny steadies himself and stares Osborn down. "No, I think the fact you're a bunch of homophobic, sexist, racist idiots is pretty clear."

"*Danny,*" Sean hisses, and his brother turns to him and Cam with a look of fury. "It's not polite to tell jerks they're jerks to their faces."

"Well, I—" Susan huffs, and Kayla starts to protest too.

"We're gonna go wait by the car," Sean says, pulling Danny away. "Great to see everyone, as always. Just a delight." Cam watches as the brothers hurry out of the church, and Sean says something he can't hear.

"Well, that was bracing," Susan grumbles. Cameron can't tell if she's embarrassed, furious, or both. "Kayla, Courtney wanted to talk to us about her shower. Come along."

"I'll be right back," Kayla says, rushing after Susan.

"I have to go… elsewhere. See you next week," Osborn says and disappears as well, leaving Cameron alone with his brothers.

"Quite a firecracker you've got there in young Danny," Vince says with warmth that surprises Cameron.

"At least he's clear about what he thinks," Luke remarks and gives Cam a dark look. "Rather than pretending to be respectful and not meaning it. You won't be bringing them along to Thanksgiving, will you?"

"I hadn't even considered that. We're going to your house this year?" Cameron says, weary already.

"Well, Kayla and Mom can't cook, and I had it last year," Vince replies. "I don't see why Danny and Sean shouldn't be there. It could be great entertainment."

"We'll see," Cameron says, casting about to see where Kayla and his mother have gone. Instead, his eyes land on the two people he wants to see least in the world: Jeremiah, with Arnold Isaacs right by his side. And heading his way. "Oh no."

"Arnold, it's been too long!" Luke crows, embracing Isaacs as he joins them. "And Jeremiah, good to see you again. You both know Vince, and of course Cameron."

"It's actually Cameron that we want to talk to," Isaacs says with a terrible smile.

"Though of course support from the two of you would be excellent as well," Jeremiah adds.

"Support?" Vincent asks. "For what?"

"We're formally calling on Osborn to fire that pervert Drew Barons," Jeremiah says plainly. "He's a pernicious influence on the congregation. Far too liberal and disruptive. Just yesterday, he was going on about how our work at the mission could do more for illegals and queers."

Cameron wants to throw up. Or scream. Or beat the living shit out of Jeremiah just like he did to Sean. Either cowardice or good sense keeps him in check.

"We're putting together a letter, and we'll be bringing our concerns to Osborn in the coming weeks. We'd be happy for signatures and testimonials from all of you," Isaacs goes on.

"Cameron here knows him best," Jeremiah says, smug and smiling. "And can verify his radical positions for us."

"Are you asking Lee to join you?" Cameron asks back, his jaw clenched and fists tight.

"Lee hasn't been returning my calls. I believe it's because she and Mr. Barons have... Well, I won't speculate." Jeremiah looks Cameron right in the eyes, and it's chilling." You know how rumors can hurt people. Especially vulnerable ones."

Cameron stares Jeremiah down. So it's blackmail, not outright exposure, with the perfect ally in Isaacs. Of course. Cameron has never hated one person this much.

"Consider it, Cameron," Isaacs says darkly. The two men nod and leave the Stewards, walking with identical dangerous smiles on their faces.

"What the hell was that?" Vince asks, staring at Cameron.

"Obviously, they've got some axes to grind," Luke says. "Even if they're right about that hippie Drew. You should sign that letter, Cam, even if they were assholes in the way they asked."

Cameron sighs. He can't do that. He's made so many bad choices, but he won't be part of this. "I don't think what I say matters," Cameron mutters, because it's true.

26

Ramble on

sean

EVERYTHING IS FADING. SEAN keeps thinking that as he looks out over the salvage yard. The leaves are almost all gone, and the few left on the skeletal trees are pale and withered, barely hanging on before the next storm takes them away to who knows where. It's the same at home. No. At the Steward place. Not home. He doesn't know where home is, and that's freaking him out. Danny's been with them for over two weeks, and it should be getting easier by now, but it's all just fading into silence.

They go through the same routines each day. He and Cam look at each other over Danny's head and don't talk. Cam sleeps in a separate room to avoid talking to Kayla at all costs. If she had some grand plan for Cam to want Sean so much that it drives him back to her, it's not working. Yet.

It's just a matter of time before Cam gives up; Sean knows it. Before his anger and resolve fade. Maybe he's waiting until Sean's gone, but doesn't say so. Sean has to go. Sooner rather than later, and no one wants to talk about that, not even Kayla.

It was weird for a few days after Danny chewed out the asshole pastor (and they hadn't returned the next week). Sean had been proud but also freaked. He had no idea if Osborn was petty enough to report him for something. Luckily, Kayla hadn't made a big deal about it – probably trying to stay in Danny's or Cam's good graces as much as possible. Danny made sure to tell Sean he didn't judge Cam by his church, but he left Kayla out of that, which was accurate but worrying.

Danny and Cam still get along like a house on fire. They even went running together a few nights ago. Sean tried to join, but he started dying after half a block and gave up. He said it was his hip, and no one had to know he was breathing so hard he was worried a lung was gonna fall out. Well, no one but Wanda, who was walking Fergus at the time and caught him. He enjoyed a stroll with her before Barry and Kid Flash made it back, then got to introduce Danny. He's not sure who liked Danny more, Wanda or Fergus.

Sean's managing to survive on those little moments of joy. Like last Thursday, when it was just the three of them. He missed having alone time with Cam, but playing Monopoly – and losing horribly to the two geniuses he's stuck with – was better than sex (in its way). That's not to say he can't stop looking at Cam or wanting him. He does, and sometimes it's so intense he can barely breathe. But the three of them, together for a few hours as a family? That's good too. Good enough to keep going and carry on for another day.

Gardner wants Sean to get his own place, and Sean knows he's got to do it, but the idea of a week away from Danny when he just got him back and leaving Cam forever is… Well, it's the reason Sean's staring out Bill's window at the dying leaves. He keeps waiting for the wind to blow him away, but he's hanging on.

"You done with the Jones order?" Bill asks, and Sean jumps. "Oh, I'm sorry, did I interrupt your quiet meditation?"

"I was just thinking."

"About Danny or about Cam?" Bill asks, wheeling back to his desk.

"Both. Don't really know what to do about… anything," Sean mutters as he sinks into the old couch.

"Why don't you start by finally putting this in that fancy new bank account you got?" Sean startles as the envelope of money he'd been trying not to think about lands in his lap. It's heavier than he remembers.

"Now, I know you think you shouldn't use that cash because of what you had to do for it, but by my thinking, you did what you could, and you came out alive on the other side. There ain't no shame in that. No point letting it sit in my desk drawer doing nothing."

Sean doesn't want to get into an argument he knows he's gonna lose. "Fine. I need first and last month's rent for an apartment deposit, *apparently*."

"You find anything good yet?" Bill chuckled.

Sean shakes his head. "I gotta stay in the same school district cause I'm not making Danny move again, and I guess I don't want a commute out here either. But everything round here is expensive, and they want credit checks or whatever."

"That's rough." Bill watches thoughtfully as Sean tucks the money away. "If you need some extra cash, I may have a side job for you. Just a few hours, under the counter."

"I ain't giving you a pedicure, no matter how much you pay me."

Bill turns to look at the decrepit staircase that mainly functions as a bookshelf. "I wanna clean up the top floor. I've got three rooms up there and a bathroom that I'd like to get habitable. Figure it's a good job for a hooligan with time on his hands."

"I'm a hooligan now?"

"You can get up the stairs. That's all I need."

Sean looks over Bill. There's something lurking behind his smirk. "Why clean it up now?"

"All your talk about finding a place got me thinking. I could rent it out, make some extra cash." Bill finally turns to Sean and fixes him with an earnest look. "I hear this place is in a prime school district."

"Bill…" Sean looks to the stairs leading to the rooms he knows Bill wouldn't even make him pay for. It's all too familiar, but for the life of him, he can't imagine what Bill wants from him. "Why're you doing this?"

"Why else? I'm a lonely old cripple and I wanna see some life in this house before I burn it to the ground for the insurance money."

"You sure a reformed hustler and a kid too smart for his own good will be good company?"

"Better than the bad memories around here." There's a gentleness below the surface of Bill's gruff words. He's not offering. He's asking.

"I gotta talk to Danny before I say yes, and..." Sean bites his lip. He doesn't need Cam's permission. "The social worker."

"Sean." He looks up at Bill, surprised by the tender tone of his voice. "Cam's welcome here too. To visit or otherwise."

Sean's mouth goes dry at the same time his eyes go wet. "He and I don't have an otherwise. Never did."

"And never will?"

"Not if I want to keep Danny." Sean picks at the worn corner of the envelope. "Fuck. I don't even want to think about it. I'll get started upstairs."

The upstairs hall is dusty and quiet; the cold sort of quiet that settles on a place that hasn't felt human warmth in years. It's a hall, just like Cam and Kayla's, but it's so different. The walls are covered in ancient, flowered wallpaper peeling where it meets the wainscoting. No one ever bothered to shut the curtains on one window, so years of sun have bleached the carpet pale in some places. Sean turns the nob on the closest door, and it gives with a stiff creak. It's a bedroom. Small, tidy; maybe meant to be for a guest, back when Bill and Linda had them.

The next room is the bathroom. There are water stains and rust around the sink, and Sean doesn't even want to think about checking the pipes. The room across from that must have been the master bedroom. It's untouched from the last time Linda Farnell woke up there, Sean knows it. There are still wrinkles on the quilt and a hairbrush on the nightstand.

Dust and cobwebs cover the wedding photo by the window. It's faded too, but Sean can still make out the faces, smiling in the sun. It's a strange mirror of the picture of Cam and Kayla hanging in their front hall. It's different the way the house is different. Bill and Linda look happy; Cam looks lonely. This empty room is full of reminders of the love that used to fill each void. It's deep in the walls, settled like the dust.

Kayla's house (because that's what it is) never held love like that. It's just endless, empty quiet of clean lines and pristine carpets where a stain or flaw would never be allowed.

Sean doesn't take off his shoes when he comes in. It's something he's been doing more lately, waiting for Kayla to say something. Today is Thursday, though, so he doesn't have to worry. He's home late after stopping by the bank and making a deposit that had the teller giving him a weird look. It was worth it to see such a healthy number on the account balance. Danny has his homework spread out in front of him on the kitchen counter, and there's no Cam in sight.

"Hey, short stuff," Sean says, ruffling Danny's hair. "What'd Cam pick up for dinner?"

"Burger stuff!" Danny says as Sean opens the fridge to check for himself. To Sean's surprise, there's a six-pack of beer next to the ground beef that's already missing a bottle.

"And beer? Where *is* Cam?"

"On the porch," Danny says, grimacing as Sean looks at him. "I think he had a bad day."

Sean grabs two bottles and closes the fridge with a sigh. "How much homework you got left?"

"Uh, gotta finish these math problems then do my history reading."

"Cool, I'll do dinner when you're done, I'm gonna…" He pops the caps from the bottles and shows them to Danny.

"Thanks. I didn't really know what to say to him."

Sean's glad he didn't bother taking off his jacket yet when he steps out into the biting November air. Cam has his old coat on too. He looks like a pale shadow in the dim light; faded and small.

"You're in my spot," Sean says as he plunks himself next to Cam on the lounger, close enough that their legs and shoulders touch. Cam's empty bottle is between his feet, and he takes the fresh one from Sean with a half-smile, their fingers brushing. "Why we drinkin'?"

Cam takes a long sip. "I finally had that talk with the hospital lawyer."

"The giant bitch you were telling me about?"

Cam gives him an annoyed look as Sean takes a swig. "It's inappropriate to call women bitches. Though Abigail Beecher does meet the traditional parameters."

"That bad?" It has to be to have Cam looking this depressed.

"She's been called in to review my entire department's performance. She says they've found irregularities in our accounts. Starting with the write off for you."

Sean's stomach falls. All he knows is that Sean said something to someone, and his bills went away, but he never knew how. "Shit, Cam. I thought that was kosher?"

"It *was.* Almost. I offered someone a favor, but that was the only time. I started reviewing our files since then and…" Cam takes another deep drink. "I should have noticed. Something has been going on."

"What? And what do you mean favor?" Sean doesn't like that this all started with him.

"Kayla performed a procedure that Arnold Isaacs objected to. He wanted the patient to pay for the sin, literally. He threatened me first, but I finally agreed to look the other way because of you, so we could write you off. I didn't know her insurance was still billed."

"So the hospital got paid twice?" Sean asks, brow furrowed.

Cam shakes his head and pinches the bridge of his nose. "The money never made it into the hospital accounts and it looks like that wasn't the first or last time it's happened."

"Someone's been skimming you mean?" Sean doesn't like the sound of this at all.

"The money's going somewhere," Cam says, taking another long draw of his beer. "I have a meeting with Miss Beecher on Tuesday. I have to investigate before then, but the person that's probably behind it…" Another drink. "It's Nate," Cam says, completely grim.

Now that's a surprise. Sean only knows of Nate vaguely, but he doesn't seem like a bad guy. "Damn. He's just a kid."

"He's two years older than you."

"Yeah, well, I'm old for my age. Why do you think he's doing it?"

"I don't know." Cam looks so defeated and tired, Sean can barely stand it. "I can't go to the administration because Isaacs knows what I did. Hell, he may be involved, and if I implicate *him*—"

"He's gonna fire you from the boring job you hate?" Sean tries to joke, but it doesn't land.

"Isaacs has always been suspicious of me." Cam takes another swig of beer. Sean echoes the movement. "I haven't been cooperative with him lately."

"What's that mean?"

"It's not important."

"Cam."

"Maybe I won't go to church on Sunday," Cam says wistfully. "I don't want to see anyone there anymore. Do you think God will mind?"

"Nah, you see him every day," Sean smiles, and Cam does the thing where he squints and tilts his head and makes Sean really want to kiss him. "Isn't that the schtick? God is all around you. In the stars and the earth and the trees or some shit?" Sean gestures to the night sky, stained pale orange by the streetlights. It's hard to imagine God there, but maybe if you squint, you can find him.

"That's God's creation, not God." Cam sounds genuinely offended.

"What's the difference?"

Cam stares at him, gears turning in his head. "That's a pagan sentiment."

"Hey, you're the pagan, Mr. Halloween."

Cam laughs. A small, bitter sound somewhere between a sigh and a hiccup. But it's a laugh and a real smile, and that's good enough for Sean. "How was your day?" Cam asks.

"Eh. Boring. Bill's got me working on a thing." Sean takes a sip of beer to cover. He's not ready to have this conversation. "Speaking of lawyers. I got a message from mine. I gotta meet him on Monday while Danny does the same.."

"Sounds exciting."

"Oh yeah, it's gonna be awesome." Cam leans against Sean with his head on his shoulder, intimate and exhausted. Sean wishes he could kiss him, but that's a bad idea for a lot of reasons. So is the cuddling, but this, Sean's willing to take a risk for.

They stay that way for a while, finishing their beers in silence. When Sean takes Cam's hand, it's freezing.

"Sorry you had a shitty day," Sean murmurs.

"Thanks."

cameron

Cameron needs more coffee than the single-cup coffeemaker, or possibly the world, can provide. He stretches as he watches the coffee drip into his mug, his neck popping loudly as he does.

"Wow. That couch can't be comfortable." He turns to look where Kayla leans meekly against the wall. "Sounds like it's taking a toll."

"I actually tried the floor last night. It wasn't much better." He keeps his eyes on the coffee. It's Saturday. He just has to get through breakfast, then he can get away.

"Or you could sleep in your bed. *Our* bed." Kayla looks tired too. It reminds him of the way she used to look in the first year of medical school, when she'd come to his apartment exhausted and he'd hold her on the couch until she fell asleep. Sometimes she'd do the same for him, and it was peaceful and safe. He misses it.

"Kayla, I don't want to talk about this right now."

"Alright, when are we going to talk about it? Because soon, it's going to be just us again and we're going to have to make this work."

"Are you asking me what I want?" Cameron shoots back. "Because that would be new."

"That is not fair, I have *always* done what you wanted," Kayla replies, voice tense and thick. "I have been trying for years to be whatever it was you needed. I was patient and turned a blind eye because I knew you were struggling. You never asked for a change. I thought you wanted to make this work, to make *us* work."

Cameron swallows. "I did. You know I did."

"That's why I can't give up now. You married me, knowing you had these feelings and urges. You didn't ever leave, you didn't ever even talk about it. You didn't give up on getting better. You kept trying, and I loved that you didn't give up on us. I kept Sean here to make it better. I brought Danny here to keep Sean around and help them because I care. What does it change that I'm trying to help you the same way you helped yourself? Was I really doing something so wrong trying to help you this whole time when you stayed by me too?"

"No," Cameron says without reservation. That whole time he'd prayed and fought and tried and tried to change, and it wasn't until he met Sean – until he fucked Sean – that he knew trying to change was useless. Even then, he hadn't left. He used his desire to stay where he was, unmoving. Kayla saw that, so how could he blame her?

"So why would you give up now when everything is out in the open?"

"Because holding Danny's welfare over Sean to get him to stay just so he can be used is wrong," Cameron replies, and he doesn't know if he's speaking for himself or Sean when he says it. "You're using people and lying—"

"Are you saying you weren't using him? That you weren't lying to me the whole time?" Kayla's face has turned from sadness to stone, her eyes clear and penetrating.

"I'm sorry for that, I truly am. I—"

"Never meant to hurt me? That means you never wanted me to know. That means you wanted to keep going and stay together."

Cameron stares at her, trying to see her the way he used to: his best friend. A beacon of hope for the normal life he was supposed to love. "I did want that."

"And if you could get better? Wouldn't you want to? Don't you want to be normal? To try? To be at peace with God and let go of sin?" Kayla is so sincere, and he can see his own suffering reflected in her eyes. And he knows she doesn't want to see him hurting.

He's tired of hurting too. He's tired of fighting.

"Hey, guys!" Danny, with Sean behind him, explodes into the room and makes Cameron and Kayla jump. "We got bagels! Oh." Danny looks between them, and Sean looks just as worried when he joins him.

"Is everything okay?" Sean asks carefully.

"It's fine," Cameron says, and Kayla sighs.

"Cool! Then I can ask you my question!" Danny exclaims.

"Danny, I told you, *no*," Sean growls.

"But..." Danny starts.

Sean turns to Cameron and Kayla, looking harassed. "He wants to go along with you to the volunteer thing."

"He what?" Cameron asks.

Sean shakes his head. "For some reason, I was trying to talk him down from thinking everyone at your church was a raging asshole and mentioned the volunteering. He got on some tear about colleges looking for that sort of thing." Sean scrubs a hand over his face. "He wants me to come, and I think he's got some idea about seeing my old stomping grounds or whatever."

"I don't think that's a good idea," Cameron says, and Sean brightens.

"Why? It could be educational, and it would be good for Danny to get another perspective on the church," Kayla counters, and Danny brightens.

"I don't want him getting educated about that sort of thing," Sean nearly hisses.

Cameron's phone starts buzzing in his pocket before he can argue more. He's perplexed by the caller ID. "It's Drew."

"Speak of the devil," Sean says. "Or the opposite of the devil."

Cameron rolls his eyes and answers. "Hello?"

"Hey, Cam," His voice is even shakier than usual. "I wanted to call you and, uh, alert you that the volunteer meeting and community outreach at the mission have been canceled. Today. And for the rest of the year."

"What?" Cam asks, as Sean and Kayla both give him interested looks. "Why is it canceled? Do you not have enough volunteers?"

"There's been some pushback on the recent changes and, well, Ted says he wants to reevaluate the program entirely. Or something. I just wanted you to know."

"Thank you," Cameron stammers. "I guess I'll see you tomorrow?"

"I hope so." Drew doesn't sound like he's joking at all.

"Damnit," Cameron says as he ends the call.

Sean looks equally unsettled. "They're shutting down the sandwich brigade?"

"It would seem so," Cameron says. "I know it was never much, but—"

"It was the only meal some folks got that day," Sean counters. "It matters, and getting rid of it sucks."

Cameron stares silently at Sean. He'd never said anything like that before. It's good to know it helped, even a bit.

"Why can't we do it ourselves?" They all turn to Danny, whose eyes are wide and hopeful. "We can go to the store, get some sandwich stuff, and give them out. We don't need your church's permission to help people."

"No, we don't," Cameron smiles.

"I'd like to help you too, if you don't mind," Kayla says like a peace offering. "You can still hand them out on your own."

Sean gives him a look and a shrug, and Cameron nods.

It's not the worst way to spend a morning. After a grocery run, the four of them get an assembly line going and have several boxes of sandwiches ready to go in an hour.

"Can I come now, since the assholes won't be there?" Danny asks, once everything is packed and Kayla has quietly retreated upstairs to paint.

"Danny, I don't need you to see that part of my life," Sean answers plaintively. "It ain't pretty and it ain't romantic. It's a sad, shitty place."

"Sean, I've seen bad stuff too. Remember, child of the system?" Danny says it so casually, and Cam hates to think of what the two of them have endured. "I want to help because *you* were down there."

Sean purses his lips, annoyed. "Cam, what'd you think?"

Cam is surprised to be asked. "I think it's good to see the sad parts of the world. It makes the good ones matter more. If Danny wants to help people, that's good too."

"Okay, fine," Sean huffs. "But we're not hanging around, okay? I'm gonna hand this shit to Orson, check on Lyle, then we're done."

"Lyle is at the VA," Cam says, to Sean's obvious surprise. "We got him in last week, finally. I'm sorry I forgot to let you know. I was distracted."

"That's awesome." Cam smiles at the warmth from Sean, probably for too long, because Danny has to clear his throat to remind them it's time to go.

It's strange driving downtown *with* Sean instead of to him. It occurs to Cam that this is the first time Sean's been to the neighborhood since the accident, and he wonders what it's like. The last time Sean saw the park, it was summer, not that it makes much of a difference in the grey waste of the city. Even so, the leaves are gone, and the sky is as bleak as the dirty streets.

Cam watches both Lockwoods as they make their way through the place that used to be Sean's backyard. He wonders if Danny is seeing Sean's face on each person huddled in a doorway to hide from the rain or peeking out from tattered tents under the bridge. They give out sandwiches and water to some panhandlers and campers, and Cam watches Danny's expression darken with shock when they distribute some to a few kids who can't be much older than him.

"Look what the cat dragged in," Orson says when they reach the tent camp. He gives Sean a sly smile and shakes his hand, but doesn't rise from behind the desk.

"Hey, Orson. Thought I'd help with the delivery today," Sean says. "Check to see you were keeping everyone in line."

"Oh, we're doing fine," Orson says. "Angel face here probably told you Lyle got a bed at the VA. Some bleeding hearts fixed everyone up with blankets and a few fresh tarps and tents last week, which was awful nice. Lots of socks too." Cameron looks away, humbled and guilty at the same time. It's never enough.

"That's good to hear," Sean says. Danny nudges Sean. "Orson, this is Danny. My brother."

"You in a good enough place to get him back?" Orson asks, eyebrow raised.

"Something like that," Sean says.

Orson turns his attention to Cam, his expression dark. "You better not let me see either of these boys back on my side of things again, you hear, Mr. Steward?"

"I assure you I won't ever let that happen," Cam replies, utterly meaning it.

"Good. Now, hand those over. We're an embarrassment of riches today with your twitchy friend bringing an entire bakery," Orson says.

"Drew was here?" Cam asks.

"And his friends," Orson answers. Cam wonders who Orson means, maybe Lee and... Well, he can't actually think of many others who would help. Strange. It still inspires him that Drew also kept up the good work on his own.

"That's good to hear. We'll see you." Cam nods.

"Bye, Orson, nice to meet you," Danny adds as they walk away. "That wasn't so bad."

"It wasn't so good either," Sean mutters. "Let's get back to the burbs before – crap."

Cam follows Sean's gaze to where a figure in a large, tattered jacket is running towards him.

"Sean, oh my God! I thought you were dead!" the man with a mess of curls pants when he reaches them.

"Get out of my face, Eli," Sean growls, grabbing Danny and striding quickly around the stranger. Cam rushes after him, flanking Sean as the trails behind.

"Wait, I just wanna talk!" Eli calls.

"You nearly got me killed, Eli, there ain't nothing to talk about!" Sean calls back. Cam winces. So this was the wannabe pimp. He suddenly feels very violent. "Fuck off!" Sean drags them away from Eli, his face deadly serious. They're quiet all the way back to the car.

"Who was that guy?" Danny finally asks once they're a few blocks away.

"The guy I was with when I got hurt," Sean answers tightly.

"I thought you said you were in a car accident," Danny says, voice uneasy.

"I was. Sorta," Sean evades.

"Sean," Danny pleads.

"I said *no*, Danny," Sean snaps with a finality that makes both Danny and Cam wince.

Cam feels like a fool now for bringing Danny along. Sean was right, Danny didn't need to guess or learn how Sean survived. He doesn't think Danny would hate Sean for it, but he might tell the wrong person and ruin everything.

What would that even mean for them? If Kayla or Jeremiah made good on the threat to expose Sean? Would Sean be left on his own without Danny? Would Danny be sent somewhere else to add another horror story from the system to his memories? Cam has no idea and doesn't know who to ask. The idea stays with him all the way home, where Kayla is waiting in the kitchen, washing green and blue paint from her hands.

"Hey, guys. That was fast. How was—" Danny goes straight upstairs, and Sean disappears into his room with twin door slams before Kayla can even finish her greeting. She turns to Cameron and sighs. "Are you going to run away from me too?"

"I was considering it." Kayla closes her eyes, and Cameron instantly regrets the callousness of the words. "I'm sorry. I shouldn't have said that."

"No, I deserve it," Kayla says. "I'm taking my punishment. I just want to know how long I'm going to have to wait."

"I don't know, Kay," Cameron replies, resolve fraying. "I don't know what's going to happen tomorrow or a month from now. I don't know what to do. I've been given no choice in anything. At the same time, every choice I make hurts people more."

"It doesn't have to be that way, babe, I swear. It doesn't have to hurt. I'm serious about working with you to fix this." Kayla looks like she's about to cry. She reaches a tentative hand to Cameron, and he doesn't flinch when she touches his arm. If he's trapped here, is it wrong to take comfort? "We can get better and forgive. Move forward. Together."

"You really think that's possible?" He had her faith once, that a merciful God could save him, change him, heal him. The idea that she still has the same faith is so tempting. Maybe miracles are still possible.

"I do. Do you?"

He doesn't know anymore. He hasn't known where his faith lay for a very long time. What God does he even believe in now? The one he prayed to when Sean was in the hospital, or the one who would condemn him for that love? Kayla's and his mother's God that can change him and wants nothing more than for him to build a family of his own, or Sean's God among the trees and stars. He doesn't know. It would be so much easier to let someone else decide.

"I…"

Sean's door opens, and Cameron pulls his hand back like he was burned.

"Hey," Sean says, looking between them. "I was gonna ask if you wanted some lunch."

"No, thank you, I already ate," Kayla says stiffly, leaving the kitchen with a frown.

"You hungry, Cam?" Sean asks, watching Kayla go. "I figure Danny is. No better way to apologize to a teen than with food."

Cameron feels like his stomach is about to eat itself and explode in a ball of fire, but it's so normal nowadays that he doesn't even care. If Sean wants to eat, he'll eat.

"Yes, please. What are you in the mood for?"

sean

Sean knows he's gonna be twitchy within two blocks of a courthouse his whole life, and the public defender's office is right next to the township court *and* the police station, so he's extra jumpy. It's also a few blocks away from the child services building where Danny is meeting with Gardner and his lawyer. Kayla was the one to pick Danny up from school and bring him over because, apparently, that's something a foster parent had to do. Sean will join them there after his own meeting, which he's super not excited for. He hates lawyers.

He can't even remember the names of the lawyers he went through as a kid. They're just a bunch of bored faces in ill-fitting suits that didn't care at all about a punk kid getting busted for shoplifting or being moved to another group home. He's been damn lucky to avoid talking with more lawyers since he aged out of the system. Even Danny's lazy washout in Ohio hadn't bothered to call Sean. Now he has to talk to his own underpaid Atticus Finch and be told exactly how he's going to fuck this all up.

The office is rundown, and the elevator, which takes a full minute to climb two floors, smells like pee. The magazines in the waiting room are from 1996, and the furniture is straight out of a garage sale. Sean has to ask for a second pen to fill out the paperwork after the first dies. Fifteen minutes after Sean's scheduled time, a man with a bald head and a five o'clock shadow steps into the waiting room. His suit is cheap and rumpled to match his scuffed shoes, like Sean expected.

"Sean Lockwood? Ron Horner. Come on back. Sorry about the mess."

There are boxes overflowing with manila folders and papers piled high in the halls between dented file cabinets and a giant printer wheezing away like it's about to explode. Ron walks through a barren kitchen that smells like stale tuna and opens the door to an office, also stuffed with boxes and shelves of files. They sit, and Ron flips open a thin file.

"Alright, Sean. Let's get the rules out of the way. Everything you say to me is privileged and confidential, so you don't have to worry about lying or anything. I've got twenty other juvenile clients and a criminal load too, so I probably won't even remember."

"That's encouraging."

"Just honest. But I am here to help you get your son back."

Sean groans. "Danny's my brother."

"Oh. Right. Sorry." Ron leafs through the file, brows knit. "There's not a lot about you in here. Says you were homeless until recently?"

"Yeah, but I have a job now and—"

Ron's eyes widen as he reads. "You're living with the foster family, that's *different*."

"It's complicated."

"You need to move out, you know that, right?"

"Yeah. I found a place. It's the top floor of my boss's house, but it would be legit. It's not too far from Danny's school and I can drive him and—"

"Good. You need to be there yesterday. Your hearing is in a week." Ron sounds more bored than concerned. "Mr. Gardner will likely administer a surprise drug test today when you meet with him."

"That's fine. I'm clean."

Ron looks slightly interested in that. "Was there a time when you weren't? Says here your dad overdosed."

"I never did anything harder than weed and booze, and I was never an addict," Sean replies, tense.

Ron shrugs and looks back at the file. "So, were you a dealer?"

"What?"

"Police report on your assault says a bad drug deal was the working theory. That'll raise some red flags."

Sean stares Ron down. Time to test the confidentiality. "It wasn't a drug deal gone wrong. It was sex. Or it was supposed to be."

"Ah, hooker. That makes sense, face like yours," Ron says, as if Sean just admitted he sold used cars.

"Gardner doesn't know about that. Neither does Danny."

"Good, if that came out, getting custody would be nearly impossible," Ron replies, confirming everything Sean knew. "You out of the business now?"

"Yeah, now I fix cars."

"Very good. Stay with that, and hopefully Judge Wu will see a fine upstanding young man on the mend and hand Danny over." Ron closes the file and smiles.

"Is that it?"

"Is there anything else I need to know?"

Sean chews his lip. Screw it. *He* needs to know. "How would the court feel if I had a thing with Danny's foster parent?"

"You and Mrs. Steward? That'd be pretty scandalous," Ron asks, chuckling.

"It's Doctor Steward. But no. Her husband."

For the first time, Ron looks surprised. "Oh boy, you don't want anyone knowing that. Not out here in the sticks. They'd have Danny out of there and away from you so fast it'd make your head spin."

"Great. Good to know." Sean doesn't really feel like that final nail in the coffin makes much of a difference. The hope had been dead for a while.

"Now, you've got my number. Call me if you have any questions."

Sean walks back through the kitchen, past the files, and into the waiting room, where the clock tells him he still has half an hour before meeting up with Danny down the street. He finds himself walking, lost in thought, until he's standing in front of the gray cement walls of the police department. He turns abruptly after reading the sign. This is the last place he needs to be.

"Sean?" Fuck. Of course, Detective Hodge is here now. He can almost hear God laughing.

"Hi," Sean says, turning fully to the detective.

"What are you doing here, Sean? You got something you want to talk about?" Hodge asks, serious but kind. Sean wants to turn and run.

"I'm heading to a meeting with my brother and his social worker," Sean says, meaningfully.

"Ah. So. No new memories coming up," Hodge asks with a frown. Sean shakes his head. "Would it change your mind if you knew I was looking to talk to you about two more recent assaults?"

Sean squints at her, his skin crawling. "What?"

"Two other young men – working boys, if you know what I mean – were seriously assaulted in the last month on the job. No one knew the assailant or could make an ID."

A cold sweat breaks on Sean's skin, and his nerves vibrate beneath it. "Did they say it was a middle-aged guy? Goatee?" Maybe it's not him.

"Yeah. Grayish hair. Medium build." The detective looks so hopeful, and Sean hates it.

"Goddamnit."

"Sean, if you have information…" He has a *name*. Hell, if he tried, he could have an address. But if he shares it, everything is over.

"I have my word against his, and I can't talk, Detective. I'd lose people," Sean murmurs.

"Cam Steward?" Hodge asks, pity in her voice. Of course, she knows that too. "He's married, Sean."

"No. Well, yes, but it's not him. It's my brother." Sean looks up to the building where Danny is waiting for him with nothing but hope. "I could get custody if I play things straight, and I can't screw his life up again. I can't let him down."

Tamara sighs and shakes her head. "You're a good man, Sean, you know that?"

"Not really."

"Good people have to make tough calls," she goes on, with more compassion than Sean will ever deserve. "I understand whatever you choose to do. Just think about calling me."

"I'll think about it," Sean lies. He's not going to do anything to jeopardize Danny and that makes him want to punch God in the face. How does doing the right thing screw over everyone? Jeremiah is still out there giving other guys religion with his fists, and no one can touch him. Maybe he is blessed.

He stews in the waiting room of the child protective services building until Gardner emerges and leads him to a small, windowless conference room where Kayla is waiting. With Cam beside her.

"Hey," Sean says, blinking in case this is a dream. "Didn't know you'd be here."

"I called him in," Gardner says. "I wanted to speak to both Cameron and Kayla about Danny, as well as how you're doing and their plans and their availability if Danny can't transition to your custody after the next hearing."

"Oh. Great," Sean says as he sinks into a chair. Cam looks absolutely defeated as Kayla takes his hand.

"My husband and I had nothing but good things to say, Sean," Kayla says. Sean wonders if he's imagining the threat in her voice.

"Thanks, that's... great," Sean says. Are they sitting closer? Has Cam finally cracked?

"But Anthony has been very clear about his concerns," Cam adds, and Sean's stomach falls even farther.

"We still need to know what your plans are," Gardner goes on. "Before Danny finishes his meeting with Miss Hernandez, I wanted to know if you've secured a residence of your own."

Sean stares down at the chipped gray surface of the conference table. What is it? Linoleum? Formica? Who knows. It doesn't matter. He tears his eyes away and up to meet Cam's. He should enjoy those eyes while he still can, even when they're so fucking sad, before it all fades to nothing.

"I have actually. If I need to, I can be out tomorrow."

27

DayLIGHT

cameron

CAMERON HASN'T OPENED A single document all morning. He sent one email. He hasn't touched his coffee. He hasn't looked up from the files sitting on his desk, hard copies of what he's sent to Abigail Beecher. He just ended Nate's career. All that remains is to explain, and he doesn't know if he can even speak. Or if it matters.

Sean is leaving tonight.

Danny was sad when they told him, but they assured him that the separation was temporary and for the best. They lied like adults are supposed to and said it would all be alright. They didn't tell anyone at church. There was no need. All the talk was of Drew getting fired. The one person there who Cam could have maybe talked to: gone.

They're going to have a goodbye dinner tonight, and then Sean is leaving. They'll see him for Thanksgiving, when they bring Danny to Bill Farnell's house (Cameron's mother made it very clear no Lockwoods are welcome at the Steward family holiday). Then Gardner will inspect the residence on Friday. If everything goes well, Danny will go home with Sean after the hearing on Monday.

Then Cameron will be alone.

He stares at his phone, numb, and scrolls down the voicemail menu to deleted messages. There's one from 3:42 A.M. on August 24th. Kayla's voice is thick with tears when he listens.

"Cam? Shit. I know. I want you to know that I know, and I'm begging you: please don't leave. Please, think about us and all we have and your soul, please. I'm so sorry I haven't been good enough, but I'll try harder. Babe, I love you so much, and I'm so sorry, just please don't do this. I'll do anything. Please don't ruin our lives for this stranger."

What would have happened if she hadn't deleted that message? Would he have confessed? Let Sean go? Left with him? Cameron doesn't think he could ever be that brave. He's spent his whole life a coward: afraid of his family, terrified of hell, desperate not to hurt others. He's managed to damn himself and hurt everyone, even so.

Maybe there's no point in being afraid.

His door bursts open, jolting him from his thoughts. Flor is there with Lee behind her.

"Alright, we waited long enough," Flor demands, charging in. "Cam, you look like you're dying. What the hell is going on?"

"It's personal," Cam says weakly.

"Are you and Kayla finally splitting the hell up?" Flor asks, and Lee smacks her on the arm.

"Flor, that is *not* appropriate," Lee says. Cam feels like he's going to be ill. When was the last time he was able to eat?

"No. Screw appropriate. He's been doing shitty for months!" Flor snaps back.

"It's not anyone's business. If Cameron wants to share anything, it's up to him when and how."

"If he doesn't talk, he's going to keel over and die of an ulcer!" Flor's eyes are sharp and dark, and Lee glares back at her. Cameron sits awestruck, staring at them. It's surreal to see two people arguing about what's best for you right in front of you as if you're not there. Then again, he should be used to other people deciding what's best for him by now. He's sick of it.

"I'm gay."

He lets out a shaky breath in the silence that meets him, unable to meet anyone's eyes. He said it. He said it aloud to two people, and the world is still spinning. The vice around his heart feels slightly loosened.

"Well, duh," Flor says, and Cam and Lee give her twin shocked looks. "Oh, come on. I've worn shirts so slutty that Nate nearly had a stroke, and you never even noticed."

Cam looks at Lee. She's as implacable as usual, but curious. "Are you going to tell me you're worried for me? Or my soul?"

"No, Cam. I've seen you struggling too," Lee says softly. "I'm glad you finally said something."

"Did *anyone* not suspect?" Coming out isn't quite as liberating when it turns out everyone knows.

"Most people don't," Lee replied. "Especially considering your marriage. I've just been thinking a great deal lately about how our church has failed many people. Even myself. I've been talking with Drew about it, trying to reconcile my feelings with God, and he's been very supportive."

Drew. Cam winces at the reminder. "Do you know that he—"

"That my horrible cousin got him fired? Yes," Lee spits. "I was planning on leaving the church anyway. This was just another reason."

"Back to you getting divorced," Flor interjects, rolling her eyes.

"I'm not getting divorced," Cam corrects. The shock he was waiting for finally flashes onto Flor and Lee's faces.

"Cam, I know this is, like, a process, but, if you're gay, being married to a chick is kinda wrong," Flor says. "For everyone."

"I am well aware of the difficulties of my situation, thank you. There are other factors at work beyond what I want." Cam feels the familiar sting of acid in his throat as he speaks.

"How is this fair to Kayla? Or you?" Flor demands.

"Or Sean," Lee adds quietly. Wonderful, something else that he thought was secret was evident to anyone willing to look.

"Sean?" Flor echoes, brows knit. "What does he have to – oh *shit*."

"This is not what I wanted to talk about." Cam doesn't want more of a conversation that will highlight what a damned fool he is.

"Then why did you tell us?" Flor asks. Her concern is uncharacteristic and therefore even more touching.

"Because I needed to tell someone." It feels affirming somehow that someone will at least know when this is all said and done.

"Does this have anything to do with why Abby wants to meet with all of us?" Flor demands.

"No, but I know she's on her way." Cam stands, bracing himself. "Please call Nate in."

Before Cameron can move, Nate peeks in the door. "I'm sorry. I tried not to listen and I… Cameron, I'm so sorry for your struggles." He looks guilty as sin.

"You should have let us know you could hear," Lee says, eyes hard and defensive.

"I was too shocked, I'm sorry." Nate looks down, shaking his head. "But I don't understand. Cameron is married and—"

"It is not our job to explain these things to you, Nate. You have the internet," Lee says.

"God hasn't abandoned you," Nate pleads, turning to Cameron.

Flor rolls her eyes. "Not the point, nugget."

"I didn't call you in for a sermon, Nate. This is more serious." Cameron says. "Miss Beecher was suspicious about fraud and irregularities in our department. I know you're behind it." That's all he knows, though. He hadn't been able to track the funds once they were in the hospital coffers.

"Oh," Nate says as Flor and Lee turn to him in shock. "You noticed that."

"Nate, why would you do this?" Cameron asks, a different kind of heaviness settling in his chest.

"It was only a few people!" Nate protests, eyes wide and innocent, and Cameron shakes his head. "They were wicked. God marked for punishment already. We were doing God's work,"

"Nate, this is not right," Lee says. "That's not your judgment to make."

"Screw judgment. It's illegal and—" Flor's mouth snaps closed at the sound of the outer door. The group files out of Cameron's office to find Abigail Beecher waiting, arms crossed in her immaculate suit and not a single black hair out of place. "Hey, Abby, how are you?"

"Underpaid," Beecher says, eyes scanning the group and settling on Nate.

"Miss Beecher, I can explain," Nate starts, his voice shaking. Before he can go on, the last person Cam wants to see steps in behind the hospital lawyer.

"Don't say anything you'd regret, Mr. Pike." Arnold Isaacs's deep voice is even more self-satisfied and dangerous than usual, a dark smile on his lips. "I can't say I'm surprised to hear of shenanigans in *this* office. But I'm sure that things will be cleared up soon, Mr. Pike."

"Are you protecting him?" Flor demands. "Nate *just* admitted—"

"Nathaniel here likely reacted in panic when it appeared he was being used as a scapegoat," Isaacs smirks, savoring what Cam knows he's about to say. "For Mr. Steward."

"What?" Flor and Lee both exclaim. Cameron himself can only stare, his panic rising as Isaacs smirks and Beecher rolls her eyes.

"Miss Beecher, I thought my report to you made clear—" Cam stammers, as he tries to keep a grip on the moment and not dissociate.

"That you failed to notice ongoing fraud in your own department," Beecher says, unimpressed. "We're going to launch a full investigation of *everyone's* conduct, but for now, both you and Mr. Pike are suspended without pay." Nate looks down in shame, and Cameron fixes Isaacs with a pitiful glare.

"That seems unfair," Cameron says. "I'm not the one who's passing judgment on our patients. Nor do I think Nate did this alone."

Isaacs only smiles. "I have no idea what you're implying, Cameron, and I would advise you to think before making any allegations," he purrs.

"I want everyone to go home and calm down," Beecher says, stepping between Cameron and Isaacs. "I'll schedule interviews with all of you *after* the holiday."

Perfect, Cameron can lose his job and the Lockwoods in the same week. He was an idiot to think he wouldn't be targeted in all of this. The squeaky wheel that gets thrown to the curb or some other tortured metaphor.

He looks at Lee and Flor, both wearing different dumbstruck expressions. "You two can manage things while I'm away."

"We'll have it all waiting for when you come back," Flor says, with an acidic look towards Isaacs. Cameron feels a new stab of worry for Flor and what will happen to her without him there. He can't even consider that now.

"Come on, Nate," Cameron says, taking the younger man by the arm to walk out past Abigail and Isaacs's glares. They stay silent all the way to the elevator to the garage. The wait is interminable, and Cameron considers taking the stairs until Nate sniffles. Cameron turns to him to see tears in his eyes as the elevator arrives.

"I thought I was doing a good thing," Nate says as they step in and the door slides closed. "I—"

"I'm not interested in your excuses, Nate," Cameron replies. "I know you thought you were doing good. We all do when we make mistakes."

"Arnold said it was the right thing!" Nate blurts out, and Cam sighs at the confirmation.

"It wasn't," Cameron mutters.

"It was going to the church! To God's work!" Nate goes pale as the words leave his mouth. He knows he's said too much.

"The church?" Cameron echoes. Suddenly, Osborn and Isaac's distaste for Drew makes more sense. They wouldn't want someone with morals snooping into the finances if the church was benefitting from Isaacs' schemes. The elevator pings, and the door opens to the cold, damp employee parking lot. They walk slowly down the row of cars, and Cameron wonders if he'll ever come back.

"Are you going to be honest with Miss Beecher when she interviews you?" Cameron asks, trying to imagine the story Isaacs will ask him to weave. "Or has the plan always been to blame me when this was inevitably discovered?"

"Cameron, you may be a sinner, but I would never do that," Nate whimpers.

Cameron doesn't bother hiding his contempt. "This has nothing to do with my sexuality." From between the rows of cars, a low laugh echoes, and Cameron spins to see Isaacs emerge. "Are you a cartoon villain? What are you doing here?"

"Giving my friend a ride to lunch. Nathaniel and I have a lot to talk about," Isaacs smiles. He presses the key fob in his hand, and a shiny black Lexus unlocks next to him. "But I couldn't help but hear. You're right, the blame for this will be laid at your feet. You'd be wise not to contest that."

"And be prosecuted for your crimes?" Cameron snarls back.

"The police won't be involved, Miss Beecher has assured me," Isaacs replies, relaxed and smiling. "Someone will need to be disciplined, quietly, and this is probably for the best. We can't have your kind working in a hospital."

"My kind?" Cameron braces his shoulders, his body vibrating in offence.

"I don't think we should discuss this anymore," Nate stammers, stepping in between Cameron and Isaacs, but the older man just sneers over his head.

"Then again, Cameron, we could probably come to an agreement to make us all happy," Isaacs muses, still calm and smiling. "I can think of ways for you to be useful. We wouldn't want any of your friends to be hurt by this either." If he means Sean or Flor or Drew or Kayala or all of them, Cameron doesn't know. All he knows is he's done.

"Arnold, may I say, in light of all of this," Cameron begins, fists tight and jaw tense. "Go fuck yourself."

Both Isaacs and Nate recoil as if Cameron punched them both, which he wishes he had the bravery to really do. He gets into the car and slams the door, gripping the wheel tight in unfocused anger, and peels out of the lot, not looking back.

It takes him half the ride home before the anger morphs into a numb sort of disgust that Isaacs will most certainly get away with all of this.

Maybe Isaacs is blessed. Maybe he *is* righteous, and God has given him protection. This is Cameron's punishment for his sins. For loving Sean. Even now, when he should be fuming at the loss of his livelihood, what scares him more is the threat to Sean.

He finds himself at a red light, staring past it to the slate sky.

"Why?" he asks, as usual, not expecting an answer from on high. "Is this all you want from me? To suffer?"

The light turns green.

His fury stays with him until he turns down his street and sees the Bel Air blocking the driveway. Sean shouldn't be home yet.

Cam parks crooked in the street and walks inside through the open garage door. The duffel bag he loaned Sean last night is full next to the door inside, but Sean isn't on the ground floor. Cameron's heart starts racing as he climbs the stairs. Every door is closed except the one to the master bedroom, and sure enough, Sean is standing inside, holding a paper bag in his hands as he stares at the bed.

"What are you doing up here?"

Sean's eyes snap to Cam, wide and guilty. "I was returning the stuff I had that was yours."

"Oh." Sean sets the bag on the bed. Inside, Cam can make out bottles and books. "I thought it was clear you could keep those."

"It wasn't," Sean replies, face unreadable. "What the hell are you doing home?"

"Were you going to leave without saying goodbye?" Cam asks back, his mind filling with the thought of coming home to find every trace of Sean gone without warning. That would have broken him entirely.

"No! Bill said I was a useless sadsack today, so he sent me home. I was getting this done so I'd have more time with you and Danny, you moron. What are *you* doing home?"

"You were upset at work?" Cam steps too close into Sean's space. Close enough to make out the details of his freckles and the way his eyes aren't as bright green in this light. He smells like rain and sweat, mixed with the soap from his morning shower.

"Yeah, I was upset. I'm messed up about leaving," Sean snarls. "But—"

"You are?" Cam squints.

"Of course! Why would you–"

"It's hard sometimes, with you. You don't always show people what you're really feeling." Sean looks so offended it's comical. Cam doesn't laugh; it wouldn't be polite. He touches Sean's face instead, a gentle graze of his fingertips along his cheekbones. The first time he spoke to Sean, when he found him outside that strip club, he hadn't been sure he was real. Even now, he's like a dream that Cam knows he has to wake from soon.

"What the hell is going on, Cam? *Why are you here?*"

"I brought up the fraud to the lawyer, and now I'm suspended pending an investigation." There it is, the anger that flares like a distant siren, echoing the horror in Sean's face and taking Cam back to his cold, hopeless reality.

"You're *what?*"

"Nate is suspended as well." His voice sounds distant, even to him, like he's talking about someone else's life. "But I'll be blamed and fired. Isaacs is behind it."

"Cam, what the hell? You're not gonna roll over and let them do that, are you? You could go to jail!" Sean is furious. It's anger bright as the sun, and Cameron feels like his own rage is a dim fire in comparison. He's beautiful, and he's about to leave Cam in the dark.

"I don't have any other choice," he says slowly. "I won't go to jail. Isaacs assured me it wouldn't come to that. Of course, then I did tell him to fuck himself."

"Good, so you can stand up for yourself. Nice to know it's actually possible."

Cam kisses Sean instead of hitting him. He kisses Sean because he's angry, because he's hurt and desperate, and Sean is leaving, and he's angry too. He doesn't push Cam away; instead, he reacts like a reflex, hands twining into Cam's hair and tugging hard. Their mouths slot together, and it's two pieces fitting together perfectly, their bodies pressed close.

Cam didn't realize how cold he was until now, pressed against Sean's heat, arms wrapped around him, grabbing fistfuls of his shirt. It's been three weeks since they last kissed, and it feels like coming home.

"Cam, what are you–" Sean pants as Cam mouths at his jaw and neck.

"I'll stop if you want."

"Don't you fucking *dare*."

Sean knows exactly what Cam does: they're alone for the first time in weeks, and this might be their last chance. It doesn't matter that it's over and everything is falling apart; they have this. They have each other, and Cam can defy heaven one more time before everything is gone. Cam moans against Sean's lips and starts tearing at his shirt.

"Here?" Sean asks, pulling back in shock.

"Is that a problem? Nothing good has ever happened in this bed, and I'd like to take my one chance to change that."

"Cam, this is—" Cam cuts him off, kissing Sean again, rough and seeking, his tongue insistent. This is a bad idea on every level, but for the first time in weeks, Cam feels something other than hopeless, trapped, or damned, and he refuses to let that go. His hands slide down Sean's back to his ass and then between them to where Sean is already hardening in his jeans. Sean gasps as Cam gropes him through the fabric. "Fuck, never mind."

Sean yanks off Cameron's coat and jacket, then practically rips off his shirt, sending a button flying. They separate enough to fumble with belts, first Sean's, then Cam's. They tumble to the bed, chest to chest and skin to skin. The bag Sean was holding crunches underneath them, and a shampoo bottle stabs Cam in the hip as they move up the mattress in a tangled mess. They struggle out of pants and shoes, grinding together and kissing ravenously, all the while.

It feels better than anything, holding Sean close and tasting his breath. Sean parts from Cam to push the debris around them away, his mouth kiss-swollen and slick, and his eyes heavy. He's beautiful, so beautiful, and Cam is going to lose him. In a second, Sean is back, smiling down at Cam from above with a small bottle in his hands. Lube.

"You were returning that too?" Cam asks. He can't decide if he should laugh or cry.

"It was your birthday present," Sean replies, as if that makes it better. "Works out though, huh?"

"Fuck me."

Sean stares, his breath slowing as if he's trying to translate what Cam just said. Strange, since Cameron thought it was quite clear. "You want me to—"

"Fuck me. I want to feel you in me before you're gone."

Sean's mouth hangs slack, and not for the first time, Cam wishes he could read his thoughts. "Okay," Sean breathes, then nods. "Jesus. Okay."

"Will you…"

"Yeah." Sean's voice quavers, but he kisses Cam with a desperate urgency that's a complete contrast. Cam wraps his legs around him, savoring each burst of friction as they move together until Sean sinks between his thighs, kissing at his hips and nuzzling his stomach. Cam sighs in contentment when Sean's lips encircle his cock, his tongue hot and velvet smooth. His mouth is scorching and skilled, but his hands shake as they trail down Cam's length and behind his balls.

Cam breathes deep as Sean stills and his hands disappear. He listens to the snap of a lid, moves readily when Sean nudges his legs further apart, and gasps at the first cold press of Sean's finger. It's different than the other times he's done this to himself, more focused and intense, but the moment Sean slides inside, Cam keens.

"It's okay. I got ya," Sean whispers against Cam's thigh. "It's okay."

Cam closes his eyes and lets Sean in. It's not relaxation, not really. It's more like floating, letting go of everything and trusting the water to keep you up. Sean licks and sucks at him, keeping him hard as he pumps his finger into Cam's core. When he adds the second, he finds Cam's prostate and Cam moans, arching off the bed into the pleasure. "There."

"I got that." There's laughter in Sean's voice, warm and perfect, and Cam loves it. He loves this man more with each frantic beat of his heart.

Sean adds a third finger with ease, wringing more moans from Cam. He's on the edge of coming just like this when Sean pulls off and kisses up his body, fingers spreading Cam wide and ready. "You good?"

"Yes. Yes, please, Sean…" Cam pants. Then he's empty. He opens his eyes to watch Sean slick himself up, then lean close above him and lay a gentle kiss on Cam's cheek.

"Tell me if I hurt you."

Cam isn't sure what that means. Sometimes just looking at Sean hurts, but it hurts in that terrible, beautiful way that reminds him he's alive. That proves he still *can* hurt. His life before Sean was gray. With this miraculous man, he can see every color, even the ugly ones. Sean kisses him, careful and adoring as he pushes in. His cock is impossibly hot and stretches Cam more than he thinks he can bear, but it's glorious and searing, and he's so full. He's so full, and he loves Sean so much he might explode, and it does hurt, and it's perfect.

He stares up into Sean's eyes, and it's bright and beautiful. This is what he wants, what he was created to adore and love. He doesn't care that it's a sin. It's his. It's theirs.

Sean is still, eyes locked with Cam's, asking for permission. Cam nods and, slowly, Sean begins to move. It's so different on this side of things. He feels possessed, needed, taken. And ecstatic. He wants to close his eyes, let himself be taken away by the pleasure, but he can't look away from Sean. He wants to remember everything about this moment: the way Sean breathes, the way his broad shoulders flex, and how the flush on his skin makes his freckles disappear. He wants to remember the last time as clearly as the first.

"You feel like heaven." He said it then, in that dingy, dark motel room. He says it now in the dim light of day in his own marriage bed. He means it. If this is as close as he gets, maybe that's enough.

"Cam, I…" Sean bites his lips and clamps his eyes shut. He thrusts fast, hitting Cam's prostate on every other stroke and driving him mad. "Fuck."

"Come in me, Sean, please."

"I…" Sean shifts and fists Cam's cock, matching the rhythm of his hips, and Cam moans, the crescendo rising in him without warning. He comes with a gasp, waves of pleasure pulsing through him as Sean kisses him. Sean's hips stutter, and Cam feels the pulse inside him and sighs.

They collapse onto the mattress, filthy and sated. The glow of it holds Cam for a few beautiful seconds before he remembers that this was the last time. Sean is still there, for now, leaning over Cam and touching his cheeks. He wonders how he sweated enough that they're so wet.

"You're not allowed to cry, okay? This is already shitty enough."

Oh.

"I'm sorry. I didn't mean to."

"I'm sorry too," Sean says softly, his forehead on Cam's.

"There's nothing to apologize for." Cam means it with his whole heart.

"I screwed up your entire life. Your job and your family, and now I'm bailing and… I'm sorry." Cam hates the pain in Sean's voice. He hates that he can feel guilt radiating off of him like heat.

"My life was a mess before you," Cam whispers. "I wouldn't take back a single moment with you because you have always made it better."

Sean's eyes glisten as he looks at Cam, but no tears fall. "Same."

It feels like a terrible rehearsal for the goodbye they'll need to say soon, and Cam can't bear it. "What if we just go?"

"What?"

"We get in your car and get Danny, and drive until an ocean stops us and start fresh." It's a beautiful idea, the three of them finally free on the open road, leaving everything behind.

"You're serious."

"*Yes.* Why not?"

Sean smiles, wistful and sad. "We'd be arrested for kidnapping for one. And Danny'd kill me for moving him again."

The small ember of hope that was growing in Cam's heart starts to fade. "We could convince him."

"And you're still married."

Cam never thought of that as an obstacle, not really. He never thought of his marriage as real because of the lack of love and lust. Sean never seemed to care before, but maybe he just doesn't want to run away.

"It was a stupid idea anyway," Cam murmurs.

"Bailing, yeah, but maybe—" A door slams downstairs, and they both jump. "What the hell? Danny isn't done with school for hours," Sean exclaims, springing up and scrambling for his clothes.

"I don't know." Cam winces as he stands. He grabs his shirt and starts scrubbing himself with it as steps approach. Cam pulls on his briefs, shaking in panic.

"Crap," Sean says as he yanks on his jeans, and the door creaks open.

Of the faces Cameron expected to see, his mother's was not among them. Nor is he expecting her utter annoyance.

"Really, Cameron? I thought you were done with this."

28

intervention

sean

SEAN'S NOT A HATEFUL person. Stubborn, maybe, and sure, he can hold a grudge, but despite the shit sandwich of bigots and zealots and just plain dicks life keeps throwing at him, he doesn't *hate* most people. But right now, he fucking hates Susan Steward.

"What the hell?" Sean exclaims, and Susan turns to him with the kind of bored disdain usually reserved for dogs peeing on the carpet. "What are you—"

"Please finish dressing before you berate me, Sean. I can't take you seriously otherwise," Susan sighs. "You too, Cameron. I'll be downstairs. Be quick about it. I didn't drive across town in the middle of the day to be kept waiting."

Susan turns on her heel and leaves Cam and Sean staring at each other. "What the hell?" Sean repeats. Cam shakes his head and gets back to dressing. He's pale and shaking, and Sean wishes he could *do something* to help him for once. "Cam, I'm sorry," Sean says for what feels like the thousandth time after he pulls on his shirt.

"It's fine." Cam's hands are quivering as he buttons up his shirt.

"No, it's not. This isn't how people want to come out to their parents."

"I said *it's fine*, Sean," Cam snaps, and Sean flinches. "Apparently, I don't need to come out to anyone."

"What?"

Cam doesn't reply. They finish getting decent quickly and quietly, which only ups Sean's anger and apprehension. When they file downstairs, Susan is in the kitchen, staring into the open refrigerator.

"You have a child in the house, and your stomach must be acting up with all this stress; why don't you have any *milk*, Cameron?"

"Danny finished it this morning," Sean answers numbly.

Susan levels him with a new glare. "I asked my son, Sean, not you."

"Mother," Cam hisses.

"In fact, don't you have a job you should be at right now?" Susan goes on, and from the corner of his eye, Sean sees Cam's fist contract. "Or has that failed?"

"I'm taking the day off," Sean growls.

"To continue your corruption of my son, I see. Well, you're no longer needed, so you can go." Susan waves her hand, and Sean wants to break it.

"Sean isn't going anywhere," Cam counters and slams the fridge door out of his mother's hands. "What are you doing here, Mother?"

"I received an extremely concerning call from Nathaniel Pike," Susan replies, stepping a safe distance away from her son and Sean.

"Nate told you about Sean and me?" Cam asks. Sean turns to him, because why would Nate learn that? "I came out to Lee and Flor," Cam whispers to Sean. He has no time to be proud.

"No, he would never discuss something so scandalous over the phone. I honestly can't believe you brought your colleagues into this." Sean's reaching the breaking point, and the only thing holding him back is Cam. "I am here because Nate informed me you might be fired? Is this true?"

"You're here about his *job*?" Sean asks, aghast.

"Of course, I am," Susan groans, rolling her eyes. "And, again, we don't need color commentary, Sean. This is a family matter."

"Like hell it is," Sean huffs.

Susan braces a hand on her hips and scowls. "Cameron, I've already been on the phone with Arnold Isaacs. He's extremely disappointed in you, but he's open to discussing this with you with Ted Osborn as a mediator."

"I don't want to discuss anything with Isaacs," Cam replies.

"He indicated you'd be amenable," Susan replies.

"Because he's blackmailing him!" Sean yells, and Susan turns to him with a look of pure fury.

"Mr. Isaacs is a good Christian and American. He's leveraging the one thing any of us seems to be able to use to get through to Cameron – you. For some reason, my son thinks it's important to allow a deviant to get custody of a child. Appalling as that is, I support it since it will mean getting you and your filth out of his life forever."

Sean grits his teeth so hard it hurts. He truly, completely, *hates* this woman. "Getting rid of me won't change Cam."

"Of course it will. It removes the temptation and will allow him to recover and heal from your unsettling influence."

"His what?" Cam asks as his mother turns to him with a look of pity.

"I'm sure he's spent months filling your head with nonsense: telling you that you were born like this, that it's not a sin, that God cannot help you," Susan sighs. "These are the teachings of the devil, Cameron."

"And yours are the teachings of a bunch of crazy, bigoted assholes!" Sean bellows back.

"Please, mind your language, Sean, this is still a Christian household, despite your efforts."

Sean throws his hands. "Cam, are you—"

"So you knew?" Cam asks, his eyes still on his mother, a look of heartbreak on his face. "That I'm—"

"That you think you're a so-called homosexual? Yes, of course." Susan sounds frustrated and bored, and it's worse than anger. "I'm your mother. I've seen the signs since you were young, but until recently, I thought you were controlling your *urges*." She gives Sean a sneer at that word for good measure.

"Why did you never talk to me about it?" Cam demands, and Susan rolls her eyes again.

"I did. I *told you* time and again that was the way of sin. That was all I needed to say. You handled it, and when you deviated, you had Kayla to help you. In the past few months, with this one's – well, help isn't the word – you were able to be a complete husband at last. Now it's time to continue that without him."

Sean can't even speak. This was her. It was all her, and she'd known all along.

"I have been dying keeping this inside me for years, and you knew?" Cam croaks. "You both knew, and you did nothing?"

"Nothing?" Susan scoffs. "I have guided you. I have reminded you of who you need to be and how to be. I got rid of that filthy professor years ago. I helped Kayla understand you. I helped her use the sins and crimes you commit with this one to help you."

"So this whole fucked up conversion thing was your idea? Awesome," Sean snorts, and Susan steps towards him with cold fire in her eyes.

"It's not conversion, Sean, it's salvation." Susan's eyes narrow, boring into Sean like little hate lasers. "You people. You're so quick to judge those of us who are willing to stand up for God's commandments and the natural order. Do you really care about Cameron? About his soul or his life?"

"Of course I—" Sean starts, even though he's shrinking.

"Then stay away from him," Susan snaps. "You're an infection. How many lives do you need to destroy to feel better about the mess you've made of yours? Was your father not enough? I have to say, I worry for that poor brother of yours, but I can't intervene there. I have to protect my own children. And that's what I'm doing, Sean, protecting my family because I know the road you want him to walk is only disease, stigma, loneliness, and disappointment, all leading to *hell*. You may not believe in his soul, but *I do*, and someone has to protect it. The walk of righteousness is long and hard, but I will see my son make it."

Sean wants to say something smartass. He wants to fight and chew this bitch out, but he can't because she's right. No matter what Cam says about making it better or Sean being good, Susan sees right through him. She's not like Jeremiah, who thinks he should be punished, or Kayla, who thinks he's good enough to be used. She sees him for what he is: toxic.

"Cam is a good person," Sean says finally, his voice thick.

"He's trying to be, no thanks to you." Susan turns her focus to Cam, who looks as meek as a prisoner.

"Mother—" Cam and Sean jump as the door from the garage slams, and Kayla rushes in. Great. "Kayla. What are you—"

"Susan called me," Kayla says, breathless and obviously confused to find Sean and Susan there. "She said you were *fired*?"

"Suspended," Cam mutters. "I didn't think to call you."

"Of course not, you never do," Kayla says, shaking her head before looking at Sean. "Did he call you?"

"No," Sean replies instantly. "I was here to pack."

"Is that the story you're telling?" Susan scoffs.

"It's the truth," Sean counters. Seeing Cam walk in was as unexpected as the news that he was suspended. Then they'd fucked, and it had felt so good even when it was so wrong. He'd been idiotically on the edge of telling Cam he loved him and throwing his whole damn life away, but at least there was one bullet dodged. "I wanted to—"

"Then you just happened to take advantage of my son's emotional distress," Susan crows, disgusted. "So you could force him into more depravity in the bed he should share with his *wife*."

Susan could have slapped them, and Sean would have taken it better. Kayla looks as sickened as Cam, and Sean's never felt so ashamed.

"In *our* bed?" Kayla asks, her voice small and her eyes filling with tears.

"I'm sorry." Cam whispers, head bowed. The person Sean's looking at is so different from the man he was just with. He's more lost and broken than when Sean first met him, and it's Sean's fault.

"Don't you see it now, Cameron? This is a *sickness*. You have fallen to sin, and all it does is hurt people. Including yourself," Susan says, then turns back to Sean. "And you. You do nothing but make it worse."

"In fact, I think it's time that you leave," Kayla says darkly, face shifting to stone as she straightens. "For good."

"What?" Sean asks. Cam looks up, but he doesn't protest. "I was gonna say goodbye to Danny—"

"Perhaps you should have thought about that before you decided to defile yourself," Susan snaps.

"You'll see Danny on Thursday," Kayla adds. "Please go, Sean."

"Kayla, come on," Sean pleads. Kayla glares at him, her cheeks wet with tears.

"I should never have invited you into this house," Kayla says, and Sean turns away. She's not wrong, but he can't undo what's been done. He can't just abandon someone he loves when they're hurting so much. Stupidly, he grabs Cam's hand, and Susan winces.

"Cam. Come on. I'll go if you want me to, but please, tell me you won't listen to these psychos?" Cam meets his eyes, and Sean begs him silently for some hope that he's willing to fight. "Do you really want me to go?"

"*Cameron*," Susan growls.

Cam yanks his hand away and shakes his head. "Goodbye, Sean."

That's it then.

Sean grabs his bag and walks out, the door slamming like a prison gate behind him. If Cam doesn't want him there, he has no reason to stay. If Cam won't fight for himself, that's not Sean's job.

He drives. He's not even sure where he's going until he pulls into the parking lot of Danny's school. He doesn't know if he'll get in trouble for being here, but Sean doesn't care.

He stares at his dash for a long time.

How did this happen? How did he mess this up so badly? How did he let Cam do this to himself? Maybe Cam and Susan are right. Maybe this is a punishment from God. He has one good thing left, and that's Danny. He's the only reason he didn't bodily haul Cam out of that house despite what everyone said.

"Sean?"

Sean startles at Danny's voice, accompanied by a knock on the window. Sean unlocks the door, and Danny slides into the shotgun seat. "Hey, short stuff."

"What are you doing at my school? Some kids saw your car and think you're a murderer lurking out here. Did you get fired or something?"

"What? No! I…" Sean sighs. "I needed you to know I'm moving over to Bill's this afternoon. I won't be around tonight like we planned, but I'll see you on Thursday. We're gonna give Bill a real Thanksgiving, okay?"

Danny, smart kid that he is, sees through the bullshit immediately. "Why aren't you staying?"

"It's complicated." Danny gives Sean his bitchiest glare. "It's complicated grown-up stuff, okay? But it's fine. It's gonna be fine."

"Did Kayla find out about you and Cam?"

"Did she – *what*? Jesus Christ, how did you know?" Sean sputters, and Danny heaves a sigh.

"Sean, come on. You and Cam act more like a couple than he and Kayla ever do. He doesn't sleep in their room, and the other night on the porch, you two were sorta… cuddling."

"We were not cuddling!"

"Sean. I don't think you're less of a man for going gay for Cam; I'm not gonna judge for cuddling."

Sean rolls his eyes. In this trying time, it's nice to know his brother will always be a little shit. "Okay, for one, I didn't go gay for Cam. And two…" Danny raises an eyebrow as Sean flounders. "I'm bi, okay! Always have been."

"Okay." Danny looks sincere, and Sean's not sure what to do with it. "Okay?"

"Okay. You're my brother, and I love you. I want you to be happy. I guess that's gonna be with Cam? I mean, was I right? Did Kayla find out?"

"Sorta. She…" Sean shakes his head. He really doesn't want to lie to Danny, but he also doesn't want him to know everything, especially the part where he was Cam's whore. "Cam and I are over. Not that we ever even started. It was just sex, and none of it matters anymore."

"Of course it matters." Danny tilts his head, considering. "Wait, you *slept* with him?"

"Uh. Yeah. I thought you guessed."

"That you guys, like, fell in love! Not that you banged! Sean, he's still *married*, even if he's gay." Danny looks so offended, and his naiveté would be cute if it didn't make Sean feel like garbage.

"Danny, like I said, it's complicated and…" The record in Sean's brain scratches. "Wait, did you say in love?"

"Yeah. Duh."

"You mean me, right? Because Cam he… he doesn't." Sean can't think that. He can't *comprehend* that, especially after everything. If Cam loved him, he'd fight for him.

"Wow. You are dumb."

"No. I mean, yeah, I am, but—"

"But it's complicated. You keep saying that, but you won't tell me how or what even happened today." Danny looks so worried, Sean can't stand it. He doesn't deserve this kid.

"Cam's having issues at work, okay? I was home early to pack up, and he came home cause he got suspended and shit happened. Then his mom came home and—"

"His *mom*? Wait, while you two were—"

"No! Jesus. This is not what I'm here to talk about! It was a giant mess, and Cam made it pretty clear that he's got no plans to change things. Not that he can. So, I need you to go back to the Stewards tonight and be cool. I wanted to tell you myself because I didn't want you to think I was ditching you." Again. He's suddenly so fucking tired, but he just has to get them through this week. "I need you to be okay."

"I am. Sean, what are you not telling me? Is something else wrong?"

"I'll see you day after tomorrow." Danny can tell he's deflecting, but he just has to get them through this week, and they'll be okay.

"Alright. Just promise to tell me when I'm older, okay?" Danny gives him a weak smile, and Sean tries to return it. It's more of a grimace, but it's good enough. Danny gets out of the car and gives Sean a wave as he runs to join the students streaming out of the school.

Sean revs the Bel Air's monstrous engine and drives. He should have said yes to Cam, caught him when he was still brave, before Susan crushed it out of him. He should have been faster to say: 'Maybe we can try to do this for real.'

But they can't. Cam never asked for that. Cam never wanted it. He ran away to Sean and asked to run away with him. Cam only ever wanted Sean as a rebellion or an escape. Now he's being punished for that, and he's taking it like a good little soldier in some holy army.

The liquor store is pretty busy for a Tuesday afternoon. Must be people getting ready for the holiday. Sean shows the ID Kayla helped him get, and pays with money Cam helped him earn, and he wonders if he'll ever get away from them or the shadow of what he's done.

Bill yells at him when he comes inside, something gruff and folksy, and Sean yells back that he's fine. Not like he's gonna share the booze with Bill. Not that Bill would mind, but Sean wants to do this alone.

He turns off his phone. He sits on the floor by the new bed and turns on the radio. He drinks, listening to Zepp until he stops imagining what might have been. What is and what shall never be.

cameron

It hurts. It's hurt for three days now, and Cameron just wants it to stop.

"Take your medicine."

Cameron doesn't argue. At this point, he's just glad to be home and not in a hospital again. He hadn't wanted to go, which was stupid of him, but he'd been past caring, and if his mother hadn't seen the blood when he threw up, who knows what would have happened.

She had been the one to take him, his mother, and he felt like a child when she bundled him into her car and scowled the entire drive. At least she took him to St. Louis General, not Sullivan Mercy. He didn't want to see anyone he knew. Kayla had stayed to take care of Danny. He still doesn't know what she told him about where he was, or why Sean was gone.

He wonders: if Danny knew, would he have tried to tell Sean? Not that Sean would have been allowed anywhere near him. Cameron didn't have any calls or messages when he got his phone back. He would be lying if he said he wasn't disappointed. He'd been weak and sent one himself.

Just 'I miss you.'

There was no reply

"Cameron. Your pills."

He blinks at his mother and complies, swallowing his pills down with the glass of milk provided.

They prodded him and filled him with drugs, and he slept or dissociated through most of the ordeal. He stared at ceilings and contemplated how the physical reminder of his sin and all he's kept inside for so long had finally broken out, the same day that he owned up to what he was, and everyone already knew.

When the pain cleared, his thoughts filled with worry about Sean. And Kayla. About Drew and Nate and Lee and Danny. His doctor had hilariously cautioned him to avoid stress. He also berated Cameron for not being on a full prescription before. He had some choice words about Kayla's attempts to control things via diet and Cameron's constant undermining of that. The medication should help. He should have been on it years ago.

He should have done so much years ago.

"Are you sure you should be driving? Kayla can take Danny." Cameron looks up at his mother. He feels like he's in college again, with her asking if he's sure he's up for living in the dorms. She has a point though. She always has a point.

"I'm fine." He wanders from the kitchen to find his coat and keys. "I know how to get there. Kayla doesn't."

"You being alone with that man is not in your best interest right now." Once again, she's not wrong. Seeing Sean is just going to make him feel worse. He doesn't need the reminder of his cowardice, or his sin, or what he's lost.

"Well, I don't care."

"What do you care about, Cameron? I'd truly like to know. For this man, you've nearly destroyed your career—"

"That wasn't Sean's fault—"

"And your marriage. Not to mention, risked your soul. You've broken my heart and Kayla's over and over, and for what? Unnatural lusts?" Cameron turns away in searing shame. It's so much worse with her knowing and being able to say this all to his face. "Cameron, you cannot keep avoiding this. We are going to have this conversation."

A quiet cough comes from the stairs. Danny looks embarrassed to have walked in on the argument, as does Kayla, who hovers behind him.

"Um. I brought some clothes," Danny says, holding up a backpack. "Anthony said it was okay for me to stay the night. He wants to talk to me tomorrow when he comes to inspect stuff or whatever."

"Did he really?" Susan asks, and Danny gives her a scowl that would get him grounded if Susan were a blood relative.

"Yes," Danny replies. "Kayla was listening while I was on the phone. I asked her to help me call because I miss my brother. Who is a way better person than you, by the way."

"Danny, that's very rude," Kayla says quietly.

"Oh, are we still pretending everything is normal here and being polite? Really?" Danny scoffs. "Can we just go, please?"

Cameron nods and sends one last weary look to Kayla before leading Danny to the car. They're quiet for a few minutes of the journey, Danny fiddling with the fraying holes in his jeans, just like Sean does.

"I know about you guys," Danny says when they hit a red light, and Cam's shoulders slump. "You and Sean, I mean. I'm okay with him and you being, uh, that way. I really am."

"But?" There's always a 'but.'

"But I think Sean's really hurting and I don't know if this is good for him?" Danny mutters. "I don't know how things happened with you guys or whatever, but he's been doing really good up until now, and I hope this doesn't mess him up."

"What do you mean?" The medicine Cameron is on is strong enough to dull the acid that was tearing at his insides, so he knows the tightness in his chest has nothing to do with that. It's fear and hurt, pure and simple.

"Just don't lead him on if you can't follow through, okay? I know 'it's complicated.' Sean keeps saying that." Danny shakes his head, long bangs flopping into his eyes. "He really cares about you, and I know you care about him. But people that care like that shouldn't keep hurting each other, okay?"

Cameron keeps his eyes on the road, blinking them clear. Danny is right. Everyone around him is right. Everything is broken, and he's the one who broke it.

"You're a very wise young man, Danny."

The rest of the ride is silent, and the crush of gravel under his wheels as he pulls up to Bill's house is deafening. He knows he shouldn't, but he gets out with Danny and walks him to the door.

It's cold, the threat of snow in the air. The dog on the porch growls at them until Danny kneels to pet her. She has no tail, so she wags her entire body as Danny scratches under her chin. Danny's bright smile makes Cameron's heart ache as much as anything. The door opens before either of them can knock to reveal Bill Farnell looking even more disgruntled than usual.

"Next you'll be asking me to bring her inside," Bill says as Danny stands.

"What's her name? Oh, I'm Danny by the way." Danny holds out his hand. "Nice to meet you, Mister Farnell." Bill scowls at Danny's hand until he drops it.

"Dog's name is Taylor, and if you call me Mister Farnell again, I'll roll over your toes. Come on in. Sean's in the kitchen." Bill moves to let Danny through the door, then rolls to block Cam when he tries to follow. "No. I don't know what you and your shithead family said to that boy, but this morning is the first time he's crawled out of the bottle in two days. Unless you're ready to make this right, don't bother."

"He's been drinking? Is he alright?" Cam doesn't want to think about Sean hurting himself because of Cam's cowardice and inaction.

"He's fine. I'll keep him in line." Bill fixes him with a withering look. "You ready to help?"

"I *can't*," Cameron whispers. "Sean knows why I can't and why we can't—"

"I thought as much. Sean'll bring Danny back after the inspection. Go be with your *family*." Bill closes the door before Cameron can say anything else.

Sean doesn't want to see him, quite rightly. He must be disgusted with Cameron. There is no one he hasn't failed, and now he gets to enjoy the torture of Thanksgiving with his family. At least it might be better than the hospital, but Cameron isn't optimistic.

Luke's house is rustic and full of character, as you'd expect from a farmhouse that's over a hundred years old out in the middle of nowhere. Alone in a barren field, full of chaos, it looks how Cameron feels: isolated and ready to burst.

Dinner is passable. Cameron responds when spoken to like a normal person. He pets Luke's dog. He plays with the kids. Useless conversation about the weather and sports passes through Cameron like smoke through a screen.

In the blink of an eye, he's elbow-deep in tepid water on dish duty with Courtney while Jillian watches the children. It's calming work, and Courtney doesn't say much. Soon it will be over. Not that he's looking forward to going home.

"Cameron?" He turns to see his mother at the door of the kitchen, her face more solemn than during dinner. "Please join us in the parlor."

"What?" Cameron blinks as Courtney takes the plate he was washing from his hands and gives him a towel.

"I told you," Susan says. "We're having the conversation."

"I don't understand," Cameron says, terror rising.

Even so, he dries his hands and follows his mother into Luke's front parlor. The room looks smaller with so many people in it. Luke and Vince share a couch, while Kayla sits in a wingback chair in the corner. On the other couch... sits Ted Osborn, looking grim and condescending at the same time. How did he get here? Cameron's mother gestures for Cameron to sit in the remaining chair, right in the middle, in front of everyone, and takes the empty place next to Osborn.

Cameron remains standing defiantly. "What's going on?"

"Cameron, we want to speak with you. As a family," Susan begins.

"I don't recall how we're related to Mr. Osborn," Cameron says.

"He's here as a man of the Lord to offer his counsel and help," Vince replies, eerily kind. "He's as concerned for you as we are."

"Concerned?" Cameron repeats.

"I've explained to your brothers what your situation is at work," Susan says. Cameron squints and finally sits. He'd almost forgotten his career was in flames.

"Arnold Isaacs is a good friend," Osborn adds. "And a pillar of our church and community. He's very disturbed that you've made such poor choices or want to make Nate Pike's clerical mistakes into some conspiracy."

"But he..." Cameron starts, but his mother's glare silences him.

"But your mother and I have talked with Arnold, and our other friends on the board, and he's willing to help you retain your position," Osborn goes on with a false smile. "However, there are conditions. Your family is here to help you understand them."

"Conditions?" Cameron feels nauseous. His brothers' faces are concerned and sincere, his mother's dark, and Kayla won't even look at him.

"You need to renounce your sins, Cameron," Susan says, eyes boring into Cameron with conviction.

"My what?" Cameron whispers.

"Do you really need a reminder of what you and that vagrant have done, brother?" Luke says, shaking his head in disgust.

"An affair is terrible enough," Vince adds, and Cameron feels the blood leave his face. "But with a man? A *prostitute*?"

"You—you told them?" He looks to Kayla, and she shakes her head vehemently.

"No. I didn't want anyone to know," Kayla stammers. God, she looks so ashamed. "Your mother decided to involve everyone."

"You need our full support to make a positive change, and your family needs all the information to make that happen," Susan explains, like it's simple.

"That's why your family wanted me here, to assure you that this is part of God's plan for you," Osborn says with a smile that makes Cameron's fists clench. "We can't have an unrepentant deviant working in a hospital, but praise be to God, you can choose to change."

"So this is an intervention," Cameron says. "But instead of drugs, you want to save me from being gay."

"You're not 'gay,' Cameron," Luke says in the same tone of voice Cameron has heard him use with children. "You're just confused."

"People keep telling me that," Cameron murmurs.

"Cam, we were all at your wedding," Vince says. "We saw how happy you and Kayla were. We know that you love each other. You two have been through so much. School. Loss. You can make it through this."

"Through God's grace, your wife has forgiven your transgressions and wants to help you," Osborn goes on, simpering.

"It's true," Kayla says, forcing a smile. "Babe, I know this isn't how you'd want this to go. I'm so sorry for how I've hurt and failed you, but this can be a fresh start for both of us."

"We forgive you too, Cameron," Susan says, her tone gentler than Cameron has heard in years. "We love you. We worry for your soul."

"And us," Luke adds and gets a glare from Kayla. "What? Someone has to say it. I run a Christian business, Cameron. I can't have customers knowing my brother chose to be a deviant. So does Vince."

"We can't have you around our children either," Jillian adds with a sickening sneer. "Unless you repent." Courtney nods as well, a hand straying to her pregnant belly.

Cameron feels naked; flayed and exposed. He's dreaded a moment like this his whole life. Every sin revealed and condemned by the people he loves, with nowhere left for him to hide. The disgust in their eyes isn't his imagination.

"If I am such a monster, why are you even speaking to me?"

Suddenly, his mother is kneeling before him, taking his hand in hers and stroking his hair tenderly, like when he'd fall as a child. "Because you are not your sins," Susan says, warm and loving. "We love and care for *you*."

"With prayer and the strength of God, I know you can do it," Kayla adds. "I know you want to make this right. Or else you wouldn't be here."

"What do you want me to do? And what does this have to do with Isaacs?" Cameron asks, tired and resigned. Susan squeezes his hands, smiling as if this is a victory.

"Like we said, renounce your sins," Osborn replies. "On Sunday, before all the congregation, we want you to witness. Testify about your crimes and fraud at work before God and admit that awful tramp led you into it with lust and sin. Confess it all and be absolved and reborn."

"Is that all?" Cameron murmurs. They make it sound so simple. "And if I don't?"

"Then we will have no choice but to contact the proper authorities about Sean Lockwood's past and your crimes," Osborn says, his voice cold and terrifying. "Isaacs is a friend. As is Nathanial Pike. They're good Christian men that I won't let you drag through the mud to hide your sins."

"I see," Cameron says. He feels like he's watching himself from a great distance.

"This is a chance for a new beginning in the Lord," Susan says, clutching his hand tight. Cameron can see the force of her prayer and call to God in her face. "He is waiting for you, Cameron. He always has been, and when you do this, when you let this darkness go and let his light into your heart, you'll be healed."

He nods.

He asked God days ago what he wanted from him. It seems he has an answer at last, clear and cruel as day.

29
counsel

sean

SEAN'S GLAD HE'S NOT hungover for the visit from Gardner. It's a nice change from the last two mornings. Danny's a good influence. Gardner takes less time to look over things than Sean expected. He talks earnestly with Danny out of earshot, and then with Bill. When Danny and Gardner come outside to retrieve Sean from where he's leaning on an old Impala some numbskull beat up, everyone is smiling.

It gives Sean hope, which is pretty new for him. He still hasn't heard a word from Cam, not that he's expecting it, but the absence follows Sean like a shadow. Thanksgiving was the first Thursday they'd missed in a long time, but it's something he's got to get used to, isn't it?

"Things look good, Sean," Gardner says with a kind smile. "Unless something unexpected comes up, I have very high hopes for Judge Wu's decision on Monday."

It's better news than Sean could even dream. "That's… wow."

"I told my lawyer I really want to be with you, too," Danny adds.

"Thanks, short stuff," is all Sean can say. He looks back at Gardner. "You've still got good reports from Cam and Kayla?"

"I was going to meet with them on Wednesday, actually, but they weren't available due to Mr. Steward's medical issues," Gardner says, and Sean's brain screeches to attention.

"Medical issues?" He turns to Danny. The look of absolute guilt on the kid's face is all Sean needs. "Cam's sick, and *you didn't tell me?*"

"You were mad at him!" Danny protests.

"No, I—" Sean snaps his mouth closed, horribly conscious of Gardner's eyes on him. "Danny, that doesn't mean I don't care if he's *sick*."

"Oh." Danny looks guilty as all get-out, and Gardner looks awkward.

"It sounds like you two have a bit to talk about on the way back to the Stewards," Gardner says. "I'll be touching base with them on Sunday. I'll see you on Monday, Sean."

"Can't wait," Sean mutters. Danny walks Gardner to his car and gets a hug for his troubles before sulking back to Sean. "What the hell happened to Cam?" Sean asks before Gardner's even down the driveway.

"I don't know, okay! I got home from school on Tuesday, and he was already gone! Turns out he was at the hospital. I guess his mom took him? I heard Kayla talking on the phone about him throwing up blood?"

"*What?*" Sean yelps, and Taylor raises her head in concern.

"He's fine! He came back Thursday morning, and he was fine." Danny's voice cracks on the last word.

"You don't throw up blood if you're fine!" Sean snaps. This is his fault too. Cam's sick, and it's his fault. "Come on, get in the car. I'll ask him what happened myself."

Danny obeys and keeps quiet on the drive until they pull up to the Steward house. Of course, Susan's ugly-ass Buick is parked in Sean's spot.

"Sean," Danny says before they get out. "I really had a good Thanksgiving with you. I like Bill and I really want to stay there with you. I mean it. I know it's a day late, but I'm thankful for you."

Sean looks down, focusing on the inseam of his jeans. It *was* nice. They watched the dog show, then football, and ate until their sides ached. Somehow, Bill and Sean started explaining to Danny how a car engine worked, and his little nerd brain exploded, especially once Bill brought out the books. It was good and warm, and the fact that Cam hadn't texted back when Sean sent him a "happy Thanksgiving" message should have hurt less because of it. It only stung more because Sean spent the whole time wishing Cam was there.

"Same, short stuff." Sean forces himself to look at Danny and remind himself why this is all worth it. "Don't get all weepy on me, okay?"

"Not now. No promises for Monday. We're almost there, Sean." Danny smiles, and Sean tries to echo it. They get out of the car, and to Sean's surprise, Kayla is already walking outside the house to meet them.

"Uh. Hey," Sean says. There's really no conversation they can have to make up for the whole the fucking her husband on her bed thing. She looks as tired as Sean feels.

"Hi, Danny," she says. "Sean."

"Is Cam around? Danny told me he was sick," Sean asks carefully.

"I'll see if he's feeling up to it," Kayla replies. "You can wait out here. Danny, come on inside. We've got some leftovers if you're hungry."

"Awesome!" Danny cheers. He gives Sean one more hug before rushing inside with Kayla at his heels.

"He ate like an hour ago!" Sean calls after them, and Danny waves him off. "Teenagers."

He waits in front of the house, kicking at the dirt by the roses. They're dormant now. No leaves or flowers left, just sticks covered in thorns. The door opens, and Sean looks up, heart leaping, then plummeting. It's Susan. "No offense, but I was hoping to talk to a different Steward."

"So I gathered, but Cameron doesn't want to see you," Susan says with a triumphant smirk. "He realizes what a dangerous influence you are."

Sean takes a step back, steadying himself. He's an expert in bullshit, and he knows it when he hears it. "I don't buy that."

"You don't need to, but you're no longer welcome in this house. For your own good, and young Daniel's." There's a threat in her smug, pale face now.

"So you're on the 'tattle about me to the social workers and fuck over Danny' bandwagon too, great." Sean shakes his head. "All so you can keep Cam shoved in the closet when it's literally killing him." He can't even think about how Cam felt at the hospital with this woman beside him, telling him how the stress she caused that had him puking blood was some judgment from God.

"I care about my son, Sean." The corner of her mouth ticks up.

"Some loving mother you are." Sean wants to throttle her, or at least slash her tires, but she holds every card and she knows it.

"In fact, I am," Susan replies, advancing. "I know you aren't familiar with how real parents treat their children, since you have none, but good mothers fight for their sons. You have attempted to destroy Cameron in every possible way, while I'm just trying to protect him. I don't want to see him abandoned or destroyed by disease, poverty, and ostracism. Can you and your kind offer anything beyond that? You're a prostitute, Sean, a liar, a criminal, and the child of an addict. How do you expect Cameron to ever trust anything you do or say?"

"I wouldn't—"

"I'm not interested in your lies. Cameron *does not want to see you.* Now or ever again."

Sean wants to spit in her face, tell her she's the liar, but now he's not sure. Nothing she's saying about him is wrong, so why would she lie about Cam? "You're a real piece of work, you know that?"

Susan reaches into her pocket. She pulls out a neatly folded stack of money. "Here. Sean, for your services," she says, holding it out to him.

He wants to scream. Slap it out of her hands and spit in her face. But he doesn't. He's not the beast she thinks he is, not entirely. He doesn't take the money. "Fuck you, Susan."

He turns and leaves, knowing full well he'll never look at the Steward house again.

cameron

Cam wakes up cold. And confused. He's not sure when he fell asleep after coming home from Luke's. He was too distracted to check the time, and there's no clock in Sean's room now. Because it's not Sean's room anymore. The sheets have been washed, but Cam can still smell a trace of Sean in the linens. In the air like a ghost. That's the last thing he remembers thinking before falling asleep in the small hours of the morning. Alone.

He knows sleeping here was cruel, but he wanted a few more hours of freedom. He can't give up entirely yet. Kayla hadn't questioned it. They didn't speak in the car after she'd made an abortive attempt at an apology. He knows she didn't have anything to do with planning the confrontation, but it doesn't matter.

Cameron pushes himself out of the sheets and stretches. He's wanted to wake up in Sean's bed for a long time, but this wasn't how he imagined it. He always thought it *would* happen, somehow. He thought a lot of things would happen, eventually. He was a fool, but that's not a thought worth pursuing so early in the morning. If it is early.

The muffled sounds of screeching tires and gunfire break him out of his stupor. He shuffles out of the room to find Danny curled on the couch while an action movie plays on the TV.

"Oh, hey, sorry. I didn't mean to wake you. Kayla said you're still feeling bad?" Danny looks worried and guilty, but what's more concerning to Cam is that he missed seeing Sean *again* when he dropped Danny off.

"I'm fine. The pills are working. What time is it?"

"Like ten-thirty."

"Shit."

Danny's eyes widen in shock. "Sorry. Your mom said not to wake you."

"She was here again?" Beyond the intervention, his mother obviously feels the need to monitor him like an addict who might sneak off for a new fix. She isn't wrong.

"I guess. I think she and Kayla went out to the black Friday sales or something after I got in." Danny looks sheepish and fiddles with the remote. "She said something about buying a new mattress."

"Wonderful." Cameron feels terrible; mentally, emotionally, and even physically, but he suddenly has to get out of the house. "I think I'm going to go for a run."

"It's kind of cold."

Cam shrugs and heads upstairs. He ignores the bed when he walks by it into the bathroom to get ready. He wonders if Kayla actually slept there after learning what he'd done. It's not like there was any other place in the house she could go that he and Sean hadn't defiled. Maybe she'll make them buy a new house to go with the new start everyone insists they'll have.

He stretches in the front hall, eyes tracking over the wedding pictures, scriptures, and crosses on the walls. There's nothing about this house that he chose or that he cares about, except the books and records all kept discreetly out of sight. He'd be happy to leave, but any new place would be the same.

He steps into the frigid air and runs. He can see his breath in front of him, and his lungs sting with the cold, but it feels good. Each stride takes him further from his house, his family, and the past. Everything. It gives him the illusion of freedom. He doesn't want to turn back, and he doesn't care where he's going. He follows the road past house after house, past a family setting up a plastic nativity scene in the front yard already, and another writing "Christ is Come!" on their roof in lights.

He runs and runs and runs, sweat pouring down his back and face and chest, until he feels like he's back in his body for the first time in days. For the first time since he and Sean made love.

That's a strange term for it, he guesses, one that Sean would roll his eyes at, but it felt like more than just fucking. It felt important and beautiful, not base. Not filthy, the way everyone thought of it. He hates that they see it that way. He hates that part of him sees it that way too.

He runs harder, pushing every thought out of his mind until there's nothing but the pounding of his feet on the pavement and the cold air on his face. He runs until he turns a corner, and suddenly he's right back on his own street, heading home.

"Fuck," he whispers, coming to a halt within sight of his house.

"You watch your mouth in front of my boy, Cameron Steward."

He looks up to see Wanda with Fergus on his leash, looking up at him with a tongue lolling out of his mouth.

"Apologies. I'm having a rough morning."

"It's nearly noon, honey, that sounds pretty rough." Wanda looks Cam up and down. "I was actually heading your way to see if your strapping young man would help me get my Christmas decorations out of the garage."

Cam fights very hard not to turn and run away again. "Sean's not—"

"I meant the little one," Wanda replies, giving Cam a discerning look. "I assume Sean's working. Is everything alright?"

"Nothing is alright, but I'm sure Danny would be happy to help you. I would be as well."

"Perfect. I can heat up some cocoa for you. Ease your weary heart. Come on, Fergus, time for lunch."

Kayla's car is still gone when Cameron gets home. He showers in the downstairs bathroom and gets dressed there. There are no messages on his phone despite a text sent to Sean in the early hours of the morning. 'I need to talk to you.' He adds a 'please' to the thread.

He heads upstairs to find Danny. At least at Wanda's, they can be of some use while they wait for everything to end.

sean

Joe's bar hasn't changed. Same dirty walls, sticky bar, and cheap whiskey. Same spot at the end of the bar reserved for a dumb kid with a pretty face and wandering eyes, hoping to get on his knees. This time it's not Sean, but the guy Sean's looking at over the lip of his glass might as well be, down to the sandy hair and fading bruise under his eye.

The kid catches Sean staring and sends him a wink. Shit.

Sean sighs as the kid sidles over, and Joe conveniently goes to serve someone else.

"You look lonely," Sean's new friend says with a smile, and Sean can't help rolling his eyes.

"Come on, man, you gotta be more subtle than that," Sean chuckles, and the guy balks. "Most johns, they're deep in the closet or just like getting their dick sucked, doesn't matter by who. You don't wanna make 'em feel too gay."

"I wasn't—" the guy stammers.

"Yeah, you were. You think I don't know my own kind?" The kid scowls, but instead of walking away, he takes the seat next to Sean and waves to Joe for refills. "Are you even old enough to drink?"

"Joe ain't checking IDs," the kid says. "So, are you gonna tell me to get off your turf or something? You look a little white bread for this scene, I gotta say."

"Nah, I'm out," Sean replies, and damn if it doesn't feel sorta good to say it.

"Good, because I don't want to have to fight for business." The kid holds out a hand. "I'm Brice, by the way."

"Hope that's not your real name," Sean replies, shaking Brice's hand. "You get that doing business?" He points to the fading bruise on Brice's cheek.

"Yeah. Some fucking nut. Jumped me and tried to break my skull a few weeks ago, cost me a job." Brice says it with the weary resignation of the streets, and Sean recognizes that too. "Kept yelling about the lord or some shit. Fuckers like him are gonna get a nasty surprise when they pack it in for good and don't find the pearly gates on the other side."

Sean closes his eyes and shakes his head. Of course. "You tell the cops?"

Brice laughs, dry and hollow. "You think they'd believe me? Or care? Even if I could ID the asshole, there's no point."

"I guess not." Sean knocks back the last of his whiskey. Brice does the same and looks Sean up and down.

"So, you sure you're not interested in blowing off some steam? Show me a few moves?" Brice gives Sean a suggestive smile. "No charge."

"Nah, man," Sean says, shaking his head. "Like I said, I'm out. Of all of it."

Brice shrugs. "Fair enough. Can I ask you one more question?"

"Sure, why not."

"How'd you do it? Get out?" The bravado is gone from Brice's face, replaced by a genuine look of hope, and perhaps wonder.

"I got lucky. Someone found me who wanted to help, even when I didn't wanna be saved," Sean answers. He's not even sure now how it happened. If he'd never been in all those wrong places at the right times, he might never have met Cam or fallen into the mess that still somehow saved his pathetic life. "I certainly didn't deserve it. Still don't."

"Sounds like a damn miracle," Brice says. "Glad someone could make it out."

"Well, I'll be damned, you two starting a union?" Sean looks up and nearly throws his drink. Eli is there, his goatee restored and wearing a cheap, shiny suit.

"You got a gig for me, boss?" Brice asks before Sean can tell Eli to fuck off.

"Yeah, midnight," Eli says, grinning. "This guy isn't convincing you to retire, is he?"

"Screw you, Eli. I don't want you getting another kid almost killed," Sean growls.

"Hey, I want that asshole behind bars as much as anyone. He's bad for business," Eli snaps back.

"The guys that you let nearly murder me got to Brice here too!" Sean sneers. The other bar patrons look up at them, and Eli comes closer, threatening.

"I had nothing to do with Brice getting jumped. Okay? That was his own job. I've been warning guys and girls around the neighborhood about the jerk, even the good cops, and no one cares. You didn't even care when I tried to tell you!"

"I care!" Sean snarls.

"You're the one whose car got beat up?" Brice asks, eyes wide. "I saw Eli's pics. That was messed up."

"I don't see you doing anything now that you've joined the Jesus freaks," Eli scoffs, ignoring the kid. "If you ever do, I'm more than happy to help when you're done with the PTA meetings."

Sean stares Eli down, ready to call his bluff, but for what? He can't do anything. His cowardice churns together with the whiskey in his stomach, mixing with the guilt. How can he go legit, live safely, and pretend to be happy with Danny when Jeremiah is still hurting people and Cam is stuck in the prison of his marriage?

"Screw you," Sean mutters.

"Nah, I outsource my screwing," Eli smirks. "But here's my number if you change your mind. Or you need a job." Eli holds out a damn business card. Sean grabs it and shoves it in his pocket, slaps a twenty on the counter, and hopes Joe keeps the change.

He stews and scowls the entire bus ride, and the cold walk from the drop-off back to Bill's has him sober by the time he slinks in the door.

"You done drowning your sorrows?" Bill asks from the desk. "Or am I gonna have to report you to the authorities?"

"I'm fine. For now." Sean slumps into the chair next to Bill. "Met an old friend at the bar and made a new one."

"And?" Bill can tell there's more Sean's carrying, like a mark from God for his sins.

"Jeremiah is still out there, and he's still hurting people," Sean says, staring at nothing. "Cam sees him every week. He sits in church and congratulates himself for doing the Lord's work. He's walking free and *I'm letting him.*"

"You're doing what you have to," Bill says automatically. "There ain't no changing people like him. Get rid of him and there's another asshole waiting to take his place."

"Does that mean it ain't worth fighting?" Sean replies. Bill meets Sean's eyes with a sincere look. "Does that mean all the guys he's hurt don't get justice? Me included?"

"Being a hero can be damn scary. It can get ya hurt," Bill begins, thoughtful. Sean agrees. Cam tried to be that, even when his God told him he was a monster, and look what it cost him. "But, you don't stand up and fight for someone else, or even for God, because you're afraid. You do it because it's right. You do it so you can look at *yourself* in the mirror and be proud. You think you can do that?"

Sean looks away from Bill and through his dirty window to the starless sky. He doesn't know the answer.

cameron

Today, Cameron plans his run better. Kayla and Danny are asleep when he wakes up, so he doesn't bother with excuses like yesterday, when he and Danny came home from Wanda's, or after dinner, when Kayla had asked him what he thought of the new bed. He gets dressed and he's out of the house into the quiet morning without a word to anyone.

It's colder than yesterday. Cold enough that he had to wear track pants and a jacket. He doesn't mind the looks from the people he passes. He focuses on the route. The plan is getting away from home, and that will never happen if he stays on autopilot.

Maybe that's what he's been doing his whole damn life. He's done as he was told, followed the route he was given by God and his family, because they were all the same thing. He questioned their wisdom in the deepest parts of his heart, but he never stood up in the daylight and disobeyed, not outright. He thought he could get away with secret defiance and stolen indulgences. Then a few more. Until he was certain he had escaped, but he was just right back where he started, begging God for a sign. At least today, he plans on doing that part right.

He has to walk the final mile and a half to the church. It's strange how a building so suburban and plain can hold so much power. Even in his mind, when Cameron hears the word 'church,' he thinks of steeples and grand cathedrals far away. Sean had gone on a tirade one night about how, at least the Catholics know how to build a place that makes you feel like God's there. Not a beige building in need of new siding with a sign out front that currently reads, "Rejoice and give thanks in th Lord!" Cam wonders where the last E went.

The side entrance is unlocked, and the chapel is silent and cold in a way that magnifies the emptiness and makes Cameron's steps twice as loud. He takes a seat in the usual pew and, for the first time in a long while, sets his eyes on the cross above the altar and prepares to pray.

It feels like getting ready to jump off a cliff. Will it feel this way on Sunday if he does what everyone wants? He kneels, knees smarting, grasps his hands, and begins. "God, please help me. I don't know what to do—"

A crash from behind the door to the rectory cuts Cameron off. It's followed by raised voices – both male – arguing.

"Is someone there?" Cameron calls.

"You said no one would be here!" one voice yelps, getting closer.

"Shit! I told you this was stupid!" The second voice is extremely familiar.

"Drew?"

The door bursts open, and Drew Barons stumbles out, a second man behind him. He's taller than Drew by an inch or two, with curly, light hair and an anemic mustache. "Cam? Wha-what are you doing here?"

Cameron looks down at his still-clasped hands. "Praying."

"Oh." Drew gulps.

"What are *you* doing here?" Cameron asks, rising, and Drew turns pale. "I thought you were fired."

"I was. But, I, uh—"

"We're breaking into ol' Teddy Bear's files," the other man interrupts, grinning. Drew hangs his head.

"We're just looking for my final paycheck records," Drew mutters, unconvincing.

"Are you lying? *In a church?*" the other man gasps, clasping a hand to his chest, then looking at Cam. "We're trying to find where Ted's been getting all that money he doesn't want Drew knowing about."

"Miles!" Drew snaps. Miles (he looks like a Miles somehow, like someone who likes alternative, indie music and gemhounding) smirks, smug and calm.

"Oh, that makes sense," Cameron says.

Miles jabs Drew in the arm and wags his eyebrows. "See. Told you everyone hates that blowhard. You aren't gonna call the cops or report us, are you? I'd hate to have to kill you."

"No. I just came here to get some quiet. Or help." Cameron is beginning to think that's impossible.

"Hon, why don't you do your walk on water thing with your friend here, and I'll work my magic on figuring out Ted's password," Miles says, tousling Drew's hair.

"No, don't—" Before Drew can finish, Miles dashes back through the door towards (Cameron assumes) Osborn's office. "Great." Drew sighs and joins Cameron in the pew, his shoulders slumping as he sits.

"Who is that, if you don't mind me asking?" Cam begins, sitting next to Drew.

"My ex. Well, ex-ex, now. We're—I don't know. He came to visit a week ago and hasn't left." Cam stares at Drew's profile, trying to process that information.

"You're gay?"

"Bi," Drew replies like he's simply admitting his favorite color. "Not that it mattered to Ted. He said that made it even more likely I was a predator and pervert that shouldn't be allowed near Christian children. Fucker."

"How did he find out?"

"Caught me and Miles holding hands coming out of the movies. That's it. Just holding hands."

Cam smiles bitterly, remembering what Sean confessed to him about Drew. "You don't think the blackmail that, I'm assuming, Miles had on him had anything to do with it?"

"I was never gonna use that. Because *I'm* a nice person," Drew grumbles. "But Miles was pissed, and he started hacking and digging. He thought it was fishy I'd get fired the day after I asked Ted where most of the money he keeps talking about comes from."

"Fired for digging into fraud *and* for your sexuality," Cameron sighs. "Common story, it seems."

"You came out?" Drew asks with a proud smile, and Cam nods.

"Sort of. It turns out most people already knew." He gives Drew a meaningful look. "It wasn't pleasant."

"I get that. And you got canned too? Rough." It's nice to talk to someone who sounds genuinely sorry for him for once.

"Suspended, for now. There's been financial malfeasance. It's under investigation." Cam slumps against the hard back of the pew.

"They think you did it?"

"They know Nate Pike did it, with Arnold Isaacs egging him on. But they – being Osborn and Isaacs and my entire family would like *me* to admit to it. Someone has to be the sacrificial lamb. But they promise if I do, then they'll just make it go away."

"What the hell?"

"They want me to witness tomorrow. Say that I did it because I was under the influence of an evil man tempting me to sin." Cameron shakes his head. "I also have to tell the congregation that I'm gay. Or was. They say that once I do, the Lord will help me to heal and I'll be reborn free of sin."

It sounds so easy, laid out like that. One testimony and all his problems will go away if he just puts his faith in God, truly and sincerely, for the first time. Maybe the miracle he's been asking for will finally happen.

"You know that's bullshit, right?"

Cam squints at the former Pastor. "It's the teaching of Christ. I thought you, of all people, would be aware of that. Though you do seem remarkably at peace with your damnation."

"Cam, I don't think I'm going to hell for being queer," Drew says, earnest and calm. "I say that as a man of faith. There's nothing like that in the Bible. Hell, don't even think there *is* a hell."

"What?" Drew could be speaking in tongues for all the sense it makes to Cam. The kindness in his face doesn't make sense either.

"Let me guess: you've been carrying this inside you for a long time – the gay thing. You spent your whole life praying for God to fix you or cleanse you or whatever."

"But he never did."

Drew gives him a lopsided, tired smile. "You ever think that's because you didn't need to be fixed?"

Cam closes his eyes, remembering the first time Sean told him he wasn't broken. The idea seems so foolish, even now. "After a while, I just started praying for help. It never came. I thought I must be so terrible in God's eyes, so sinful, to not even merit that."

Drew shakes his head with a sigh. "You ever hear that joke about the drowning man?"

Cam looks back up at Drew, confused again. "I don't see where this is going."

"So, this guy is drowning, and he prays, 'Oh God, please save me! I have faith in you!' And a lifeboat comes by and offers him help, but he says, 'No thanks. God will save me. I have faith.' So the lifeboat goes off, and the guy drowns."

"This isn't very hopeful."

"So he's up in heaven and he meets God and he says, 'God! I prayed to you! Why didn't you save me?' And God says, '*What do you think the lifeboat was for?*'"

Cam stares at Drew, his mind working both too fast and not fast enough. "Are you telling me that God... works in mysterious ways?"

Drew sighs again. "I'm saying the same thing I've been telling Miles for years. God shows his love for us through us. He thinks because good people suffer, that God is either not there or must be a total asshole. I try to explain that God gave us free will, and through that, suffering happens, but also so much good. We just have to take the chances to show love and take hope, and that's where we find him and his work. Ephesians 4:2: 'Whoever lives in love, lives in God, and God in them.'

God is found in the love between us, Cam. When we help each other, when we love each other, no matter how, that's God."

In a lifetime of sermons and gospel, Cam has never heard anything so clear. The closest he can remember is Sean talking about seeing God in the stars and trees. There had been no trees to look at that night, no leaves to enjoy. It had made him think of Sean's eyes.

"You think God sent me a lifeboat and I didn't see it?" Cam asks carefully.

"I'm kinda certain of it."

"Oh, honey!" They look up to see Miles returning to the chapel. "Merry Christmas, I got us in. Let's take a look-see!"

"We don't even know what to look for," Drew groans. "Or that he's even doing anything."

"He is," Cam says, finally certain of something. "The extra money would come in as donations from the hospital."

"Ooo, I like this one." Miles grins. "You wanna get to work?"

"As long as you're okay?" Drew says, looking at Cam.

"I'm not, but, you have given me some things to think about."

"Are you gonna go through with it? Tomorrow?" Drew asks.

"Do you think God wants me to?"

Drew shakes his head. "I can't speak for him. You gotta figure out the path to walk that's right for you. The rest will work itself out."

"Nice to meet ya," Miles says with a wave.

The two leave Cameron alone in the empty sanctuary. He doesn't feel much like praying anymore. Or maybe he doesn't feel like God is there to listen. He walks out of the church and onto the road, trying to remember a time when he did feel that way. To him, holy places were always marked by the absence of something more than what they held.

Cameron gets colder as he walks, even when he switches to a jog. It's not a short journey, and with a mile to go before he reaches home, it begins to snow. Icy, dry flakes that dust the world like powdered sugar. It's beautiful.

He remembers watching out the window as a child any time there was a chance of snow, believing he could smell it in the air. He stayed up late, praying and waiting for the first flakes to be visible in the beams of the streetlights. You can't simply see snow at night; you have to look for it. Find it in the light. Then wait for it to change the world into something beautiful. Even now, with a light dusting, Cam loves how it makes the world quiet and clean. It fills his soul with wonder that something so simple can be so beautiful.

He doesn't want to go inside when he reaches home, but he can't feel his hands or face, so it's probably a wise decision to do so. Kayla is waiting in the kitchen when he gets in.

"Oh my God, babe, you were running?" She jumps up to hug him then winces back. "I'll make you some tea."

"Thank you." Kayla sets the kettle to boil and grabs a sweater from the closet to hand to Cameron. "I didn't expect you to want to do anything for me."

"I'm still your wife." Kayla keeps saying that like it means everything. Should it?

"Why though?" Cameron asks, the thought striking him suddenly. "Why keep up this marriage when I hurt you? Why marry me at all or remain with me, knowing my sins?"

Kayla smiles sadly. "Because you've always been my best friend, and I love you. I always have, and I want to be with you for the rest of my life. No matter what you've done or choose to do tomorrow, I still love you."

Is that the kind of love Drew was talking about? The kind where he could find God?

"If I do this – if I stand up in front of everyone and beg God's forgiveness – do you really think that can be a new beginning for us?" Cameron asks softly.

"Yes. I do. I know you don't have a choice tomorrow, if you want to protect Danny, and I'm sorry it's come to that. I'm sorry I've spent so long trying to change you, or control you, the way your mom does," Kayla goes on, approaching him like he's a feral animal that might snap at her. "I can change too. I can be what you need. If it takes you a while to trust me or touch me again, I understand that too."

"And if I can't touch you?" He read the articles that Vince forwarded him, about how God loves all his children but hates their sin. As long as he's celibate…

"We'll find ways. And if you want…" Kayla gulps and bites her lips. "To see Sean."

Cameron's stomach twists at how much he wants it. How easy it could be. The sound of a door closing upstairs jolts him from the thought. "No. I won't do that. I'm doing this to protect Sean and Danny."

"I won't put Danny at risk, I swear. I do care about him and Sean." He knows Kayla isn't lying, which makes all of it worse.

"It doesn't matter. If my mother found out…" Cameron shakes his head. It doesn't even matter. "Sean doesn't want anything to do with me now anyway. He won't answer my calls or texts."

"Then what have you got to lose tomorrow? Certainly not him." Kayla lays a hand over Cameron's, and he doesn't pull away. "You have everything to gain. Peace. Forgiveness. Family. Salvation."

Is this the lifeboat? If it is, shouldn't it feel less like drowning?

30
THE WALK

sean

SEAN TAKES A fiNAL look at the room. It's not half as nice as Danny's room at the Steward place, or even half the size, but it's got a desk and a twin bed with new sheets and a window with a view of the front gate. The window in Sean's room looks over the few trees Bill has growing on the edge of his land. He figured out this morning that it faces East when the light of dawn woke him to pound on his head and hangover.

He switches off the light. The room's good enough. It should make Sean feel hopeful and happy, not like he's drowning in guilt. Maybe he did inherit some Catholic tendencies from Mom.

He's not expecting the doorbell. Mainly because he didn't know Bill *had* a doorbell. Taylor starts barking from inside. (It took all of five minutes on Thanksgiving for Danny to convince Bill to let her in, and she's been parked in front of the space heater under Bill's desk since.) By the time Sean's down the stairs, she's whining and scratching at the door as the visitor keeps ringing and knocking.

"Get back," Sean hisses at the dog as he opens the door. "Sorry, Bill's out right now, but – Danny?"

Danny shoves inside, brushing snow off his windbreaker. "Took you long enough to get the door. It's freezing."

"Danny, what the hell?" Sean demands, rushing after Danny to the living room. Danny scratches behind Taylor's ears as he sits by the heater. "How'd you get here?"

"I took the bus."

"Jesus Christ, why?" Sean pulls out his phone and starts scrolling through his contacts. "I'm calling Gardner right now."

"No!" Danny yelps and grabs the phone from Sean's hands.

"Hey! You're not supposed to be here. I know Kayla is a pain sometimes, but—"

"I'm here because Kayla and Cam's mom are gonna make Cam do something horrible, and I can't call you, so I had to tell you in person!"

Sean freezes. "What are you talking about? What are they gonna make him do?"

"They want him to testify or something in church? The weird thing where they stand up and talk about their sins. They're making *Cam* do that and say God's gonna make him not be gay or something."

Sean has to sit down. He can't believe Kayla would... No, this has Susan's stink all over it. "What the hell? Why would Cam ever—"

"I don't know!" Danny yelps. "I heard him and Kayla talking. It sounds like his mom is making him because of me?"

Fuck.

"Are they gonna take me away from you?" Danny pushes on. "Because I'll tell Anthony they're lying. I will. Is it the bi thing? Because that does *not* matter."

"No, it's not that. I—" Sean's skin feels too tight. He can't breathe.

"Sean, please, just tell me. Unless you like, murdered someone, I promise it's okay." Sean looks into his brother's eyes. There's nothing but love and faith there. He doesn't deserve it, but goddamnit, he's got to believe in it.

"I didn't kill anyone, okay? But I did bad things. I needed money, and I had nothing else and..." Sean chews his lip as Danny's brows furrow.

"Did you sell drugs or something?" Danny looks so innocent, and Sean braces himself to ruin that.

"No. I sold myself." He watches Danny blink slowly as understanding dawns and waits for the hate and pity and disgust to eclipse the confusion. It doesn't happen. "Do I need to be clearer? I was a hooker."

"I got that. Sean, I'm..." Sean braces himself. "I'm sorry. I bet that was really hard."

He was not expecting that. "You're not angry?"

"It's not great, but you did what you had to do, right?"

"Yeah..."

Danny shrugs. "Then I can be okay. I still think you're a good person."

"I'm not though." Sean closes his eyes and sees Cam's face. And Eli's and Tamara's and Brice's, and they all dissolve into Jeremiah laughing.

"Why do you think that?" Danny asks, all sincere and innocent, because he doesn't know how bad the world can be and how Sean's letting it stay bad.

"Because I'm selfish," Sean hisses. "I'm letting bad people get away with bad shit because I don't want the world to know what I did. And I'm not just talkin' about Cam and his stupid family."

Sean dares to look at Danny. He looks like he's trying to reconcile his hero big brother with the lying, failure of a whore he's looking at now. "So Cam knows? About what you did?"

Sean gives a dry laugh. "How do you think we met?"

"Oh." Now Danny looks like he's revising everything he ever thought about Cam too, and Sean doesn't want that.

"He wasn't ever like other clients, okay? Never. He was always special. Always good."

Danny's face melts into a warm smile. "You guys fell in love while he was paying you for sex? I've seen that movie."

"I told you, Cam doesn't—"

"Yes, he does." Danny sounds absolutely sure of it, and Sean has to close his eyes to block out the conviction in Danny's face. "If Susan's making him do this by threatening to – what? Tell the authorities about you and get me taken away? That means he's doing it because he loves you."

"Danny—"

"And if *you* love him, you won't let him do that."

"I can't stop him. I can't do fuckall because I love *you*. I won't let them take you away." Sean scrubs a hand over his face. "Cam doesn't want me interfering. If he did, he'd answer my damn calls and tell me himself."

"What? He said you weren't calling *him* back," Danne squawks. "He's totally depressed. He might want to do this because he thinks you're okay with it!"

"That's Cam's choice," Sean says, shaking his head. "I can't make it for him."

Danny scowls at him. "Okay, then, what do *you* want?"

"What?" Sean doesn't understand. What he's wanted has never mattered.

"Do you *want* to make the bad guys pay?"

"Well, yeah." Sean doesn't even think that's a question.

"Do you want to be with Cam?"

Sean looks down. He doesn't know why the answer fills him with shame. "More than anything, but that's not on the table."

"Sean, I love you too, but helping people is more important than me," Danny says with total earnestness. "I don't want to be the reason that people get hurt, whether it's strangers or you or Cam. If Anthony knowing what you did gets me taken away, we'll deal with it. But I don't want to be a hostage, and I sure as hell don't want to be the thing that keeps you from being happy with the person you love."

Sean swallows, not even fighting the tears filling his eyes. "Danny..."

He's not prepared for the hug, and it knocks the wind out of him. "Sean, I believe in you, and I believe if we do the right thing, it'll work out."

"That's a stretch," Sean murmurs, blinking the moisture from his eyes as he looks at the kid who somehow is the best of every person that's raised him.

"Call it faith," Danny says, and Sean's heart stutters again. Their mom would be so damn proud.

"Thanks, kid," Sean whispers into his brother's hair. "Now, give me my phone."

"Why?"

"Because I'm still calling Gardner to take you home," Sean replies. "Then I've got a lot of other calls to make."

cameron

Cameron's alarm goes off at the same time as usual. He's always hated that anemic beeping, and the last few weeks of using his phone had been a welcome relief. Today, it's his alarm clock on the nightstand. Black plastic. Red numbers. Sitting on pale maple. The windows are closed, and he can't see the bare tree branches outside gilded with snow. He can't stand to turn around and see Kayla beside him.

He looks at the painting on the wall. It's new. Splashes of red and blue at war, violent and jarring. They don't blend, but the green around them does. It makes the blue deeper but turns the red a rusted brown. He never tried to find meaning in Kayla's art. He accepted the beauty, but he needed poetry to tell a story. Perhaps that was a mistake. She's been showing him her heart for years – seeing them as two colors that will never merge.

"Good morning," Kayla says softly from beside him. "Did you sleep okay?"

"No."

The evening was quiet and fraught. After Gardner brought Danny home, Kayla had been furious and sent him to his room, over Cameron's protests. Danny wasn't even allowed to explain. Cam escaped after a silent dinner and tried to call Sean again. He tried to call Bill Farnell. He tried to call Drew. No one had answered, and he gave up. Danny's door was shut against him, and Kayla asked him, humble and gentle, to sleep in their bed.

He gave up again and regretted it instantly. He spent hours staring at the ceiling and thinking of God and lifeboats and love and obligation, and then he gave up again and took a pill. Because he thought he was tired of the fight and the search.

He was wrong. Waking up next to Kayla makes that clear. He isn't tired of the fight. He's tired of giving up. Cam is tired of drowning.

He doesn't say another word to Kayla. He showers and shaves, combs his hair, and dresses in his best suit. He ties his blue tie with extra care and goes downstairs to make coffee.

He heads outside while his cup fills. Sean's seat at the corner is vacant and covered with snow. There are no leaves left, and the world is silent and empty. Sean saw God here, in this emptiness. Somewhere between the trees and sky. The memory of Sean's faith, Sean's defiance, Sean's light: It makes Cam consider praying, one more time.

He's tired of prayers of surrender and desperation. To this day, there was only one time he prayed unselfishly; when he begged God to save the man he loved. He thought that was the only prayer God ever answered, and he never considered why.

He doesn't pray for a sign or for a miracle. Just forgiveness.

Danny is waiting by the coffee when Cam comes inside. "Cam, you don't have to do this. Whatever they're gonna make you do, you don't have to," Danny says without prelude.

"Is that why you were at Sean's? You heard us talking and wanted him to stop this?" Cam asks, bemused.

"Yeah. And he thinks it's crap too and—" Danny gulps.

"He didn't say that, did he?"

"He implied it," Danny huffs.

"We're going to be late. Your mother is waiting outside," Kayla says, her voice tight and tense as she enters the kitchen. "Danny, please stay put while we're out."

"And if I don't?" Danny snaps back. "Are you gonna make me write how bad I was on a chalkboard until God likes me again or something?"

"*Danny,*" Kayla gasps. "Don't talk about things you don't understand."

"I understand that you're screwing with *my* life because—"

The sound of a key in the front door stops Danny. Cam doesn't even have to look to know it's his mother walking in. "What is all this yelling about? Cameron, Kayla, I don't like to be kept waiting."

"It's nothing, Susan," Kayla replies. "Danny, you have homework."

Danny glares at Kayla and turns away, muttering.

"Danny," Cam calls. Danny turns to him with hope in his face that breaks his heart. "Thank you." Danny nods and goes upstairs.

"It's time to go," his mother says, annoyed, and Cam won't debate that.

Cam has never been sent to execution, obviously, so he doesn't know if that's what this feels like; the creeping dread, the world crumbling under his feet if he doesn't take the right steps. There's a chasm waiting to swallow him if he falls.

He rides in the back seat, like an errant child, and watches the snow. It's already melting, leaving puddles of gray mush on the side of the road. He wonders if the people downtown are warm. He imagines Sean sleeping in the Bel Air, covered in snow. He thinks of Sean's eyes and street lights on snowflakes and hidden gods in quiet places.

Everyone is at the church. Vince and Courtney stand next to Luke and Jillian. The children are already downstairs for Sunday school. Their parents certainly don't want them exposed to the filthy things Cam is going to confess. They file in together, Susan leading the clan to the front pew.

Cam sees so many people he knows in the crowd. Nate is seated in a middle row, next to his parents. He won't meet Cam's gaze. Isaacs is right in front, looking calm and satisfied. Jeremiah is beside him, and he stares Cam down like he can send him straight to the fires with the sheer force of his hate. Lee isn't beside him, but she's there in the crowd, at the back... with Drew and Miles sitting next to her. That's interesting.

Cam knows he won't be allowed to speak to them. He certainly doesn't want Osborn to know they're there. His eyes drift to the rest of the crowd. Friends and acquaintances too numerous to name. People he's grown up with and works with. An entire life in one room. All ready to know his sin.

Osborn appears to greet them, embracing Susan before turning to Cam. "So, will you be testifying today?"

Cam feels his family hold their breath, waiting, the eyes of the congregation on him already. "Yes," he answers, surprised by his own calm. Kayla sighs in absolute relief, and his mother looks triumphant.

"I'm glad to hear that, Cameron," Osborn says and heads back to the pulpit to begin the service.

"So am I," Susan adds.

Cam sits, listens to the quiet fall over the congregation, and waits.

"Good morning, all," Osborn begins. "I hope you all had a blessed holiday. I myself had a very interesting time, and it got me thinking. The human soul... is like a turkey."

Cam sighs. He really has to listen to this whole thing before his doom.

"The soul is raw and unclean at first," Osborn goes on. "Because it is full of sin. All of us are born sinning and unclean. We are born flawed, and it is only through following God's laws that we can be saved. It is only through accepting that Christ died for your sins that our turkeys can be cooked in the fire of God's love, and we are finally ready to be one with the Lord. Yes, I see some of you smiling. It's a silly metaphor, but it's not wrong. We must all face that fiery forge of salvation. We must all place our trust in God's light or be cast into the eternal fires of hell."

"Amen," Susan says beside Cameron, her eyes alight with hope and devotion.

"In light of that, I'd like to open the floor up to you, my friends. As we return from giving thanks, it is time for you to open your hearts, let the light of God in, and cleanse yourself of sin. It is time to be reborn."

Cam closes his eyes and listens to the quiet one more time. Someone coughs. A door opens as someone enters late. Another person whispers. There's no more waiting.

"I would like to testify," Cam says, opening his eyes. His voice is unsteady and rough, muffled by the attention focused on him. He trembles as he stands, and a murmur goes up.

"Brother Cameron, please come forward," Osborn says with a grin. Cam keeps his steps steady, keeps his eyes down as he walks forward. "What would you like to say, here in the sight of God? Remember, my friends, these confessions are sacred and are not to be judged or shared. These words are between Cameron and his God."

"Your God," Cam corrects softly, finally raising his eyes to Osborn and the empty altar behind him.

"Excuse me?" Osborn stammers.

"This is your God, not mine. He was never mine," Cam goes on as the whispers of the congregation break into a murmur. "And he never will be."

"Cameron," his mother hisses from behind him. "We have been over this. Think of that boy before you do something *stupid*."

He does think of Danny – and Sean – and he falters. He is being stupid and selfish, but…

"Hey, excuse me!"

Cam spins, blinking because he's not sure if what he's seeing is a dream. Or a miracle. "Sean."

"Sorry, we're kinda late," Sean says, bright and defiant as he walks down the aisle with Danny right beside him. At the back of the chapel by the door is Tamara Hodge, of all people, with another woman in uniform beside her. "Glad I made it, though. Heard it was show and tell time. Oh, heya, Cam."

"What are you doing here?" Susan demands, standing up with such aggression that Cam is worried for Sean's safety.

"Are you gonna call the manager on me? I thought everyone was welcome in the house of the Lord?" Sean replies, smirking, and another wave of chatter ripples around him. "And I got shit to say."

"You'll need to wait your turn," Osborn sneers.

"Never been one for waiting, actually." Sean stops halfway down the aisle. "You mind me horning in on your time, Cam?"

"Not at all," Cam replies, voice soft with wonder.

"Cool. I figure I need some practice testifying, since I'm gonna be doing it in court someday soon. See, folks, I'm a big ol' queer. Always have been, no matter what my dad wanted. Oh, I'm also a whore. Or I was. And you know what? I ain't ashamed of that." The congregation is too shocked to even whisper, but Cam finds himself beginning to smile. "I did what I had to do to survive. I refuse to be ashamed because I did survive. I even survived an asshole who thought it was okay to beat the shit out of a guy and wreck his car because he's queer. I'm talking about this asshole by the way."

Sean points, and every set of eyes in the congregation falls on the target: Jeremiah.

"This is absurd!" Jeremiah blusters, rising and moving to rush at Sean.

Danny steps in front of him, face full of fire. "You try to hurt my brother again, and I will break your face."

"And I'll help you." Lee rises from the back of the church and advances, fixing her cousin with a look of wrath. "I'll be happy to testify against my dear cousin with you, Sean. I'm sure I can confirm some things."

"You still have no evidence!" Jeremiah yelps as the crowd begins to murmur in earnest.

"Actually, I do." Sean looks back at Cam and gives him a wink. "Turns out I have a friend with some real interesting pictures and emails. My other friend Tamara's here to take you in, but if you want to stay for the rest of the show, you're welcome to."

"This is an outrage!" Jeremiah huffs, looking between Sean, Osborn, and Tamara for some chance of escape.

"Yeah, it really is, because you give all these people a bad name," Sean says and turns back towards the front of the church. "You too, Teddy. You talk about God's love and grace, but it's all a bunch of BS. You only believe in hate. Hating people for who they screw or how they vote or where they come from or what they look like or what they believe. That's the opposite of what your guy JC taught, and it sure ain't God. It's fear, and I'm not going to let you use it to hurt..." Sean inhales, locking eyes with Cam. "To hurt someone I love."

Cam takes a shuddering breath. Maybe the sun came out, maybe reality shifted, but the colors of the world suddenly seem brighter, especially the green of Sean's eyes.

"Sorry to say this so public, but I think someone blocked my number on your phone," Sean goes on with a crooked smile. He takes a step closer to Cam, then another, his voice growing softer. "Cam, I don't know if I believe in God, or heaven, or any of it. But I believe in *you*. You're the best person I know, and I'm not going to let these assholes tell you otherwise. I'm not going to let what I did or who I am get used against you anymore, or let you pretend to be something you don't want to be because of fear. Now everyone knows what I am and what I've done. So, you can make your big confession however you want, but don't do it for me. Don't do it for them. Do what you want for *you*. I'll love you either way."

It's strange. Cam heard similar words from Kayla yesterday, but this means so much more.

"Do you hear that, Cameron? You still have a chance," Susan hisses, stepping closer and grabbing his arm. "Think about your future. Think about your *soul*."

Cam doesn't look at her or Kayla, or any of the people staring at him, waiting. He can't look away from Sean, or he'll fall, and right now is his chance to fly.

"I love you," Cam says, plain and easy. The most important words he'll ever say.

Sean smiles and takes his hand.

"I've never loved anyone more than I love you. I didn't know for a long time what that meant. I have been searching my whole life for something, asking God for a sign or to save me. I thought he didn't hear me, but I was wrong. He sent me you. Every time I have needed faith, you were there. Every time I fell, you found me. Every step has led me to you. I have never felt holier than when I am with you."

Cam places a hand on Sean's face, tender and reverent, and his mother gasps. Sean has tears in his eyes.

"Someone told me recently that God is the love between us. And with all my heart and soul, I love you, Sean, and *that is not a sin.*"

Everything happens quickly. Someone starts clapping, someone else starts yelling, but Cam still doesn't look away from Sean. He closes the distance between them and kisses the man he loves in the sight of God and all the world. The congregation explodes around them with voices crying out in horror and hollers of approval. It doesn't matter.

Sean kisses him back, wraps him in his arms, and finally, Cam is reborn.

Free.

31
Prayer

Sean

SEAN SHOULD BE USED to doing things in public, but it's always been back alleys and borrowed spaces, nothing quite like this. It's one thing to tell a guy you love him, but it's another thing to say it in front of a few hundred people in his goddamn *church*. And yet, kissing Cam has never felt so intimate or so right. He pulls back to see those blue eyes again and smiles. It's only them, with the world crashing all around, and it's perfect.

"Did we just get married?" Sean asks softly.

"I should get divorced first," he murmurs back, arms around Sean's waist.

"And maybe take me on a real date."

"Excuse me!" someone yells at them, but neither of them looks away.

"Hope you don't mind me crashing your party," Sean says. "I almost didn't make it. Danny made me promise to take him. Emma and Tamara got here before us."

Sean spent most of last night at the police station, explaining everything to Tamara in minute detail, including Eli's evidence that cemented everything. Brice ID'd Jeremiah from a photo to and it was enough for a warrant.

"It was quite dramatic," Cam replies. "I had a speech prepared, you know, and you ruined it. I was going to tell everyone that their God could go fuck himself and that I would rather live alone than live a lie."

"Sorry," Sean murmurs. "But you don't have to do the alone thing. Not anymore."

Cam kisses him again, and the chatter around them gets louder and angrier. It still doesn't matter because Sean loves this idiot, and by some miracle, Cam loves him back.

"Uh, guys, I think someone's getting arrested?" Danny interrupts, pulling at Sean's sleeve. They part reluctantly and turn to see Jeremiah and Isaacs arguing loudly with Tamara and Emma, the other officer. Drew, Lee, (and some other dude Sean doesn't know) crowd around him, Danny and Cam as they approach the spectacle.

"Now, Sirs," Officer Emma says, calmly cutting through the yelling. She's at least six feet of muscle, and Sean would be scared to take her on. "We can do this hard or easy. We're only here for Mr. Fowler."

"How can you arrest this man when there are *trespassers* right there!" Osborn yells, jabbing the air in the direction of Sean and Cam as Tamara steps around him and grabs Jeremiah. "They are not welcome here and are engaging in public indecency!"

Tamara gives them a look over Jeremiah's head as she secures his cuffs. "I don't see anything indecent there, Mr. Osborn, just two people in love." Jeremiah winces as Tamara claps the cuffs on Jeremiah with an extra hard yank. "You have the right to remain silent, by the way, and anything you say can and will be used against you in a court of law."

"You're all going to hell," Jeremiah growls, because apparently, he wants to incriminate himself more.

"I don't think you get to decide that, Mr. Fowler," Tamara says. "And if anyone is interested, All Souls over on Burnaby street welcomes *everyone*, if you'd like a different place next Sunday." Tamara sends Sean and Cam a wink.

"Well, these degenerates are certainly not welcome here!" Arnold Isaacs thunders, advancing towards the melee. Sean doesn't know Cam's ex-boss very well, but he sure wouldn't mind punching him.

Emma steps in front of Isaacs before Sean can, placing a hand on his chest. "Like I said, sir, this doesn't have to be hard."

"Get your hands off me, you filthy cunt," Isaacs growls and swats Emma's hand away. In one smooth movement, Emma grabs his arm and twists it behind him, and pulls out her cuffs.

"Don't ya know that threatening an officer is a bad idea?" Emma says with a smile as Isaacs grunts in frustration. "But at least your friend here will have company in custody."

"We may have some information that will keep him there for a while." It's Nate Pike (at least that's who Sean assumes the twink is, he hasn't been introduced formally) who says it, from the back of the group. Isaacs opens his mouth, but Cam stops him with a glare.

"I'll be happy to forward the police everything I sent Miss Beecher as well," Cam says firmly. Sean grins.

"This is insane! The District Attorney will be hearing from me! These men are the criminals!"

Osborn bellows, bald head red as a cranberry, as he points at Sean and Cam. Sean squeezes Cam's hand, even though he seems unbothered.

"Let he among you without sin be the first to cast a stone," Cam replies with deadly calm, and Osborn freezes.

"Oh, I got the stones," the weird guy next to Drew pipes up, raising a finger. "Everyone on the church email list! Yeah, all of you watching, check your inbox for some *fascinating* video subscription and financial information about your beloved Mr. Osborn *and* Mr. Isaacs here."

Drew groans and shakes his head. "Miles. You didn't."

"Hells yeah, I did," Miles grins. "In fact, Officer! I'd love to share some info with you too!"

"Really?" Tamara asks, and Osborn looks like he's about to have a stroke.

"Oh, baby, I have so much dirt on these fuckers, you can call me mole man," Miles says and grins. "You want the flash drive now?"

"Gimme a second to get these two in the squad car, and we'll talk," Tamara smiles, before turning to Osborn. "I wouldn't go too far, sir."

"Go sit in a corner and think about what you've done, Teddy," Miles snickers and turns to Drew, beaming. "Told you no one fires my boo and gets off scot-free."

Drew closes his eyes, and Sean's pretty sure he's praying for the strength not to commit murder in a church. "Thanks, and please never call me your boo again."

"You have no sense of romance," Miles shrugs.

"This is outrageous! I want everyone who is not here for the true message of God to get OUT!" Osborn yells, face red and mouth frothing, as Jeremiah and Isaacs are escorted out. He doesn't need to watch. They don't matter anymore.

"Oh, but we're having fun!" Miles laughs, elbowing Drew. "Before we go, can we do the making-out thing too? I think Pantsuit over there might actually burst into flames if she sees more man-on-man action."

Sean follows Miles's gaze to Susan. She approaches with Cam's brothers and Kayla clustered behind her like the most depressing gang that ever lived.

"You've been asked to leave," Susan says calmly, eyes fixed on Sean. "Please do so."

"No one wants to stay here in your stupid church anyway," Danny sneers back. Kayla finally looks up, meeting Sean's eyes with a look of deep pain before turning to Danny.

"Actually, Danny, you have to stay," Kayla says quietly. "You're still placed at our house until the court makes a decision tomorrow."

It's Cam's turn to clench Sean's hand in comfort. He breathes through the anger. They knew this was coming. Still, Danny turns to him with worry in his face. "Sean..."

"It's okay, short stuff," Sean says. "I'll see you tomorrow."

Danny nods and pulls Sean into a hug. "I'm really proud of you," he says, smiling up at him. He turns to Cam and locks him in a hug as well. Sean loves the way Cam's face softens from surprise to affection. "You too, Cam."

"Thank you, Danny," Cam whispers into Danny's mop of brown hair.

Danny walks to the Stewards with heavy steps as Susan stares them down. "Tomorrow certainly will be interesting," she says.

"Mother, it's over. No more threats," Cam says, and Sean's heart swells with pride.

Susan shakes her head. She doesn't look angry anymore, just resigned and so, so disappointed. "You're right. It is over. Or it will be if you insist on living like this."

"I'm not insisting on anything," Cam replies. Sean retakes the hand he'd let go of to hug Danny. Whatever Cam is going to say or do, Sean wants him to know he's not doing it alone. "I'm gay. It's who I am. The only choice here is for you to accept it or not."

"I don't accept it," Susan says without a second of hesitation. "If you walk out of here with *him*, you have no place in this family, this church, or in my life."

"Then I'm sorry for hurting you, all of you, I truly am." Cam looks at Kayla when he says it. "I'm sorry for the mistakes I've made and the lies I've told. But I won't be sorry for living my life and being who I am going forward. Exactly as God intended me to be. Goodbye."

Sean doesn't let go of Cam's hand as they walk back down the aisle. He holds tight and watches Cam, who doesn't look back. Sean does though, because there's noise behind them, the sound of movement and murmurs too loud for only Drew, Miles, and Lee. Sure enough, at least a third of the congregation is walking out behind them. Cam doesn't see until they get out into the parking lot, but his face fills with awe as he does.

"Guess you inspired some folks," Sean says. He notices a pair of teen girls standing by a car, one crying and the other saying something fervently before hugging her. Then they kiss. "Like, *really* inspired."

Cam doesn't say anything, but his eyes look moist.

"That was amazing, Cam," Drew says, joining them and following Sean's eyeline to the young couple. "Looks like Casey and Meredith liked it."

"It was. We're all quite impressed," Lee adds, more cheerful than Sean has ever seen her. "What are you going to do now?"

"I don't know," Cam says with a wry smile. "I should probably figure out where I'm going to be sleeping tonight."

"Dude," Sean sighs. "You're coming to Bill's."

"Am I?" Cam asks back.

"Well, he doesn't have a guest room, but I think we can find a spot for ya."

"I think I could be agreeable to that." Cam smiles; that real, warm, perfect smile that Sean can't get enough of, and it makes perfect sense to kiss him. He could get used to this out in public thing.

"Aw, see how cute they are, honey," Miles says, breaking the moment. When Sean looks over, Miles has his eyes on Drew. "That could be us, but you playin'."

"That is—" Drew sputters. "What does that even mean? I am not playing!"

"Who is this guy again?" Sean asks.

"My sorta boyfriend," Drew mutters.

"Don't undersell it, I'm the love of his goddamn life," Miles replies with a smirk.

"Fuck you," Drew grumbles.

"Later," Miles shoots back.

Lee has obviously had enough. "Let's go find lunch or anything else and get out of Sean and Cam's hair. I'm sure they have a lot to talk about."

"Ooo, waffles?" Miles asks with a grin. "Then I think we have a date at the police station."

"Sure, fine," Drew says, but doesn't leave. "As long as you're both okay?"

"We're fine, or we will be," Cam says. "Thank you, Drew. For everything."

"Call me anytime," Drew replies.

They wave, and the trio heads towards a beat-up Nissan as Cam and Sean walk hand in hand to the Bel Air. They let go long enough to get inside.

"Before you go calling Drew, we should probably un-fuck your phone," Sean says, as they settle in the bench seat.

"And then I need to get a few clothes. If you don't mind driving me to the store."

"Anywhere you want," Sean replies, and Cam looks at him with such adoration that it makes him blush. "As long as we're finally getting you some goddamn jeans."

They huddle in the car and unblock Sean, Drew, Bill, and a slew of others from Cam's phone and correct his phonebook as well. It makes Sean furious to know Susan was working so hard to keep them apart and doubly so to see how much it hurts Cam. He kisses Cam to comfort him and spite her as well.

He stays close to Cam in the store, even when he sees an old woman with white hair and a pink jacket give them a *look*. He stares her down while Cam looks for his size of jeans, and she huffs away. She won't be the last to look at them that way, and Sean hates it, but it's better than hiding. He holds Cam's hand going into the market and through the drive-through and all the way up Bill's front steps because he can.

"So, you got him?" Bill asks, wheeling from the kitchen as soon as they're inside. Cam raises an eyebrow.

"Yeah, I got him," Sean says.

"And Danny?"

Sean's anxiety spikes like an icicle to the gut. "We'll find out tomorrow."

"Well, one ain't bad," Bill says, looking Cam over. "I'm glad to have ya, son."

Seeing Cam smile at Bill makes Sean's heart hurt in the best way. "Come on, I'll give you the tour."

Sean shows Cam around the downstairs, then leads him up to his room. The door creaks as they enter. Cam trails his fingers over the spines of books and traces the fading filigree on the wallpaper. He tests the quilt between his fingertips and turns back to Sean, eyes bright.

"You like it? I know it's not perfect," Sean asks.

"That's what I like about it."

Sean closes the distance between them, leaving a breath of space between their bodies. Cam lifts a handy to Sean's face and caresses him with the same reverence and care he gave the rest of the room. It makes Sean tremble.

"Are you okay?" Cam asks.

"I should be the one asking you that, you've had a big day."

"I'm not. There's a lot to adjust to. And I asked you first."

Sean finally dares to touch Cam back, tracing the solid line of his jaw. "I'm scared."

"Me too."

"I'm scared that we're not gonna get Danny back, and I'm scared that when I'm not some forbidden thing that you're not gonna want me. I'm scared that you're gonna decide God doesn't want you—"

He's so relieved when Cam kisses him. It's soft and loving and everything he needs. Everything they need. He holds Cam carefully, part of him still afraid he'll disappear like a dream.

"Can you say it again?" Sean asks, barely above a whisper.

"I love you."

"I love you too."

He kisses Cam again, putting every ounce of longing and love he can into it. He's pretty sure he's not ready to get naked right now, but simply touching Cam without fear is enough. He pulls him onto the bed and keeps kissing him.

They are not perfect, and things are not okay, but they are here together, and it's good enough for now.

cam

Cam wakes in sheets that smell of Sean. They're soft with age, and warm, but the space beside him is cold and empty. Cam sits up in worry. It's still dark out; a few hints of light on the horizon visible through the window. Cam can't find a sweater or robe, so he throws his coat over his boxers and sleep shirt and pads through the quiet house.

Sean isn't in the living room or kitchen, but the coffee maker is gurgling away, and Taylor is sulking by the front door. Cam steps outside into the cold to see Sean leaning on the Bel Air, looking at the sky.

"Sean?"

"Hey," Sean replies, smiling at Cam. "I was gonna bring you some coffee."

"I don't know if I should. My new pills are still at… the other house." He can't call it home anymore, can he?

"Like that ever stopped you," Sean smirks as Cam joins him by the car. The ground is freezing through his socks, and the metal of the Bel Air even more so when he leans on it, but Sean is warm. "Glad you're finally taking care of yourself."

"I'm slightly more motivated to not let my anxiety literally kill me from the inside," Cam says with a shrug. Now that he thinks of it though, his stomach has felt just fine since Sean walked into that church. "I will say: this is an interesting method you have for making coffee. Does the hypothermia bring out the flavor?"

"Anyone ever tell you you're kind of a dick?"

"I was under the impression you liked that about me. Or did you mean my actual dick?" Sean laughs quietly and shakes his head. His smile is still the most beautiful thing Cam has ever seen, even in the pale twilight. "Why are you out here, Sean? Did I do something wrong?"

"What? No! You're fucking awesome!"

Cam smiles at that. They were quiet last night. Sean had explained the situation with Tamara and Eli. There had been a few texts and calls with Lee, Flor, and Drew, but nothing of great import. He had also sent one to Kayla, asking her to bring some of his things with her to Danny's hearing. He didn't receive a reply.

Then it was only him and Sean, alone in a bedroom that no one had to leave when things were done. Neither of them had really known what to do with that. It was unspoken that they could take things slowly, and they did, kissing and touching and embracing until they fell asleep, tangled together in shared warmth. It was wonderful, but Cam worried anyway.

"Good. So why are you out in the cold instead of in bed with me?"

"You're gonna laugh at me," Sean sighs.

"I promise I won't."

"I was… praying."

Cam stares at Sean in confusion and wonder. "To who?"

"What do you mean to who?" Sean scoffs and gestures at the brightening sky. "Fuckin' God or Mother Mary or the universe or whatever!"

Cam looks up at the sky, a smile tugging at the corner of his mouth. "I didn't think you believed."

"I don't know what I believe or how much, but, hell, I figure we can use all the help we can get today." Cam treasures this: that Sean lets him see when he's afraid. "I was just getting around to Saint Anthony, asking for help to make what's lost found."

Cam smiles, a surge of love filling his heart. Love that makes him believe. "Then I'll pray too."

"Really?" Sean asks with the same touched expression he has whenever Cam offers him something he doesn't think he deserves.

"You know, I prayed for you when you were unconscious in the hospital. It was the first time praying ever felt right, because it wasn't about me."

"Guess it worked then." Sean smiles.

"I hope it works now." Cam leans close as they both look up at the sky. The sun is behind clouds, but Cam can still pinpoint the moment it peeks above the horizon. He watches deep blue become gray and prays that when it's dark again, Danny will be home with them. For the first time in decades, he feels something like hope as he calls to the divine. An answering whisper from the universe that perhaps he was heard. It could just be the cold, of course, but he wants to believe in it.

"Let's get inside," Sean says after a while. "Coffee's probably done."

Cam lets Sean fiddle in the kitchen while he showers. The pipes bang, and it's awkward in the old clawfoot tub, but warm water brings the feeling back into his skin. Cam feels exposed crossing the hall to the bedroom in a towel, but Sean looking him up and down and wolf whistling is worth it.

"I gather you're in a better mood," Cam smiles.

"I'm in a room with my naked boyfriend, it's hard not to be."

Cam tilts his head, pushing a few stray drops of water from his eyes. "Your boyfriend?"

"Is that not okay? Were we supposed to have a talk first?"

"No, it's fine." Cam approaches Sean, smiling. "I like it."

"Good. Okay."

"You seem nervous."

"Of course I'm nervous! I've got this damn hearing in a few hours *and* I don't want to screw things up with you before they've even started!" Sean's voice is tight, and his breathing is too fast for Cam's comfort.

"You don't have to worry about that second one," Cam says, laying a hand on Sean's shoulder.

"Really? Because I don't know what the hell I'm doing. Making a big show in front of the church is one thing, but being a human person in a *relationship*? I'm lost. I've had sex with a lot of people, but I've never dated anyone."

"And I've dated one person, and we saw how that worked out," Cam says, stepping too close and forcing Sean to look at him. "Nothing about our relationship is typical. We'll figure it out together, okay?"

"Okay. And the hearing?"

"All we can do is hope and pray, and we already did that."

"That's comforting."

"I try."

"Try harder."

Cam crowds into Sean's space, gently pushing him until the back of Sean's legs hit the bed and he's forced to sit. Cam follows him, straddling his lap and dropping his towel. "Is this alright?"

"This your way of trying to relax me?"

"Is it working?"

"Mmm. Maybe." Sean kisses him, pulling him flush against his chest. He tastes of chicory coffee and cinnamon, and his hair is soft and silken between Cam's fingers. The kiss deepens easily, only breaking so they can remove Sean's shirt.

"You'll need to change for the hearing anyway," Cam mutters as he fumbles with Sean's belt and buttons. The fact that he's getting hard makes that particularly challenging in this position.

"What?" Sean asks against Cam's neck.

"You can't wear jeans to court."

Sean huffs as he flips them, trapping Cam under him as he shimmies out of said jeans. "Fucking watch me."

"Do you even own a suit?"

"You helped me buy everything I own, you know I don't."

"Maybe you can—" Talking while kissing is very difficult, especially when Sean is doing things with his hips and mouth that are making Cam's brain overheat. "—borrow one of Bill's."

"God no."

Cam grabs the globes of Sean's ass and bucks his hips, earning a grunt of pleasure. Sean responds in kind, building the friction between them. "You have – oh fuck – khakis," Cam gasps.

"I would rather die. Just for suggesting that, I get to come first," Sean says.

Cam laughs as he flips them again and kisses his way down Sean's body. "Fine," he murmurs before taking Sean in his mouth. "But you still can't wear jeans."

sean

The juvenile court isn't even in the main courthouse. It's next door in a two-story white building that looks like it could be any old office from the outside. The only thing that really gives it away is the metal detectors they have to walk through to get inside. It makes Sean nervous, and he hates taking off his shoes to go through, but Cam is right there with him. Bill raising hell about getting his chair past is pretty damn entertaining at least.

The lobby is small, with twenty gray chairs on bluish gray carpet and two big wooden doors with "Courtroom" signs above them, and Sean doesn't know which he's supposed to go into. He doesn't know anything that's going to happen, and he doesn't see Danny, and he's going to throw up.

"Mr. Lockwood!"

Sean spins at the voice. Ron is just coming through the security. He looks like he shaved, but his suit is still wrinkled and he has a hand-sewed patch on the shoulder. "Hey, Ron."

"What, you didn't trust me, so you hired someone fancy?" Ron says as he meets their trio, looking Cam up and down. He's got some major sex hair going, but he's in his church suit, so he looks pretty respectable. Sean's wearing a pair of dark slacks that Bill found somewhere and his best shirt.

"Told ya that you looked like a lawyer," Sean smirks at Cam. "Ron, this is Bill Farnell, my boss and landlord, and this… is Cameron Steward."

"The foster dad?" Ron asks, eyes widening. "The one you had a fling with?"

"The one I have a relationship with. Present tense," Sean says. "And, uh, better to just tell you. Everyone knows. Like the whole town. I also let the cat out of the bag about me turning tricks."

"You *what*?" Ron balks.

"He went to the police about his assault," Cam explains, puffing up protectively.

"To put a bad character in jail," Bill adds. "He's being a hero."

"And there were other factors at work," Cam adds.

"I don't care about other factors. Sean, this isn't good," Ron says, his expression dire. "Wu isn't super-conservative, but 'ex-hooker who's banging the foster dad' doesn't look good *to anyone*! Are you telling me you two are *together*?"

"Yeah," Sean replies. "Cam came out. It was a big thing. He's staying with me at Bill's for now." Cam flinches at that, and Bill smacks Sean on his bad hip. "For good, actually."

"Okay. I guess I can try and spin that as, uh, continuity for Danny and an extra income," Ron mutters.

"I'm unemployed right now, actually. Or I will be once I officially quit," Cam says.

"Wait, what?" Sean asks, turning to Cam. This is news.

"You know you're screwed, right?" Ron asks, scrubbing his face with his hand.

Sean's stomach twists, and Cam takes his hand. "I know. Maybe we'll get some grace."

"We'll try," Ron replies.

One of the courtroom doors opens, and a tall redhead in glasses comes out. She's wearing an ID badge around her neck, so she must be a court employee. "In the matter of Daniel Lockwood?" she calls into the lobby.

"Here!" Ron says. "We're still waiting on the agency, kid, and Miss Hernandez."

"They're all inside already," the clerk says. "The judge is about to take the bench."

"Shit," Ron says. "I wanted to talk to the worker and Carrie – Danny's attorney."

"You didn't yet?" Sean demands, his panic rising.

"Until now, this was a pretty open and shut case!" Ron snaps back.

"Guys," the clerk says. "We have six more hearings after you, and we're already running late, so we need you to get in here."

"Sean." Cam's voice is calm as he squeezes Sean's hand. "Just breathe. Let's go."

"Okay," Sean whispers and lets Ron lead the way inside.

The courtroom is small and reminds Sean to an uncomfortable degree of a church. There are rows of scuffed benches on either side of a central aisle, with tables at the front facing the raised judge's bench. There are flags and seals, and it's like they're looking at an altar waiting for God.

The courtroom is also more crowded than Sean anticipated. Gardner is seated at the right table next to two women, one preppy white lady with long blonde hair and a sturdy Latina in a mismatched suit. Beside her is Danny, so she must be his lawyer. Sean has no idea who the blonde is. Danny turns and waves meekly to Sean. Ron leads Sean to the empty table on the left, and Cam takes a spot on the bench directly behind them.

"I'll get the judge," the clerk says and disappears.

Sean turns to look at Cam and finally notices the rest of the crowd in the courtroom. Holy shit. They're not strangers waiting for another hearing. Drew is there with Miles, Lee, and a Latina woman Sean doesn't recognize. One row behind them, next to where Bill parked, is Tamara Hodge. On the other side of the courtroom, alone in a middle row is *Vince*. That can't be a good thing, but at least Susan and Luke aren't here. Kayla is seated in the back next to Dawn, the nurse Sean's pretty sure ratted Cam out to Kayla all that time ago.

"All rise," the clerk calls. Sean jumps to his feet to watch Judge Wu, a stern-looking Chinese man, enter and take his seat on the bench.

"Please be seated," Judge Wu says, and everyone but Gardner sits. "Looks like we have a guest worker today."

"Yes," Gardner says. "The St. Louis County Child Protection Unit has been very welcoming. However, if this case is not dismissed today, I will be transferring this fully to Miss Hawkins."

"Do you anticipate that, Mr. Gardner?" the Judge asks. "Your report was optimistic."

The blonde – Miss Hawkins – rises. "That report was filed before certain information about the elder Mr. Lockwood's past and his inappropriate relationship with the foster family came to light." Sean decides right then and there that he does not like Miss Hawkins at all. She uses the same tone Susan does, implying everything is beneath her. "In addition, we've received multiple calls of concern about Danny Lockwood's placement from members of the community. Including the foster parent, Mr. Steward's own mother."

"Well, don't keep me in suspense, Miss Hawkins, what information is this?" Judge Wu asks. "By the way, this whole courtroom is sworn in, and if anyone lies, it's perjury."

JESSICA MASON

Miss Hawkins puffs up, a smug look on her face. "Sean Lockwood is a prostitute. He has ties to other criminals, and his association with the Stewards began when Mr. Steward paid him for extramarital sex."

The judge turns his eyes to Sean, and he feels like something smaller and dirtier than a worm. He's absolutely screwed. "Okay, then," the judge says. "Does this change the agency's recommendation on placement and dismissal?"

"Yes," Miss Hawkins says.

"No," Gardner says at the same moment.

"What?" Sean asks aloud and gets glares for it.

Gardner clears his throat. "Sean *was* a sex worker, yes, and I'm disappointed he didn't share this information earlier. However, the facts in my report remain the same: he is fully employed now in a different field with a stable residence, free of drugs, and is in a good position to take care of Danny."

"And the foster father?" the judge asks, still looking in Sean's direction. "I assume this is Mr. Steward we have with Mr. Lockwood?"

Ron stands, hands spread on the table. "Yes, Your Honor, Mr. Steward and Mr. Lockwood informed me – *this morning* – that they are in a committed relationship and that, apparently, Mr. Steward will be living with Mr. Lockwood for the foreseeable future." Sean keeps his eyes on the judge, trying to read any sign of what he's thinking, but there's nothing. "I think this is a good thing. It's another adult Danny knows and trusts in his life to help care for him."

"*Or*," Miss Hawkins cuts in. "Placing Daniel with another person with a history of criminal activity and moral—"

"Hey, I'm going to stop you there and object." The court's attention turns to Danny's lawyer, who also stands. All these lawyers standing up and talking about him makes Sean feel pretty damn small. "If Miss Hawkins is taking Mr. Lockwood's sexuality or his relationship with Mr. Steward into consideration, that is blatantly unconstitutional."

The judge fixes Miss Hawkins with a hard look. "Miss Hernandez is correct. Miss Hawkins, do you have any concerns about Mr. Lockwood that are *not* related to this?"

"There are the calls from the community," Miss Hawkins stammers.

"From homophobes," Miss Hernandez cuts in again. "And one of those community members, Ted Osborn, was arrested yesterday."

Sean can't help him smile at hearing that news.

"I've shared everything I have," Miss Hawkins grumbles and sits down.

"Miss Hernandez," the judge asks, looking implacable. "Do you have anything more to add?"

"Yes," Miss Hernandez says, smiling over at Danny. "My client wants to be with his brother *and* Mr. Steward. He has been very, *very* clear on this and, in my opinion, it is in his best interest to be placed with Sean and that jurisdiction be dismissed."

Sean lets out a breath and smiles at Danny.

"Alright, Mr. Horner. Anything more from you or your client?" the judge asks. Ron nudges Sean.

Sean's mouth goes dry as he stands up. He's shaking, and he wants to look to Ron or Cam for help, but that's not going to do anything. Instead, he thinks about walking into that church yesterday. He knew he was doing the right thing then, and he knows he can do it now.

"Your Honor, I've messed up – a lot, but Cam here, and Kayla too, actually, they helped me get my life back," Sean says, though he's not brave enough to look at Kayla yet. "Yeah, it was for some screwed up reasons, but what matters is that I'm doing good now. I'm steadier than I've ever been in my life, and I am ready to take care of Danny."

"No one doubts that you're ready, Mr. Lockwood," the judge replies. "The question is: are you fit? Is Mr. Steward fit, for that matter?"

Sean's mouth goes dry. Crap. This is where it ends…

"Your Honor," Tamara says from the back. Sean and the lawyers turn around to look at her.

"Detective Hodge, nice to see you. Do you have something to say?" Judge Wu asks as Sean's heart starts racing.

"Yes, Your Honor," Tamara replies. "Mr. Lockwood was nearly killed in the incident that led him to move in with the Stewards to recover. Sean has provided evidence alleging that he was beaten by a religious fanatic because of his sexuality and profession. He won't tell you that, because he doesn't think it's important, but, even knowing that bringing those charges would put Danny's placement with him in jeopardy, he came to me and made his report. Because Sean did the right thing at a huge risk to himself, bad people will hopefully get punished. Sean is not one of those bad people. He's one of the very good ones. He has no arrests as an adult; I can verify that, but he has the gratitude of the St. Louis PD. And he has my faith as a member of law enforcement that he will be exactly the person his brother needs to have the best chance at happiness."

Tamara meets Sean's eyes, and he has to blink a few times to keep his stupid tears at bay. "Thank you," he mouths. Tamara smiles, then sits back down.

"It looks like we have some other community members here," the judge says. "Sir?"

It's Drew who stands and speaks, his voice shaking. "Hi. Uh. Your Honor. My name is Drew Barons, and until recently, I was assistant pastor at First Christian, where I got to know both Sean and Mr. Steward. I can tell you, without any reservation, as both a person of faith and a person in general, that these are good people. They made mistakes, but they're making up for them, and I know that Danny belongs with them." Drew gives a nervous smile and sits back down as quickly as possible.

"And you two?" Judge Wu nods to Lee and the woman beside her, and they glance at Cam.

"We're here to speak for Cameron," Lee says as both stand. "My name is Lee Fowler. This is Flor Guerra. We're Cam Steward's former co-workers."

"I don't know Sean," Flor says. "But I know Cam. He's not just a good guy; he's hard-working and believes in people. He'd be a good person for anyone to have in their life."

"We also have a letter of support from a neighbor, Wanda Brook, who has nothing but praise. But I wanted you and Cam to know he's an inspiration, not just in spite of his mistakes, but because he has learned from them and overcome," Lee adds with a proud smile. "He's helped me more than he knows."

"I was gonna say the same things about Sean," Bill interjects gruffly, grabbing the court's attention. "Hope you're not offended if I don't stand."

"It's fine, I'm getting the idea," Judge Wu smiles. "What about you, sir?" he asks Vince.

Sean glances at Cam as Vince rises. His heart is pounding, even though he knows what's coming. He could probably recite the speech about how they've disappointed Jesus and save Vince the trouble.

"Your Honor, my name is Vincent Steward, Cameron is my brother," Vince begins. His eyes linger on Cam apologetically. "I don't know Sean well. I won't lie to you and say I'm not disappointed in how Sean and Cam met. It's not right, and it shows some disregard for the law and other people which is troubling." Vince looks over at Kayla for emphasis, but she won't meet his eyes.

Sean braces himself as Vince turns back to the judge.

"But my brother is a good man," Vince goes on, and Sean blinks in shock. "He was cornered into doing a bad thing. As far as I can tell, so was Sean here. They did what they had to because no one ever told them there was another way or, heaven forbid, let them walk it. I may not really know Sean, but I know brothers. I love my brother, and I'd do anything to take care of him if I had to. I think that's what Sean will do for Danny here, so I urge you to make that happen."

Sean can't believe it, but when he looks at Cam and sees the tears on his face, he knows this is real. "Holy shit," he whispers to Cam.

"This is all very moving," Judge Wu says, looking entirely unmoved. "Would the foster parent *not* dating Mr. Lockwood like to have a say?"

Sean's stomach drops as Vince sits, and Kayla rises. She takes a deep breath, holding onto Dawn's hand.

"Sean came to our house because of me," Kayla starts. "I was the one who invited him. I was the one who brought in Danny as well. I did this because I knew, in my heart, that my husband loved Sean, and I didn't want to lose my husband. I was afraid..." Kayla's voice hitches, and Sean feels like he's swallowed an entire cave of bats. "I used them when I should have been helping them, and I trapped someone when I should have been letting him go. I made as big a mistake as Cam in doing that, but I want to fix it."

Sean feels sick. If Kayla says one more time that she wants to save Cam...

"Danny belongs with Sean, and Sean... He belongs with Cam. Keeping Danny away from his family would be a huge mistake. We've all made enough mistakes lately, so please don't add another."

Sean lets out a shaking breath as Kayla meets his eyes. He's feeling too many emotions to process.

"Mr. Steward, do you have anything to say?" the judge asks. "Since everyone else got a chance."

Cam rises uneasily with a hand on Sean's shoulder. "Everyone said it already: Sean is the best man I know, and he loves Danny and will take care of him. I love Danny too, and I love Sean more than anything. I want to be part of their life – both of their lives – as long as possible. We all want to start making things right. If you'll let us."

Sean can't help but smile. Things are already better because Cam is there, and he isn't going anywhere.

"Alright then, well–" the judge begins before Danny stands up.

"Can I talk?" Danny asks.

Wu's eyebrows go high. "Your attorney already made a statement."

"Yeah, but *I* want to tell you that I'll be safe with Sean and—"

Judge Wu sighs and rolls his eyes. "And that he's the best thing since sliced bread, yes, I get the idea. The agency recommendation, whatever it is, is noted, but I am ruling that Danny should be placed with his brother. I trust the agency to create a robust safety plan and Mr. Lockwood to get formal custody papers sorted out. Jurisdiction and the case are dismissed. Congrats."

The judge bangs his gavel for good measure, and Sean gets one warning whoop before Danny flies across the room to tackle him. He jumps up and hugs him so tight neither of them can breathe, and it doesn't matter because finally they're a family. All of them.

32

Awake

cam

IT'S CHAOS ALL AROUND Cam, but for once it's joyful chaos. Cam is right there in the middle of it, hugging Danny and Sean and thanking God with all his heart.

"Holy shit," Sean says, shaking his head as he looks around.

Ron looks even more amazed than they are. "Congrats, I guess."

"I'm so happy!" It's Danny's lawyer who says it. Cam doesn't know where she came from, but she's jumping up and down in excitement. "Guys, since I'm not Danny's lawyer after this, if you need any legal help with anything, let me know, okay?"

"Us?" Sean asks, looking between him and Cam.

"Yeah, like if anyone gives you crap about the queer thing or you need help in court with the criminal stuff or custody or—" Ron takes her by the shoulder.

"They got it, Carrie. Everyone has our cards; we need to clear out," Ron says.

"Sean, Danny, we need to talk with you," Anthony calls from the door, the other social worker beside him looking like she just drank spoiled milk. It's extremely satisfying.

"You okay?" Sean asks Cam.

"I'm fine. I'll wait," Cam replies. Sean and Danny follow Anthony and Miss Hawkins out of the courtroom and to a quiet corner of the lobby.

"Cameron."

He turns to see Lee smiling next to Flor, Drew, and Miles. "Thank you all for coming," Cam gets out before he's caught in a fierce hug from Flor. Lee is more restrained with her hug, but her smile is warm. "How are you even here?"

"Drew called us," Lee explains. "And we took the day off."

"Our boss is apparently not coming back, so he can't discipline us," Flor smirks. "Even though Abby knows Isaacs and Nate did it all."

"I'm sorry to leave you with a mess, but I never liked that job. It was just another thing I did because I was told to do it," Cam says, and only gets smiles in return. "I want to find something I care about."

"That's very commendable," Lee says, beaming.

"You and I can commiserate on navigating new employment horizons," Miles says with a conspiratorial grin.

"I thought you worked for a porn company?" Cam asks, squinting at him.

"Not much longer," Miles says, looking at Drew with an affectionate smile. "Some bleeding heart says there are better things I can do with my life if I want to keep seeing him. I can't commute to the valley from St. Louis anyway."

"So, you're staying here?" Cam asks, and Miles nods. Cam looks at Drew. "But you got fired. You don't have to stay here."

"Actually, I want to. I have a new job already. Miles might too if he passes the interview with the board," Drew says, smiling. "I'm working with the city and a new endowment to expand the shelter and services downtown. We're setting up a whole new non-profit."

"Really?" Cam can't think of anyone better for such a project, nor a better way for Drew to really do God's work.

"The pay is shitty and there are no benefits, but they needed IT. Now we're looking for a numbers guy," Miles says with a sly smile. Cam glances at Drew, wondering if this offer was the plan all along.

"See, man," Drew smiles. "Lifeboat."

"Thank you," Cam says. "I have to think about it. I was also considering going back to school at some point. There's a degree I'd like to get."

"Take all the time you need, it'll take us a while to get going anyway," Drew replies. "For now, enjoy yourself."

"And enjoy that sweet ass you get to shack up with," Miles adds, tilting his head as he looks at said ass across the lobby. Drew and Lee both hit him. Flor looks like she's met her new best friend."

"Call us if you need anything," Lee says. "We'll see you for Christmas, no matter what." Her last words are delivered with a pointed look over Cam's shoulder. Cam turns to see Vince waiting, awkward and alone.

"Thank you all," Cam says. They exchange goodbye hugs, and he watches his friends walk away.

"You need someone who can speak Spanish?" Flor asks Miles as they leave. "Because I wanna talk…"

Cam chuckles to himself before he turns to make his way to his brother. "I can't believe you came," he says warmly as Vince gives him a crooked smile.

"Mother told me not to," Vince says tiredly. "Said she would never forgive me."

"And?"

"And I told her to shove it."

Cam grins. "I'm sure she liked that."

"She'll come around," Vince replies with a shrug.

"I doubt that."

"Hey." Vince sets a hand on Cam's shoulder. "I did."

"Did you really?"

Vince gives him a true big brother look that makes Cam feel small and protected at the same time. "Cam, I'm not gonna say that I understand you or that I approve, but I'm working on it. I am. You and Sean said a lot of things yesterday that I'm still thinking about. And you're my family, you being—" Vince gulps, bracing himself. "You being *gay* doesn't undo that, okay?"

"Okay. That's a good start." It's not perfect, but it's more than Cam ever expected from anyone in his family. "Come here. I promise the homosexuality isn't contagious." Vince comes easily as Cam pulls him into a hug. It makes Cam feel like he did when he was young: that someone is watching out for him, and maybe that's a bit of God too.

"Don't be a stranger, okay?" Vince says.

"You too. And check your phone, Mom likes to block numbers," Cam replies. "Bye, Vince."

"Bye, little brother."

Cam watches his brother go and then turns to see Danny hugging Gardner, while his lawyer talks animatedly with Bill. Sean catches Cam's eye and smiles brightly, then frowns. Cam turns to see the focus of his expression. Kayla stands with Dawn beside her, a folder clutched to her chest. "Hello, Kayla. Dawn."

"I'm here for Kayla. As far as I'm concerned, you and lover boy can eat shit," Dawn sneers.

"Dawn, please. Go somewhere else. I'm okay. Cam, would you come with me? I have Danny's stuff in the car." Cam follows Kayla out to the parking lot by the courthouse. Her back seat is surprisingly full.

"That's all Danny's?" Cam asks.

"No, most of it is yours. The big lumps there are the records and the player. I hope I got all the books."

Cam blinks, still amazed after everything. "Kay, you didn't have to bring all this. I only needed pills and pants."

"I did though. I need to start… moving on." Her voice is unsteady, but her face is resolved. "I also filed these this morning since we were here." Kayla hands Cam the folder she was holding. He opens it to find a stack of papers, the top one emblazoned with the words 'Petition for Dissolution of Marriage.' "If you want, you can sign them tonight. It's all down the middle. No support, of course. I'll sell the house and you get half the profit."

"That sounds fair," Cam murmurs.

"Look it over anyway, to be safe. Don't just trust me."

Cam finally finds the bravery to look Kayla in the eye and smiles. It's ending. All the years of lies and silence, and over a decade of friendship. Maybe, someday, they can salvage the last part. "Thank you. What will you do now?"

"I don't know." Kayla looks happy about the answer. "I don't even know if I'll stay in town once my residency is done. I think I need some time with myself, only myself. I've never been alone before, and I want to see how that feels. It'll be good for me." Kayla takes a careful breath, as if she's afraid she might break if she inhales too hard.

"It will be. You're stronger than you know, Kay. You never needed me to do all that you did." For once, Cam said the right thing, because Kayla smiles, and it's hopeful and real.

"I hope you're right."

"I'll pray for you; that you find happiness," Cam says and means it with his whole heart. Kayla looks at him with an expression that's both sad and grateful. "I'm so sorry for hurting you."

"I'm sorry too. I wish things had happened differently," Kayla replies. Cam isn't sure he agrees with that, but he doesn't say so. "I'll pray for you too. And your boys. Speaking of."

Cam turns around to see Danny, Sean, and Bill coming towards them. "Need any help?" Sean asks.

"Yes, please," Kayla replies.

Moving the bags and boxes with five people isn't hard at all, and before they know it, Dawn is back by Kayla's side, and they're all standing awkwardly in the cold.

"Kayla," Danny starts. "Thank you, for... Well, thank you."

"I want to be kept up to date on you, Danny," Kayla says with a smile. "You're going to do great things. And Sean?" Sean straightens up where he stands next to Cam. "Take care of him."

"I promise," Sean replies without hesitation.

"Goodbye, Cam," Kayla says with a finality that hurts, but in the way taking off a Band-Aid might. It means the last of the hurt is over.

"Goodbye, Kayla."

Cam watches her and Dawn get into the car and drive away as Sean turns to him. "Come on, Cam, let's get home."

sean

Sean makes burgers for dinner, and even manages some oven-roasted potatoes with Old Bay that are pretty dang close to fries. They sit around the table all together, Danny and Cam talk about math and the history of the actual Saint Louis (who bought the crown of thorns on resale or something), and William Butler Yates, then Bill chimes in about T. S. Elliott and Sean has to spend half the meal trying not to get too sentimental.

Dessert is ice cream, Moose Tracks for Bill and Danny, and coffee for Sean and Cam. They fight with spoons over the last bites while Bill and Danny laugh at them. They argue over what movie to watch (*Dirty Dancing* doesn't count as a chick flick because it's Swayze, Danny) and end up on *Top Gun* because it's a crime that Cam and Danny haven't seen it.

Bill falls asleep in his recliner halfway through, but Danny likes it. Sean likes that Cam spends the whole movie snuggled against him on the sagging couch and remarks that it's "remarkably homoerotic," and it's not surprising at all that Sean enjoys it so much.

"Okay, kids, time for bed," Sean says as the credits roll.

"Should we wake him up?" Danny asks, looking at Bill. He snorts and shifts deeper into the recliner. Sean smiles at him fondly. The old man turned down a drink at dinner and smiled more tonight than Sean's ever seen.

"Nah, he's good. Come on, short stuff."

Walking upstairs with Danny and Cam next to him is so different from the first time he came up these stairs. The quiet and emptiness are gone, replaced with something warm and comforting. It reminds him of the nights alone with Cam, but it's more. It's not going anywhere, and it's... beautiful.

"I'll wait for you," Cam says in the hall outside Danny's door. "Goodnight, Danny."

"Night, Cam," Danny replies. He turns to Sean once they're alone in the hall. "I like my room."

"You do?"

"Yeah, it's cool. I'm glad Kayla brought all my stuff. Including the old phone and headphones. Which I'm gonna use to listen to some loud music. *As soon as I get in there.*"

"You've got school tomorrow," Sean scowls.

His brother gives him an annoyed look. "You don't."

"Oh. *Oh.* Jesus, Danny."

"And I can get to school on my own or with Bill if you need, like, more time."

"*Danny.*"

"What? I'm happy for you!" He yelps.

"I'm happy you're here, kid." Sean sighs. "But I don't need your help to get me laid."

"Okay, I just wanted you to know." Sean's not sure if Danny's ever looked more satisfied with himself.

"I get that." Sean shakes his head. Is this how it's gonna be? "We'll have more room. Eventually."

"You want to move?" Danny asks, and Sean sees him deflate.

"Not soon. Just one day, okay? You deserve a real home."

"Sean, this is a home. It's got you in it. That's all I need."

Sean stares at Danny, one last knot uncoiling in his chest. Maybe that's what he was feeling before – home. Christ, if this kid makes him tear up again, he's going to break something. He settles for one more hug for his stupid little brother, who he gets to deal with every day for the foreseeable future. "Thanks, Danny."

"For what?"

"For sticking with me."

"Ditto. I love you, dork."

Sean smiles against Danny's hair, crap, soon this kid *is* gonna be taller than him. At least Sean will be there to see it. "Love you too, kiddo."

"Now go do stuff with your boyfriend."

Sean breaks away, rolling his eyes. "You keep that music up loud."

Danny grins as he closes his door, and Sean turns to his own room. His and Cam's room. In a home. Which he has. Holy crap.

Cam is standing by the window, looking out into the night, when Sean gets in.

"What you looking at?"

Cam turns to him with a gentle smile. "The snow."

"What snow? It was dry as a bone out there last I checked." Sean crosses the room to stand by Cam between the window and the bed. He can feel the cold through the glass.

"It's coming. I can smell it."

Sean chuckles. "You do that too?"

"Since I was a kid."

"I could always tell it was coming when I was downtown. Always meant it was gonna be a shitty, cold night. Made it sort of hard to enjoy." Sean shivers at the memory.

"I can imagine."

Sean slips his arms around Cam's waist, eyes still on the window, and he hooks his chin over Cam's shoulder. "It was still nice sometimes. It made everything pretty and clean for a while, before it turned into a mess."

"Nothing lasts." Cam doesn't sound sad, simply thoughtful.

"Some things do. The rest, we just gotta appreciate it while we can."

"That's very enlightened of you."

"I'm a regular philosopher, didn't you know? Speaking of, when were you gonna tell me you quit your job?"

Cam shrinks in Sean's arms. "Sorry. There's been a lot going on. But Drew and Miles may have an opportunity for me. I could do some good."

"But is it what you want to do?" Cam furrows his brow. Sean knows that the concept is sort of new for Cam. Hell, he's working on it too. If Cam asked him what he wanted for his future beyond being with the people he loves, he wouldn't be able to say.

"I'm not sure. But I have time to figure it out."

"That we do. Maybe you can go back to classics. Or poetry," Sean muses, pulling Cam a bit tighter against him.

"Oh, yes, very lucrative."

"Doesn't have to be lucrative, just has to make you happy." Sean kisses the back of Cam's neck. "You deserve to be happy."

"I think I am." Sean can see the reflection of Cam's wistful smile in the window.

"You *think*? Well, I think we can do better than that." Sean kisses along Cam's shoulder and rolls his hips.

"Was that a proposition?"

"Hell yeah." Cam laughs, warm and deep as he turns in Sean's arms and kisses him properly. It feels so good, kissing Cam, and knowing he's entirely Sean's. "It's been too long since I've had you in me," Sean whispers.

"I can accommodate that."

Cam pushes him back, and Sean lets him lower them onto the bed. The old springs groan when they move, and the headboard jostles against the wall. Sean gets stuck getting out of his stupid slacks, and Cam snickers. "Very sexy."

"Shut up, I ain't a professional anymore. I'm allowed." Sean says it before he can think, and panic bursts in his chest. He still shouldn't bring that shit up.

"No, you're not," Cam replies, as warm and kind as ever, like it didn't matter at all. "You're just mine."

Sean's skin is suddenly covered in goosebumps, and it has nothing to do with the fact that they're naked. "Some poet you are, that's an old line."

"Still true," Cam whispers and kisses him again.

Cam takes his time – they both do. He's gentle and thorough opening Sean up, taking him apart, and laying his soul bare with tenderness. Sean's heavy breath and soft moans fade into the flowered wallpaper, and more goosebumps rise on his skin as Cam whispers back his name. He slides home into Sean, slow and inevitable, and he feels whole.

In all the back alleys and dirty bathroom stalls, or under the bleachers or in the back of a car when he was just fooling around, it was never like this. It was just bodies. Just cash and survival. Before Cam, he never knew what it was to give or to receive in return. He never knew until Cam took his hand what it meant to feel at *home*.

He wants to speak, to tell Cam that and everything else he feels, but words escape him. They move together, steady as a heartbeat, pleasure cresting and ebbing and rising again until Sean is falling apart in Cam's arms and they finally break, together.

"I love you," someone whispers, and Sean can't say who.

They lie together, breath slowing in the dim gold light of the bedside lamp. There's nowhere to run, nothing to hide. It's getting cold, and they should clean up, but for now, Sean just wants to stay here together. He is exactly where he belongs, right now.

Home.

cam

Cam wakes to brightness that stings his eyes as the sun crests the horizon beyond the window. It takes several blinks to register that it's not just the dawn that's blinding, but the reflection of the sun on the newly fallen snow. The world outside is pristine and quiet, but not half as beautiful as the sight inside. Sean, next to him, sharing Cam's bed in the new morning at last.

Cam settles back on his pillow, studying Sean's face: the freckles, his long lashes, and full lips. He watches as the sky beyond the window brightens and listens to voices downstairs discuss winter coats and when the bus comes. He knows they should say goodbye to Danny, but leaving this bed is unthinkable.

Instead, he prays. Or perhaps that is not the word for it. He thanks the universe for the love and peace he feels in this moment. Tries to preserve it and tuck it away, like a holy relic. He lets it fill his heart with light that might be divine.

Sean groans at long last, covering his eyes and burrowing closer to Cam.

"Good morning, Sean."

"Morning. How long you been up?" Sean asks through a yawn.

"Not long. It snowed last night."

"Told you it would."

"I think I was the one who told you."

Sean shrugs and finally opens his eyes, smiling at Cam with adoration that's impossible to mistake. "So, whatcha gonna do today, you useless layabout? Take it easy?"

Cam smiles. "Maybe. I was thinking about what you said last night. Maybe I'll write down some poems."

"Really? Will you let me read them when you're done?"

"Of course. I was thinking of one just now, if you want to hear it."

"Always, Cam."

Cam presses a kiss onto Sean's forehead and pulls him close as he speaks:

Weep not for me,
For lost years I have suffered.
Mourn not for my seeking
Pity not my long walk.
My burden has shaped me
And led me to heaven.
My road was to paradise
Here in your arms.
For I have found my God now
In the light of the morning,
In the silence of snow,
In the green trees and stars
In the love in your eyes.
Found by my hope
Where once I was fallen.
Home with you at last
Amen.

ACKNOWLEDGEMENTS

There are so many people who are responsible for the existence of th, both as the story it began as and the book it has now become. For one, this book exists because it is needed. I needed to write it and I know there are people out there that need to read it.

This book exists in large part because of the people who tried to save my soul in my small town high school. I was grew up among Christians who couldn't see past dogma to the people who mattered and understand that love is love. I thought as I grew older that the world would become more open minded, and in many ways it has. But in others we're still stuck in the hateful thinking of the past. I hope this book reaches someone who wants to be free of that. I hope it brings someone some hope and helps you feel less alone.

This book exists thanks to fandom, which taught me so many lessons, both beautiful and painful. To everyone who ever left a comment about how my work made you feel inspired or seen or just enjoyed it, thank you. It means the world.

Thank you to the friends and family that helped this book along the way: Heidi for your nerdiness and your love of yacht rock, Tam for reminding me what life is all about and helping me name several character; Mom for never turning away from me; Dad and Pat, for teaching me that good Christians exist, I'll always light candles for you. To Marlon and our newest family member, Penny, thank you for making our house a home. Thank you to Ana, Barbara and Alisa for your eyes and imput.

This book is dedicated to the memory of Elizabeth "Betty" Farnell and William "Bill" Montgomery.

And finally, this book is for every queer kid who has felt alone and for anyone they system has failed. I attempted to depicting houselessness and the conditions of unhoused individuals with as much compassion and clarity as I could, but fiction cannot be our only action. With that in mind, a portion of all the profits of *Fallen and Found* will be donated to Northwest Housing Alternatives, an organization I have worked with for many years and I am proud to support. If you are moved to donate or offer your support to any community as well, I hope you do.

Thank you for reading.

Carry on.

ABOUT THE AUTHOR

Jessica Mason lives near Portland, Oregon with her wife, daughter, and various dogs. She has studied opera, practiced law, and worked as a fandom journalist and podcaster, among many varied careers. But first and foremost she has always been a storyteller. When she manages to stop writing, she enjoys gardening, travel, music, and witchcraft. She is passionate about stories of all kinds and loves to discuss and create them.

To learn more, please visit:

www.JessicaMasonAuthor.Com

Find her on social media: @ByJessicaMason

ALSO BY Jessica Mason

The Phantom Saga:
Angel's Mask
Angel's Kiss
Angel's Fall
Erik's Tale
Angel's Flight

The Witch of Versailles
The Binge Watcher's Guide to Supernatural: An Unofficial Companion
The Binge Watcher's Guide to the Marvel Cinematic Universe: An
Unofficial Companion